# On The Beach

## By

## Nevil Shute

# Chapter One

Lieutenant Commander Peter Holmes of the Royal Australian Navy woke soon after dawn. He lay drowsily for a while, lulled by the warm comfort of Mary sleeping beside him, watching the first light of the Australian sun upon the cretonne curtains of their room. He knew from the sun's rays that it was about five o'clock; very soon the light would wake his baby daughter Jennifer in her cot, and then they would have to get up and start doing things. No need to start before that happened; he could lie a little longer.

He woke happy, and it was some time before his conscious senses realized and pinned down the origin of this happiness. It was not Christmas, because that was over. He had illuminated the little fir tree in their garden with a string of coloured lights with a long lead to the plug beside the fireplace in the lounge, a small replica of the great illuminated tree a mile away outside the town hall of Falmouth. They had had a barbecue in the garden on the evening of Christmas Day, with a few friends. Christmas was over, and this— his mind turned over slowly—this must be Thursday the 27th. As he lay in bed the sunburn on his back was still a little sore from their day on the beach yesterday, and from sailing in the race. He would do well to keep his shirt on today. And then, as consciousness came fully to him, he realized that of course he would keep his shirt on today. He had a date at eleven o'clock in the Second Naval Member's office, in the Navy Department up in Melbourne. It meant a new appointment, his first work for seven months. It could even mean a seagoing job if he were very lucky, and he ached for a ship again.

It meant work, anyway. The thought of it had made him happy when he went to sleep, and his happiness had lasted through the night. He had had no appointment since he had been promoted lieutenant commander in August and in the circumstances of the time he had almost given up hope of ever working again. The Navy Department, however, had maintained him on full pay throughout these months, and he was grateful to them.

The baby stirred, and started chuntering and making little whimpering noises. The naval officer reached out and turned the switch of the electric kettle on the tray of tea things and baby food beside the bed, and Mary stirred beside him. She asked the time, and he told her. Then he kissed her, and said, "It's a lovely morning again."

She sat up, brushing back her hair. "I got so burned yesterday. I put some calamine stuff on Jennifer last night, but I really don't think she ought to go down to the beach again today." Then she, too, recollected. "Oh—Peter, it's today you're going up to Melbourne, isn't it?"

He nodded. "I should stay at home, have a day in the shade."

"I think I will."

He got up and went to the bathroom. When he came back Mary was up, too; the baby was sitting on her pot and Mary was drawing a comb through her hair before the glass. He sat down on the edge of the bed in a horizontal beam of sunlight, and made the tea.

She said, "It's going to be very hot in Melbourne today, Peter. I thought we might go down to the club about four, and you join us there for a swim. I could take the trailer and your bathers."

They had a small car in the garage, but since the short war had ended a year previously it remained unused. However, Peter Holmes was an ingenious man and good with tools, and he had contrived a tolerable substitute. Both Mary and he had bicycles. He had built a small two-wheeled trailer using the front wheels of two motor bicycles, and he had contrived a trailer hitch both on Mary's bicycle and his own so that either could pull this thing, which served them as a perambulator and a general goods carrier. Their chief trouble was the long hill up from Falmouth.

He nodded. "That's not a bad idea. I'll take my bike and leave it at the station."

"What train have you got to catch?"

"The nine-five. He sipped his tea and glanced at his watch. "I'll go and get the milk as soon as I've drunk this."

He put on a pair of shorts and a singlet and went out. He lived in the ground floor flat of an old house upon the hill above the town that had been divided into apartments; he had the garage and a good part of the garden in his share of the property. There was a verandah, and here he kept the bicycles and the trailer. It would have been logical to park the car under the trees and use the garage, but he could not bring himself to do that. The little Morris was the first car he had ever owned, and he had courted Mary in it. They had been married in 1961 six months before the war, before he sailed in *H.M.A.S. Anzac* for what they thought would be indefinite separation. The short, bewildering war had followed, the war of which no history had been written or ever would be written now, that had flared all-round the Northern Hemisphere and had died away with the last seismic record of explosion on the thirty-seventh day. At the end of the third month he had returned to Williamstown in *Anzac* on the last of her fuel oil while the statesmen of the Southern Hemisphere gathered in conference at Wellington in New Zealand to compare notes and assess the new conditions, had returned to Falmouth to his Mary and his Morris Minor car. The car had three gallons in the tank; he used that unheeding and another five that he bought at a pump before it dawned upon Australians that all oil came from the Northern Hemisphere.

He pulled the trailer and his bicycle down from the verandah on to the lawn and fitted the trailer hitch; then he mounted and rode off. He had four miles to go to fetch the milk and cream, for the transport shortage now prevented all collections from the farms in his district and they had learned to make their own butter in the Mixmaster. He rode off down the road in the warm morning sunlight, the empty billies rattling in the trailer at his back, happy in the thought of work before him.

There was very little traffic on the road. He passed one vehicle that once had been a car, the engine removed and the windscreen knocked out,

3

drawn by an Angus bullock. He passed two riders upon horses, going carefully upon the gravel verge to the road beside the bitumen surface. He did not want one; they were scarce and delicate creatures that changed hands for a thousand pounds or more, but he had sometimes thought about a bullock for Mary, He could convert the Morris easily enough, though it would break his heart to do so.

He reached the farm in half an hour, and went straight to the milking shed. He knew the farmer well, a slow-speaking, tall, lean man who walked with a limp from the Second World War. He found him in the separator room, where the milk flowed into one churn and the cream into another in a low murmur of sound from the electric motor that drove the machine. "Morning, Mr. Paul," said the naval officer. "How are you today?"

"Good, Mr. Holmes." The farmer took the milk billy from him and filled it at the vat. "Everything all right with you?"

"Fine. I've got to go up to Melbourne, to the Navy Department. I think they've got a job for me at last."

"Ah," said the farmer, "that'll be good. Kind of wearisome, waiting around, I'd say."

Peter nodded. "It's going to complicate things a bit if it's a seagoing job. Mary'll be coming for the milk, though, twice a week. She'll bring the money, just the same."

The farmer said, "You don't have to worry about the money till you come back, anyway. I've got more milk than the pigs will take even now, dry as it is. Put twenty gallons in the creek last night—can't get it away. Suppose I ought to raise more pigs, but then it doesn't seem worthwhile. It's hard to say what to do. . . ." He stood in silence for a minute, then he said, "Going to be kind of awkward for the wife, coming over here. What's she going to do with Jennifer?"

"She'll probably bring her over with her, in the trailer."

"Kind of awkward for her, that." The farmer walked to the alley of the milking shed and stood in the warm sunlight, looking the bicycle and trailer over. "That's a good trailer," he said. "As good a little trailer as I ever saw. Made it yourself, didn't you?"

"That's right.'

"Where did you get the wheels, if I may ask?"

"They're motor bike wheels. I got them in Elizabeth Street."

"Think you could get a pair for me?"

"I could try," Peter said. "I think there may be some of them about still. They're better than the little wheels—they tow more easily." The farmer nodded. "They may be a bit scarce now. People seem to be hanging on to motor bikes."

"I was saying to the wife," the farmer remarked slowly, "if I had a little trailer like that I could make it like a chair for her, put it on behind the push bike and take her into Falmouth, shopping. It's mighty lonely for a woman in a place like this, these days," he explained. "Not like it was before the war, when she could take the car and get into town in twenty minutes. The bullock cart takes three and a half hours, and three and a half hours back; that's seven hours for travelling alone. She did try to learn to ride a bike but she'll never make a go of it, not at her age and another baby on the way. I wouldn't want her to try. But if I had a little trailer like you've got I could take her into Falmouth twice a week, and take the milk and cream along to Mrs. Holmes at the same time." He paused. "I'd like to be able to do that for the wife," he remarked. "After all, from what they say on the wireless, there's not so long to go."

The naval officer nodded. "I'll scout around a bit today and see what I can find. You don't mind what they cost?"

The farmer shook his head. "So long as they're good wheels, to give no trouble. Good tires, that's the main thing—last the time out. Like those you've got."

The officer nodded. "I'll have a look for some today."

"Taking you a good bit out of your way."

"I can slip up there by tram. It won't be any trouble. Thank God for the brown coal."

The farmer turned to where the separator was still running. "That's right. We'd be in a pretty mess but for the electricity." He slipped an empty chum into the stream of skim milk deftly and pulled the full chum away. "Tell me, Mr. Holmes," he said. "Don't they use big digging machines to get the coal? Like bulldozers, and things like that?" The officer nodded. "Well, where do they get the oil to run those things?"

"I asked about that once," Peter said. "They distill it on the spot, out of the brown coal. It costs about two pounds a gallon."

"You don't say!" The farmer stood in thought. "I was thinking maybe if they could do that for themselves, they might do some for us. But at that price, it wouldn't hardly be practical. . ."

Peter took the milk and cream billies, put them in the trailer, and set off for home. It was six-thirty when he got back. He had a shower and dressed in the uniform he had so seldom worn since his promotion, accelerated his breakfast, and rode his bicycle down the hill to catch the 8:15 in order that he might explore the motor dealers for the wheels before his appointment.

He left his bicycle at the garage that had serviced his small car in bygone days. It serviced no cars now. Horses stood stabled where the cars had been, the horses of the business men who lived outside the town, who now rode in in jodhpurs and plastic coats to stable their horses while they commuted up to town in the electric train. The petrol pumps served them as hitching posts. In the evening they would come down on the train, saddle their horses, strap the attaché case to the saddle, and ride home again. The tempo of business life was slowing down and this was a help to them; the 5:03 express train from the city had been cancelled and a 4:17 put on to replace it.

Peter Holmes travelled to the city immersed in speculations about his new appointment, for the paper famine had closed down all the daily newspapers and news now came by radio alone. The Royal Australian Navy was a very small fleet now. Seven small ships had been converted from oil burners to most unsatisfactory coal burners at great cost and effort; an attempt to convert the aircraft carrier Melbourne had been suspended when it proved that she would to too slow to allow the aircraft to land on with safety except in the strongest wind. Moreover, stocks of aviation fuel had to be husbanded so carefully that training programmes had been reduced to virtually nil, so that it now seemed inexpedient to carry on the Fleet Air Arm at all. He had not heard of any changes in the officers of the seven minesweepers and frigates that remained in commission. It might be that somebody was sick and had to be replaced, or it might be that they had decided to rotate employed officers with the unemployed to keep up seagoing experience. More probably it meant a posting to some dreary job on shore, an office job in the barracks or doing something with the stores at some disconsolate, deserted place like Flinders Naval Depot. He would be deeply disappointed if he did not get to sea, and yet he knew it would be better for him so. On shore he could look after Mary and the baby as he had been doing, and there was now not so long to go.

He got to the city in about an hour and went out of the station to get upon the tram. It rattled unobstructed through streets innocent of other vehicles and took him quickly to the motor dealing district. Most of the shops here were closed or taken over by the few that remained open, the windows still encumbered with the useless stock. He shopped around here for a time searching for two light wheels in good condition that would make a pair, and finally bought wheels of the same size from two makes of motorcycle, which would make complications with the axle that could be got over by the one mechanic still left in his garage.

He took the tram back to the Navy Department carrying the wheels tied together with a bit of rope. In the Second Naval Member's offices he reported to the secretary, a paymaster lieutenant who was known to him. The young man said, "Good morning, sir. The admiral's got your posting on his desk. He wants to see you personally. I'll tell him that you're here."

The lieutenant commander raised his eyebrows. It seemed unusual, but then in this reduced navy everything was apt to be a bit unusual. He put the wheels down by the paymaster's desk, looked over his uniform with some concern, picked a bit of thread off the lapel of his jacket, and tucked his cap under his arm.

"The admiral will see you now, sir."

He marched into the office and came to attention. The admiral, seated at his desk, inclined his head. "Good morning, Lieutenant Commander. You can stand easy. Sit down."

6

Peter sat down in the chair beside the desk. The admiral leaned over and offered him a cigarette out of his case, and lit it for him with a lighter. "You've been unemployed for some time."

"Yes, sir."

The admiral lit a cigarette himself. "Well, I've got a sea-going appointment for you. I can't give you a command, I'm afraid, and I can't even put you in one of our own ships. I'm posting you as liaison officer in *U.S.S. Scorpion.*"

He glanced at the younger man. "I understand you've met Commander Towers."

"Yes, sir." He had met the captain of *Scorpion* two or three times in the last few months, a quiet, soft-spoken man of thirty-five or so with a slight New England accent. He had read the American's report upon his ship's war service. He had been at sea in his atomic-powered submarine on patrol between Kiska and Midway when the war began, and opening his sealed orders at the appropriate signal he submerged and set course for Manila at full cruising speed. On the fourth day, somewhere north of Iwo Jima, he came to periscope depth for an inspection of the empty sea as was his routine in each watch of the daylight hours and found the visibility to be extremely low, apparently with some sort of dust; at the same time the detector on his periscope head indicated a high level of radioactivity. He attempted to report this to Pearl Harbor in a signal but got no reply; he carried on, the radioactivity increasing as he neared the Philippines. Next night he made contact with Dutch Harbor and passed a signal in code to his admiral, but was told that all communications were now irregular, and he got no reply. On the next night he failed to raise Dutch Harbor. He carried on upon his mission, setting course around the north of Luzon. In the Balintang Channel he found much dust and the radioactivity far above the lethal level, the wind being westerly, force 4 to 5. On the seventh day of the war he was in Manila Bay looking at the city through his periscope, still without orders. The atmospheric radioactivity was rather less here though still above the danger level; he did not care to surface or go up on to the bridge. Visibility was moderate; through the periscope he saw a pall of smoke drifting up above the city and formed the opinion that at least one nuclear explosion had taken place there within the last few days. He saw no activity on shore from five miles out in the bay. Proceeding to close the land he grounded his ship unexpectedly at periscope depth, being then in the main channel where the chart showed twelve fathoms; this reinforced his previous opinion. He blew his tanks and got off without difficulty, turned round, and went out to the open sea again.

That night he failed again to raise any American station, or any ship that could relay his signals. Blowing his tanks had used up much of his compressed air, and he did not care to take in the contaminated air in that vicinity. He had been submerged by that time for eight days; his crew were still fairly fit through various neuroses were beginning to appear, born of

7

anxiety about conditions in their homes. He established radio contact with an Australian station at Port Moresby in New Guinea; conditions there appeared to be normal, but they could not relay any of his signals.

It seemed to him that the best thing he could do would be to go south. He went back round the north of Luzon and set course for Yap Island, a cable station under the control of the United States. He got there three days later. Here the radioactive level was so low as to be practically normal; he surfaced in a moderate sea, blew out the ship with clean air, charged his tanks, and let the crew up on the bridge in batches. On entering the roads he was relieved to find an American cruiser there. She directed him to an anchorage and sent a boat; he moored ship, let the whole crew up on deck, and went off in the boat to put himself under the command of the captain of the cruiser, a Captain Shaw. Here he learned for the first time of the Russian-Chinese war that had flared up out of the Russian-NATO war, that had in turn been born of the Israeli-Arab war, initiated by Albania. He learned of the use of cobalt bombs by both the Russians and the Chinese; that news came deviously from Australia, relayed from Kenya. The cruiser was waiting at Yap to rendevous with a Fleet tanker; she had been there for a week and in the last five days she had been out of communication with the United States. The captain had sufficient bunker fuel to get his ship to Brisbane at her most economical speed, but no further.

Commander Towers stayed at Yap for six days while the news, such as it was, grew steadily worse. They did not succeed in making contact with any station in the United States or Europe, but for the first two days or so they were able to pick up news broadcasts from Mexico City, and that news was just about as bad as it could be. Then that station went off the air, and they could only get Panama, Bogota, and Valparaiso, who knew practically nothing about what was going on up in the northern continent. They made contact with a few ships of the U.S. Navy in the South Pacific, most of them as short of fuel as they were themselves. The captain of the cruiser at Yap proved to be the senior officer of all these ships; he made the decision to sail all U.S. ships into Australian waters and to place his forces under Australian command. He made signals to all ships to rendezvous with him at Brisbane. They congregated there a fortnight later, eleven ships of the U.S. Navy, all out of bunker fuel and with very little hope of getting any more. That was a year ago; they were there still.

The nuclear fuel required for *U.S.S. Scorpion* was not available in Australia at the time of her arrival, but it could be prepared. She proved to be the only naval vessel in Australian waters with any worth-while radius of action so she was sailed to Williamstown, the naval dockyard of Melbourne, being the nearest port to the headquarters of the Navy Department. She was, in fact, the only warship in Australia worth bothering about. She stayed idle for some time while her nuclear fuel was prepared till, six months previously, she had been restored to operational mobility. She then made a cruise to Rio de Janeiro, carrying supplies of fuel for another American nuclear submarine that had taken refuge there, and returned to Melbourne to undergo a fairly extensive refit in the dockyard.

All this was known to Peter Holmes as the back-ground of Commander Towers, U.S.N., and it passed quickly through his mind as he sat before the admiral's desk. The appointment that he had been offered was a new one; there had been no Australian liaison officer in *Scorpion* when she had made her South American cruise. The thought of Mary and his little daughter troubled him now and prompted him to ask, "How long is this appointment for, sir?"

The admiral shrugged his shoulders slightly. "We could say a year. I imagine it will be your last posting, Holmes."

The younger man said, "I know, sir. I'm very grateful for the opportunity." He hesitated, and then he asked, "Will the ship be at sea for much of that time, sir? I'm married, and we've got a baby. Things aren't too easy now, compared with what they used to be, and it's a bit difficult at home. And anyway, there's not so long to go."

The admiral nodded. "We're all in the same boat, of course. That's why I wanted to see you before offering this posting. I shan't hold it against you if you ask to be excused, but in that case I can't hold out much prospect of any further employment. As regards seatime, at the conclusion of the refit on the fourth—" he glanced at the calendar "—that's in a little over a week from now—the ship is to proceed to Cairns. Port Moresby, and Port Darwin to report upon conditions in those places, returning to Williamstown. Commander Towers estimates eleven days for that cruise. After that we have in mind a longer cruise for her, lasting perhaps two months."

"Would there be an interval between those cruises, sir?"

"I should think the ship might be in the dockyard for about a fortnight."

"And nothing on the programme after that?"

"Nothing at present."

The young officer sat in thought for a moment revolving in his mind the shopping, the ailments of the baby, the milk supply. It was summer weather; there would be no firewood to be cut If the second cruise began about the middle of February he would be home by the middle of April, before the weather got cold enough for fires. Perhaps the farmer would see Mary right for firewood if he was away longer than that, now that he had got him the wheels for his trailer. It should be all right for him to go, so long as nothing further went wrong. But if the electricity supply failed, or the radioactivity spread south more quickly than the wise men estimated . . . Put away that thought.

Mary would be furious if he turned down this job and sacrificed his career. She was a naval officer's daughter born and brought up at Southsea in the south of England; he had first met her at a dance in Indefatigable when he

9

was doing his sea time in England with the Royal Navy. She would want him to take this appointment. ...

He raised his head. "I should be all right for those two cruises, sir," he said. "Would it be possible to review the situation after that? I mean, it's not so easy to make plans ahead—at home—with all this going on."

The admiral thought for a moment. In the circumstances it was a reasonable request for a man to make, especially a newly married man with a young baby.

The case was a new one, for postings were now so few, but he could hardly expect this officer to accept sea duty outside Australian waters in the last few months. He nodded. "I can do that, Holmes," he said. "I'll make this posting for five months, till the thirty-first of May. Report to me again when you get back from the second cruise."

"Very good, sir."

"You'll report in *Scorpion* on Tuesday, New Year's Day. If you wait outside a quarter of an hour you can have your letter to the captain. The vessel is at Williamstown, lying alongside *Sydney* as her mother ship."

"I know, sir."

The admiral rose to his feet. "All right, Lieutenant Commander." He held out his hand. "Good luck in the appointment."

Peter Holmes shook hands. "Thank you for considering me, sir." He paused before leaving the room. "Do you happen to know if Commander Towers is on board today?" he asked. "As I'm here, I might slip down and make my number with him, and perhaps see the ship. I'd rather like to do that before joining."

"So far as I know he is on board," the admiral said. "You can put a call through to *Sydney*—ask my secretary." He glanced at his watch. "There's a transport leaving from the main gate at eleven-thirty. You'll be able to catch that."

Twenty minutes later Peter Holmes was seated by the driver in the electric truck that ran the ferry service down to Williamstown, bowling along in silence through the deserted streets. In former days the truck had been a delivery van for a great Melbourne store; it had been requisitioned at the conclusion of the war and painted naval grey. It moved along at a steady twenty miles an hour unimpeded by any other traffic on the roads. It got to the dockyard at noon, and Peter Holmes walked down to the berth occupied by H.M.A.S. *Sydney*, an aircraft carrier immobilized at the quay side. He went on board, and went down to the wardroom.

There were only about a dozen officers in the great wardroom, six of them in the khaki gabardine working uniform of the U.S. Navy. The captain of *Scorpion* was among them; he came forward smiling to meet Peter. "Say, Lieutenant Commander, I'm glad you could come down."

10

Peter Holmes said, "I hoped you wouldn't mind, sir. I'm not due to join till Tuesday. But as I was at the Navy Department I hoped you wouldn't mind if I came down for lunch, and perhaps had a look through the ship."

"Why, sure," said the captain. "I was glad when Admiral Grimwade told me he was posting you to join us. I'd like you to meet some of my officers." He turned to the others. "This is my executive officer, Mr. Farrell and my engineering officer, Mr. Lundgren." He smiled. "It takes a pretty high-grade engineering staff to run our motors. This is Mr. Benson, Mr. O'Doherty, and Mr. Hirsch." The young men bowed, a little awkwardly. The captain turned to Peter. "How about a drink before lunch, Commander?"

The Australian said, "Well—thank you very much. I'll have a pink gin." The captain pressed the bell upon the bulkhead. "How many officers have you in *Scorpion*, sir?"

"Eleven, all told. She's quite a submarine, of course, and we carry four engineer officers."

"You must have a big wardroom."

"It's a bit cramped when we're all sitting down together but that doesn't happen very often in a submarine. But we've got a cot for you, Commander."

Peter smiled. "All to myself, or is it Box and Cox?" The captain was a little shocked at the suggestion. "Why, no. Every officer and every enlisted man has an individual berth in *Scorpion*"

The wardroom steward came in answer to the bell. The captain said, "Will you bring one pink gin and six orangeades?"

Peter was embarrassed, and could have kicked himself for his indiscretion. He checked the steward.

"Don't you drink in port, sir?"

The captain smiled. "Why, no. Uncle Sam doesn't like it. But you go right ahead. This is a British ship."

"I'd rather have it your way, if you don't mind," Peter replied. "Seven orangeades." '

"Seven it is," said the captain nonchalantly. The steward went away. "Some navies have it one way and some another," he remarked. "I never noticed that it made much difference in the end result."

They lunched in Sidney, a dozen officers at one end of one of the long, empty tables. Then they went down into *Scorpion*, moored alongside. She was the biggest submarine that Peter Holmes had ever seen; she displaced about six thousand tons and her atomic-powered turbines developed well over ten thousand horsepower. Besides her eleven officers she carried a crew of about seventy petty officers and enlisted men. All these men messed and slept amongst a maze of pipes and wiring as is common in all submarines, but she was well equipped for the tropics with good air conditioning and a very large cold store. Peter Holmes was no submariner and could not judge her from a

11

technical point of view, but the captain told him that she was easy on controls and quite manoeuvrable in spite of her great length.

Most of her armament and warlike stores had been taken off her during her refit, and all but two of her torpedo tubes had been removed. This made more room for mess decks and amenities than is usual in a submarine, and the removal of the aft tubes and torpedo stowage made conditions in the engine room a good deal easier for the engineers. Peter spent an hour in this part of the ship with the engineering officer, Lieutenant Commander Lundgren. He had never served in an atomic-powered ship, and as much of the equipment was classified for security a great deal of it was novel to him. He spent some time absorbing the general layout of the liquid sodium circuit to take heat from the reactor, the various heat exchangers, and the closed cycle helium circuits for the twin high-speed turbines that drove the ship through the enormous reduction gears, so much larger and more sensitive than the other units of the power plant.

He came back to the captain's tiny cabin in the end. Commander Towers rang for the coloured steward, ordered coffee for two, and let down the folding seat for Peter. "Have a good look at the engines?" he asked.

The Australian nodded. "I'm not an engineer," he said. "Much of it is just a bit over my head, but it was very interesting. Do they give you much trouble?"

The captain shook his head. "They never have so far. There's nothing much that you can do with them at sea if they do. Just keep your fingers crossed and hope they'll keep on spinning around."

The coffee came and they sipped it in silence. "My orders are to report to you on Tuesday," Peter said. "What time would you like me here, sir?"

"We sail on Tuesday on sea trials," the captain said. "It might be Wednesday, but I don't think we'll be so late as that. We're taking on stores Monday and the crew come aboard."

"I'd better report to you on Monday, then," said the Australian. "Some time in the forenoon?"

"That might be a good thing," said the captain. "I think we'll get away by Tuesday noon. I told the admiral I'd like to take a little cruise in Bass Strait as a shakedown, and come back maybe on Friday and report operational readiness. I'd say if you're on board any time Monday forenoon that would be okay."

"Is there anything that I can do for you in the meantime? I'd come aboard on Saturday if I could help at all."

"I appreciate that, Commander, but there's not a thing. Half the crew are off on leave right now, and I'm letting the other half go off on week-end pass tomorrow noon. There'll be nobody here Saturday and Sunday barring one officer and six men on watch. No, Monday forenoon will be time enough for you."

12

He glanced at Peter. "Anybody tell you what they want us to do?"

The Australian was surprised. "Haven't they told you, sir?"

The American laughed. "Not a thing. I'd say the last person to hear the sailing orders is the captain."

"The Second Naval Member sent for me about this posting," Peter said. "He told me that you were making a cruise to Carins, Port Moresby, and Darwin, and that it was going to take eleven days."

"Your Captain Nixon in the Operations Division, he asked me how long that would take," the captain remarked. "I haven't had it as an order yet."

"The admiral said, this morning, that after that was over there'd be a much longer cruise, that would take about two months."

Commander Towers paused, motionless, His cup suspended in mid-air. "That's news to me," he remarked. "Did he say where we were going?"

Peter shook his head. "He just said it would take about two months."

There was a short silence. Then the American roused himself and smiled. "I guess if you look in around midnight you'll find me drawing radiuses on the chart," he said quietly. "And tomorrow night, and the night after that."

It seemed better to the Australian to turn the conversation to a lighter tone. "Aren't you going away for the week-end?" he asked.

The captain shook his head. "I'll stick around. Maybe go up to the city one day and take in a movie." It seemed a dreary sort of programme for his weekend, a stranger far from home in a strange land. On the impulse Peter said, "Would you care to come down to Falmouth for a couple of nights, sir? We've got a spare bedroom. We've been spending most of our time at the sailing club this weather, swimming and sailing. My wife would like it if you could come."

"That's mighty nice of you," the captain said thoughtfully. He took another drink of coffee while he considered the proposal. Northern Hemisphere people seldom mixed well, now, with people of the Southern Hemisphere. Too much lay between them, too great a difference of experience. The intolerable sympathy made a barrier. He knew that very well, and more, he knew that this Australian officer must know it in spite of his invitation. In the line of duty, however, he felt that he would like to know more about the liaison officer. If he had to communicate through him with the Australian naval command he would like to know what sort of man he was; that was a point in favour of this visit to his home. The change would certainly be some relief from the vile inactivity that had tormented him in the last months; however great the awkwardness, it might be better than a week-end in the echoing, empty aircraft carrier with only his own thoughts and memories for company.

He smiled faintly as he put his cup down. It might be awkward if he went down there, but it could be even more awkward if he churlishly refused

13

an invitation kindly meant from his new officer. "You sure it wouldn't be too much for your wife?" he asked. "With a young baby?"

Peter shook his head. "She'd like it," he said. "Make a bit of a change for her. She doesn't see many new faces, with things as they are. Of course, the baby makes a tie as well."

"I certainly would like to come down for one night," the American said. "I'll have to stick around here tomorrow, but I could use a swim on Saturday. It's a long time since I had a swim. How would it be if I came down to Falmouth on the train Saturday morning? I'll have to be back here on Sunday."

"I'll meet you at the station." They discussed trains for a little. Then Peter asked, "Can you ride a push bike?" The other nodded. "I'll bring another bike down with me to the station. We live about two miles out."

Commander Towers said, "that'll be fine." The red Oldsmobile was fading to a dream. It was only fifteen months since he had driven it to the airport, but now he could hardly remember what the instrument panel looked like or on which side the seat adjustment lever lay. It must be still in the garage of his Connecticut home, untouched perhaps, with all the other things that he had schooled himself not to think about. One had to live in the new world and do one's best, forgetting about the old; now it was push bikes at the railway station in Australia.

Peter left to catch the ferry truck back to the Navy Department; he picked up his letter of appointment and his wheels, and took the tram to the station. He got back to Falmouth at about six o'clock, hung the wheels awkwardly on the handlebars of his bicycle, took off his jacket, and trudged the pedals heavily up the hill to his home. He got there half an hour later sweating profusely in the heat of the evening, to find Mary cool in a summer frock in the refreshing murmur of a sprinkler on the lawn.

She came to meet him. "Oh Peter, you're so hot!" she said. "I see you got the wheels."

He nodded. "Sorry I couldn't get down to the beach."

"I guessed you'd been held up. We came home about half-past five. What happened about the appointment?"

"It's a long story," he said. He parked the bicycle and the wheels on the verandah. "I'd like to have a shower first, and tell you then."

"Good or bad?" she asked.

"Good," he replied. "Seagoing until April. Nothing after that."

"Oh Peter," she cried, "that's just perfect! Go on and have your shower and tell me about it when you're cool. I'll bring out the deck chairs and there's a bottle of beer in the frig."

A quarter of an hour later, cool in an open-necked shirt and light drill trousers, sitting in the shade with the cold beer, he told her all about it In the end he asked, "Have you ever met Commander Towers?"

14

She shook her head. "Jane Freeman met them all at the party in *Sydney*. She said he was rather nice. What's he going to be like to serve under?"

"All right, I think," he replied. "He's very competent. It's going to be a bit strange at first, in an American ship. But I liked them all, I must say." He laughed. "I put up a blue right away by ordering a pink gin." He told her.

She nodded. "That's what Jane said. They drink on shore but not in a ship. I don't believe they drink in uniform at all. They had some kind of a fruit cocktail, rather dismal. Everybody else was drinking like a fish."

"I asked him down for the week-end," he told her. "He's coming down on Saturday morning."

She stared at him in consternation. "Not Commander Towers?"

He nodded. "I felt I had to ask him. He'll be all right."

"Oh . . . Peter, he won't be. They're never all right. It's much too painful for them, coming into people's homes."

He tried to reassure her. "He's different. He's a good bit older, for one thing. Honestly, he'll be quite all right."

That's what you thought about that R.A.F. squadron leader," she retorted. "You know—I forget his name. The one who cried."

He did not care to be reminded of that evening. "I know it's difficult for them," he said. "Coming into someone's home, with the baby and everything. But honestly, this chap won't be like that."

She resigned herself to the inevitable. "How long is he staying for?"

"Only the one night," he told her. "He says he's got to be back in *Scorpion* on Sunday."

"If it's only for one night it shouldn't be too bad . . ." She sat in thought for a minute, frowning a little. "The thing is, we'll have to find him plenty to do.

Keep him occupied all the time. Never a dull moment. That's the mistake we made with that R.A.F. bloke. What does he like doing?"

"Swimming," he told her. "He wants to have a swim."

"Sailing? There's a race on Saturday."

"I didn't ask him. I should think he sails. He's the sort of man who would."

She took a drink of beer. "We could take him to the movies," she said thoughtfully.

"What's on?"

"I don't know. It doesn't really matter, so long as we keep him occupied."

"It might not be so good if it was about America," he pointed out. "We might just hit on one that was shot in his home town."

15

She stared at him in consternation. "Wouldn't that be awful! Where is his home town, Peter? What part of

America?"

"I haven't a clue," he said. "I didn't ask him."

"Oh dear. We'll have to do something with him in the evening, Peter. I should think a British picture would be safest, but there may not be one on."

"We could have a party," he suggested.

"We'll have to, if there's not a British picture. It might be better, anyway." She sat in thought, and then she asked, "Was he married, do you know?"

"I don't. I should think he must have been."

"I believe Moira Davidson would come and help us out," she said thoughtfully. "If she isn't doing anything else."

"If she isn't drunk," he observed.

"She's not like that all the time," his wife replied. "She'd keep the party lively, anyway."

He considered the proposal. "That's not a bad idea," he said. "I should tell her right out what she's got to do. Never a dull moment" He paused, thoughtful. "In bed or out of it."

"She doesn't, you know. It's all on the surface."

He grinned. "Have it your own way."

They rang Moira Davidson that evening and put the proposition to her. "Peter felt he had to ask him," Mary told her. "I mean, he's his new captain. But you know how they are and how they feel when they come into someone's home, with children and a smell of nappies and a feeding bottle in a saucepan of warm water and all that sort of thing. So we thought we'd clean the house up a bit and put all that away, and try and give him a gay time—all the time, you know. The trouble is, I can't do much myself with Jennifer. Could you come and help us out, dear? I'm afraid it means a camp bed in the lounge or out on the verandah, if you'd rather. It's just for Saturday and Sunday. Keep him occupied, all the time—that's what we thought. Never a dull moment. I thought we'd have a party on Saturday night, and get some people in."

"Sounds a bit dreary," said Miss Davidson. "Tell me, is he a fearful stick? Will he start weeping in my arms and telling me I'm just like his late wife? Some of them do that."

"I suppose he might," said Mary uncertainly. "I've never met him. Half a minute while I ask Peter." She came back to the telephone. "Moira? Peter says he'll probably start knocking you about when he gets a skinful."

"That's better," said Miss Davidson. "All right, I'll come over on Saturday morning. By the way, I've given up gin."

"Given up gin?"

"Rots your insides. Perforates the intestine and gives you ulcers. I've been having them each morning, so I've given it away. It's brandy now. About six bottles, I should think—for the week-end. You can drink a lot of brandy."

On Saturday morning Peter Holmes rode down to Falmouth station on his push bike. He met Moira Davidson there. She was a slightly built girl with straight blonde hair and a white face, the daughter of a grazier with a small property at a place called Harkaway near Berwick. She arrived at the station in a very smart four-wheeled trap, snatched from some junk yard and reconditioned at considerable expense a year before, with a good-looking, high-spirited grey mare between the shafts. She was wearing slacks of the brightest red and a shirt of the same colour, with lips, fingernails, and toenails to match. She waved to Peter, who went to the horse's head, got down from her outfit, and tied the reins loosely to a rail where once the passengers had stood in line before boarding the bus. "Morning, Peter," she said. "Boyfriend not turned up?"

"He'll be on this train coming now," he said. "What time did you leave home?" She had driven twenty miles to Falmouth.

"Eight o'clock. Ghastly."

"You've had breakfast?"

She nodded. "Brandy. I'm going to have another one before I get up in that jinker again."

He was concerned for her. "Haven't you had anything to eat?"

"Eat? Bacon and eggs and all that muck? My dear child, the Symes had a party last night. I'd have sicked it up."

They turned to walk together to meet the train. "What time did you get to bed?" he asked.

"About half-past two."

"I don't know how you can keep it up. I couldn't."

"I can. I can keep it up as long as I've got to, and that's not so long now. I mean, why waste time in sleeping?" She laughed, a little shrilly. "Just doesn't make sense."

He did not reply because she was quite right, only it wasn't his own way. They stood and waited till the train came in, and met Commander Towers on the platform. He came in civilian clothes, a light grey jacket and fawn drill trousers, slightly American in cut, so that he stood out as a stranger in the crowd.

Peter Holmes made the introductions. As they walked down the ramp from the platforms the American said, "I haven't ridden a bicycle in years. I'll probably fall off."

"We're doing better for you than that," Peter said, "Moira's got her jinker here."

17

The other wrinkled his brows. "I didn't get that."

"Sports car," the girl said. "Jaguar XK. 140. Thunderbird to you, I suppose. New model, only one horsepower, but she does a good eight miles an hour on the flat. Christ, I want a drink!"

They came to the jinker with the grey standing in the shafts; she went to untie the reins. The American stood back and looked it over, gleaming in the sun and very smart. "Say," he exclaimed, "this is quite a buggy you've got!"

Moira stood back and laughed. "A buggy! That's the word for it. It's a buggy, isn't it? All right, Peter— that's not dirty. And anyway, it is. We've got a custom-line sitting in the garage, Commander Towers, but I didn't bring that. It's a buggy. Come on and get up into it, and I'll step on it and show you how she goes."

"I've got my bike here, sir," Peter said. "I'll ride that up and meet you at the house."

Commander Towers climbed up into the buggy and the girl got up beside him; she took the whip and turned the grey and trotted up the road behind the bicycle. "One thing I'm going to do before we leave town," she told her companion, "and that's have a drink. Peter's a dear, and Mary too, but they don't drink enough. Mary says it gives the baby colic. I hope you don't mind. You can have a Coke or something if you'd rather."

Commander Towers felt a little dazed, but refreshed. It was a long time since he had had to deal with this sort of a young woman. "I'll go along with you," he said. "I've swallowed enough Cokes in the last year to float my ship, periscope depth. I could use a drink."

"Then there's two of us," she remarked. She steered her outfit into the main street, not unskilfully. A few cars stood abandoned parked diagonally by the curb; they had been there for over a year. So little traffic used the streets that they were not in the way, and there had been no petrol to tow them away. She drew up outside the Pier Hotel and got down; she tied the reins to the bumper of one of these cars and went with her companion into the Ladies' Lounge.

He asked, "What can I order for you?"

"Double brandy."

"Water?"

"Just a little, and a lot of ice."

He gave the order to the barman and stood considering for a moment while the girl watched him. There never had been any rye, and there had been no Scotch for many months. He was unreasonably suspicious of Australian whisky. "I never drank brandy like that," he remarked. "What's it like?"

"No kick," the girl said, "but it creeps up on you. Good for the guts. That's the reason why I drink it."

18

"I guess I'll stick to whisky." He ordered, and then turned to her, amused. "You drink quite a lot, don't you?"

"That's what they tell me." She took the drink he handed to her and produced a pack of cigarettes from her bag, blended South African and Australian tobacco. "Have one of these things? They're horrible, but they're all that I could get."

He offered one of his own, equally horrible, and lit it for her. She blew a long cloud of smoke from her nostrils. "It's a change, anyway. What's your name?"

"Dwight," he told her. "Dwight Lionel."

"Dwight Lionel Towers," she repeated. "I'm Moira Davidson. We've got a grazing property about twenty miles from here. You're the captain of the submarine, aren't you?"

"That's right."

"Happy in your job?" she asked cynically.

"It was quite an honor to be given the command," he said quietly. "I reckon it's quite an honor still."

She dropped her eyes. "Sorry I said that. I'm a bit of a pig when I'm sober." She tossed off her drink.

"Buy me another, Dwight."

He bought her another, but stood himself upon his whisky.

"Tell me," the girl asked, "what do you do when you're on leave? Play golf? Sail a boat? Go fishing?"

"Fishing, mostly," he said. A far-off holiday with Sharon in the Gaspe Peninsula floated through his mind, but he put the thought away. One must concentrate upon the present and forget the past. "It's kind of hot for golf," he said. "Commander Holmes said something about a swim."

"That's easy," she said. "There's a sailing race this afternoon, down at the club. Is that in your line?"

"It certainly is," he said, with pleasure in his voice. "What kind of a boat does he have?"

"A thing called a Gwen Twelve," she said. "It's a sort of watertight box with sails on it. I don't know if he wants to sail it himself. I'll crew for you if he doesn't."

"If we're going sailing," he said firmly, "we'd better stop drinking."

"I'm not going to crew for you if you're going to be all U.S. Navy," she retorted. "Our ships aren't dry, like yours."

"Okay," he said equably. "Then I'll crew for you." She stared at him. "Has anyone ever bashed you over the head with a bottle?"

He smiled. "Lots of times."

She drained her glass. "Well, have another drink."

"No, thank you. The Holmes will be wondering what's become of us."

"They'll know," the girl said.

"Come on. I want to see the world from up in that jinker." He steered her towards the door.

She went with him unresisting. "It's a buggy," she said.

"No, it's not. We're in Australia now. It's a jinker."

"That's where you're wrong," she said. "It's a buggy —an Abbott buggy. It's over seventy years old. Daddy says it was built in America."

He looked at it with new interest. "Say," he exclaimed, "I was wondering where I'd seen it before. My grandpa had one just like it in the woodshed, up in Maine, when I was a boy."

She mustn't let him think about the past "Just stand by her head as I back out of this," she said. "She's not so good in reverse." She swung herself up into the driving seat and tweaked the mare's mouth cruelly, so that he had plenty to do. The mare stood up and pawed at him with her forefeet; he managed to get her headed round towards the street and swung up beside the girl as they dashed off in a canter. Moira said, "She's a bit fresh. The hill'll stop her in a minute. These bloody bitumen roads. . . The American sat clinging to his seat as they careered out of town, the mare slithering and sliding on the smooth surfaces, wondering that any girl could drive a horse so badly.

They came to the Holmes' house a few minutes later with the grey in a lather of sweat. The lieutenant commander and his wife came out to meet them. "Sorry we're late, Mary," the girl said coolly. "I couldn't get Commander Towers past the pub."

Peter remarked, "Looks like you've been making up lost time."

"We had quite a ride," the submarine commander observed. He got down and was introduced to Mary. Then he turned to the girl. "How would it be if I walk her up and down a little, till she cools off?"

"Fine," said the girl. "I should unharness her and put her in the paddock—Peter'll show you. I'll give Mary a hand with the lunch. Peter, Dwight wants to sail your boat this afternoon."

"I never said that," the American protested.

"But you do." She eyed the horse, glad that her father wasn't there to see. "Give her a rub down with something—there's a cloth in the back underneath the oats. I'll give her a drink later on, after we've had one ourselves."

That afternoon Mary stayed at home with the baby, quietly preparing for the evening party; Dwight Towers rode unsteadily with Peter and Moira to the sailing club on bicycles. They went with towels round their necks and swimming trunks tucked into pockets; they changed at the club in anticipation of a wet sail. The boat was a sealed plywood box with a small cockpit and an

20

efficient spread of sail. They rigged and launched her and got to the starting line with five minutes to spare, the American sailing the boat, Moira crewing for him, and Peter watching the race from the shore.

They sailed in bathing costumes, Dwight Towers in an old pair of fawn trunks and the girl in a two-piece costume mainly white; they had shirts with them in the boat in case of sunburn. For a few minutes they manoeuvred about in the warm sun behind the starting line, milling around amongst a dozen others of mixed classes in the race. The commander had not sailed a boat for some years and he had never handled a boat of that particular type before; she handled well, however, and he quickly learned that she was very fast He had confidence in her by the time the gun went, and they were fifth over the line at the start of a race three times round a triangular course.

As is the case on Port Phillip Bay, the wind blew up very quickly. By the time they had been round once, it was blowing quite hard and they were sailing gunwale under; Commander Towers was too busy with the sheet and tiller keeping the boat upright and on her course to have much attention for anything else. They started on the second round and beat up to the further turning point in brilliant sunshine and clouds of spray like diamonds; so occupied was he that he failed to notice the girl's toe as she kicked a coil of mainsheet round the cleat and laid a tangle of jib sheet down on top of it. They came to the buoy and he bore away smartly, putting up the tiller and letting out the sheet, which ran two feet and fouled. A gust came down on them and laid the vessel over, the girl played dumb and pulled the jib sheet in, and the boat gave and laid her sails down flat upon the water. In a moment they were swimming by her side.

She said accusingly, "You held on to the main-sheet!" And then she said, "Oh, hell, my bra's coming off!"

Indeed, she had contrived to give the knot between her shoulder blades a tweak as she went into the water, and it now floated by her side. She grabbed it with one hand and said, "Swim round to the other side and sit on the centre-board. She'll come up all right." She swam with him.

In the distance they saw the white motorboat on safety patrol turn and head toward them. She said to her companion, "Here's the crash boat coming now. Just one thing after another. Help me get this on before they come, Dwight." She could have done it perfectly well herself, lying face down in the water. "That's right—a good hard knot. Not quite so tight as that; I'm not a Japanese. That's right. Now let's get this boat up and go on with the race."

She climbed on to the centre-board that stuck out horizontally from the hull at water level and stood on it holding on to the gunwale while he swam below, marvelling at the slim lines of her figure and at her effrontery. He bore his weight down on the plate with her and the boat lifted sodden sails out of the water, hesitated, and then came upright with a rush. The girl tumbled over the topsides into the cockpit and fell in a heap as she cast off the mainsheet, and Dwight clambered in beside her. In a minute they were under

21

way again, the vessel tender with the weight of water on her sails, before the crash boat reached them. "Don't do that again," she said severely. "This is my sun-bathing suit. It's not meant for swimming in."

"I don't know how I came to do it," he apologized. "We were doing all right up till then."

They completed the course without further incident, finishing last but one. They sailed in to the beach, and Peter met them waist deep in the water. He caught the boat and turned her into the wind. "Have a good sail?" he asked. "I saw you bottle her."

"It's been a lovely sail," the girl replied. "Dwight bottled her and then my bra came off, so one way and another we've had a thrilling time. Never a dull moment. She goes beautifully, Peter."

They jumped over into the water and pulled the boat ashore, let down the sails, and put her on the trolley on the slipway to park her up on the beach. Then they bathed off the end of the jetty and sat smoking in the warm evening sun, sheltered from the offshore wind by the cliff behind them.

The American looked at the blue water, the red cliffs, the moored motorboats rocking on the water. "This is quite a place you've got here," he said reflectively. "For its size it's as nice a little club as any that I've seen."

"They don't take sailing too seriously," Peter remarked. "That's the secret."

The girl said, "That's the secret of everything. When do we start drinking again, Peter?"

"The crowd are coming in at about eight o'clock," he told her. He turned to his guest. "We've got a few people coming in this evening," he said. "I thought we'd go down and have dinner at the hotel first Eases the strain on the domestic side."

"Sure. That'll be fine."

The girl said, "You're not taking Commander Towers to the Pier Hotel again?"

"That's where we thought of going for dinner."

She said darkly, "It seems to me to be very unwise." The American laughed. "You're building up quite a reputation for me in these parts."

"You're doing that for yourself," she retorted. "I'm doing all I can to whitewash you. I'm not going to say a word about you tearing off my bra."

Dwight Towers glanced at her uncertainly, and then he laughed. He laughed as he had not laughed for a year, unrestrained by thoughts of what had gone before. "Okay," he said at last. "We'll keep that a secret, just between you and me."

"It will be on my side," she said primly. "You'll probably be telling everyone about it later on this evening when you're a bit full."

Peter said, "Maybe we'd better think about changing. I told Mary we'd be back up at the house by six." They walked down the jetty towards the dressing rooms, changed, and rode back on their bicycles. At the house they found Mary on the lawn watering the garden. They discussed ways and means of getting down to the hotel, and decided to harness up the grey and take the buggy down. "We'd better do that for Commander Towers," the girl said. "He'd never make it back up the hill after another session in the Pier Hotel."

She went off with Peter to the paddock to catch the grey and harness her. As she slipped the bit between the teeth and pulled the ears through the bridle she said, "How am I doing, Peter?"

He grinned. "You're doing all right. Never a dull moment"

"Well, that's what Mary said she wanted. He's not burst into tears yet, anyway."

"More likely to burst a blood vessel if you keep going on at him."

"I don't know that I'll be able to. I've worked through most of my repertoire." She laid the saddle over the mare's back.

"You'll get a bit more inspiration as the night goes on," he remarked.

"Maybe."

The night went on. They dined at the hotel and drove back up the hill more moderately than before, unharnessed the horse and put her in the paddock for the night, and were ready to meet the guests at eight o'clock. Four couples came to the modest little party; a young doctor and his wife, another naval officer, a cheerful young man described as a chook farmer whose way of life was a mystery to the American, and the young owner of a tiny engineering works. For three hours they danced and drank together, sedulously avoiding any serious topic of conversation. In the warm night die room grew hotter and hotter, coats and ties were jettisoned at an early stage, and the gramophone went on working through an enormous pile of records, half of which Peter had borrowed for the evening. In spite of the wide-open windows behind the fly wire, the room grew full of cigarette smoke. From time to time Peter would throw the contents of the ash trays into the wastepaper bin; from time to time Mary would collect the empty glasses, take them out to the kitchen to wash them, and bring them back again. Finally at about half-past eleven she brought in a tray of tea and buttered scones and cakes, the universal signal in Australia that the party was coming to an end. Presently the guests began to take their leave, wobbling away on their bicycles.

Moira and Dwight walked down the little drive to see the doctor and his wife safely off the premises. They turned back towards the house. "Nice party," said the submarine commander. "Really nice people, all of them."

It was cool and pleasant in the garden after the hot stuffiness of the house. The night was very still. Between the trees they could see the shore line of Port Phillip running up from Falmouth towards Nelson in the bright light of the stars. "It was awfully hot in there," the girl remarked. "I'm going to stay out here a bit before going to bed, and cool off."

"I'd better get you a wrap."

"You'd better get me a drink, Dwight."

"A soft one?" he suggested.

She shook her head. "About an inch and a half of brandy and a lot of ice, if there's any left."

He left her and went in to get her drink. When he came out again, a glass in each hand, he found her sitting on the edge of the verandah in the darkness. She took the glass from him with a word of thanks and he sat down beside her. After the noise and turmoil of the evening the peace of the garden in the night was a relief to him. "It certainly is nice to sit quiet for a little while," he said.

"Till the mosquitoes start biting," she said. A little warm breeze blew around them. "They may not, with this wind. I shouldn't sleep now if I went to bed, full as I am. I'd just lie and toss about all night"

"You were up late last night?" he asked.

She nodded. "And the night before."

"I'd say you might try going to bed early, once in a while."

"What's the use?" she demanded. "What's the use of anything now?" He did not try to answer that, and presently she asked, "Why is Peter joining you in *Scorpion*, Dwight?"

"He's our new liaison officer," he told her.

"Did you have one before him?"

He shook his head. "We never had one before."

"Why have they given you one now?"

"I wouldn't know," he replied. "Maybe we'll be going for a cruise in Australian waters. I've had no orders, but that's what people tell me. The captain seems to be about the last person they tell in this navy."

"Where do they say you're going to, Dwight?"

He hesitated for a moment. Security was now a thing of the past though it took a conscious effort to remember it; with no enemy in all the world there was little but the force of habit in it. "People are saying we're to make a little cruise up to Port Moresby," he told her. "It may be just a rumour, but that's all I know."

"But Port Moresby's out, isn't it?"

"I believe it is. They haven't had any radio from there for quite a while."

"But you can't go on shore there if it's out, can you?"

"Somebody has to go and see, sometime," he said. "We wouldn't go outside the hull unless the radiation level's near to normal. If it's high I

24

wouldn't even surface. But someone has to go and see, sometime." He paused and there was silence in the starlight, in the garden. "There's a lot of places someone ought to go and see," he said at last. "There's radio transmission still coming through from someplace near Seattle. It doesn't make any sense, just now and then a kind of jumble of dots and dashes. Sometimes a fortnight goes by, and then it comes again. It could be somebody's alive up there, doesn't know how to handle the set. There's a lot of funny things up in the Northern Hemisphere that someone ought to go and see."

"Could anybody be alive up there?"

"I wouldn't think so. It's not quite impossible. He'd have to be living in an hermetically sealed room with all air filtered as it comes in and all food and water stored in with him some way. I wouldn't think it practical."

She nodded. "Is it true that Cairns is out, Dwight?"

"I think it is—Cairns and Darwin. Maybe we'll have to go and see those, too. Maybe that's why Peter has been drafted into *Scorpion*. He knows those waters."

"Somebody was telling Daddy that they've got radiation sickness in Townsville now. Do you think that's right?"

"I don't really know—I hadn't heard it. But I'd say it might be right. It's south of Cairns."

"It's going to go on spreading down here, southwards, till it gets to us?"

"That's what they say."

"There never was a bomb dropped in the Southern Hemisphere," she said angrily. "Why must it come to us? Can't anything be done to stop it?"

He shook his head. "Not a thing. It's the winds. It's mighty difficult to dodge what's carried on the wind. You just can't do it. You've got to take what's coming to you, and make the best of it."

"I don't understand it," she said stubbornly. "People were saying once that no wind blows across the equator, so we'd be all right. And now it seems we aren't all right at all. . . ."

"We'd never have been all right," he said quietly.

"Even if they'd been correct about the heavy particles —the radioactive dust—which they weren't, we'd still have got the lightest particles carried by diffusion. We've got them now. The background level of the radiation here, today, is eight or nine times what it was before the war."

"That doesn't seem to hurt us," she retorted. "But this dust they talk about. That's blown about on the wind, isn't it?"

"That's so," he replied. "But no wind does blow right into the Southern Hemisphere from the Northern Hemisphere. If it did we'd all be dead right now."

"I wish we were," she said bitterly. "It's like waiting to be hung."

25

"Maybe it is. Or maybe it's a period of grace."

There was a little silence after he said that. "Why is it taking so long, Dwight?" she asked at last "Why can't the wind blow straight and get it over?"

"It's not so difficult to understand, really," he said. "In each hemisphere the winds go around in great whorls, thousands of miles across, between the pole and the equator. There's a circulatory system of winds in the Northern Hemisphere and another in the Southern Hemisphere. But what divides them isn't the equator that you see on a globe. It's a thing called the Pressure Equator, and that shifts north and south with the season. In January the whole of Borneo and Indonesia is in the northern system, but in July the division has shifted away up north, so that all of India and Siam, and everything that's to the south of that, is in the southern system. So in January the northern winds carry the radioactive dust from the fall-out down into Malaya, say. Then in July that's in the southern system, and our own winds pick it up and carry it down here. That's the reason why it's coming to us slowly."

"And they can't do anything about it?"

"Not a thing. It's just too big a matter for mankind to tackle. We've just got to take it."

"I won't take it," she said vehemently. "It's not fair. No one in the Southern Hemisphere ever dropped a bomb, a hydrogen bomb or a cobalt bomb or any other sort of bomb. We had nothing to do with it. Why should we have to die because other countries nine or ten thousand miles away from us wanted to have a war? It's so bloody unfair."

"It's that all right," he said. "But that's the way it is." There was a pause, and then she said angrily, "It's not that I'm afraid of dying, Dwight. We've all got to do that sometime. It's all the things I'm going to have to miss. . . ." She turned to him in the starlight "I'm never going to get outside Australia. All my life I've wanted to see the Rue de Rivoli. I suppose it's the romantic name. It's silly, because I suppose it's just a street like any other street But that's what I've wanted, and I'm never going to see it Because there isn't any Paris now, or London, or New York."

He smiled at her gently. "The Rue de Rivoli may still be there, with things in the shopwindows and everything. I wouldn't know if Paris got a bomb or not. Maybe it's all there still, just as it was, with the sun shining down the street the way you'd want to see it. That's the way I like to think about that sort of place. It's just that folks don't live there anymore."

She got restlessly to her feet. "That's not the way I wanted to see it. A city of dead people. . . . Get me another drink, Dwight."

Still seated, he smiled up at her. "Not on your life. It's time you went to bed."

"Then I'll get it for myself." She marched angrily into the house. He heard the tinkle of glass and she came out almost immediately, a tumbler more than half full in hand with a lump of ice floating in it. "I was going home in March," she exclaimed. "To London. It's been arranged for years. I was to have six months in England and on the Continent, and then I was coming back through America. I'd have seen Madison Avenue. It's so bloody unfair."

She took a long gulp at her glass, and held it away from her in disgust. "Christ, what's this muck I'm drinking?"

He got up and took the glass from her and smelled it. "That's whisky," he told her.

She took it back from him and smelled it herself. "So it is," she said vaguely. "It'll probably kill me, on top of brandy." She lifted the glass of neat liquor and tossed it down, and threw the ice cube out upon the grass.

She faced him, unsteady in the starlight. "I'll never have a family like Mary," she muttered. "It's so unfair. Even if you took me to bed tonight I'd never have a family, because there wouldn't be time." She laughed hysterically. "It's really damn funny. Mary was afraid that you'd start bursting into tears when you saw the baby and the nappies hanging on the line. Like the squadron leader in the R.A.F. they had before." Her words began to slur. "Keep him occ . . . occupied."

She swayed, and caught a post of the verandah. "That's what she said. Never a dull moment. Don't let him see the baby or perhaps . . . perhaps he'll start crying." The tears began to trickle down her cheeks. "She never thought it might be me who'd do the crying, and not you."

She collapsed by the verandah, head down in a torrent of tears. The submarine commander hesitated for a moment, went to touch her on the shoulder and then drew back, uncertain what to do. Finally he turned away and went into the house. He found Mary in the kitchen tidying up the mess left by the party.

"Mrs. Holmes," he said a little diffidently. "Maybe you could step outside and take a look at Miss Davidson. She just drank a full glass of neat whisky on top of brandy. I think she might want somebody to put her to bed."


## Chapter Two

Infants take no account of Sundays or midnight parties; by six o'clock next morning the Holmes were up and doing and Peter was on the road pedalling his bicycle with the trailer attached to fetch the milk and cream. He stayed with the farmer for a while discussing the axle for the new trailer, and the towbar, and making a few sketches for the mechanic to work from. "I've got to report for duty tomorrow," he said. "This is the last time that I'll be coming over for the milk."

"That'll be right," said Mr. Paul. "Leave it to me. Tuesdays, and Saturdays. I'll see Mrs. Holmes gets the milk and cream."

He got back to his house at about eight o'clock; he shaved and had a shower, dressed, and began to help Mary with the breakfast. Commander Towers put in an appearance at about a quarter to nine with a fresh, scrubbed look about him. "That was a nice party that you had last night," he said. "I don't know when I enjoyed one so much."

His host said, "There are some very pleasant people living just round here." He glanced at his captain and grinned. "Sorry about Moira. She doesn't usually pass out like that."

"It was the whisky. She isn't up yet?"

"I wouldn't expect to see her just yet. I heard someone being sick at two in the morning. I take it that it wasn't you?"

The American laughed. "No sir."

The breakfast came upon the table, and the three of them sat down. "Like another swim this morning?" Peter asked his guest. "It looks like being another hot day."

The American Hesitated. "I rather like to go to church on Sunday morning. It's what we do at home. Would there be a Church of England church around her any place?"

Mary said, "It's just down the hill. Only about three-quarters of a mile away. The service is at eleven o'clock."

"I might take a walk down there. Would that fit in with what you're doing, though?"

Peter said, "Of course, sir. I don't think I'll come with you. I've got a good bit to sort out here before I join in *Scorpion*"

The captain nodded. "Sure. I'll be back here in time for lunch, and then I'll have to get back to the ship. I'd like to take a train around three o'clock."

He walked down to the church in the warm sunlight He left plenty of time so that he was a quarter of an hour early for the service, but he went in. The sidesman gave him a prayer book and a hymn book, and he chose a seat towards the back, because the order of the service was still strange to him and from there he could see when other people knelt, and when they stood. He said the conventional prayer that he had been taught in childhood and then he sat back, looking around. The little church was very like the church in his own town, in Mystic, Connecticut. It even smelled the same.

The girl Moira Davidson certainly was all mixed up. She drank too much, but some people never could accept things as they were. She was a nice kid, though. He thought Sharon would like her.

In the tranquillity of the church he set himself to think about his family, and to visualize them. He was, essentially, a very simple man. He would be going back to them in September, home from his travels. He would see them all again in less than nine months' time. They must not feel when he rejoined them, that he was out of touch, or that he had forgotten things that were important in their lives. Junior must have grown quite a bit; kids did at that age. He had probably outgrown the coonskin cap and outfit, mentally and physically. It was time he had a fishing rod, a little Fiberglas spinning rod, and learned to use it. It would be fun teaching Junior to fish. His birthday was July the 10th. Dwight couldn't send the rod for his birthday, and probably he couldn't take it with him, though that would be worth trying. Perhaps he could get one over there.

Helen's birthday was April the 17th; she would be six then. Again, he'd missed her birthday unless something happened to *Scorpion*. He must remember to tell her he was sorry, and he must think of something to take her between now and September. Sharon would explain to her on the day, would tell her that Daddy was away at sea, but he'd be coming home before the winter and he'd bring his present then. Sharon would make it all right with Helen.

He sat there thinking of his family throughout the service, kneeling when other people knelt and standing when they stood. From time to time he roused himself to take part in the simple and uncomplicated words of a hymn, but for the rest of the time he was lost in a daydream of his family and of his home. He walked out of the church at the end of the service mentally refreshed. Outside the church he knew nobody and nobody knew him; the vicar smiled at him uncertainly in the porch and he smiled back, and then he was strolling back uphill in the warm sunlight, his head now full of *Scorpion*, the supplies, and the many chores he had to do, the many checks he had to make, before he took her to sea.

At the house he found Mary and Moira Davidson sitting in deck chairs on the verandah, the baby in its pram beside them. Mary got up from her chair as he walked up to them. "You look hot," she said. "Take off your coat and come and sit down in the shade. You found the church all right?"

"Why, yes," he said. He took his coat off and sat down on the edge of the verandah. "You've got a mighty fine congregation," he observed. "There wasn't a seat vacant."

"It wasn't always like that," she said drily. "Let me get you a drink."

"I'd like something soft," he said. He eyed their glasses. "What's that you're drinking?"

Miss Davidson replied, "Lime juice and water. All right, don't say it."

He laughed. "I'd like one of those, too." Mary went off to get it for him, and he turned to the girl. "Did you get any breakfast this morning?"

"Half a banana and a small brandy," she said equably. "I wasn't very well."

"It was the whisky," he said. "That was the mistake you made."

"One of them," she replied. "I don't remember anything after talking to you on the lawn, after the party. Did you put me to bed?"

He shook his head. "I thought that was Mrs. Holmes' job."

She smiled faintly. "You missed an opportunity. I must remember to thank Mary."

"I should do that. She's a mighty nice person, Mrs. Holmes."

"She says you're going back to Williamstown this afternoon. Can't you stay and have another bathe?"

He shook his head. "I've got a lot to do on board before tomorrow. We go to sea this week. There's probably a flock of messages on my desk."

"I suppose you're the sort of person who works very hard, all the time, whether you've got to or not."

He laughed. "I suppose I must be." He glanced at her. "Do you do any work?"

"Of course. I'm a very busy woman."

"What do you work at?"

She lifted her glass. "This. What I've been doing ever since I met you yesterday."

He grinned. "You find that the routine gets tedious, sometimes?"

"Life gets tedious," she quoted. "Not sometimes. All the time."

He nodded. "I'm lucky, having plenty to do."

She glanced at him. "Can I come and see your submarine next week?"

He laughed, thinking of the mass of work there was to do on board. "No, you can't. We go to sea next week." And then, because that seemed ungracious, he said, "You interested in submarines?"

"Not really," she said a little listlessly. "I kind of thought I'd like to see it, but not if it's a bother."

"I'd be glad to show it to you," he told her. "But not next week. I'd like it if you'd come down and have lunch with me one day when things are quiet and we're not dashing around like scalded cats. A quiet day, when I could show you everything. And then maybe we could go up to the city and have dinner someplace."

"That sounds good," she said. "When will that be, so that I can look forward to it?"

He thought for a moment. "I couldn't say right now. I'll be reporting a state of operational readiness around the end of this coming week, and I'd think they'd send us off on the first cruise within a day or so. After that we ought to have a spell in the dockyard before going off again."

"This first cruise—that's the one up to Port Moresby?"

"That's right. I'll try to fit it in before we go away on that, but I couldn't guarantee it. If you'll give me your telephone I'll call you around Friday and let you know."

"Berwick 8641," she said. He wrote it down. "Before ten o'clock is the best time to ring. I'm almost always out in the evening."

He nodded. "That'll be fine. It's possible we'll still be at sea on Friday. It might be Saturday before I call. But I will call, Miss Davidson."

She smiled. "Moira's the name, Dwight."

He laughed. "Okay."

She drove him to the station in the buggy after lunch', being herself on her way home to Berwick. As he got down in the station yard she said, "Good-bye, Dwight. Don't work too hard." And then she said, "Sorry I made such a fool of myself last night."

He grinned. "Mixing drinks, that's what does it. Let that be a lesson to you."

She laughed harshly. "Nothing's a lesson to me, ever. I'll probably do that again tomorrow night, and the night after."

"It's your body," he said equably.

"That's the trouble," she replied. "Mine, and nobody else's. If anybody else became involved it might be different, but there's no time for that. Too bad."

He nodded. "I'll be seeing you."

"You really will?"

"Why, sure," he said. "I'll call you like I said."

He travelled back to Willamstown in the electric train, while she drove twenty miles to her country home. She got there at about six o'clock, unharnessed the mare and put her in the stable. Her father came to help her, and together they pushed the buggy into the garage shed beside the unused Customline, gave the mare a bucket of water and a feed of oats, and went into the house. Her mother was sitting in the screened verandah, sewing.

"Hullo, dear," she said. "Did you have a nice time?"

"All right," the girl replied. "Peter and Mary threw a party last night. Quite good fun. Knocked me back a bit, though."

Her mother sighed a little, but she had learned that it was no use to protest. "You must go to bed early tonight," she said. "You've had so many late nights recently."

"I think I will."

"What was the American like?"

"He's nice. Very quiet and navy."

"Was he married?"

"I didn't ask him. I should think he must have been."

"What did you do?"

The girl repressed her irritation at the catechism; Ma was like that, and there was now too little time to spend it in quarrelling. "We went sailing in the afternoon." She settled down to tell her mother most of what had

31

happened during the week-end, repressing the bit about her bra and much of what had happened at the party.

At Williamstown Commander Towers walked into the dockyard and made his way to *Sydney*. He occupied two adjoining cabins with a communicating door in the bulkhead, one of which was used for office purposes. He sent a messenger for the officer of the deck in *Scorpion* and Lieutenant Hirsch appeared with a sheaf of signals in his hand. He took these from the young man and read them through. Mostly they dealt with routine matters of the fuelling and victualling, but one from the Third Naval Member's office was unexpected. It told him that a civilian scientific officer of the Commonwealth Scientific and Industrial Research Organisation had been ordered to report in *Scorpion* for scientific duties. This officer would be under the command of the Australian liaison officer in *Scorpion*. His name was Mr. J. S. Osborne.

Commander Towers held this signal in his hand, and glanced at the lieutenant. "Say, do you know anything about this guy?"

"He's here right now, sir. He arrived this morning. I put him in the wardroom and got the duty officer to allocate a cabin for him for tonight."

The captain raised his eyebrows. "Well, what do you know? What does he look like?"

"Very tall and thin. Mousey sort of hair. Wears spectacles."

"How old?"

"A little older than me, I'd say. Under thirty, though."

The captain thought for a minute. "Going to make things kind of crowded in the wardroom. I think we'll berth him with Commander Holmes. You got three men aboard?"

"That's right. Isaacs, Holman, and de Vries. Chief of the Boat Mortiner is on board, too."

"Tell the chief I want another cot rigged on the forward side of Bulkhead F, transverse to the ship, head to starboard. He can take one out of the forward torpedo fiat."

"Okay, sir."

Commander Towers ran through the routine matters in the other signals with his officer, and then sent the lieutenant to ask Mr. Osborne to come to the office. When the civilian appeared he motioned him to a chair, gave him a cigarette, and dismissed his officer. "Well, Mr. Osborne," he said, "this is quite a surprise. I just read the order posting you to join us. I'm glad to know you."

"I'm afraid it was rather a quick decision," the scientist said. "I only heard about it the day before yesterday."

"That's very often the way it is in service matters," said the captain. "Well, first things first. What's your full name?"

"John Seymour Osborne."

"Married?"

"No."

"Okay. Aboard *Scorpion*, or aboard any naval vessel, you address me as Captain Towers, and every now and then you call me 'sir.' On shore, off duty, my name is Dwight to you—not to the junior officers."

The scientist smiled. "Very good, sir."

"Ever been to sea in a submarine before?"

"No."

"You'll find things just a little cramped till you get used to it. I'm fixing you a berth in Officer's Country, and you'll mess with the officers in the wardroom." He glanced at the neat grey suit upon the scientist. "You'll probably need clothing. See Lieutenant Commander Holmes about that when he comes aboard tomorrow morning, and get him to draw clothing for you from the store. You'll get that suit messed up if you go down in *Scorpion* in that."

"Thank you, sir."

The captain leaned back in his chair and glanced at the scientist, noting the lean, intelligent face, the loose, ungainly figure. "Tell me, what are you supposed to be doing in this outfit?"

"I'm to make observations and keep records of the radioactive levels, atmospheric and marine, with special reference to the subsurface levels and radioactive intensity within the hull. I understand you're making a cruise northwards."

"That's what everybody understands but me. It must be right, and I'll be told one day." He frowned slightly. "Are you anticipating a rise in the radioactive level inside the hull?"

"I don't think so. I very much hope not. I doubt if it could happen when you are submerged, except under very extreme conditions. But it's just as well to keep an eye on it. I take it that you'd want to know at once of any significant rise."

"Sure I would."

They proceeded to discuss the various techniques involved. Most of the gear that Osborne had brought with him was portable and involved no installation in the ship. In the evening light he put on an overall suit lent him by the captain and went down with Dwight into *Scorpion* to inspect the radiation detector mounted on the aft periscope and formulate a programme for its calibration against a standard instrument as they went down the bay. A similar check was to be made upon the detector installed in the engine room, and a small amount of engineering was required at one of the two remaining torpedo tubes for the sampling of sea water. It was practically dark when they climbed back into *Sydney*, to take supper in the great, echoing, empty wardroom.

33

Next day was a turmoil of activity. When Peter came aboard in the forenoon his first job was to telephone a friend in the Operations Division and point out that it would be courteous, to say the least, to tell the captain what was common knowledge to the Australian officers under his command, and to make a signal requesting his comments on a draft operation order. By evening this signal had come in and had been dealt with, John Osborne was suitably clothed for life in a submarine, the work on the aft door of the torpedo tube was finished, and the two Australians were packing their gear into the little space that had been allocated to them for personal effects. They slept that night in *Sydney*, and moved into *Scorpion* on Tuesday morning. A few more chores were finished in a couple of hours, and Dwight reported readiness to proceed upon sea trials. They were cleared for sea, had lunch at noon beside the *Sydney*, and cast off. Dwight turned his ship and set a course at slow speed down the bay towards the Heads.

All afternoon they carried out their radioactive trials, cruising around a barge with a mildly radioactive element on board anchored in the middle of the bay, while John Osborne ran around noting the readings on his various instruments, barking his long shins upon steel manholes as he clambered up and down the conning tower to the bridge, cracking his tall head painfully on bulkheads and control wheels as he moved quickly in the control room. By five o'clock the trials were over; they left the barge to be disposed of by the shore party of scientists who had put it there, and set course for the open sea.

They stayed on the surface all night, settling into the sea routine as they proceeded westward. At dawn they were off Cape Banks in South Australia, in a fresh southwesterly breeze and a moderate sea. Here they submerged and went down to about fifty feet, returning to periscope depth for a look round once an hour. In the late afternoon they were off Cape Borda on Kangaroo Island, and set course up the strait at periscope depth towards Port Adelaide. By about ten o'clock on Wednesday night they were looking at the town through the periscope; after ten minutes the captain turned around without surfacing and made for the open sea again. At sunset on Thursday they were off the north of King Island and setting course for home. They surfaced as they neared the Heads and passed into Port Phillip Bay at the first light of dawn, and berthed alongside the aircraft carrier at Williamstown in time for breakfast on Friday, with nothing but minor defects to be rectified.

That morning the First Naval Member, Vice Admiral Sir David Hartman, came down to inspect the only ship in his command that was worth bothering about. That took about an hour, and he spent a quarter of an horn; with Dwight and Peter Holmes in the office cabin discussing with them the modifications that they had proposed to the draft operation order. He left then for a conference with the Prime Minister, at that time in Melbourne; with no aircraft flying on the airlines, federal government from Canberra was growing difficult, and parliamentary sessions there were growing shorter and less frequent.

That evening Dwight rang Moira Davidson, as he had promised. "Well," he said, "we got back in one piece. There's just a little being done on board the ship, but nothing very much."

She asked, "Does that mean I can see her?"

"I'd be glad to show her to you. We shan't be going off again before Monday."

"I'd like to see her, Dwight. Would tomorrow or Sunday be the best?"

He thought for a moment. If they were to sail on Monday, Sunday might be busy. "I'd say tomorrow would be best."

In turn, she thought rapidly. She would have to run out on Anne Sutherland's party, but it looked like a dreary sort of party anyway.

"I'd love to come tomorrow," she said. "Do I come to Williamstown station?"

"That's the best way. I'll meet you there. What train will you be coming on?"

"I don't know the times. Let's say the first one after eleven-thirty."

"Okay. If I should be all tied up, I'll get Peter Holmes or else John Osborne to go down and meet you."

"Did you say John Osborne?"

"That's right. Do you know him?"

"An Australian—with C.S.I.R.O.?"

"That's the one. A tall guy with spectacles."

"He's a sort of relation—his aunt married one of my uncles. Is he in your party?"

"Definitely. He joined us as scientific officer."

"He's dippy," she informed him. "Absolutely mad. He'll wreck your ship for you."

He laughed. "Okay. Come down and see it before he pulls the bung out."

"I'd love to do that, Dwight. See you on Saturday morning."

He met her at the station the next morning, having nothing particular to do in the ship. She came in a white outfit, white pleated skirt, white blouse with coloured thread embroidery, vaguely Norwegian in style, white shoes. She was pleasant to look at, but there was concern in him as he greeted her; how in hell he was going to get her through the cramped maze of greasy machinery that was *Scorpion* with her clothes unsullied was a problem, and he was to take her out in the evening.

"Morning, Dwight," she said. "Have you been waiting long?"

"Just a few minutes," he replied. "Did you have to start very early?"

"Not as early as last time," she informed him. "Daddy drove me to the station, and I got a train soon after nine. Early enough, though. You'll give me a drink before lunch, won't you?"

He hesitated. "Uncle Sam doesn't like it aboard ship," he said. "It'll have to be Coke or orangeade."

"Even in *Sydney*?"

"Even in *Sydney*" he said firmly. "You wouldn't want to drink hard liquor with my officers when they were drinking Cokes."

She said restlessly, "I want to drink hard liquor, as you call it, before lunch. I've got a mouth like the bottom of the parrot's cage. You wouldn't want me to throw a screaming fit in front of all your officers." She glanced around. "There must be a hotel here somewhere. Buy me a drink before we go on board, and then I'll just breathe brandy at them while I'm drinking Coke."

"Okay," he said equably. "There's a hotel on the corner. We'll go in there."

They walked together to the hotel; he entered and looked around, unsure of his surroundings. He led her into the Ladies' Lounge. "I think this must be it."

"Don't you know? Haven't you ever been in here before?"

He shook his head. "Brandy?"

"Double," she said. "With ice, and just a little water. Don't you come in here?"

"I've never been in here," he told her.

"Don't you ever want to go out on a bender?" she inquired. "In the evenings, when you've got nothing to do?"

"I used to just at first," he admitted. "But then I went up to the city for it. Don't mess on your own doorstep. I gave it up after a week or two. It wasn't very satisfactory."

"What do you do in the evenings, when the ship's not at sea?" she asked.

"Read a magazine, or else maybe a book. Sometimes we go out and take in a movie." The barman came, and he ordered her brandy, with a small whisky for himself.

"It all sounds very unhealthy," she observed. "I'm going to the Ladies'. Look after my bag."

He managed to detach her from the hotel after her second double brandy and took her into the dockyard and to *Sydney*, hoping that she would behave herself in front of his officers. But he need have had no fears; she was demure and courteous to all the Americans. Only to Osborne did she reveal her real self.

"Hullo, John," she said. "What on earth are you doing here?"

36

"I'm part of the ship's company," he told her. "Scientific observation. Making a nuisance of myself generally."

"That's what Commander Towers told me," she observed. "You're really going to live with them in the submarine? For days on end?"

"So it seems."

"Do they know your habits?"

"I beg your pardon?"

"All right, I won't tell them. It's nothing to do with me." She turned away to talk to Commander Lundgren.

When he offered her a drink she chose an orangeade; she made an attractive picture in the wardroom of *Sydney* that morning, drinking with the Americans, standing beneath the portrait of the Queen. While she was occupied the captain drew his liaison officer to one side. "Say," he observed in a low tone, "she can't go down in *Scorpion* in those clothes. Can you rustle up an overall for her?"

Peter nodded. "I'll draw a boiler suit. About size one, I should think. Where's she going to change?"

The captain rubbed his chin. "Do you know any place?"

"Nothing better than your sleeping cabin, sir. She wouldn't be disturbed there."

"I'll never hear the last of it—from her."

"I'm sure you won't," said Peter.

She lunched with the Americans at the end of one of the long tables, and took coffee with them in the anteroom. Then the junior officers dispersed to go about their business, and she was left with Dwight and Peter. Peter laid a clean, laundered boiler suit upon the table. "There's the overall," he said.

Dwight cleared his throat. "It's liable to be greasy in a submarine, Miss Davidson," he said.

"Moira," she interrupted.

"Okay, Moira. I was thinking maybe you should go down in an overall. I'm afraid you might get that dress pretty dirty down in *Scorpion*."

She took the boiler suit and unfolded it. "It's a comprehensive change," she observed. "Where can I put it on?"

"I was thinking you might use my sleeping cabin," he suggested. "You wouldn't be disturbed there."

"I hope not, but I wouldn't be too sure," she said. "Not after what happened in the boat." He laughed. "All right, Dwight, lead me to it. I'll try everything once."

He took her to the cabin and went back to the anteroom himself to wait for her. In the little sleeping cabin she looked about her curiously. There were photographs there, four of them. All showed a dark-haired young woman with two children, a boy eight or nine years old and a girl a couple of years

37

younger. One was a studio portrait of a mother with two children. The others were enlargements of snapshots, one at a bathing place with the family seated on a springboard, perhaps at a lake shore. Another was apparently taken on a lawn, perhaps the lawn before his home, a long car showed in the background and a portion of a white wooden house. She stood examining them with interest; they looked nice people. It was hard, but so was everything these days. No good agonizing about it.

She changed, leaving her outer clothes and her bag on the bunk, scowled at her appearance in the little mirror, and went out and down the corridor to find her host. He came forward to meet her. "Well, here I am," she said. "Looking like hell. Your submarine will have to be good, Dwight, to make up for this."

He laughed, and took her arm to guide her. "Sure it's good," he said. "Best in the U.S. Navy. This way." She repressed the comment that it was probably the only one in the U.S. Navy; no sense in hurting him.

He took her down the gangplank to the narrow deck and up on to the bridge, and began explaining his ship to her. She knew little of ships and nothing about submarines, but she was attentive and once or twice surprised him with the quick intelligence of her questions. "When you go down, why doesn't the water go down the voice pipe?" she asked.

"You turn off this cock."

"What happens if you forget?"

He grinned. "There's another one down below."

He took her down through the narrow hatchways into the control room. She spent some time at the periscope looking around the harbour and got the hang of that, but the ballasting and trim controls were beyond her and she was not much interested. She stared uncomprehending at the engines, but the sleeping and messing quarters intrigued her, so did the galley. "What happens about smells?" she asked. "What happens when you're cooking cabbage underwater?"

"You try not to have to do it," he told her. "Not fresh cabbage. The smell hangs around for quite a while. Finally the deodorizer deals with it, as the air gets changed and reoxygenated. There wouldn't be much left after an hour or two."

He gave her a cup of tea in the tiny cubicle that was his cabin. Sipping it, she asked him, "Have you got your orders yet, Dwight?"

He nodded. "Cairns, Port Moresby, and Darwin.

Then we come back here."

"There isn't anybody left alive in any of those places, is there?"

"I wouldn't know. That's what we've got to find out."

"Will you go ashore?"

He shook his head. "I don't think so. It all depends upon the radiation levels, but I wouldn't think we'd land. Maybe we won't even go outside the hull. We might stay at periscope depth if the conditions are really bad. But that's why we're taking John Osborne along with us, so we'll have somebody who really understands what the risks are."

She wrinkled her brows. "But if you can't go out on deck, how can you know if there's anyone still living in those places?"

"We can call through the loud hailer," he said. "Get as close inshore as we can manage, and call through the loud hailer."

"Could you hear them if they answer?"

"Not so well as we can talk. We've got a microphone hooked up beside the hailer, but you'd have to be very close to hear a person calling in reply. Still, it's something."

She glanced at him. "Has anybody been into the radioactive area before, Dwight?"

"Why, yes," he said. "It's okay if you're sensible, and don't take risks. We were in it quite a while the war was on, from Iwo Jima to the Philippines and then down south to Yap. You stay submerged, and carry on as usual. Of course, you don't want to go out on deck."

"I mean—recently. Has anyone been up into the radioactive area since the war stopped?"

He nodded. "The Swordfish-—that's our sister ship —she made a cruise up in the North Atlantic. She got back to Rio de Janeiro about a month ago. I've been waiting for a copy of Johnny Dismore's report—he's her captain—but I haven't seen it yet. There hasn't been a ship across to South America for quite a while.

I asked for a copy to be sent by teleprinter, but it's low priority on the radio."

"How far did she get?"

"She got all over, I believe," he said. "She did the eastern states from Florida to Maine and went right into New York Harbor, right on up the Hudson till she tangled with the wreck of the George Washington Bridge. She went to New London and to Halifax and to St. John's, and then she crossed the Atlantic and went up the English Channel and into the London River, but she couldn't get far up that. Then she took a look at Brest and at Lisbon, and by that time she was running out of stores and her crew were in pretty bad shape, so she went back to Rio." He paused. "I haven't heard yet how many days she was submerged—I'd like to know. She certainly set a new record, anyway."

"Did she find anyone alive, Dwight?"

"I don't think so. We'd certainly have heard about it if she did."

She stared down the narrow alleyway outside the curtain forming the cabin wall, the running maze of pipes and electric cables. "Can you visualize it, Dwight?"

"Visualize what?"

"All those cities, all those fields and farms, with nobody, and nothing left alive. Just nothing there. I simply can't take it in."

"I can't, either," he said. "I don't know that I want to try. I'd rather think of them the way they were."

"I never saw them, of course," she observed. "I've never been outside Australia, and now I'll never go. Not that I want to, now. I only know all those places from the movies and the books—that's as they were. I don't suppose there'll ever be a movie made of them as they are now."

He shook his head. "It wouldn't be possible. A cameraman couldn't live, as far as I can see. I guess nobody will ever know what the Northern Hemisphere looks like now, excepting God." He paused. "I think that's a good thing. You don't want to remember how a person looked when he was dead—you want to remember how he was when he was alive. That's the way I like to think about New York."

"It's too big," she repeated. "I can't take it in."

"It's too big for me, too," he replied. "I can't really believe in it, just can't get used to the idea. I suppose it's lack of imagination. I don't want to have any more imagination. They're all alive to me, those places in the States, just like they were. I'd like them to stay that way till next September."

She said softly, "Of course."

He stirred. "Have another cup of tea?"

"No, thanks."

He took her out on deck again; she paused on the bridge rubbing a bruised shin, breathing the sea air gratefully. "It must be the hell of a thing to be submerged in her for any length of time," she said. "How long will you be underwater for this cruise?"

"Not long," he said. "Six or seven days, maybe."

"It must be terribly unhealthy."

"Not physically," he said. "You do suffer from a lack of sunlight. We've got a couple of sunray lamps, but they're not the same as being out on deck. It's the psychological effect that's worst. Some men—good men in every other way—they just can't take it. Everybody gets kind of on edge after a while. You need a steady kind of temperament. Kind of placid, I'd say." She nodded, thinking that it fitted in with his own character. "Are all of you like that?"

"I'd say we might be. Most of us."

"Keep an eye on John Osborne," she remarked. "I don't believe he is."

He glanced at her in surprise. He had not thought of that, and the scientist had survived the trial trip quite well. But now that she had mentioned it, he wondered. "Why—I'll do that," he said. "Thanks for the suggestion."

They went up the gangway into *Sydney*. In the hangar of the aircraft carrier there were still aircraft parked with folded wings; the ship seemed dead and silent. She paused for a moment. "None of these will ever fly again, will they?"

"I wouldn't think so."

"Do any aeroplanes fly now, at all?"

"I haven't heard one in the air for quite a while," he said. "I know they're short of aviation gas."

She walked quietly with him to the cabin, unusually subdued. As she got out of the boiler suit and into her own clothes her spirits revived. These morbid bloody ships, these morbid bloody realities! She was urgent to get away from them, to drink, hear music, and to dance. Before the mirror, before the pictures of his wife and children, she made her lips redder, her cheeks brighter, her eyes sparkling. Snap out if it! Get right outside these riveted steel walls, and get out quick. This was no place for her. Into the world of romance, of make-believe and double brandies! Snap out of it, and get back to the world where she belonged!

From the photograph frames Sharon looked at her with understanding and approval.

In the wardroom he came forward to meet her. "Say," he exclaimed in admiration, "you look swell!" She smiled quickly. "I'm feeling lousy," she said. "Let's get out of it and into the fresh air. Let's go to that hotel and have a drink, and then go up and find somewhere to dance."

"Anything you say."

He left her with John Osborne while he went to change into civilian clothes. "Take me up on to the flight deck, John," she said. "I'll throw a screaming fit if I stay in these ships one minute longer."

"I'm not sure that I know the way up to the roof," he remarked. "I'm a new boy here." They found a steep ladder that led up to a gun turret, came down again, wandered along a steel corridor, asked a rating, and finally got up into the island and out on to the deck. On the wide, unencumbered flight deck the sun was warm, the sea blue, and the wind fresh. "Thank God I'm out of that," she said.

"I take it that you aren't enamoured of the navy," he observed.

"Well, are you having fun?"

He considered the matter. "Yes, I think I am. It's going to be rather interesting."

"Looking at dead people through a periscope. I can think of funnier sorts of fun."

41

They walked a step or two in silence. "It's all knowledge," he said at last. "One has to try and find out what has happened. It could be that it's all quite different to what we think. The radioactive elements may be getting absorbed by something. Something may have happened to the half-life that we don't know about Even if we don't discover anything that's good, it's still discovering things. I don't think we shall discover anything that's good, or very hopeful. But even so, it's fun just finding out."

"You call finding out the bad things fun?"

"Yes, I do," he said firmly. "Some games are fun even when you lose. Even when you know you're going to lose before you start. It's fun just playing them."

"You've got a pretty queer idea of fun and games."

"Your trouble is you won't face up to things," he told her. "All this has happened, and is happening, but you won't accept it. You've got to face the facts of life someday."

"All right," she said angrily, "I've got to face them. Next September, if what all you people say is right. That's time enough for me."

"Have it your own way." He glanced at her, grinning. "I wouldn't bank too much upon September," he remarked. "It's September plus or minus about three months. We may be going to cop it in June for all that anybody knows. Or, then again, I might be buying you a Christmas present."

She said furiously, "Don't you know?"

"No, I don't," he replied. "Nothing like this has ever happened in the history of the world before." He paused, and then he added whimsically, "If it had, we wouldn't be here talking about it."

"If you say one word more I'm going to push you over the edge of that deck."

Commander Towers came out of the island and walked across to them, neat in a double-breasted blue suit. "I wondered where you'd got to," he remarked.

The girl said, "Sorry, Dwight. We should have left a message. I wanted some fresh air."

John Osborne said, "You'd better watch out, sir. She's in a pretty bad temper. I'd stand away from her head, if I were you, in case she bites."

"He's been teasing me," she said. "Like Albert and the lion. Let's go, Dwight."

"See you tomorrow, sir," the scientist said. "I'll be staying on board over the week-end."

The captain turned away with the girl, and they went down the stairs within the island. As they passed down the steel corridor towards the gangway he asked her, "What was he teasing you about, honey?"

"Everything," she said vaguely. "Took his stick and poked it in my ear. Let's have a drink before we start looking for a train, Dwight. I'll feel better then."

He took her to the same hotel in the main street. Over the drinks he asked her, "How long have we got, this evening?"

"The last train leaves Flinders Street at eleven-fifteen. I'd better get on that, Dwight. Mummy would never forgive me if I spent the night with you."

"I'll say she wouldn't. What happens when you get to Berwick? Is anybody meeting you?"

She shook her head. "We left a bicycle at the station this morning. If you do the right thing by me I won't be able to ride it, but it's there, anyway." She finished her first double brandy. "Buy me another, Dwight."

"I'll buy you one more," he said. "After that we're getting on the train. You promised me that we'd go dancing."

"So we are," she said. "I booked a table at Mario's. But I shuffle beautifully when I'm tight."

"I don't want to shuffle," he said. "I want to dance."

She took the drink he handed her. "You're very exacting," she said. "Don't go poking any more sticks in my ear—I just can't bear it. Most men don't know how to dance, anyway."

"You'll find me one of them," he said. "We used to dance a lot back in the States. But I've not danced since the war began."

She said, "I think you live a very restricted life."

He managed to detach her from the hotel after her second drink, and they walked to the station in the evening light. They arrived at the city half an hour later, and walked out into the street. "It's a bit early," she said. "Let's walk."

He took her arm to guide her through the Saturday evening crowds. Most of the shops had plenty of good stock still in the windows but few were open. The restaurants and cafes were all full, doing a roaring trade; the bars were shut, but the streets were full of drunks. The general effect was one of boisterous and uninhibited lightheartedness, more in the style of 1890 than of 1963. There was no traffic in the wide streets but for the trams, and people swarmed all over the road. At the comer of Swanston and Collins Streets an Italian was playing a very large and garish accordion, and playing it very well indeed. Around him, people were dancing to it. As they passed the Regal cinema a man, staggering along in front of them, fell down, paused for a moment upon hands and knees, and rolled dead drunk into the gutter. Nobody paid much attention to him. A policeman, strolling down the pavement, turned him over, examined him casually, and strolled on.

"They have quite a time here in the evenings," Dwight remarked.

"It's nothing like so bad as it used to be," the girl replied. "It was much worse than this just after the war."

43

"I know it. I'd say they're getting tired of it." He paused, and then he said, "Like I did."

She nodded. "This is Saturday, of course. It's very quiet here on an ordinary night. Almost like it was before the war."

They walked on to the restaurant. The proprietor welcomed them because he knew her well; she was in his establishment at least once a week and frequently more often. Dwight Towers had been there half a dozen times, perhaps, preferring his club, but he was known to the headwaiter as the captain of the American submarine. They were well received and given a good table in a comer away from the band; they ordered drinks and dinner.

"They're pretty nice people here," Dwight said appreciatively. "I don't come in so often and I don't spend much when I do come."

"I come here pretty frequently," the girl said. She sat in reflection for a moment. "You know, you're a very lucky man."

"Why do you say that?"

"You've got a full-time job to do."

It had not occurred to him before that he was fortunate. "That's so," he said slowly. "I certainly don't seem to get a lot of time to go kicking around on the loose."

"I do," she said. "It's all I've got to do."

"Don't you work at anything? No job at all?"

"Nothing at all," she said. "Sometimes I drive a bullock round the farm at home, harrowing the muck. That's all I ever do."

"I'd have thought you'd have been working in the city someplace," he remarked.

"So would I," she said a little cynically. "But it's not so easy as that. I took honours in history up at the Shop, just before the war."

"The Shop?"

"The university. I was going to do a course of shorthand and typing. But what's the sense in working for a year at that? I wouldn't have time to finish it. And if I did, there aren't any jobs."

"You mean, business is slowing down?"

She nodded. "Lots of my friends are out of a job now. People aren't working like they used to, and they don't want secretaries. Half of Daddy's friends—people who used to go to the office—they just don't go now. They live at home, as if they were retired. An awful lot of offices have closed, you know."

"I suppose that makes sense," he remarked. "A man has a right to do the things he wants to do in the last months, if he can get by with the money."

"A girl has a right to, too," she said. "Even if the things she wants to do are something different to driving a bullock round the farm to spread the dung."

44

"There's just no work at all?" he asked.

"Nothing that I could find," she said. "And I've tried hard enough. You see, I can't even type."

"You could learn," he said. "You could go and take that course that you were going to take."

"What's the sense of that, if there's no time to finish it, or use it afterwards?"

"Something to work at," he remarked. "Just as an alternative to all the double brandies."

"Work just for the sake of working?" she inquired. "It sounds simply foul." Her fingers drummed restlessly upon the table.

"Better than drinking just for the sake of drinking," he observed. "Doesn't give you a hangover."

She said irritably, "Order me a double brandy, Dwight, and then let's see if you can dance."

He took her out upon the dance floor, feeling vaguely sorry for her. She was in a prickly kind of mood. Immersed in his own troubles and occupations, it had never occurred to him that young, unmarried people had their own frustrations in these times. He set himself to make the evening pleasant for her, talking about the films and musicals they both had seen, the mutual friends they had. "Peter and Mary Holmes are funny," she told him once. "She's absolutely nuts on gardening. They've got that flat upon a three years' lease. She's planning to plant things this autumn that'll come up next year."

He smiled. "I'd say she's got the right idea. You never know." He steered the conversation back to safer subjects. "Did you see the Danny Kaye movie at the Plaza?"

Yachting and sailing were safe topics, and they talked around those for some time. The floor show came on as they finished dinner, and amused them for a while, and then they danced again. Finally the girl said, "Cinderella. I'll have to start and think about that train, Dwight."

He paid the bill while she was in the cloakroom, and met her by the door. In the streets of the city it was quiet now; the music was still, the restaurants and cafes were now closed. Only the drunks remained, reeling down the pavements aimlessly or lying down to sleep. The girl wrinkled her nose. "They ought to do something about all this," she said. "It never was like this before the war."

"It's quite a problem," he said thoughtfully. "It comes up all the time in the ship. I reckon a man has a right to do the things he wants to when he goes ashore, so long as he doesn't go bothering other people. Some folks just have to have the liquor, times like these." He eyed a policeman on the comer. "That's what the cops here seem to think, in this city, at any rate. I've never seen a drunk arrested yet, not just for being drunk."

45

At the station she paused to thank him and to wish him good night. "It's been a beaut evening," she said. "The day, too. Thanks for everything, Dwight."

"I've enjoyed it, Moira," he said. "It's years since I danced."

"You're not too bad," she told him. And then she asked, "Do you know when you go off up north?"

He shook his head. "Not yet. A message came in just before we left telling me to report Monday morning in the First Naval Member's offices, with Lieutenant Commander Holmes. I imagine we'll get our final briefing then, and maybe get away on Monday afternoon."

She said, "Good luck. Will you give me a ring when you come back to Williamstown?"

"Why, sure," he said. "I'd like to do that. Maybe we could go sailing again someplace, or else do this again." She said, "That'd be fun. I'll have to go now, or I'll miss this train. Good night again, and thanks for everything."

"It's been a lot of fun," he said. "Good night." He stood and watched her go till she was lost in the crowd. From the back view, in that light summer dress, she was not unlike Sharon—or could it be that he was forgetting, muddling them up? No, she really was a bit like Sharon in the way she walked. Not in any other way. Perhaps that was why he liked her, that she was just a little like his wife.

He turned away, and went to catch his train to Williamstown.

He went to church next morning in Williamstown, as was his habit on a Sunday when circumstances made it possible. At ten o'clock on Monday morning he was with Peter Holmes in the Navy Department, waiting in the outer office to see the First Naval Member, Sir David Hartman. The secretary said, "He won't be a minute, sir. I understand he's taking you both over to the Commonwealth Government Offices."

"He is?"

The lieutenant nodded. "He ordered a car." A buzzer sounded and the young man went into the inner office. He reappeared in a moment. "Will you both go in now."

They went into the inner office. The vice admiral got up to meet them. "Morning, Commander Towers. Morning, Holmes. The Prime Minister wants to have a word with you before you go, so we'll go over to his office in a minute. Before we do that, I want to give you this." He turned, and lifted a fairly bulky typescript from his desk. "This is the report of the commanding officer of U.S.S. Swordfish on his cruise from Rio de Janeiro up into the North Atlantic." He handed it to Dwight. "I'm sorry that it's been so long in coming, but the pressure on the radio to South America is very great, and there's a good deal of it. You can take it with you and look it over at your leisure."

46

The American took it, and turned it over with interest. "It's going to be very valuable to us, sir. Is there anything in it to affect this operation?"

"I don't think there is. He found a high level of radioactivity—atmospheric radioactivity—over the whole area, greater in the north than in the south, as you'd expect. He submerged—let's see—" he took the typescript back and turned the pages quickly "—submerged in latitude two south, off Pamaiba, and stayed submerged for the whole cruise, surfacing again in latitude five south off Cape Sao Roque."

"How long was he submerged, sir?"

"Thirty-two days."

"That might be a record."

The admiral nodded. "I think it is. I think he says so, somewhere." He handed back the typescript. "Well, take it with you and study it. It gives an indication of conditions in the north. By the way, if you should want to get in touch with him, he's moved his ship down into Uruguay. He's at Montevideo now." Peter asked, "Are things getting hot in Rio, sir?"

"It's getting a bit close."

They left the office in the Navy Department, went down into the yard, and got into an electric truck. It took them silently through the empty streets of the city, up tree-lined Collins Street to the Commonwealth Offices. In a few minutes they found themselves seated with Mr. Donald Ritchie, the Prime Minister, around a table.

He said, "I wanted to see you before you sailed, Captain, to tell you a little bit about the purpose of this cruise, and to wish you luck. I've read your operation order, and I have very little to add to that. You are to proceed to Cairns, to Port Moresby, and to Darwin for the purpose of reporting on conditions in these places. Any signs of life would be particularly interest-mg, of course, whether human or animal. Vegetation, too. And sea birds, if you can gather any information about those."

"I think that's going to be difficult, sir," Dwight said.

"Yes, I suppose so. Anyway, I understand you're taking a member of the C.S.I.R.O. with you."

"Yes, sir. Mr. Osborne."

The Prime Minister passed his hand across his face, an habitual gesture. "Well. I don't expect you to take risks. In fact, I forbid it. We want you back here with your ship intact and your crew in good health. You will use your own discretion whether you expose yourself on deck, whether you expose your ship upon the surface, guided by your scientific officer. Within the limits of that instruction, we want all the information we can get. If the radiation level makes it possible, you should land and inspect the towns. But I don't think it will." The First Naval Member shook his head. "I very much doubt it. I think you may find it necessary to submerge by the time you get to

47

twenty-two south." The American thought rapidly. "That's south of Townsville."

The Prime Minister said heavily, "Yes. There are still people alive in Townsville. You are expressly forbidden to go there, unless your operation order should be modified by a signal from the Navy Department." He raised his head, and looked at the American. "That may seem hard to you, Commander. But you can't help them, and it's better not to raise false hopes by showing them your ship. And after all, we know what the conditions are in Townsville. We still have telegraphic contact with them there."

"I understand that, sir."

"That leads me to the last point that I have to make," the Prime Minister said. "You are expressly forbidden to take anybody on board your ship during this cruise, except with the prior permission of the Navy Department obtained by radio. I know that you will understand the obvious necessity that neither you or any member of your crew should be exposed to contact with a radioactive person. Is that quite clear?"

"Quite clear, sir."

The Prime Minister rose to his feet. "Well, good luck to all of you. I shall look forward to talking to you again, Commander Towers, in a fortnight's time."


## Chapter Three

Nine days later *U.S.S. Scorpion* surfaced at dawn. In the grey light, as the stars faded, the periscopes emerged from a calm sea off Sandy Cape near Bundaberg in Queensland, in latitude twenty-four degrees south. She stayed below the surface for a quarter of an hour while the captain checked his position by the lighthouse on the distant shore and by echo soundings, and while John Osborne checked the atmospheric and sea radiation levels, with fingers fumbling irritably upon his instruments. Then she slid up out of the depths, a long grey hull, low in the water, heading south at twenty knots. On the bridge deck a hatch clanged open and the officer of the deck emerged, followed by the captain and by many others. In the calm weather the forward and aft torpedo hatches were opened and clean air began to circulate throughout the boat. A lifeline was rigged from the bow to the bridge structure and another to the stern, and all the men off duty clambered up on deck into the fresh morning air, white faced, rejoicing to be out of it, to see the rising sun. They had been submerged for over a week.

Half an hour later they were hungry, hungrier than they had been for several days. When breakfast was sounded they tumbled below quickly; the cooks in turn came up for a spell on deck. When the watch was relieved more men came quickly up into the bright sunlight. The officers appeared upon the bridge, smoking, and the ship settled into a normal routine of surface operation, heading southwards on a blue sea down the Queensland coast. The radio mast was rigged, and they reported their position in a signal. Then they began to receive the broadcasting for entertainment, and light music filled the hull, mingling with the murmur of the turbines and the rushing noise of water alongside.

On the bridge the captain said to his liaison officer, "This report's going to be just a little difficult to write."

Peter nodded. "There's the tanker, sir."

Dwight said, "Sure, there's the tanker." Between Cairns and Port Moresby, in the Coral Sea, they had come upon a ship. She was a tanker, empty and in ballast, drifting with her engines stopped. She was registered in Amsterdam. They cruised around her, hailing through the loud hailer, and getting no response, looking at her through the periscope as they checked her details with Lloyds Register. All her boats were in place at the davits, but there seemed to be nobody alive on board her. She was rusty, very rusty indeed. They came to the conclusion finally that she was a derelict that had been drifting about the oceans since the war; she did not seem to have suffered any damage, other than the weather. There was nothing to be done about her, and the atmospheric radiation level was too high for them to go on deck or make any attempt to board her, even if it had been possible for them to get up her sheer sides. So, after an hour, they left her where they found her, photographing her through the periscope and noting the position. This was the only ship that they had met throughout the cruise.

The liaison officer said, "It's going to boil down to a report on Honest John's radioactive readings."

"That's about the size of it," the captain agreed. "We did see that dog."

Indeed, the report was not going to be an easy one to write, for they had seen and learned very little in the course of their cruise. They had approached Cairns upon the surface but within the hull, the radiation level being too great to allow exposure on the bridge. They had threaded their way cautiously through the Barrier Reef to get to it, spending one night hove-to because Dwight judged it dangerous to navigate in darkness in such waters, where the lighthouses and leading lights were unreliable. When finally they picked up Green Island and approached the land, the town looked absolutely normal to them. It stood bathed in sunshine on the shore, with the mountain range of the Atherton tableland behind. Through the periscope they could see streets of shops shaded with palm trees, a hospital, and trim villas of one storey raised on posts above the ground; there were cars parked in the streets and one or two flags flying. They went on up the river to the docks. Here there was little to be seen except a few fishing boats at anchor up the river, completely normal; there were no ships at the wharves. The cranes were trimmed fore and aft along the wharves and properly secured. Although they were close in to shore, they could see little here, for the periscope reached barely higher than the wharf decking and the warehouses then blocked the view. All that they could see was a silent waterfront, exactly as it would have looked upon a Sunday or a holiday, though then there would have been activity among the smaller craft. A large black dog appeared and barked at them from a wharf.

They had stayed in the river off the wharves for a couple of hours, hailing through the loud hailer at its maximum volume in tones that must have sounded all over the town. Nothing happened, for the whole town was asleep.

They turned the ship around, and went out a little way till they could see the Strand Hotel and part of the shopping centre again. They stayed there for a time, still calling and still getting no response. Then they gave up, and headed out to sea again to get clear of the Barrier Reef before the darkness fell. Apart from the radioactive information gathered by John Osborne, they had learned nothing, unless it was the purely negative information that Cairns looked exactly as it always had before. The sun shone in the streets, the flame trees brightened the far hills, the deep verandahs shaded the shop windows of the town. A pleasant little place to live in in the tropics, though nobody lived there except, apparently, one dog.

Port Moresby had been the same. From the sea they could see nothing the matter with the town viewed through the periscope. A merchant ship registered in Liverpool lay at anchor in the roads, a Jacob's ladder up her side. Two more ships lay on the beach, probably having dragged their anchors in some storm. They stayed there for some hours, cruising the roads and going in to the dock, calling through the loud hailer. There was no response, but there seemed to be nothing the matter with the town. They left after a time, for there was nothing there to stay for.

Two days later they reached Port Darwin and lay in the harbour beneath the town. Here they could see nothing but the wharf, the roof of Government House, and a bit of the Darwin Hotel. Fishing boats lay at anchor and they cruised around these, hailing, and examining them through the periscope. They learned nothing, save for the inference that when the end had come the people had died tidily. "It's what animals do," John Osborne said. "Creep away into holes to die.

They're probably all in bed."

"That's enough about that," the captain said.

"It's true," the scientist remarked.

"Okay, it's true. Now let's not talk about it anymore."

The report certainly was going to be a difficult one to write.

They had left Port Darwin as they had left Cairns and Port Moresby; they had gone back through the Torres Strait and headed southward down the Queensland coast, submerged. By that time the strain of the cruise was telling on them; they talked little among themselves till they surfaced three days after leaving Darwin. Refreshed by a spell on deck, they now had time to think about what story they could tell about their cruise when they got back to Melbourne.

They talked of it after lunch, smoking at the wardroom table. "It's what Swordfish found, of course," Dwight said. "She saw practically nothing either in the States or in Europe."

Peter reached out for the well-thumbed report that lay behind him on the cupboard top. He leafed it through again, though it had been his constant reading on the cruise. "I never thought of that," he said slowly. "I missed that angle on it, but now that you mention it, it's true. There's practically nothing here about conditions on shore."

"They couldn't look on shore, any more than we could," the captain said. "Nobody will ever really know what a hot place looks like. And that goes for the whole of the Northern Hemisphere."

Peter said, "That's probably as well."

"I think that's right," said the commander. "There's some things that a person shouldn't want to go and see."

John Osborne said, "I was thinking about that last night. Did it ever strike you that nobody will ever— ever—see Cairns again? Or Moresby, or Darwin?" They stared at him while they turned over the new idea. "Nobody could see more than we've seen," the captain said.

"Who else can go there, except us? And we shan't go again. Not in the time."

"That's so," Dwight said thoughtfully. "I wouldn't think they'd send us back there again. I never thought of it that way, but I'd say you're right. We're the last living people that will ever see those places." He paused. "And we saw practically nothing. Well, I think that's right."

Peter stirred uneasily. "That's historical," he said. "It ought to go on record somewhere, oughtn't it? Is anybody writing any kind of history about these times?"

John Osborne said, "I haven't heard of one. I'll find out about that. After all, there doesn't seem to be much point in writing stuff that nobody will read."

"There should be something written, all the same," said the American. "Even if it's only going to be read in the next few months." He paused. "I'd like to read a history of this last war," he said. "I was in it for a little while, but I don't know a thing about it. Hasn't anybody written anything?"

"Not as a history," John Osborne said. "Not that I know of, anyway. The information that we've got is all available, of course, but not as a coherent story. I think there'd be too many gaps—the things we just don't know."

"I'd settle for the things we do know," the captain remarked.

"What sort of things, sir?"

"Well, as a start, how many bombs were dropped? Nuclear bombs, I mean."

51

"The seismic records show about four thousand seven hundred. Some of the records were pretty weak, so there were probably more than that."

"How many of those were big ones—fusion bombs, hydrogen bombs, or whatever you call them?"

"I couldn't tell you. Probably most of them. All the bombs dropped in the Russian-Chinese war were hydrogen bombs, I think—most of them with a cobalt element."

"Why did they do that? Use cobalt, I mean?" Peter asked.

The scientist shrugged his shoulders. "Radiological warfare. I can't tell you any more than that."

"I think I can," said die American. "I attended a commanding officers' course at Yerba Buena, San Francisco, die month before the war. They told us what they thought might happen between Russia and China. Whether they told us what did happen six weeks later—well, your guess is as good as mine."

John Osborne asked quietly, "What did they tell you?"

The captain considered for a minute. Then he said, "It was all tied up with the warm water ports. Russia hasn't got a port that doesn't freeze up in the winter except Odessa, and that's on the Black Sea. To get out of Odessa on to the high seas the traffic has to pass two narrow straits both commanded by NATO in time of war—the Bosporus and Gibraltar. Murmansk and Vladivostok can be kept open by icebreakers in the winter, but they're a mighty long way from any place in Russia that makes things to export." He paused. "This guy from Intelligence said that what Russia really wanted was Shanghai."

The scientist asked, "Is that handy for their Siberian industries?"

The captain nodded. "That's exactly it. During the Second War they moved a great many industries way back along the Trans-Siberian railway east of the Urals, back as far as Lake Baikal. They built new towns and everything. Well, it's a long, long way from those places to a port like Odessa. It's only about half the distance to Shanghai."

He paused. "There was another thing he told us," he said thoughtfully. "China had three times the population of Russia, all desperately overcrowded in their country. Russia, next door to the north of them, had millions and millions of square miles of land she didn't use at all because she didn't have the people to populate it. This guy said that as the Chinese industries increased over the last twenty years, Russia got to be afraid of an attack by China. She'd have been a great deal happier if there had been two hundred million fewer Chinese, and she wanted Shanghai And that adds up to radiological warfare..."

Peter said, "But using cobalt, she couldn't follow up and take Shanghai."

"That's true. But she could make North China uninhabitable for quite a number of years by spacing the bombs right. If they put them down in the right places the fall-out would cover China to the sea. Any leftover would go around the world eastwards across the Pacific; if a little got to the United States I don't suppose the Russians would have wept salt tears. If they planned it right, there would be very little left when it got around the world again to Europe and to western Russia. Certainly she couldn't follow up and take Shanghai for quite a number of years, but she'd get it in the end."

Peter turned to the scientist. "How long would it be before people could work in Shanghai?"

"With cobalt fall-out? I wouldn't even guess. It depends on so many things. You'd have to send in exploratory teams. More than five years, I should think —that's the half-life. Less than twenty. But you just can't say."

Dwight nodded. "By the time anyone could get there, Chinese or anyone else, they'd find the Russians there already."

John Osborne turned to him. "What did the Chinese think about all this?"

"Oh, they had another angle altogether. They didn't specially want to kill Russians. What they wanted to do was to turn the Russians back into an agricultural people that wouldn't want Shanghai or any other port. The Chinese aimed to blanket the Russian industrial regions with a cobalt fall-out, city by city, put there with their intercontinental rockets. What they wanted was to stop any Russian from using a machine tool for the next ten years or so. They planned a limited fallout of heavy particles, not going very far around the world. They probably didn't plan to hit the city, even —just to burst maybe ten miles west of it, and let the wind do the rest." He paused. "With no Russian industry left, the Chinese could have walked in any time they liked and occupied the safe parts of the country, any that they fancied. Then, as the radiation eased, they'd occupy the towns."

"Find the lathes a bit rusty," Peter said.

"I'd say they might be. But they'd have had an easy war."

John Osborne asked, "Do you think that's what happened?

"I wouldn't know," said the American. "Maybe no one knows. That's just what this officer from the Pentagon told us at the commanding officers' course." He paused. "One thing was in Russia's favour," he said thoughtfully. "China hadn't any friends or allies, except Russia. When Russia went for China, nobody else would make much trouble—start war on another front, or anything like that."

They sat smoking in silence for a few minutes. "You think that's what flared up finally?" Peter said at last. "I mean, after the original attacks the Russians made on Washington and London?"

John Osborne and the captain stared at him. "The Russians never bombed Washington," Dwight said. "They proved that in the end."

He stared back at them. "I mean, the very first attack of all."

"That's right. The very first attack. They were Russian long-range bombers, Il 626's, but they were Egyptian manned. They flew from Cairo."

53

"Are you sure that's true?"

"It's true enough. They got the one that landed at Puerto Rico on the way home. They only found out it was Egyptian after we'd bombed Leningrad and Odessa and the nuclear establishments at Kharkov, Kuibyshev, and Molotov. Things must have happened kind of quick that day."

"Do you mean to say, we bombed Russia by mistake?" It was so horrible a thought as to be incredible.

John Osborne said, "That's true, Peter. It's never been admitted publicly, but it's quite true. The first one was the bomb on Naples. That was the Albanians, of course. Then there was the bomb on Tel Aviv. Nobody knows who dropped that one, not that I've heard, anyway. Then the British and Americans intervened and made that demonstration flight over Cairo. Next day the Egyptians sent out all the serviceable bombers that they'd got, six to Washington and seven to London. One got through to Washington, and two to London. After that there weren't many American or British statesmen left alive."

Dwight nodded. "The bombers were Russian, and I've heard it said that they had Russian markings. It's quite possible."

"Good God!" said the Australian. "So we bombed Russia?"

"That's what happened," said the captain heavily.

John Osborne said, "It's understandable. London and Washington were out—right out. Decisions had to be made by the military commanders at dispersal in the field, and they had to be made quick before another lot of bombs arrived. Things were very strained with Russia, after the Albanian bomb, and these aircraft were identified as Russian." He paused. "Somebody had to make a decision, of course, and make it in a matter of minutes. Up at Canberra they think now that he made it wrong."

"But if it was a mistake, why didn't they get together and stop it? Why did they go on?"

The captain said, "It's mighty difficult to stop a war when all the statesmen have been killed."

The scientist said, "The trouble is, the damn things got too cheap. The original uranium bomb only cost about fifty thousand quid towards the end. Every little pipsqueak country like Albania could have a stockpile of them, and every little country that had that, thought it could defeat the major countries in a surprise attack, That was the real trouble."

"Another was the aeroplanes," the captain said. "The Russians had been giving the Egyptians aeroplanes for years. So had Britain for that matter, and to Israel, and to Jordan. The big mistake was ever to have given them a long-range aeroplane."

Peter said quietly, "Well, after that the war was on between Russia and the Western powers. When did China come in?"

The captain said, "I don't think anybody knows exactly. But I'd say that probably China came in right there with her rockets and her radiological warfare against Russia, taking advantage of the opportunity. Probably they didn't know how ready Russia was with radiological warfare against China." He paused. "But that's all surmise," he said. "Most of the communications went out pretty soon, and what were left didn't have much time to talk to us down here, or to South Africa. All we know is that the command came down to quite junior officers, in most countries."

John Osborne smiled wryly. "Major Chan Sze Lin." Peter asked, "Who was Chan Sze Lin, anyway?"

The scientist said, "I don't think anybody really knows, except that he was an officer in the Chinese Air Force, and towards the end he seems to have been in command. The Prime Minister was in touch with him, trying to intervene to stop it all. He seems to have had a lot of rockets in various parts of China, and a lot of bombs to drop. His opposite number in Russia may have been someone equally insignificant. But I don't think the Prime Minister ever succeeded in making contact with the Russians. I never heard a name, anyway."

There was a pause. "It must have been a difficult situation," Dwight said at last. "I mean, what could the guy do? He had a war on his hands and plenty of weapons left to fight it with. I'd say it was the same in all the countries, after the statesmen got killed. It makes a war very difficult to stop."

"It certainly made this one. It just didn't stop, till all the bombs were gone and all the aircraft were unserviceable. And by that time, of course, they'd gone too far."

"Christ," said the American softly, "I don't know what I'd have done in their shoes. I'm glad I wasn't."

The scientist said, "I should think you'd have tried to negotiate."

"With an enemy knocking hell out of the United States and killing all our people? When I still had weapons in my hands? Just stop fighting and give in? I'd like to think that I was so high-minded but— well, I don't know." He raised his head. "I was never trained for diplomacy," he said. "If that situation had devolved on me, I wouldn't have known how to handle it."

"They didn't, either," said the scientist. He stretched himself, and yawned. "Just too bad. But don't go blaming the Russians. It wasn't the big countries that set off this thing. It was the little ones, the Irresponsibles."

Peter Holmes grinned, and said, "It's a bit hard on all the rest of us."

"You've got six months more," remarked John Osborne. "Plus or minus something. Be satisfied with that. You've always known that you were going to die sometime. Well, now you know when. That's all." He laughed. "Just make the most of what you've got left."

"I know that," said Peter. "The trouble is I can't think of anything that I want to do more than what I'm doing now."

"Cooped up in bloody *Scorpion*?"

"Well—yes. It's our job. I really meant, at home."

"No imagination. You want to turn Mohammedan and start a harem."

The submarine commander laughed. "Maybe he's got something there."

The liaison officer shook his head. "It's a nice idea, but it wouldn't be practical. Mary wouldn't like it." He stopped smiling. "The trouble is, I can't really believe it's going to happen. Can you?"

"Not after what you've seen?"

"Peter shook his head."

"No. If we'd seen any damage..."

"No imagination whatsoever," remarked the scientist. "It's the same with all you service people. That can't happen to me" He paused. "But it can. And it certainly will."

"I suppose I haven't got any imagination," said Peter thoughtfully. "It's—it's the end of the world. I've never had to imagine anything like that before."

John Osborne laughed. "It's not the end of the world at all," he said. "It's only the end of us. The world will go on just the same, only we shan't be in it. I dare say it will get along all right without us."

Dwight Towers raised his head. "I suppose that's right. There didn't seem to be much wrong with Cairns, or Port Moresby either." He paused, thinking of the flowering trees that he had seen on shore through the periscope, cascaras and flame trees, the palms standing in the sunlight. "Maybe we've been too silly to deserve a world like this," he said.

The scientist said, "That's absolutely and precisely right."

There didn't seem to be much more to say upon that subject, so they went up on to the bridge for a smoke, in the sunlight and fresh air.

They passed the Heads at the entrance to *Sydney* Harbour soon after dawn next day and went on southwards into the Bass Strait. Next morning they were in Port Phillip Bay, and they berthed alongside the aircraft carrier at Williamstown at about noon. The First Naval Member was there to meet them and he was piped aboard *Scorpion* as soon as the gangway was run out.

Dwight Towers met him on the narrow deck. The admiral returned his salute. "Well, Captain, what sort of a cruise did you have?"

"We had no troubles, sir. The operation went through in accordance with the orders. But I'm afraid you may find the results are disappointing."

"You didn't get very much information?"

"We got plenty of radiation data, sir. North of twenty latitude we couldn't go on deck."

The admiral nodded. "Have you had any sickness?"

"One case that the surgeon says is measles. Nothing of a radioactive nature."

They went below into the tiny captain's cabin. Dwight displayed the draft of his report, written in pencil upon sheets of foolscap with an appendix of the radiation levels at each watch of the cruise, long columns of small figures in John Osborne's neat handwriting. "I'll get this typed in *Sydney* right away," he said. "But what it comes to is just this—we found out very little."

"No signs of life in any of those places?"

"Nothing at all. Of course, you can't see very much, at periscope height from the waterfront. I never realized before we went how little we'd be able to see. I should have, perhaps. You're quite a ways from Cairns out in the main channel, and the same at Moresby. We never saw the town of Darwin at all, up on the cliff. Just the waterfront." He paused. "There didn't seem to be much wrong with that."

The admiral turned over the pencilled pages, stopping now and then to read a paragraph. "You stayed some time at each place?"

"About five hours. We were calling all the time through the loud hailer."

"Getting no answer?"

"No, sir. We thought we did at Darwin just at first, but it was only a crane shackle squeaking on the wharf. We moved right up to it and tracked it down."

"Sea birds?"

"None at all. We never saw a bird north of latitude twenty. We saw a dog at Cairns."

The admiral stayed twenty minutes. Finally he said, "Well, get in this report as soon as you can, marking one copy by messenger direct to me. It's a bit disappointing, but you probably did all that anybody could have done."

The American said, "I was reading that report of Swordfish, sir. There's very little information about things on shore in that, either in the States or in Europe. I guess they didn't see much more than we did, from the waterfront." He hesitated for a moment. "There's one suggestion that I'd like to put forward."

"What's that, captain?"

"The radiation levels aren't very high, anywhere along the line. The scientific officer tells me that a man could work safely in an insulating suit—helmet, gloves, and all, of course. We could put an officer on shore in any of those places, rowing in a dinghy, working with an oxygen pack on his back."

"Decontamination when he comes on board again," said the admiral. "That makes a problem. Probably not insuperable. I'll suggest it to the Prime Minister and see if he wants information upon any specific point. He may not think it worthwhile. But it's an idea."

He turned to the control room to go up the ladder to the bridge.

"Will we be able to give shore leave, sir?"

"Any defects?"

"Nothing of importance."

"Ten days," said the admiral. "I'll make a signal about that this afternoon."

Peter Holmes rang up Mary after lunch. "Home again, all in one piece," he said. "Look, darling, I'll be home sometime tonight—I don't know when. I've got a report to get off first, and I'll drop it in myself at die Navy Department on my way through—I've got to go there, anyway. I don't know when I'll be back. Don't bother about meeting me—I'll walk up from the station."

"It's lovely to hear you again," she said. "You won't have had supper, will you?"

"I shouldn't think so. I'll do myself some eggs or something when I get in."

She thought rapidly. "I'll make a casserole, and we can have that any time."

"Fine. Look, there's just one thing. We had a case of measles on board, so I'm in a kind of quarantine."

"Oh, Peter! You've had it before, though, haven't you?"

"Not since I was about four years old. The surgeon says I can get it again. The incubation time is three weeks. Have you had it—recently?"

"I had it when I was about thirteen."

"I think that makes you pretty safe."

She thought quickly. "What about Jennifer, though?"

"I know. I've been thinking about her. I'll have to keep out of her way."

"Oh dear. . . . Can anyone get measles when she's as young as Jennifer?"

"I don't know, darling. I could ask the surgeon commander."

"Would he know about babies?"

He thought for a moment. "I don't suppose he's had a great deal of experience with them."

"Ask him, Peter, and I'll ring up Dr. Halloran. We'll fix up something, anyway. It's lovely that you're back."

He rang off and went on with his work, while Mary settled down to her besetting sin, the telephone. She rang up Mrs. Foster down the road who was going into town to a meeting of the Countrywomen's Association and asked her to bring out a pound of steak and a couple of onions. She rang the doctor who told her that a baby could get measles and that she must be very

58

careful. And then she thought of Moria Davidson who had rung her up die night before to ask if she had any news of *Scorpion*. She got her at teatime at the farm near Berwick.

"My dear," she said. "They're back. Peter rang me from die ship just now. They've all got measles."

"They've got what?"

"Measles—like you have when you're at school." There was a burst of laughter on the line, a little hysterical and shrill. "It's nothing to laugh about," Mary said. "I'm thinking about Jennifer. She might catch it from Peter. He's had it once, but he can get it again. It's all so worrying...."

The laughter subsided. "Sorry, darling, but it seems so funny. It's nothing to do with radioactivity, is it?"

"Oh, I don't think so. Peter said it was just measles." She paused. "Isn't it awful?"

Miss Davidson laughed again. "It's just the sort of thing they would do. Here they go cruising for a fortnight up in parts where everyone is dead of radiation, and all that they can catch is measles! I'll have to speak to Dwight about it, very sharply. Did they find anyone alive up there?"

"I don't know, darling. Peter didn't say anything about it. But anyway, that's not important. What am I going to do about Jennifer? Dr. Halloran says she can catch it, and Peter's going to be contagious for three weeks."

"He'll have to sleep and have his meals out on the verandah."

"Don't be silly, darling."

"Well, let Jennifer sleep and have her meals out on the verandah."

"Flies," said her mother. "Mosquitoes. A cat might come and lie on her face and smother her. They do, you know."

"Put a mosquito net over the pram."

"I haven't got a mosquito net."

"I think we've got some somewhere, that Daddy used to use in Queensland. They're probably full of holes."

"I do wish you'd have a look, darling. It's the cat I'm worried about."

"I'll go and have a look now. If I can find one I'll put it in the post tonight. Or I might bring it over. Are you going to have Commander Towers down again, now that they're home?"

"I really hadn't thought. I don't know if Peter wants to have him. They may be hating the sight of each other after a fortnight in that submarine. Would you like us to have him over?"

"It's nothing to me," said the girl carelessly. "I don't care if you do or don't."

"Darling!"

"It's not. Stop poking your stick in my ear. Anyway, he's a married man."

Puzzled, Mary said, "He can't be, dear. Not now."

"That's all you know," the girl replied. "It makes things a bit difficult. I'll go and look for that net."

When Peter arrived home that evening he found Mary to be somewhat uninterested in Cairns but very much concerned about the baby. Moira had rung up again to say that she was sending a mosquito net, but it would clearly be some time before it could arrive. As a makeshift Mary had secured a long length of butter muslin and had draped this round the pram on the verandah, but she had not done it very well and the liaison officer spent some time on his first evening at home in fashioning a close-fitting cover to the pram hood from the muslin. "I do hope she'll be able to breathe," his wife said anxiously. "Peter, are you sure she'll get enough air through that?"

He did what he could to reassure her, but three times in the night she left his side to go out to the verandah to make sure that the baby was still alive.

The social side of *Scorpion* was more interesting to her than the technical achievements of the ship. "Are you going to ask Commander Towers down again?" she inquired.

"I really hadn't thought about it," he replied. "Would you like to have him down?"

"I quite liked him," she said. "Moira liked him a lot. So funny for her, because he's such a quiet man. But you never can tell."

"He took her out before we went away," he said. "Showed her the ship and took her out. I bet she leads him a dance."

"She rang up three times while you were away to ask if we had any news," his wife said. "I don't believe that was because of you."

"She was probably just bored," he remarked.

He had to go up to town next day for a meeting at the Navy Department with John Osborne and the Principal Scientific Officer. The meeting ended at about noon; as they were going out of the office the scientist said, "By the way, I've got a parcel for you." He produced a brown paper packet tied with string. "Mosquito net. Moira asked me to give it to you."

"Oh—thanks. Mary wanted that badly."

"What are you doing for lunch?"

"I hadn't thought."

"Come along to the Pastoral Club."

The young naval officer opened his eyes; this was somewhat upstage and rather expensive. "Are you a member there?"

John Osborne nodded. "I always intended to be one before I died. It was now or never."

They took a tram up to the club at the other end of the town. Peter Holmes had been inside it once or twice before, and had been suitably impressed. It was an ancient building for Australia, over a hundred years old, built in the spacious days in the manner of one of the best London clubs of the time. It had retained its old manners and traditions in a changing era; more English than the English, it had carried the standards of food and service practically unaltered from the middle of the nineteenth century to the middle of the twentieth. Before the war it had probably been the best club in the Commonwealth. Now it certainly was.

They parked their hats in the hall, washed their hands in the old-fashioned washroom, and moved out into the garden cloister for a drink. Here they found a number of members, mostly past middle age, discussing the affairs of the day. Amongst them Peter Holmes noticed several state and federal ministers. An elderly gentleman waved to them from a group upon the lawn and started towards them.

John Osborne said quietly, "It's my great-uncle— Douglas Froude. Lieutenant General—you know." Peter nodded. Sir Douglas Froude had commanded the army before he was born and had retired soon after that event, fading from great affairs into the obscurity of a small property near Macedon, where he had raised sheep and tried to write his memoirs. Twenty years later he was still trying though he was gradually abandoning the struggle. For some time his chief interest had lain in his garden and in the study of Australian wild birds; his weekly visit into town to lunch at the Pastoral Club was his one remaining social activity. He was still erect in figure though white haired and red of face. He greeted his great-nephew cheerfully.

"Ha, John," he said. "I heard last night that you were back again. Had a good trip?"

John Osborne introduced the naval officer. "Quite good," he said. "I don't know that we found out very much, and one of the ship's company developed measles. Still, that's all in the day's work."

"Measles, eh? Well, that's better than this cholera thing. I hope you none of you got that. Come and have a drink—I'm in the book."

They crossed to the table with him. John said, "Thank you, Uncle. I didn't expect to see you here today. I thought your day was Friday."

They helped themselves to pink gins. "Oh no, no. It used to be Friday. Three years ago my doctor told me that if I didn't stop drinking the club port he couldn't guarantee my life for longer than a year. But everything's changed now, of course." He raised his glass of sherry. "Well, here's thanks for your safe home-coming. I suppose one ought to pour it on the ground as a libation or something, but the situation is too serious for that. Do you know we've got over three thousand bottles of vintage port still left in the cellars of this club, and only about six months left to go, if what you scientists say is right?"

John Osborne was suitably impressed. "Fit to drink?"

"In first-class condition, absolutely first class. Some of the Fonseca may be just a trifle young, a year or two maybe, but the Gould Campbell is in its prime. I blame the Wine Committee very much, very much indeed. They should have seen this coming."

Peter Holmes repressed a smile. "It's a bit difficult to blame anyone," he said mildly. "I don't know that anybody really saw this coming."

"Stuff and nonsense. I saw this coming twenty years ago. Still, it's no good blaming anybody now. The only thing to do is to make the best of it."

John Osborne asked, "What are you doing about the port?"

"There's only one thing to do," the old man said.

"What's that?"

"Drink it, my boy, drink it—every drop. No good leaving it for the next comer, with the cobalt half-life over five years. I come in now three days a week and take a bottle home with me." He took another drink of his sherry. "If I'm to die, as I most certainly am, I'd rather die of drinking port than of this cholera thing. You say you none of you got that upon your cruise?"

Peter Holmes shook his head. "We took precautions. We were submerged and underwater most of the time."

"Ah, that makes a good protection." He glanced at them. "There's nobody alive up in North Queensland, is there?"

"Not at Cairns, sir. I don't know about Townsville."

The old man shook his head. "There's been no communication with Townsville since last Thursday, and now Bowen has it. Somebody was saying that they've had some cases in Mackay."

John Osborne grinned. "Have to hurry up with that port, Uncle."

"I know that. It's a very terrible situation." The sun shone down on them out of a cloudless sky, warm and comforting; the big chestnut in the garden cast dappled shadows on the lawn. "Still, we're doing our best. The secretary tells me that we put away over three hundred bottles last month."

He turned to Peter. "How do you like serving in an American ship?"

"I like it very much, sir. It's a bit different to our navy, of course, and I've never served in a submarine before. But they're quite a nice party to be with."

"Not too gloomy? Not too many widowers?"

He shook his head. "They're all pretty young, except the captain. I don't think many of them were married. The captain was, of course, and some of the petty officers. But most of the officers and enlisted men are in their early twenties. A lot of them seem to have got themselves girls here in Australia." He paused. "It's not a gloomy ship."

The old man nodded. "Of course, it's been some time, now." He drank again, and then he said, "The captain—is he a Commander Towers?"

"That's right, sir. Do you know him?"

62

"He's been in here once or twice, and I've been introduced to him. I have an idea that he's an honorary member. Bill Davidson was telling me that Moira knows him."

"She does, sir. They met at my house."

"Well, I hope she doesn't get him into mischief."

At that moment she was ringing up the commander in the aircraft carrier, doing her best to do so. "This is Moira, Dwight," she said. "What's this I hear about your ship all getting measles?"

His heart lightened at .the sound of her voice. "You're very right," he said. "But that's classified information."

"What does that mean?"

"Secret. If a ship in the U.S. Navy gets put out of action for a while, we just don't tell the world about it."

"All that machinery put out of action by a little thing like measles. It sounds like bad management to me. Do you think *Scorpion*'s got the right captain?"

"I'm darned sure she hasn't," he said comfortably. "Let's you and me get together someplace and talk about a replacement. I'm just not satisfied myself."

"Are you going down to Peter Holmes' this weekend?"

He hasn't asked me."

Would you go if you were asked? Or have you had him keel-hauled for insubordination since we met?"

"He never caught a sea gull," he said. "I guess that's all I've got against him. I never logged him for it"

Did you expect him to catch sea gulls?"

Sure. I rated him chief sea gull catcher, but he fell down on the job. The Prime Minister, your Mr.

Ritchie, he'll be mighty sore with me about no sea gull. A ship's captain, though, he's just so good as his officers and no better."

She asked, "Have you been drinking, Dwight?"

"I'll say I have. Coca-Cola."

"Ah, that's what's wrong. You need a double brandy—no, whisky. Can I speak to Peter Holmes?"

"Not here, you can't. He's lunching with John Osborne someplace, I believe. Could be the Pastoral Club."

"Worse and worse," she said. "If he happens to ask you down, will you come? I'd like to see if you can sail that dinghy any better this time. I've got a padlock for my bra."

He laughed. "I'll be glad to come. Even on those terms."

"He may not ask you," she pointed out. "I don't like the sound of this sea gull business at all. It seems to me that there's bad trouble in your ship."

"Let's talk it over."

"Certainly," she replied. "I'll hear what you've got to say."

She rang off, and succeeded in catching Peter on the telephone as he was about to leave the club. She came directly to the point. "Peter, will you ask Dwight Towers down to your place for the week-end? I'll ask myself."

He temporized. "I'll get he'll from Mary if he gives Jennifer measles."

"I'll tell her she caught it from you. Will you ask him?"

"If you like. I don't suppose he'll come."

"He will."

She met him at Falmouth station in her buggy, as she had before. As he passed through the ticket barrier he greeted her with, "Say, what happened to the red outfit?"

She was dressed in khaki, khaki slacks and khaki shirt, practical and workmanlike. "I wasn't sure about wearing it, meeting you," she said. "I didn't want to get it all messed up."

He laughed. "You've got quite an opinion of me!"

"A girl can't be too careful," she said primly. "Not with all this hay about."

They walked down to where her horse and buggy stood tied to the rail. "I suppose we'd better settle up this sea gull business before meeting Mary," she said. "I mean, it's not a thing one wants to talk about in mixed company. What about the Pier Hotel?"

"Okay with me," he said. They got up into the jinker and drove through the empty streets to the hotel. She tied the reins to the same bumper of the same car, and they went into the Ladies' Lounge.

He bought her a double brandy, and bought a single whisky for himself. "Now, what's all this about the sea gull?" she demanded. "You'd better come clean, Dwight, however discreditable it is."

"I saw the Prime Minister before we went off on this cruise," he told her. "The First Naval Member, he took me over. He told us this and that, and among other things he wanted us to find out all we could about the bird life in the radioactive area."

"All right. Well, did you find out anything for him?"

"Nothing at all," he replied comfortably. "Nothing about the birds, nothing about the fish, and not much about anything else."

"Didn't you catch any fish?"

He grinned at her. "If anyone can tell me how to catch a fish out of a submarine that's submerged, or a sea gull when nobody can go on deck, I'd like to know. It could probably be done with specially designed equipment.

64

Everything's possible. But this was at the final briefing, half an hour before we sailed."

"So you didn't bring back a sea gull?"

"No."

"Was the Prime Minister very much annoyed?"

"I wouldn't know. I wouldn't dare go see him."

"I'm not surprised." She paused and took a drink from her glass, and then more seriously she said, "Tell me. There's nobody alive up there, is there?"

He shook his head. "I don't think so. It's difficult to say for certain unless one was prepared to put a man on shore, in a protective suit Looking back, I think that's what we should have done in some of those places. But we weren't briefed for that this time, and no equipment on board. The decontamination is a problem, when he comes back in the ship."

"This time," she quoted. "Are you going again?" He nodded. "I think so. We've had no orders, but I've got a hunch they'll send us over to the States."

She opened her eyes. "Can you go there?"

He nodded. "It's quite a way, and it'd be a very long time underwater. Pretty hard on the crew. But yet—it could be done. Swordfish took a cruise like that, and so could we."

He told her about Swordfish and her cruise around the North Atlantic. "The trouble is, you see so very little through the periscope. We've got the captain's report on the Swordfish cruise, and, when you sum it all up, they really learned very little. Not much more than you'd know if you sat down to think it out. You can only see the waterfront, and that from a height of about twenty feet. You can see if there's been bomb damage in a city or a port, but that's about all you can see. It was the same with us. We found out very little on this cruise. Just stayed there calling on the loud hailer for a while, and when nobody came down to look at us or answer, we assumed they were all dead." He paused. "It's all you can assume."

She nodded. "Somebody was saying that they've got it in Mackay. Do you think that's true?"

"I think it is true," he said. "It's coming south very steadily, just like the scientists said it would."

"If it goes on at this rate, how long will it be before it gets here?"

"I'd say around September. Could be a bit before." She got restlessly to her feet. "Get me another drink,

Dwight." And when he brought it she said, "I want to go somewhere—do something—dancer

"Anything you say, honey."

"We can't just sit here mooning and moaning about what's coming to us!"

"You're right," he said. "But what do you want to do, more'n you're doing now?"

"Don't be sensible," she said fretfully. "I just can't bear it."

"Okay," he said equably. "Drink up and let's go up and meet the Holmes, and then go sail that boat."

They found at the flat that Peter and Mary Holmes had arranged a beach picnic supper for the evening's entertainment. Not only was it cheaper than a party and more pleasant in the heat of summer, but in Mary's somewhat muddled view the more the men were kept out of the house the less likely they were to give the baby measles. That afternoon Moira and Dwight went down to the sailing club after a quick lunch to rig the boat and sail her in the race, while Peter and Mary followed with the baby in the bicycle trailer in the middle of the afternoon.

The race went reasonably well that time. They bumped the buoy at the start, and engaged in a luffing match on the second round which ended in a minor collision because neither party knew the rules, but in that club such incidents were not infrequent, and protests very few. They finished the race in sixth place, an improvement on the time before, and in much better order. They sailed in to the beach at the conclusion of the race, parked the vessel on a convenient sandbank, and waded on shore to drink a cup of tea and eat small cakes with Peter and Mary.

They bathed in leisurely fashion in the evening sun; in bathing costumes they unrigged the boat, put away the sails, and got her up to her resting place upon the dry sand of the beach. The sun dropped down to the horizon and they changed into their clothes, took drinks from the hamper, and walked out to the jetty's end to see the sunset while Peter and Mary got busy with the supper.

Sitting with him perched upon a rail, watching the rosy lights reflected in the calm sea, savouring the benison of the warm evening and the comfort of her drink, she asked him, "Dwight, tell me about the cruise that Swordfish made. Did you say she went to the United States?"

"That's right." He paused, and then he said, "She went everywhere she could along the eastern seaboard, but all it amounted to was just a few of the small ports and harbours, Delaware Bay, the Hudson River, and, of course, New London. They took a big chance going in to look at New York City."

She was puzzled. "Was that dangerous?"

He nodded. "Minefields—our own mines. Every major port or river entrance on the eastern seaboard was protected by a series of minefields. At any rate, that's what we think. The West Coast, too." He paused for a moment in thought. "They should have been put down before the war. Whether they got them down before, or whether they were put down after, or whether they

66

were never laid at all—we just don't know. All we know is that there should be minefields there, and unless you have the plan of them to show the passage through—you can't go in."

"You mean, if you hit one it'd sink you?"

"It most certainly would. Unless you have the key chart you just daren't go near."

"Did they have the key chart when they went into New York?"

He shook his head. "They had one that was eight years old, with NOT TO BE USED stamped all over it. Those things are pretty secret; they don't issue them unless a ship needs to go in there. They only had this old one. They must have wanted to go in very much. They got to figuring what alterations could have been made, retaining the main leading marks to show the safe channels in. They got it figured out that not much alteration to the plan they had would have been possible save on one leg. They chanced it, and went in, and got away with it. Maybe there were never any mines there at all."

"Did they find out much that was of value when they got into the harbour?"

He shook his head. "Nothing but what they knew already. It's how it seems to be, exploring places in this way. You can't find out a lot."

"There was nobody alive there?"

"Oh no, honey. The whole geography was altered. It was very radioactive, too."

They sat in silence for a time, watching the sunset glow, smoking over their drinks. "What was the other place you say she went to?" the girl asked at last. "New London?"

"That's right," he said.

"Where is that?"

"In Connecticut, in the eastern part of the state," he told her. "At the mouth of the Thames River."

"Did they run much risk in going there?"

He shook his head. "It was their home port. They had the key chart for the minefields there, right up to date." He paused. "It's the main U.S. Navy submarine base on the East Coast," he said quietly. "Most of them lived there, I guess, or in the general area. Like I did."

"You lived there?"

He nodded.

"Was it just the same as all the other places?"

"So it seems," he said heavily. "They didn't say much in the report, just the readings of the radioactivity. They were pretty bad. They got right up to the base, to their own dock that they left from. It must have been kind of funny going back like that, but there was nothing much about it in the report. Most of the officers and the enlisted men, they must have been very near their homes. There was nothing they could do, of course. They just stayed there a while, and then went out and went on with the mission. The captain said in his report they had some kind of a religious service in the ship. It must have been painful."

In the warm, rosy glow of the sunset there was still beauty in the world. "I wonder they went in there," she observed.

"I wondered about that, just at first," he said. "I'd have passed it by, myself, I think. Although . . . well, I don't know. But thinking it over, I'd say they had to go in there. It was the only place they had the key chart for—that, and Delaware Bay. They were the only two places that they could get into safely. They just had to take advantage of the knowledge of the minefields that they had."

She nodded. "You lived there?"

"Not in New London itself," he said quietly. "The base is on the other side of the river, the east side. I've got a home about fifteen miles away, up the coast from the river entrance. Little place called West Mystic."

She said, "Don't talk about it if you'd rather not." He glanced at her. "I don't mind talking, not to some people. But I wouldn't want to bore you." He smiled gently. "Nor to start crying, because I'd seen the baby."

She flushed a little. "When you let me use your cabin to change in," she said, "I saw your photographs. Are those your family?"

He nodded. "That's my wife and our two kids," he said a little proudly. "Sharon. Dwight goes to grade school, and Helen, she'll be going next fall. She goes to a little kindergarten right now, just up the street."

She had known for some time that his wife and family were very real to him, more real by far than the half-life in a far comer of the world that had been forced upon him since the war. The devastation of the Northern Hemisphere was not real to him, as it was not real to her. He had seen nothing of the destruction of the war, as she had not; in thinking of his wife and of his home it was impossible for him to visualize them in any other circumstances than those in which he had left them. He had little imagination, and that formed a solid core for his contentment in Australia.

She knew that she was treading upon very dangerous ground. She wanted to be kind to him, and she had to say something. She asked a little timidly, "What's Dwight going to be when he grows up?"

"I'd like him to go to the Academy," he said. "The Naval Academy. Go into the navy, like I did. It's a good life for a boy—I don't know any better. Whether he can make the grade or not, well, that's another thing. His mathematics aren't so hot, but it's too early yet to say. He won't be ten years old till next July. But I'd like to see him get into the Academy. I think he wants it, too."

"Is he keen on the sea?" she asked.

He nodded. "We live right near the shore. He's on the water, swimming and running the outboard motor, most of the summer." He paused thoughtfully. "They get so brown" he said. "All kids seem to be the same. I sometimes think that kid get browner than we do, with the same amount of exposure."

"They get very brown here," she remarked. "You haven't started him sailing yet?"

"Not yet," he said. "I'm going to get a sailboat when I'm home on my next leave."

He raised himself from the rail that they had been sitting on, and stood for a moment looking at the sunset glow.

"I guess that'll be next September," he said quietly. "Kind of late in the season to start sailing, up at Mystic."

She was silent, not knowing what to say.

He turned to her. "I suppose you think I'm nuts," he said heavily. "But that's the way I see it, and I can't seem to think about it any other way. At any rate, I don't cry over babies."

She rose and turned to walk with him down the jetty.

"I don't think you're nuts," she said.

They walked together in silence to the beach.

## Chapter Four

Next morning, Sunday, everyone in the Holmes household got up in pretty good shape, unlike the previous Sunday that Commander Towers had spent with them. They had gone to bed after a reasonable evening, unexcited by a party. At breakfast Mary asked her guest if he wanted to go to church, thinking that the more she got him out of the house the less likely he was to give Jennifer measles.

"I'd like to go," he said, "if that's convenient"

"Of course it is," she said. "Just do whatever you like. I thought we might take tea down to the club this afternoon, unless you've got anything else you'd like to do."

He shook his head. "I could use another swim. But I'll have to get back to the ship tonight sometime, after supper, maybe."

"Can't you stay over till tomorrow morning?"

He shook his head, knowing her concern about the measles. "I'll have to get back tonight."

He went out into the garden directly the meal was over to smoke a cigarette, thinking to ease Mary's mind. Moira found him there when she came out from helping with the dishes, sitting in a deck chair looking out over the bay. She sat down beside him. "Are you really going to church?" she asked.

"That's right," he said.

"Can I come too?"

He turned his head, and looked at her in surprise. "Why, certainly. Do you go regularly?"

She smiled. "Not once in a blue moon," she admitted. "It might be better if I did. Maybe I wouldn't drink so much."

He pondered that one for a moment. "Could be," he said uncertainly. "I don't know that that's got a lot to do with it."

"You're sure you wouldn't rather go alone?'

"Why, no," he said. "I'd like your company."

As they left to walk down to the church Peter Holmes was getting out the garden hose to do some watering before the sun grew hot. His wife came out of the house presently. "Where's Moira?" she asked.

"Gone to church with the captain."

"Moira? Gone to church?"

He grinned. "Believe it or not, that's where she's gone."

She stood in silence for a minute. "I hope it's going to be all right," she said at last.

"Why shouldn't it?" he asked. "He's dinkum, and she's not a bad sort when you get to know her. They might even get married."

She shook her head. "There's something funny about it. I hope it's going to be all right," she repeated.

"It's no concern of ours, anyway," he said. "Lots of things are going a bit weird these days."

She nodded, and started pottering about the garden while he watered. Presently she said, "I've been thinking, Peter. Could we take out those two trees, do you think?"

He came and looked at them with her. "I'd have to ask the landlord," he said. "What do you want to take them out for?"

"We've got so little space for growing vegetables," she said. "They are so expensive in the shops. If we could take those trees out and cut back the wattle, we could make a kitchen garden here, from here to here" She indicated with her hands. "I'm sure we could save nearly a pound a week by growing our own stuff. And it'd be fun, too."

He went to survey the trees. "I could get them down all right," he said, "and there's a nice bit of firewood in them. It'd be green, of course, too green to bum this winter. We'd have to stack it for a year. The only thing is, getting out the stumps. It's quite a big job, that."

"There are only two of them," she said. "I could help—keep on nibbling at them while you're away. If we could get them out this winter and dig the ground over, I could plant it in the spring and we'd have vegetables all next summer." She paused. "Peas and beans," she said. "And a vegetable marrow. I'd make marrow jam."

"Good idea," he said. He looked the trees up and down. "They're not very big," he said. "It'd be better for the pine if they came out."

"Another tiling I want to do," she said, "is to put in a flowering gum tree, here. I think that'd look lovely in the summer."

"Takes about five years to come into bloom," he said.

"Never mind. A gum tree there would be just lovely, up against the blue of the sea. We could see it from our bedroom window."

He paused, considering the brilliance of the scarlet flowers all over the big tree against the deep blue sea, in the brilliant sunlight. "It'd certainly be quite a sensation when it was in bloom," he said. "Where would you put it? Here?"

"A bit more over this way, here," she said. "When it got big we could take down this holly thing and have a seat in the shade, here." She paused. "I went to Wilson's nurseries while you were away," she said. "He's got some lovely little flowering gum trees there, only ten and sixpence each. Do you think we could put in one of those this autumn?"

"They're a bit delicate," he said. "I think the thing to do would be to put in two fairly close to each other, so that you'd have one if the other died. Then take out one of them in a couple of years' time."

"The trouble is, one never does it," she observed.

They went on happily planning their garden for the next ten years, and the morning passed very quickly.

When Moira and Dwight came back from church they were still at it. They were called into consultation on the layout of the kitchen garden. Presently Peter and Mary went into the house, the former to get drinks and the latter to get the lunch.

The girl glanced at the American. "Someone's crazy," she said quietly. "Is it me or them?"

"Why do you say that?"

"They won't be here in six months' time. I won't be here. You won't be here. They won't want any vegetables next year."

Dwight stood in silence for a moment, looking out at the blue sea, the long curve of the shore. "So what?" he said at last. "Maybe they don't believe it. Maybe they think that they can take it all with them and have it where they're going to, someplace. I wouldn't know." He paused. "The thing is, they just kind of like to plan a garden. Don't you go and spoil it for them, telling them they're crazy."

71

"I wouldn't do that." She stood in silence for a minute. "None of us really believe it's ever going to happen—not to us," she said at last. "Everybody's crazy on that point, one way or another."

"You're very right," he said emphatically.

Drinks came, and put a closure on the conversation, and then lunch. After lunch Mary turned the men out into the garden, thinking them to be infectious, while she washed the dishes with Moira. Seated in deck chairs with a cup of coffee, Peter asked his captain, "Have you heard anything about our next job, sir?" The American cocked his eye at him. "Not a thing. Have you?"

"Not really. Something was said at that conference with P.S.O. that made me wonder if anything was in the wind."

"What was it that was said?"

"Something about fitting us with new directional wireless of some kind. Have you heard anything?" Dwight shook his head. "We've got plenty of radio."

"This is for taking a bearing—accurately. Perhaps when we're submerged to periscope depth. We can't do that, can we?"

"Not with our existing equipment. What do they want us to do that for?"

"I don't know. It wasn't on the agenda. It was just one of the back-room boys speaking out of turn."

"They want us to track down radio signals?"

"Honestly, I don't know, sir. How it came up was that they asked if the radiation detector could be moved to the forward periscope so that this thing could be put on the aft periscope. John Osborne said he was pretty sure it could, but he'd take it up with you."

"That's right. It can go on the forward periscope. I thought they wanted to fit two."

"I don't think so, sir. I think they want to fit this other gadget in its place on the aft one."

The American stared at the smoke rising from his cigarette. Then he said, "Seattle."

"What's that, sir?"

"Seattle. There were radio signals coming from someplace near Seattle. Do you know if they're still coming through?"

Peter shook his head, amazed. "I didn't know anything about that. Do you mean that somebody's still operating a transmitter?"

The captain shrugged his shoulders. "Could be. If so, it's somebody that doesn't know how to send. Sometimes they make a group, sometimes a word is clear. Most times it's just a jumble, like a child might make, playing at radio stations."

"Does this go on all the time?"

72

Dwight shook his head. "I don't think so. It comes on the air irregularly, now and then. I know they're monitoring that frequency most of the time. At least, they were till Christmas. I haven't heard since."

The liaison officer said, "But that must mean there's somebody alive up there."

"It's just a possibility. You can't have radio without power, and that means starting up some kind of a motor. A big motor, to run a big station with global range. But—I don't know. You'd think a guy who could start up an outfit of that size and run it—you'd think he'd know Morse code. Even if he had to spell it out two words a minute with the book in front of him."

"Do you think we're going there?"

"Could be. It was one of the points they wanted information on way back last October. They wanted all the information on the U.S. radio stations that we had."

"Did you have anything that helped?"

Dwight shook his head. "Only the U.S. Navy stations. Very little on the Air Force or the Army stations. Practically nothing on the civil stations. There's more radio on the West Coast than you could shake a stick at."

That afternoon they strolled down to the beach and bathed, leaving Mary with the baby at the house. Lying on the warm sand with the two men, Moira asked, "Dwight, where is Swordfish now? Is she coming here?"

"I haven't heard it," he replied. "The last I heard she was in Montevideo."

"She could turn up here, any time," said Peter Holmes. "She's got the range."

The American nodded. "That's so. Maybe they'll send her over here one day with mail or passengers. Diplomats, or something."

"Where is Montevideo?" asked the girl. "I ought to know that, but I don't."

Dwight said, "It's in Uruguay, on the east side of South America. Way down towards the bottom."

"I thought you said she was at Rio de Janeiro. Isn't that in Brazil?"

He nodded. "That was when she made her cruise up in the North Atlantic. She was based on Rio then. But after that they moved down into Uruguay."

"Was that because of radiation?"

"Uh-huh."

Peter said, "I don't know that it's got there yet. It may have done. They've not said anything upon the radio. It's just about on the tropic, isn't it?"

"That's right," said Dwight. "Like Rockhampton." The girl asked, "Have they got it in Rockhampton?"

73

"I haven't heard that they have," said Peter. "It said on the wireless this morning that they've got it at Salisbury, in Southern Rhodesia. I think that's a bit further north."

"I think it is," said the captain. "It's in the middle of a land mass, too, and that might make a difference. These other places that we're talking about—they're all on a coast."

"Isn't Alice Springs just about on the tropic?"

"It might be. I wouldn't know. That's in the middle of a land mass, too, of course."

The girl asked, "Does it go quicker down a coast than in the middle?"

Dwight shook his head. "I wouldn't know. I don't think they've got any evidence on that, one way or the other."

Peter laughed. "They'll know by the time it gets here. Then they can etch it on the glass."

The girl wrinkled her brows. "Etch it on the glass?"

"Hadn't you heard about that one?"

She shook her head.

"John Osborne told me about it, yesterday," He said. "It seems that somebody in C.S.I.R.O. is getting busy with a history, about what's happened to us. They do it on glass bricks. They etch it on the glass and then they fuse another brick down on the top of it in some way, so that the writing's in the middle."

Dwight turned upon his elbow, interested. "I hadn't heard of that. What are they going to do with them?"

"Put them up on top of Mount Kosciusko," Peter said. "It's the highest peak in Australia. If ever the world gets inhabited again they must go there sometime. And it's not so high as to be inaccessible."

"Well, what do you know? They're really doing that, are they?"

"So John says. They've got a sort of concrete cellar made up there. Like in the Pyramids."

The girl asked, "But how long is this history?"

"I don't know. I don't think it can be very long. They're doing it with pages out of books, though, too. Sealing them in between sheets of thick glass."

"But these people who come after," the girl said. "They won't know how to read our stuff. They may be . . . animals."

"I believe they've gone to a lot of trouble about that. First steps in reading. Picture of a cat, and then C-A-T and all that sort of thing. John said that was about all that they'd got finished so far." He paused. "I suppose it's something to do," he said thoughtfully. "Keeps the wise men out of mischief."

"A picture of a cat won't do them much good," Moira remarked. "There won't be any cats. They won't know what a cat is."

"A picture of a fish might be better," said Dwight. "F-I-S-H. Or—say—a picture of a sea gull."

"You're getting into awful spelling difficulties."

The girl turned to Peter curiously. "What sort of books are they preserving? All about how to make the cobalt bomb?"

"God forbid." They laughed. "I don't know what they're doing. I should think a copy of the Encyclopaedia Britannica would make a good kickoff, but there's an awful lot of it. I really don't know what they're doing. John Osborne might know—or he could find out."

"Just idle curiosity," she said. "It won't affect you or me." She stared at him in mock consternation. "Don't tell me they're preserving any of the newspapers. I just couldn't bear it."

"I shouldn't think so," he replied. "They're not as crazy as that."

Dwight sat up on the sand. "All this beautiful warm water going to waste," he remarked. "I think we ought to use it."

Moira stood up. "Make the most of it," she agreed. "There's not much of it left."

Peter yawned. "You two go and use the water. I'll use the sun."

They left him lying on the beach and went into the sea together. As they swam out she said, "You're pretty fast in the water, aren't you?"

He paused, treading water beside her. "I used to swim quite a lot when I was younger. I swam for the Academy against West Point one time."

She nodded. "I thought you were something like that. Do you swim much now?"

He shook his head. "Not in races. That's a thing you have to give up pretty soon, unless you've got the time to do a lot of it, and keep in training." He laughed. "I think the water's colder now than when I was a boy. Not here, of course. I mean, in Mystic."

"Were you born in Mystic?" she asked.

He shook his head. "I was born on Long Island Sound, but not at Mystic. A place called Westport. My Dad's a doctor there. He was a navy surgeon in the First World War, and then he got this practice in Westport."

"Is that on the sea?"

He nodded. "Swimming and sailing and fishing. That's the way it was when I was a boy."

"How old are you, Dwight?"

"I'm thirty-three. How old are you?"

"What a rude question! I'm twenty-four." She paused. "Does Sharon come from Westport, too?"

"In a way," he said. "Her Dad's a lawyer in New York City, fives in an apartment on West 84th Street, near the park. They have a summer home at West-port."

"So you met her there."

He nodded. "Boy meets girl."

"You must have married quite young."

"Just after graduation," he replied. "I was twenty-two, an ensign on the Franklin. Sharon was nineteen; she never finished college. We'd made our minds up more than a year before. Our folks got together when they saw that we weren't going to change, and they decided that they'd better stake us for a while." He paused. "Her Dad was mighty nice about it," he said quietly. "We could have gone on until we got some money somehow, but they thought it wasn't doing either of us any good. So they let us get married."

"They gave you an allowance."

"That's right. We only needed it three or four years, and then an aunt died and I got promoted, and we were all set."

They swam to the end of the jetty, got out, and sat basking in the sun. Presently they walked back to Peter on the beach, sat with him while they smoked a cigarette, and then went to change. They reassembled on the beach carrying their shoes, drying their feet in leisurely manner in the sun and brushing off the sand. Presently Dwight started to put on his socks.

The girl said, "Fancy going round in socks like that!"

The commander glanced at them. "It's only in the toe," he said. "It doesn't show."

"It's not only in the toe," she leaned across and picked up his foot. "I thought I saw another one. The heel's all holes across the bottom!"

"It still doesn't show," he said. "Not when I've got a shoe on."

"Doesn't anybody mend them for you?"

"They've paid off a lot of the ship's company in *Sydney* recently," he said. "I still get my bed made up, but he's too busy now to bother about mending. It never did work very well aboard that ship, anyway. I do them myself, sometimes. Most times I just throw them away and get another pair."

"You've got a button off your shirt, too."

"That doesn't show, either," he said equably. "It's way down at the bottom, goes underneath my belt."

"I think you're a perfect disgrace," she remarked. "I know what the admiral would say, if he saw you going round like that. He'd say *Scorpion* needs another captain."

"He wouldn't see it," he replied. "Not unless he made me take off my pants."

"This conversation's taking an unprofitable line," she said. "How many pairs of socks have you got in that condition?"

"I wouldn't know. It's quite a while since I went through the drawer."

"If you give them to me I'll take them home and mend them for you."

He glanced at her. "That's mighty nice of you, to offer to do that. But you don't have to. It's time I got more, anyway. These are just about done."

"Can you get more socks?" she said. "Daddy can't. He says they're going off the market, with a lot of other things. He can't get any new handkerchiefs, either."

Peter said, "That's right. I couldn't get socks to fit me, the last time I tried. The ones I got were about two inches too long."

Moira pressed the point "Have you tried to buy any more recently?"

"Well—no. The last lot I bought was sometime back in the winter."

Peter yawned. "Better let her mend them for you, sir. You'll have a job getting any more."

"If that's the way it is," Dwight said, "I'd be very grateful." He turned to the girl. "But you don't have to do it. I can do them for myself." He grinned. "I can, you know. I can do them quite well."

She sniffed audibly. "About as well as I can run your submarine. You'd better make up a parcel of everything you've got that needs mending, and let me have it. That shirt included. Have you got the button?"

"I think I lost that."

"You should be more careful. When a button comes off, you don't just chuck it away."

"If you talk to me like that," he said grimly, "I really will give you everything I've got that needs mending. I'll bury you in the stuff."

"Now we're getting somewhere," she remarked. "I thought you'd been concealing things. You'd better put it all into a cabin trunk, or two cabin trunks, and let me have them."

"There's quite a lot," he said.

"I knew it. If there's too much I'll shove some of it off on to Mummy and she'll probably distribute it all round the district. The First Naval Member lives quite near us; Mummy'll probably give Lady Hartman your underpants to mend."

He looked at her in mock alarm. "Say, *Scorpion* certainly would need another captain, then."

She said, "This conversation's going round in circles. You let me have everything that you've got that needs mending, anyway, and I'll see if I can't get you dressed up like a naval officer."

"Okay," he said. "Where shall I bring the stuff to?" She thought for a moment. "You're on leave, aren't you?"

"On and off," he said. "We're giving leave over ten days, but I don't get that much. The captain has to stick around, or thinks he has."

77

"Probably do the ship a world of good if he didn't," she said. "You'd better bring them down to me at Berwick, and stay a couple of nights. Can you drive a bullock?"

"I've never driven one," he said. "I could try."

She eyed him speculatively. "I suppose you'd be all right. If you can command a submarine you probably can't do much harm to one of our bullocks. Daddy's got a cart horse now called Prince, but I don't suppose he'd let you touch that. He'd probably let you drive one of the bullocks."

"That's all right with me," he said meekly. "What am I supposed to do with the bullock?"

"Spread the dung," she said. "The cow pats. It has a harness that pulls a chain harrow over the grass. You walk beside it, leading it with a halter. You have a stick to tap it with as well. It's a very restful occupation. Good for the nerves."

"I'm sure it is," he said. "What's it for? I mean, why do you do it?"

"It makes a good pasture," she said. "If you just leave the droppings where they are, the grass comes up in rank tufts and the animals won't eat it. Then the pasture isn't half as good next year as if you'd harrowed it. Daddy's very particular about harrowing each pasture after the beasts come out. We used to do it with a tractor. Now we do it with a bullock."

"This is all so that he'd get a better pasture next year?"

"Yes, it is," she said firmly. "All right, you needn't say it. It's good farming to harrow the paddocks, and Daddy's a good farmer."

"I wasn't going to say it. How many acres does he farm?"

"About five hundred. We do Angus beef cattle and sheep."

"You shear the sheep for the wool?"

"That's right."

"When do you do that?" he asked. "I've never seen a shearing."

"Usually we shear in October," she said. "Daddy's a bit worried that if we leave it till October this year it won't get done. He's talking of putting it forward and shearing in August."

"That makes sense," he observed gravely. He bent forward to put on his shoes. "It's a long time since I was on a farm," he said. "I'd like to come and spend a day or two, if you can put up with me. I expect I can make myself useful, one way or another."

"Don't worry about that," she said. "Daddy'll see you make yourself useful. It's going to be a godsend to him, having another man on the place."

He smiled. "And you'd really like me to bring all the mending with me?"

"I'll never forgive you if you just turn up with a couple of pairs of socks and say that your pyjamas are all right. Besides, Lady Hartman's looking forward to doing your pants. She doesn't know it, but she is."

"I'll take your word for it."

She drove him down to the station that evening in the Abbott buggy. As he got down from the vehicle she said, "I'll expect you on Tuesday, at Berwick station, in the afternoon. Give me a ring about the time of your train if you can. Otherwise I'll be there at about four o'clock, and wait."

He nodded. "I'll call you. You really mean that about bringing all the mending?"

"I'll never forgive you if you don't."

"Okay." He hesitated. "It'll be dark by the time you get home," he said. "Look after yourself."

She smiled at him. "I'll be all right. See you on Tuesday. Good night, Dwight."

"Good night," he said a little thickly. She drove off. He stood watching her until the buggy turned a corner and was out of sight.

It was ten o'clock at night when she drove into the yard outside the homestead. Her father heard the horse and came out in the darkness to help her unharness and put the buggy in the shed. In the dim light as they eased the vehicle back under cover, she said, "I asked Dwight Towers down here for a couple of days. He's coining on Tuesday."

"Coming here?" he asked, surprised.

"Yes. They've got leave before they go off on some other trip. You don't mind, do you?"

"Of course not. I hope it's not going to be dull for him, though. What are you going to do with him all day?"

"I told him he could drive the bullock round the paddocks. He's very practical."

"I could do with somebody to help feed out the silage," her father said.

"Well, I expect he could do that. After all, if he commands a nuclear-powered submarine he ought to be able to learn to shovel silage."

They went into the house. Later that night he told her mother about their visitor. She was properly impressed. "Do you think there's anything in it?"

"I don't know," he said. "She must like him all right."

"She hasn't had a man to stay since that Forrest boy, before the war."

He nodded. "I remember. Never thought much of him. I'm glad that came to an end."

"It was his Austin-Healey," her mother remarked. "I don't think she ever cared for him, not really."

"This one's got a submarine," her father said helpfully. "It's probably the same thing."

"He can't take her down the road in that at ninety miles an hour." She paused, and then she said, "Of course, he must be a widower now."

He nodded. "Everybody says that he's a very decent sort of chap."

Her mother said, "I do hope something comes of it. I would like to see her settled down, and happily married with some children."

"She'll have to be quick about it, if you're going to see that," remarked her father.

"Oh dear, I keep forgetting. But you know what I mean."

He came to her on Tuesday afternoon; she met him with the horse and buggy. He got out of the train and looked around, sniffing the warm country air. "Say," he said, "you've got some pretty nice country around here. Which way is your place?"

She pointed to the north. "Over there, about three miles."

"Up on that range of hills?"

"Not right up," she said. "Just a bit of the way up."

He was carrying a suitcase, and swung it up into the buggy, pushing it under the seat. "Is that all you've got?" she demanded.

"That's right. It's full of mending."

"It doesn't look much. I'm sure you must have more than that."

"I haven't. I brought everything there was. Honest"

"I hope you're telling me the truth." They got up into the driving seat and started off towards the village. Almost immediately he said, "That's a beech tree! There's another!"

She glanced at him curiously. "They grow round here. I suppose it's cooler on the hills."

He looked at the avenue, entranced. "That's an oak tree, but it's a mighty big one. I don't know that I ever saw an oak tree grow so big. And there's some maples!" He turned to her. "Say, this is just like an avenue in a small town in the States!"

"Is it?" she asked. "Is it like this in the States?"

"It certainly is," he said. "You've got all the trees here from the Northern Hemisphere. Parts of Australia I've seen up till now, they've only had gum trees and wattles."

"They don't make you feel bad?" she asked.

"Why, no. I just love to see these northern trees again."

"There are plenty of them round the farm," she said. They drove through the village, across the deserted bitumen road, and out upon the road to Harkaway. Presently the road trended uphill; the horse slowed to a walk and began to slog against the collar.

The girl said, "This is where we get out and walk."

He got down with her from the buggy, and they walked together up the hill, leading the horse. After the stuffiness of the dockyard and the heat of the steel ships, the woodland air seemed fresh and cool to him. He took off his jacket and laid it in the buggy, and loosened the collar of his shirt. They walked on up the hill, and now a panorama started to unfold behind them, a wide view over the flat plain to the sea at Port Phillip Bay ten miles away. They went on, riding on the flats and walking on the steeper parts, for half an hour. Gradually they entered a country of gracious farms on undulating hilly slopes, a place where well-kept paddocks were interspersed with coppices and many trees. He said, "You're mighty lucky to have a home in country like this."

She glanced at him. "We like it all right. Of course, it's frightfully dull living out here."

He stopped, and stood in the road, looking around him at the smiling countryside, the wide, unfettered views. "I don't know that I ever saw a place that was more beautiful," he said.

"It is beautiful?" she asked. "I mean, is it as beautiful as places in America or England?"

"Why, sure," he said. "I don't know England so well. I'm told that parts of that are just a fairyland. There's plenty of lovely scenery in the United States, but I don't know of any place that's just like this. No, this is beautiful all right, by any standard in the world."

"I'm glad to hear you say that," she replied. "I mean, I like it here, but then I've never seen anything else. One sort of thinks that everything in England or America must be much better. That this is all right for Australia, but that's not saying much."

He shook his head. "It's not like that at all, honey. This is good by any standard that you'd like to name." They came to a flat and, driving in the buggy, the girl turned into an entrance gate. A short drive led between an avenue of pine trees to a single-storey wooden house, a fairly large house painted white that merged with farm buildings towards the back. A wide verandah ran along the front and down one side, partially glazed in. The girl drove past the house and into the farmyard. "Sorry about taking you in by the back door," she said. "But the mare won't stand, not when she's so near the stable."

A farm hand called Lou, the only employee on the place, came to help her with the horse, and her father came out to meet them. She introduced Dwight all round, and they left the horse and buggy to Lou and went into the house to meet her mother. Later they gathered on the verandah to sit in the warm evening sun over short drinks before the evening meal. From the verandah there was a pastoral view over undulating pastures and coppices, with a distant view of the plain down below the trees. Again Dwight commented upon the beauty of the countryside.

"Yes, it's nice up here," said Mrs. Davidson. "But it can't compare with England. England's beautiful."

The American asked, "Were you born in England?"

"Me? No. I was born Australian. My grandfather came out to *Sydney* in the very early days, but he wasn't a convict. Then he took up land in the Riverina. Some of the family are there still." She paused. "I've only been home once," she said. "We made a trip to England and the Continent in 1948, after the Second War. We thought England was quite beautiful. But I suppose it's changed a lot now."

She left the verandah presently with Moira to see about the tea, and Dwight was left on the verandah with her father. He said, "Let me give you another whisky."

"Why, thanks. I'd like one."

They sat in warm comfort in the mellow evening sun over their drinks. After a time the grazier said, "Moira was telling us about the cruise that you just made up to the north."

The captain nodded. "We didn't find out much."

"So she said."

"There's not much that you can see, from the water's edge and through the periscope," he told his host. "It's not as if there was any bomb damage, or anything like that. It all looks just the same as it always did. It's just that people don't live there anymore."

"It was very radioactive, was it?"

Dwight nodded. "It gets worse the further north you go, of course. At Cairns, when we were there, a person might have lived for a few days. At Port Darwin nobody could live so long as that."

"When were you at Cairns?"

"About a fortnight ago."

"I suppose the intensity at Cairns would be worse by now."

"Probably so. I'd say it gets worse steadily as time goes on. Finally, of course, it'll get to the same level all around the world."

"They're still saying that it's going to get here in September."

"I would say that's right. It's coming very evenly, all around the world. All places in the same latitude seem to be getting it just about the same time."

"They were saying on the wireless they've got it in Rockhampton."

The captain nodded. "I heard that, too. And at Alice Springs. It's coming very evenly along the latitudes."

His host smiled, a little grimly. "No good agonizing about it Have another whisky."

"I don't believe I will, not now. Thank you."

Mr. Davidson poured himself another small one. "Anyway," he said, "it comes to us last of all."

"That seems to be so," said Dwight. "If it goes on the way it's going now, Cape Town will go out a little before *Sydney*, about the same time as Montevideo. There'll be nothing left then in Africa and South America. Melbourne is the most southerly major city in the world, so we'll be near to the last." He paused for a moment in thought. "New Zealand, most of it, may last a little longer, and, of course, Tasmania. A fortnight or three weeks, perhaps. I don't know if there's anybody in Antarctica. If so, they might go on for quite a while."

"But Melbourne is the last big city?"

"That's what it looks like, at the moment."

They sat in silence for a little while. "What will you do?" the grazier asked at last. "Will you move your ship?"

"I haven't decided that," the captain said slowly. "Maybe I won't have to decide it. I've got a senior officer, Captain Shaw, in Brisbane. I don't suppose he'll move because his ship can't move. Maybe he'll send me orders. I don't know."

"Would you move, if it was at your own discretion?"

"I haven't decided that," the captain said again. "I can't see that there's a great deal to be gained. Nearly forty per cent of my ship's company have got themselves tied up with girls in Melbourne—married, some of them. Say I was to move to Hobart. I can't take them along, and they can't get there any other way, and if they could there's nowhere there for them to live. It seems kind of rough on the men to separate them from their women in the last few days, unless there was some compelling reason in the interest of the naval service." He glanced up, grinning. "Anyway, I don't suppose they'd come. Most of them would probably jump ship."

"I suppose they would. I think they'd probably decide to put the women first."

The American nodded. "It's reasonable. And there's no sense in giving orders that you know won't be obeyed."

"Could you take your ship to sea without them?"

"Why, yes—just for a short run. Hobart would be a short trip, six or seven hours. We could take her there with just a dozen men, or even less. We wouldn't submerge if we were as short-handed as that, and we couldn't cruise for any length of time. But if we got her there, or even to New Zealand—say to Christchurch—without a full crew we could never be effective, operationally." He paused. "We'd be just refugees."

They sat in silence for a time. "One of the things that's been surprising me," the grazier said, "is that there have been so few refugees. So few people coming down from the north. From Cairns and Townsville, and from places like that."

"Is that so?" the captain asked. "It's just about impossible to get a bed in Melbourne—anywhere."

"I know there have been some. But not the numbers that I should have expected."

"That's the radio, I suppose," Dwight said. "These talks that the Prime Minister's been giving have been kind of steadying. The A.B.C.'s been doing a good job in telling people just the way things are. After all, there's not much comfort in leaving home and coming down here to live in a tent or in a car, and have the same thing happen to you a month or two later."

"Maybe," the grazier said. "I've heard of people going back to Queensland after a few weeks of that. But I'm not sure that that's the whole story. I believe it is that nobody really thinks it's going to happen, not to them, until they start to feel ill. And by that time, well, it's less effort to stay at home and take it. You don't recover from this once it starts, do you?"

"I don't think that's true. I think you can recover, if you get out of the radioactive area into a hospital where you get proper treatment. They've got a lot of cases from the north in the Melbourne hospitals right now."

"I didn't know that."

"No. They don't say anything about that over the radio. After all, what's the use? They're only going to get it over again next September."

"Nice outlook," said the grazier. "Will you have another whisky now?"

"Thank you, I believe I will." He stood up and poured himself a drink. "You know," he said, "now that I've got used to the idea, I think I'd rather have it this way. We've all got to die one day, some sooner and some later. The trouble always has been that you're never ready, because you don't know when it's coming. Well, now we do know, and there's nothing to be done about it. I kind of like that. I kind of like the thought that I'll be fit and well up till the end of August and then—home. I'd rather have it that way than go on as a sick man from when I'm seventy to when I'm ninety."

"You're a regular naval officer," the grazier said. "You're probably more accustomed to this sort of thing than I would be."

"Will you evacuate?" the captain asked. "Go someplace else when it gets near? Tasmania?"

"Me? Leave this place?" the grazier said. "No, I shan't go. When it comes, I'll have it here, on this verandah, in this chair, with a drink in my hand. Or else in my own bed. I wouldn't leave this place."

"I'd say that's the way most folks think about it, now that they've got used to the idea."

They sat on the verandah in the setting sun till Moira came to tell them that tea was ready. "Drink up," she said, "and come in for the blotting paper, if you can still walk."

Her father said, "That's not the way to talk to our guest."

"You don't know our guest as well as I do, Daddy. I tell you, you just can't get him past a pub. Any pub."

"More likely he can't get you past one." They went into the house.

There followed a very restful two days for Dwight Towers. He handed over a great bundle of mending to the two women, who took it away from him, sorted it, and busied themselves over it. In the hours of daylight he was occupied with Mr. Davidson upon the farm from dawn till dusk. He was initiated into the arts of crutching sheep and of shovelling silage up into a cart and distributing it in the paddocks; he spent long hours walking by the bullock on the sunlit pastures. The change did him good after his confined life in the submarine and in the mother ship; each night he went to bed early and slept heavily, and awoke refreshed for the next day.

On the last morning of his stay, after breakfast, Moira found him standing at the door of a small outside room beside the laundry, now used as a repository for luggage, ironing boards, gum boots, and junk of every description. He was standing at the open door smoking a cigarette, looking at the assortment of articles inside. She said, "That's where we put things when we tidy up the house and say we'll send it to the jumble sale. Then we never do."

He smiled. "We've got one of those, only it's not so full as this. Maybe that's because we haven't lived there so long." He stood looking in upon the mass with interest. "Say, whose tricycle was that?"

"Mine," she said.

"You must have been quite small when you rode around on that."

She glanced at it "It does look small now, doesn't it? I should think I was four or five years old."

"There's a Pogo stick!" He reached in and pulled it out; it squeaked rustily. "It's years and years since I saw a Pogo stick. There was quite a craze for them at one time, back home."

"They went out for a time, and then they came back into fashion," she said. "Quite a lot of kids about here have Pogo sticks now."

"How old would you have been when you had that?"

She thought for a moment. "It came after the tricycle, after the scooter, and before the bicycle. I should think I was about seven."

He held it in his hands thoughtfully. "I'd say that's about the right age for a Pogo stick. You can buy them in the shops here, now?"

"I should think so. The kids use them."

He laid it down. "It's years since I saw one of those in the United States. They go in fashions, as you say." He glanced around. "Who owned the stilts?"

"My brother had them first, and then I had them. I broke that one."

"He was older than you, wasn't he?"

She nodded. "Two years older—two and a half."

"Is he in Australia now?"

"No. He's in England."

He nodded; there was nothing useful to be said about that.

"Those stilts are quite high off the ground," he remarked. "I'd say you were older then."

She nodded. "I must have been ten or eleven."

"Skis." He measured the length of them with his eye, "You must have been older still."

"I didn't go skiing till I was about sixteen. But I used those up till just before the war. They were getting a bit small for me by then, though. That other pair were Donald's."

He ran his eye around the jumbled contents of the little room.

"Say," he said, "there's a pair of water-skis!"

She nodded. "We still use those—or we did up till the war." She paused. "We used to go for summer holidays at Barwon Heads. Mummy used to rent the same house every year. . . She stood in silence for a moment, thinking of the sunny little house by the golf links, the warm sands, the cool air rushing past as she flew behind the motorboat in a flurry of warm spray. "There's the wooden spade I used to build sand castles with when I was very little. . . ."

He smiled at her. "It's kind of fun, looking at other people's toys and trying to think what they must have looked like at that age. I can just imagine you at seven, jumping around on that Pogo stick."

"And flying into a temper every other minute," she said. She stood for a moment looking in at the door thoughtfully. "I never would let Mummy give any of my toys away," she said quietly. "I said that I was going to keep them for my children to play with. Now there aren't going to be any."

"Too bad," he said. "Still that's the way it is." He pulled the door to and closed it on so many sentimental hopes. "I think I'll have to get back to the ship this afternoon and see if she's sunk at her moorings. Do you know what time there'd be a train?"

"I don't, but we can ring the station and find out. You don't think you could stay another day?"

"I'd like to, honey, but I don't think I'd better. There'll be a pile of paper on my desk that needs attention."

"I'll find out about the train. What are you going to do this morning?"

"I told your father that I'd finish harrowing the hill paddock."

"I've got an hour or so to do around the house. I'll probably come out and walk around with you after that."

"I'd like that. Your bullock's a good worker, but he doesn't make a lot of conversation."

They gave him his newly mended clothes after lunch. He expressed his thanks for all that they had done for him, packed his bag, and Moira drove him down to the station. There was an exhibition of Australian religious paintings at the National Gallery; they arranged to go and see that together before it came off; he would give her a ring. Then he was in the train for Melbourne, on his way back to his work.

He got back to the aircraft carrier at about six o'clock. As he had supposed, there was a pile of paper on his desk, including a sealed envelope with a security label gummed on the outside. He slit it open and found that it contained a draft operation order, with a personal note attached to it from the First Naval Member asking him to ring up for an appointment and come and see him about it.

He glanced the order through. It was very much as he had thought that it would be. It was within the capacity of his ship to execute, assuming that there were no mines at all laid on the west coast of the United States, which seemed to him to be a bold assumption.

He rang up Peter Holmes that evening at his home near Falmouth. "Say," he said, "I've got a draft operation order lying on my desk. There's a covering letter from the First Naval Member, wants me to go and see him. I'd like it if you could come on board tomorrow and look it over. Then I'd say you'd better come along when I go to see the admiral."

"I'll be on board tomorrow morning, early," said the liaison officer.

"Well, that's fine. I hate to pull you back off leave, but this needs action."

"That's all right, sir. I was only going to take down a tree."

He was in the aircraft carrier by half-past nine next morning, seated with Commander Towers in his little office cabin reading through the order. "It's more or less what you thought it was going to be, sir, isn't it?" he asked.

"More or less," the captain agreed. He turned to the side table. "This is all we've got on the minefields. This radio station that they want investigated. They've pinpointed that in the Seattle area. Well, we're all right for that." He raised a chart from the table. "This is the key minefield chart of the Juan de Fuca and Puget Sound. We should be safe to go right up to Bremerton Naval Yard. We're all right for Pearl Harbor, but they don't ask us to go there. The Gulf of Panama, San Diego, and San Francisco—we've got nothing on those at all."

Peter nodded. "We'll have to explain that to the admiral. As a matter of fact, I think he knows it. I know that he's quite open to a general discussion of this thing."

"Dutch Harbor," said the captain. "We've got nothing on that."

"Would we meet any ice up there?"

"I'd say we would. And fog, a lot of fog. It's not so good to go there at this time of year, with no watch on deck. We'll have to be careful up around those parts."

"I wonder why they want us to go there."

"I wouldn't know. Maybe he'll tell us."

They pored over the charts together for a time. "How would you go?" the liaison officer asked at last.

"On the surface along latitude thirty, north of New Zealand, south of Pitcairn, till we pick up longitude one-twenty. Then straight up the longitude. That brings us to the States in California, around Santa Barbara. Coming home from Dutch Harbor we'd do the same. Straight south down one-six-five past Hawaii. I guess we'd take a look in at Pearl Harbor while we're there. Then right on south till we can surface near the Friendly Islands, or maybe a bit south of that."

"How long would that mean that we should be submerged?"

The captain turned and took a paper from the desk.

"I was trying to figure that out last night. I don't suppose that we'd stay very long in any place, like the last time. I make the distance around two hundred degrees, twelve thousand miles submerged. Say six hundred hours cruising—twenty-five days. Add a couple of days for investigations and delays. Say twenty-seven days."

"Quite a long time underwater."

"Swordfish went longer. She went thirty-two days. The thing is to take it easy, and relax."

The liaison officer studied the chart of the Pacific. He laid his finger on the mass of reefs and island groups south of Hawaii. "There's not going to be much relaxing when we come to navigate through all this stuff, submerged. And that comes at the end of the trip."

"I know it." He stared at the chart. "Maybe we'll move away towards the west a trifle, and come down on Fiji from the north." He paused. "I'm more concerned about Dutch Harbor than I am of the run home," he said.

They stood studying the charts with the operation order for half an hour. Finally the Australian said, "Well, it's going to be quite a cruise." He grinned.

"Something to tell our grandchildren about."

The captain glanced at him quickly, and then broke into a smile. "You're very right."

The liaison officer waited in the cabin while the captain rang the admiral's secretary in the Navy Department. An appointment was made for ten o'clock the following morning. There was nothing then for Peter Holmes to stay for; he arranged to meet his captain next morning in the secretary's office before the appointment, and he took the next train back to his home at Falmouth.

He got there before lunch and rode his bicycle up from the station. He was hot when he got home, and glad to get out of uniform and take a shower before the cold meal. He found Mary to be very much concerned about the baby's prowess in crawling. "I left her in the lounge," she told him, "on the hearthrug and I went into the kitchen to peel the potatoes. The next thing I knew, she was in the passage, just outside the kitchen door. She's a little devil. She can get about now at a tremendous pace."

They sat down to their lunch. "We'll have to get some kind of a playpen," he said. "One of those wooden things, that fold up."

She nodded. "I was thinking about that. One with a few rows of beads on part of it, like an abacus."

"I suppose you can get playpens still," he said. "Do we know anyone who's stopped having babies—might have one they didn't want?"

She shook her head. "I don't. All our friends seem to be having baby after baby."

"I'll scout around a bit and see what I can find," he said.

It was not until lunch was nearly over that she was able to detach her mind from the baby. Then she asked, "Oh, Peter, what happened with Commander Towers?"

"He'd got a draft operation order," he told her. "I suppose it's confidential, so don't talk about it. They want us to make a fairly long cruise in the Pacific.

Panama, San Diego, San Francisco, Seattle, Dutch Harbor, and home, probably by way of Hawaii. It's all a bit vague just at present."

She was uncertain of her geography. "That's an awfully long way, isn't it?"

"It's quite a way," he said. "I don't think we shall do it all. Dwight's very much against going into the Gulf of Panama because he hasn't got a clue about the minefields, and if we don't go there that cuts off thousands of miles. But even so, it's quite a way."

"How long would it take?" she asked.

"I haven't worked it out exactly. Probably about two months. You see," he explained, "you can't set a direct course, say for San Diego. He wants to keep the underwater time down to a minimum. That means we set course east on a safe latitude steaming on the surface till we're two-thirds of the way across the South Pacific, and then go straight north till we come to California. It makes a dog leg of it, but it means less time submerged."

"How long would you be submerged, Peter?"

"Twenty-seven days, he reckons."

"That's an awfully long time, isn't it?"

"It's quite long. It's not a record, or anywhere near it. Still, it's quite a time to be without fresh air. Nearly a month."

"When would you be starting?"

"Well, I don't know that. The original idea was that we'd get away about the middle of next month, but now we've got this bloody measles in the ship. We can't go until we're clear of that."

"Have there been any more cases?"

"One more—the day before yesterday. The surgeon seems to think that's probably the last. If he's right we might be cleared to go about the end of the month. If not—if there's another one—it'll be sometime in March."

"That means that you'd be back here sometime in June?"

"I should think so. We'll be clear of measles by the tenth of March whatever happens. That means we'd be back here by the tenth of June."

The mention of measles had aroused anxiety in her again. "I do hope Jennifer doesn't get it."

They spent a domestic afternoon in their own garden. Peter started on the job of taking down the tree. It was not a very large tree, and he had little difficulty in sawing it half through and pulling it over with a rope so that it fell along the lawn and not on to the house. By teatime he had lopped its branches and stacked them away to be burned in the winter, and he had got well on with sawing the green wood up into logs. Mary came with the baby, newly wakened from her afternoon sleep, and laid a rug out on the lawn and put the baby on it. She went back into the house to fetch a tray of tea things; when she returned the baby was ten feet from the rug trying to eat a bit of bark. She scolded her husband and set him to watch his child while she went in for the kettle.

"It's no good," she said. "We'll have to have that playpen."

He nodded. "I'm going up to town tomorrow morning," he said. "We've got a date at the Navy Department, but after that I should be free. I'll go to Myers' and see if they've still got them there."

"I do hope they have. I don't know what we'll do if we can't get one."

"We could put a belt round her waist and tether her to a peg stuck in the ground."

"We couldn't, Peter!" she said indignantly. "She'd wind it round her neck and strangle herself!"

He mollified her, accustomed to the charge of being a heartless father. They spent the next hour playing with their baby on the grass in the warm sun, encouraging it to crawl about the lawn. Finally Mary took it indoors to bathe it and give it its supper, while Peter went on sawing up the logs.

He met his captain next morning in the Navy Department, and together they were shown into the office of the First Naval Member, who had a captain from the Operations Division with him. He greeted them cordially, and made them sit down. "Well now," he said. "You've had a look at the draft operation order that we sent you down?"

"I made a very careful study of it, sir," said the captain.

"What's your general reaction?"

"Minefields," Dwight said. "Some of the objectives that you name would almost certainly be mined." The admiral nodded. "We have full information on Pearl Harbor and on the approaches to Seattle. We have nothing on any of the others."

They discussed the order in some detail for a time. Finally the admiral leaned back in his chair. "Well, that gives me the general picture. That's what I wanted." He paused. "Now, you'd better know what this is all about.

"Wishful thinking," he observed. "There's a school of thought among the scientists, a section of them, who consider that this atmospheric radioactivity may be dissipating—decreasing in intensity, fairly quickly. The general argument is that the precipitation during this last winter in the Northern Hemisphere, the rain and snow, may have washed the air, so to speak." The American nodded. "According to that theory, the radioactive elements in the atmosphere will be falling to the ground, or to the sea, more quickly than we had anticipated. In that case the ground masses of the Northern Hemisphere would continue to be uninhabitable for many centuries, but the transfer of radioactivity to us would be progressively decreased. In that case life—human life—might continue to go on down here, or at any rate in Antarctica. Professor Jorgensen holds that view very strongly."

He paused. "Well, that's the bare bones of the theory. Most of the scientists disagree, and think that Jorgensen is optimistic. Because of the majority opinion nothing has been said about this on the wireless broadcasting, and we've been spared the press. It's no good raising people's hopes without foundation. But clearly, it's a matter that must be investigated."

"I see that, sir," Dwight said. "It's very important. That's really the main object of this cruise?"

The admiral nodded. "That's right. If Jorgensen is correct, as you go north from the equator the atmospheric radioactivity should be steady for a time and then begin to decrease. I don't say at once, but at some point a decrease should be evident. That's why we want you to go as far north in the Pacific as you can, to Kodiak and to Dutch Harbor. If Jorgensen is right, there should be much less radioactivity up there. It might even be near normal. In that case, you might be able to go out on deck." He paused. "On shore, of course, ground radioactivity would still be intense. But out at sea, life might be possible."

Peter asked, "Is there any experimental support for this yet, sir?"

The admiral shook his head. "Not much. The Air Force sent out a machine the other day. Did you hear about that?"

"No, sir."

"Well, they sent out a Victor bomber with a full load of fuel. It flew from Perth due north and got as far as the China Sea, about latitude thirty north, somewhere south of Shanghai, before it had to turn back. That's not far enough for the scientists, but it was as far as the machine could go. The evidence they got was inconclusive. Atmospheric radioactivity was still increasing, but towards the northern end of the flight it was increasing slowly." He smiled. "I understand the back-room boys are still arguing about it. Jorgensen, of course, claims it as his victory. He says there'll be a positive reduction by the time you get to latitude fifty or sixty."

"Sixty," the captain said. "We can make that close inshore in the Gulf of Alaska. The only thing up there is that we'd have to watch the ice."

They discussed the technicalities of the operation again for a time. It was decided that protective clothing should be carried in the submarine to permit one or two men to go on deck in moderate conditions and that decontamination sprays should be arranged in one of the escape chambers. An inflatable rubber dinghy would be carried in the superstructure, and the new directional aerial would be mounted on the after periscope.

Finally the admiral said, "Well, that clears the decks so far as we are concerned. I think the next step is that I call a conference with C.S.I.R.O. and anybody else who may be concerned. I'll arrange that for next week. In the meantime, Commander, you might see the Third Naval Member or one of his officers about this dockyard work. I'd like to see you get away by the end of next month."

Dwight said, "I think that should be possible, sir. There's not a lot of work in this. The only thing might hold us up would be the measles."

The admiral laughed shortly. "The fate of human life upon the world at stake, and we're stuck with the measles! All right, Captain—I know you'll do your best."

When they left the office Dwight and Peter separated, Dwight to call the Third Naval Member's office, and Peter to go to find John Osborne in his office in Albert Street. He told the scientist what he had learned that morning. "I know all about Jorgensen," Mr. Osborne said impatiently. "The old man's crackers. It's just wishful thinking."

"You don't think much of what the aeroplane found out—the reduced rate of increase of the radioactivity as you go north?"

"I don't dispute the evidence. The Jorgensen effect may well exist. Probably it does. But nobody but Jorgensen thinks that it's significant."

Peter got to his feet. "I'll leave the wise to wrangle," he quoted sardonically. "I've got to go and buy a playpen for my eldest unmarried daughter."

"Where are you going to for that?"

"Myers'."

The scientist got up from his chair. "I'll come with you. I've got something in Elizabeth Street I'd like to show you."

He would not tell the naval officer what it was. They walked together down the centre of the traffic-free streets to the motorcar district of the town, turned up a side street, and then into a mews. John Osborne produced a key from his pocket, unlocked the double doors of a building, and pushed them open.

It had been the garage of a motor dealer. Silent cars stood ranged in rows along the walls, some of them unregistered, all covered in dust and dirt with flat tires sagging on the floor. In the middle of the floor stood a racing car. It was a single seater, painted red. It was a very low-built car, a very small car, with a bonnet sloping forward to an aperture that lay close to the ground. The tires were inflated and it had been washed and polished with loving care; it shone in the light from the door. It looked venomously fast.

"My goodness!" Peter said. "What's that?"

"It's a Ferrari," said John Osborne. "It's the one that Donezetti raced the year before the war. The one he won the Grand Prix of Syracuse on."

"How did it get out here?"

"Johnny Bowles bought it and had it shipped out. Then the war came and he never raced it."

"Who owns it now?"

"I do."

"You?"

The scientist nodded. "I've been keen on motor racing all my life. It's what I've always wanted to do, but there's never been any money. Then I heard of this Ferrari. Bowles was caught in England. I went to his widow and offered her a hundred quid for it. She thought I was mad, of course, but she was glad to sell it."

Peter walked round the little car with the large wheels, inspecting it. "I agree with her. What on earth are you going to do with it?"

"I don't know yet. I only know that I'm the owner of what's probably the fastest car in the world."

It fascinated the naval officer. "Can I sit in it?"

"Go ahead."

He squeezed down into the little seat behind the plastic windscreen. "What will she do, all out?"

"I don't really know. Two hundred, anyway."

Peter sat fingering the wheel, feeling the controls. The single seater felt delightfully a part of him. "Have you had her on the road?"

"Not yet."

He got out of the seat reluctantly. "What are you going to use for petrol?"

93

The scientist grinned. "She doesn't drink it."

"Doesn't use petrol?"

"She runs on a special ether-alcohol mixture. It's no good in an ordinary car. I've got eight barrels of it in my mother's back garden." He grinned. "I made sure that I'd got that before I bought the car."

He lifted the bonnet and they spent some time examining the engine. John Osborne had spent all his leisure hours since they returned from their first cruise in polishing and servicing the racing car; he hoped to try her out upon the road in a couple of days' time. "One thing," he said, grinning in delight, "there's not a lot of traffic to worry about."

They left the car reluctantly, and locked the garage doors. In the quiet mews they stood for a few moments. "If we get away upon this cruise by the end of next month," Peter said, "we should be back about the beginning of June. I'm thinking about Mary and the kid. Think they'll be all right till we get back?"

"You mean—the radioactivity?"

The naval officer nodded.

The scientist stood in thought. "Anybody's guess is as good as mine," he said at last. "It may come quicker or it may come slower. So far it's been coming very steadily all round the world, and moving southwards at just about the rate that you'd expect. It's south of Rockhampton now. If it goes on like this it should be south of Brisbane by the beginning of June—just south. Say about eight hundred miles north of us. But as I say, it may come quicker or it may come slower. That's all I can tell you."

Peter bit his lip. "It's a bit worrying. One doesn't want to start a flap at home. But all the same, I'd be happier if they knew what to do if I'm not there."

"You may not be there anyway," John Osborne said. "There seem to be quite a few natural hazards on this course—apart from radiation. Minefields, ice—all sorts of things. I don't know what happens to us if we hit an iceberg at full cruising speed, submerged."

"I do," said Peter.

The scientist laughed. "Well, let's keep our fingers crossed and hope we don't. I want to get back here and race that thing." He nodded at the car behind the door.

"It's all a bit worrying," Peter repeated. They turned towards the street. "I think I'll have to do something about it before we go."

They walked in silence into the main thoroughfare. John Osborne turned towards his office. "You going my way?"

Peter shook his head. "I've got to see if I can buy a playpen for the baby. Mary says we've got to have it or she'll kill herself."

94

They turned in different directions and the scientist walked on, thankful that he wasn't married.

Peter went shopping for a playpen, and succeeded in buying one at the second shop he tried. A folded playpen is an awkward thing to carry through a crowd; he battled with it to the tram and got it to Flinders Street station. He got to Falmouth with it at about four o'clock in the afternoon. He put it in the cloakroom till he could come and fetch it with his bicycle trailer, took his bicycle, and rode slowly into the shopping street. He went to the chemist that they dealt with, whose proprietor he knew, and who knew him. At the counter he asked the girl if he could see Mr. Goldie.

The chemist came to him in a white coat. He asked, "Could I have a word with you in private?"

"Why, yes, Commander." He led the way into the dispensary.

Peter said, "I wanted to have a talk with you about this radiation disease." The chemist's face was quite expressionless. "I've got to go away. I'm sailing in the *Scorpion*, the American submarine. We're going a long way. We shan't be back till the beginning of June, at the earliest." The chemist nodded slowly. "It's not a very easy trip," the naval officer said. "There's just the possibility that we might not come back at all."

They stood in silence for a moment. "Are you thinking about Mrs. Holmes and Jennifer?" the chemist asked.

Peter nodded. "I'll have to make sure Mrs. Holmes understands about things before I go." He paused. "Tell me, just what does happen to you?"

"Nausea," the chemist said, "That's the first symptom. Then vomiting, and diarrhoea. Bloody stools. All the symptoms increase in intensity. There may be slight recovery, but if so it would be very temporary. Finally death occurs from sheer exhaustion." He paused. "In the very end, infection or leukaemia may be the actual cause of death. The blood-forming tissues are destroyed, you see, by the loss of body salts in the fluids. It might go one way or the other."

"Somebody was saying it's like cholera."

"That's right," the chemist said. "It is rather like cholera."

"You've got some stuff for it, haven't you?"

"Not to cure it, I'm afraid."

"I don't mean that. To end it."

"We can't release that yet, Commander. About a week before it reaches any district details will be given on the wireless. After that we may distribute it to those who ask for it." He paused. "There must be terrible complications over the religious side," he said. "I suppose then it's a matter for the individual."

"I've got to see that my wife understands about it," Peter said, "She'll have to see to the baby. . . . And I may not be here. I've got to see this all squared up before I go."

"I could explain it all to Mrs. Holmes, when the time comes."

"I'd rather do it myself. She'll be a bit upset."

"Of course. . . ." He stood for a moment, and then said, "Come into the stock room."

He went through into a back room through a locked door. There was a packing case in one corner, the lid part lifted. He wrenched it back. The case was full of little red boxes, of two sizes.

The chemist took out one of each and went back into the dispensary. He undid the smaller of the two; it contained a little plastic vial with two white tablets in it. He opened it, took out the tablets, put them carefully away, and substituted two tablets of aspirin. He put the vial back in the red box and closed it. He handed it to Peter. "That is for anybody who will take a pill," he said. "You can take that and show it to Mrs. Holmes. One causes death, almost immediately. The other is a spare. When the time comes, we shall be distributing these at the counter."

"Thanks a lot," he said. "What does one do about the baby?"

The chemist took the other box. "The baby, or a pet animal—dog or cat," he said. "It's just a little more complicated." He opened the second box and took out a small syringe. "I've got a used one I can put in for you, here. You follow these instructions on the box. Just give the hypodermic injection under the skin. She'll fall asleep quite soon."

He packed the dummy back into the box, and gave it to Peter with the other.

The naval officer took them gratefully. "That's very kind of you," he said. "She'll be able to get these at the counter when the time comes?"

"That's right."

"Will there be anything to pay?"

"No charge," the chemist said. "They're on the free list."

## Chapter Five

Of the three presents which Peter Holmes took back to his wife that night, the playpen was the most appreciated.

It was a brand-new playpen, painted in a pastel green, with brightly coloured beads upon the abacus. He set it up on the lawn before he went into the house, and then called Mary out to see it. She came and examined it critically, testing it for stability to make sure the baby couldn't pull it over on top of her. "I do hope the paint won't come off," she said. "She sucks everything, you know. Green paint's awfully dangerous. It's got verdigris in it."

"I asked about that in the shop," he said. "It's not oil paint—it's Duco. She'd have to have acetone in her saliva to get that off."

"She can get the paint off most things. . . She stood back and looked at it. "It's an awfully pretty colour," she said. "It'll go beautifully with the curtains in the nursery."

"I thought it might," he said. "They had a blue one, but I thought you'd like this better."

"Oh, I do!" She put her arms round him and kissed him. "It's a lovely present. You must have had a fearful job with it on the tram. Thank you so much."

"That's all right," he said. He kissed her back. "I'm so glad you like it."

She went and fetched the baby from the house and put her in the pen. Then they got short drinks for themselves and sat on the lawn, the bars between them and the baby, smoking cigarettes and watching her reaction to the new environment. They watched her as she grasped one of the bars in a tiny fist.

"You don't think she'll get up on her feet too soon, with that to hold on to?" her mother asked, worried. "I mean, she wouldn't learn to walk without it for a long time. If they walk too soon they grow up bandy legged."

"I shouldn't think so," Peter said. "I mean, everyone has playpens. I had one when I was a kid, and I didn't grow up bandy legged."

"I suppose if she didn't pull herself up on this she'd be pulling herself up on something else. A chair, or something."

When Mary took the baby away to give her bath and make her ready for bed, Peter took the playpen indoors and set it up in the nursery. Then he laid the table for the evening meal. Then he went and stood on the verandah fingering the red boxes in his pocket, wondering how on earth he was to give his other presents to his wife.

Presently he went and got himself a whisky.

He did it that evening, shortly before she went to take the baby up before they went to bed. He said awkwardly, "There's one thing I want to have a talk about before I go off on this cruise."

She looked up. "What's that?"

"About this radiation sickness people get. There's one or two things that you ought to know."

She said impatiently, "Oh, that. It's not until September. I don't want to talk about it."

"I'm afraid we'll have to talk about it," he said.

"I don't see why. You can tell me all about it nearer the time. When we know it's coming. Mrs. Hildred says her husband heard from somebody that it isn't coming here after all. It's slowing down or something. It's not going to get here."

"I don't know who Mrs. Hildred's husband has been talking to. But I can tell you that there's not a word of truth in it. It's coming here, all right. It may come in September, or it may come sooner."

She stared at him. "You mean that we're all going to get it?"

"Yes," he said. "We're all going to get it. We're all going to die of it. That's why I want to tell you just a bit about it."

"Can't you tell me about it nearer the time? When we know it's really going to happen?"

He shook his head. "I'd rather tell you now. You see, I might not be here when it happens. It might come quicker than we think, while I'm away. Or I might get run over by a bus—anything."

"There aren't any buses," she said quietly. "What you mean is the submarine."

"Have it your own way," he said. "I'd be much happier while I'm away in the submarine if I knew you knew about things more than you do now."

"All right," she said reluctantly. She lit a cigarette. "Go on and tell me."

He thought for a minute. "We've all got to die one day," he said at last. "I don't know that dying this way is much worse than any other. What happens is that you get ill. You start feeling sick, and then you are sick. Apparently you go on being sick—you can't keep anything down. And then, you've got to go. Diarrhoea.

And that gets worse and worse, too. You may recover for a little while, but it comes back again. And finally you get so weak that you just— die."

She blew a long cloud of smoke. "How long does all this take?"

"I didn't ask about that. I think it varies with the individual. It may take two or three days. I suppose if you recover it might take two or three weeks."

There was a short silence. "It's messy," she said at last. "I suppose if everybody gets it all at once, there's nobody to help you. No doctors, and no hospitals?"

"I shouldn't think so. I think this is the thing you've got to battle through with on your own."

"But you'll be here, Peter?"

"I'll be here," he comforted her. "I'm just telling you to cover the thousand to one chance."

"But if I'm all alone, who's going to look after Jennifer?"

"Leave Jennifer out of it for the moment," he said. "We'll come to her later." He leaned towards her. "The thing is this, dear. There's no recovery.

But you don't have to die in a mess. You can die decently, when things begin to get too bad." He drew the smaller of the two red boxes from his pocket.

She stared at it, fascinated. "What's that?" she whispered.

He undid the little carton and took out the vial. "This is a dummy," he said. "These aren't real. Goldie gave it to me to show you what to do. You just take one of them with a drink—any kind of drink. Whatever you like best. And then you just lie back, and that's the end."

"You mean, you die?" The cigarette was dead between her fingers.

He nodded. "When it gets too bad—it's the way out."

"What's the other pill for?" she whispered.

"That's a spare," he said. "I suppose they give it you in case you lose one of them, or funk it."

She sat in silence, her eyes fixed on the red box.

"When the time comes," he said, "they'll tell you all about this on the wireless. Then you just go to Goldie's and ask the girl for it, over the counter, so that you can have it in the house. She'll give it to you. Everybody will be given it who wants it."

She reached out, dropping the dead cigarette, and took the box from him. She read the instructions printed on it in black. At last she said, "But, Peter, however ill I was, I couldn't do that. Who would look after Jennifer?"

"We're all going to get it," he said. "Every living thing. Dogs and cats and babies—everyone. I'm going to get it. You're going to get it. Jennifer's going to get it, too."

She stared at him. "Jennifer's going to get this sort of—cholera?"

"I'm afraid so, dear," he said. "We're all going to get it."

She dropped her eyes. "That's beastly," she said vehemently. "I don't mind for myself so much. But that's . . . it's simply vile."

He tried to comfort her. "It's the end of everything for all of us," he said. "We're going to lose most of the years of life that we've looked forward to, and Jennifer's going to lose all of them. But it doesn't have to be too painful for her. When things are hopeless, you can make it easy for her. It's going to take a bit of courage on your part, but you've got that. This is what you'll have to do if I'm not here."

He drew the other red box from his pocket and began to explain the process to her. She watched him with growing hostility. "Let me get this straight," she said, and now there was an edge in her voice. "Are you trying to tell me what I've got to do to kill Jennifer?"

He knew that there was trouble coming, but he had to face it. "That's right," he said. "If it becomes necessary you'll have to do it."

She flared suddenly into anger. "I think you're crazy," she exclaimed. "I'd never do a thing like that, however ill she was. I'd nurse her to the end. You must be absolutely mad. The trouble is that you don't love her. You never have loved her. She's always been a nuisance to you. Well, she's not a nuisance to me. It's you that's the nuisance. And now it's reached the stage that you're trying to tell me how to murder her." She got to her feet, white with rage. "If you say one more word I'll murder you!"

He had never seen her so angry before. He got to his feet. "Have it your own way," he said wearily. "You don't have to use these things if you don't want to."

She said furiously, "There's a trick here, somewhere. You're trying to get me to murder Jennifer and kill myself. Then you'd be free to go off with some other woman."

He had not thought that it would be so bad as this. "Don't be a bloody fool," he said sharply. "If I'm here I'll have it myself. If I'm not here, if you've got to face things on your own, it'll be because I'm dead already. Just think of that, and try and get that into your fat head. I'll be dead."

She stared at him in angry silence.

"There's another thing you'd better think about," he said. "Jennifer may live longer than you will." He held up the first red box. "You can chuck these in the dust bin," he said. "You can battle on as long as you can stand, until you die. But Jennifer may not be dead. She may live on for days, crying and vomiting all over herself in her cot and lying in her muck, with you dead on the floor beside her and nobody to help her. Finally, of course, she'll die. Do you want her to die like that? If you do, I don't." He turned away. "Just think about it, and don't be such a bloody fool."

She stood in silence. For a moment he thought that she was going to fall, but he was too angry now himself to help her.

"This is a time when you've just got to show some guts and face up to things," he said.

She turned and ran out of the room and presently he heard her sobbing in the bedroom. He did not go to her. Instead he poured himself a whisky and soda and went out on to the verandah and sat down in a deck chair, looking out over the sea. These bloody women, sheltered from realities, living in a sentimental dream world of their own! If they'd face up to things they could help a man, help him enormously. While they clung to the dream world they were just a bloody millstone round his neck.

About midnight, after his third whisky, he went into the house and to their bedroom. She was in bed and the light was out; he undressed in the dark, fearing to wake her. She lay with her back to him; he turned from her and fell asleep, helped by the whisky. At about two in the morning he awoke, and heard her sobbing in the bed beside him. He stretched out a hand to comfort her.

She turned to him, still sobbing. "Oh, Peter, I'm sorry I've been such a fool."

They said no more about the red boxes, but next morning he put them in the medicine cupboard in the bathroom, at the back, where they would not be obtrusive but where she could hardly fail to see them. In each box he left a little note explaining that it was a dummy, explaining what she had to do to get the real ones. He added to each note a few words of love, thinking that she might well read it after he was dead.

The pleasant summer weather lasted well on into March. In *Scorpion* there were no more cases of measles, and the work upon the submarine progressed quickly in the hands of dockyard fitters who had little else to do. Peter Holmes took down the second tree, cut it up and stacked the logs to dry out so that they could be burned the following year, and started to dig out the stumps to make the kitchen garden.

John Osborne started up his Ferrari and drove it out upon the road. There was no positive prohibition upon motoring at that time. There was no petrol available to anybody because officially there was no petrol in the country; the stocks reserved for doctors and for hospitals had been used up. Yet very occasionally cars were still seen in motion on the roads. Each individual motorist had cans of petrol tucked away in his garage or in some private hiding place, provision that he had made when things were getting short, and these reserves were sometimes called upon in desperate emergency. John Osborne's Ferrari on the road did not call for any action by the police, even when his foot slipped upon the unfamiliar accelerator on his first drive and he touched eighty-five in second gear in Bourke Street, in the middle of the city. Unless he were to kill anybody, the police were not disposed to persecute him for a trifle such as that.

He did not kill anybody, but he frightened himself very much. There was a private road-racing circuit in South Gippsland near a little place called Tooradin, owned and run by a club of enthusiasts. Here there was a three-mile circuit of wide bitumen road, privately owned, leading nowhere, and closed to the public. The course had one long straight and a large number of sinuous turns and bends. Here races were still held, sparsely attended by the public for lack of road transport. Where the enthusiasts got their petrol from remained a closely guarded secret, or a number of secrets, because each seemed to have his own private hoard, as John Osborne hoarded his eight drums of special racing fuel in his mother's back garden.

John Osborne took his Ferrari down to this place several times, at first for practice and later to compete in races, short races for the sake of fuel economy. The car fulfilled a useful purpose in his life. His had been the life of a scientist, a man whose time was spent in theorizing in an office or, at best, in a laboratory. Not for him had been the life of action. He was not very well accustomed to taking personal risks, to endangering his life, and his life had been the poorer for it. When he had been drafted to the submarine for scientific duties he had been pleasurably excited by the break in his routine, but in secret he had been terrified each time that they submerged. He had managed to control himself and carry out his duties without much of his nervous tension showing during their week of underwater cruising in the north, but he had been acutely nervous of the prospect of nearly a month of it in the cruise that was coming.

The Ferrari altered that.' Each time he drove it, it excited him. At first he did not drive it very well. After touching a hundred and fifty miles an hour or so upon the straight, he failed to slow enough to take his corners safely. Each corner at first was a sort of dice with death, and twice he spun and ended up on the grass verge, white and trembling with shock and deeply ashamed that he had treated his car so. Each little race or practice run upon the circuit left him with the realization of mistakes that he must never make again, with the realization of death escaped by inches.

With these major excitements in the forefront of his mind, the coming cruise in *Scorpion* ceased to terrify. There was no danger in that comparable with the dangers that he courted in his racing car. The naval interlude became a somewhat boring chore to be lived through, a waste of time that now was growing precious, till he could get back to Melbourne and put in three months of road racing before the end.

Like every other racing motorist, he spent a lot of time endeavouring to track down further supplies of fuel.

Sir David Hartman held his conference as had been arranged. Dwight Towers went to it as captain of *Scorpion* and took his liaison officer with him. He also took the radio and electrical officer, a Lieutenant Sunderstrom, to the conference because matters connected with the Seattle radio were likely to arise. C.S.I.R.O. were represented by the director with John Osborne, the Third Naval Member was there with one of his officers, and the party was completed by one of the Prime Minister's secretaries.

At the commencement the First Naval Member outlined the difficulties of the operation. "It is my desire," he said, "and it is the Prime Minister's instruction, that *Scorpion* should not be exposed to any extreme danger in the course of this cruise. In the first place, we want the results of the scientific observations we are sending her to make. At the low height of her radio aerial and the necessity that she remains submerged for much of the time, we cannot expect free radio communication with her. For that reason alone she must return safely or the whole value of the operation will be lost. Apart from that, she is the only long-range vessel left at our disposal for communication with South America and with South Africa. With these considerations in mind I have made fairly drastic alterations to the cruise that we discussed at our last meeting. The investigation of the Panama Canal has been struck out. San Diego and San Francisco also have been struck out. All these are on account of minefields. Commander Towers, will you tell us shortly how you stand in regard to minefields?"

Dwight gave the conference a short dissertation on the mines and on his lack of knowledge. "Seattle is open to us, and the whole of Puget Sound," he said. "Also Pearl Harbor. I'd say there wouldn't be much danger from mines up around the Gulf of Alaska on account of the ice movements. The ice constitutes a problem in those latitudes, and the *Scorpion*'s no icebreaker. Still, in my opinion we can feel our way up there without unduly hazarding the ship. If we just can't make it all the way to latitude sixty, well, we'll have done our best. I'd say we probably can do most of what you want."

They turned to a discussion of the radio signals still coming from somewhere in the vicinity of Seattle. Sir Phillip Goodall, the director of C.S.I.R.O., produced a synopsis of the messages monitored since the war. "These signals are mostly incomprehensible," he said. "They occur at random intervals, more frequently in the winter than the summer. The frequency is 4.92 megacycles." The radio officer made a note upon the paper in front of him. "One hundred and sixty-nine transmissions have been monitored. Of these, three contained recognizable code groups, seven groups in all. Two contained words in clear, in English, one word in each. The groups were undecipherable; I have them here if anyone wants to see them. The words were waters and connect."

Sir David Hartman asked, "How many hours' transmission, in all, were monitored?"

"About a hundred and six hours."

"And in that time only two words have come through in clear? The rest is gibberish?"

"That is correct."

The admiral said, "I don't think the words can be significant. It's probably a fortuitous transmission. After all, if an infinite number of monkeys start playing with an infinite number of typewriters, one of them will write a play of Shakespeare. The real point to be investigated is this—how are these transmissions taking place at all? It seems certain that there is electrical power available there still. There may be human agency behind that power. It's not very likely, but it could be so."

Lieutenant Sunderstrom leaned towards his captain and spoke in a low tone. Dwight said aloud, "Mr. Sunderstrom knows the radio installations in that district."

The lieutenant said diffidently, "I wouldn't say that I know all of them. I attended a short course on naval communications at Santa Maria Island about five years back. One of the frequencies that was used there was 4.92 kilocycles."

The admiral asked, "Where is Santa Maria Island?"

"That one is just near Bremerton in Puget Sound, sir. There's several others on the Coast. This one is the main navy communications school for that area."

Commander Towers unrolled a chart, and pointed to the island with his finger. "Here it is, sir. It connects with the mainland by a bridge to this place Manchester right next to Clam Bay."

The admiral asked, "What would be the range of the station on Santa Maria Island?"

The lieutenant said, "I wouldn't know for certain, but I guess it's global."

"Does it look like a global station? Very high aerials?"

"Oh, yes, sir. The antennas there are quite a sight. I think it's a part of the regular communication system covering the Pacific area, but I don't know that for sure. I only attended the communications school."

"You never communicated with the station direct, from any ship that you were serving in?"

"No, sir. We operated on a different set of frequencies."

They discussed the techniques of radio for a time. "If it turns out to be Santa Maria," Dwight said at last, "I'd say we can investigate it without difficulty." He glanced at the chart that he had studied before, to confirm his studies. "There's forty feet of water right close up to it," he said. "Maybe we could even lie alongside a wharf. In any case, we've got the rubber boat. If the radiation level is anywhere near reasonable, we can put an officer on shore for a while, in the protective suit, of course."

The lieutenant said, "I'd be glad to volunteer for that. I guess I know the way around that installation pretty well."

They left it so, and turned to a consideration of the Jorgensen effect, and the scientific observations that were needed to prove or to disprove it.

Dwight met Moira Davidson for lunch after the conference. She had picked a small restaurant in the city for their meeting and he was there before her. She came to him bearing an attaché case.

He greeted her and offered her a drink before lunch. She elected for a brandy and soda, and he ordered it. "Double?" he inquired, as the waiter stood by.

"Single," she said. He nodded to the waiter without comment. He glanced at the attaché case. "Been shopping?"

"Shopping!" she said indignantly. "Me—full of virtue!"

"I'm sorry," he replied. "You're going someplace?"

"No," she said, enjoying his curiosity. "I'll give you three guesses what's in it."

"Brandy," he suggested.

"No. I carry that inside me."

He thought for a moment. "A carving knife. You're going to cut one of those religious pictures out of the frame and take it away to hang in the bathroom."

"No. One more."

"Your knitting."

"I don't knit. I don't do anything restful. You ought to know that by now."

The drinks came. "Okay," he said, "you win. What's in it?"

She lifted the lid of the case. It contained a reporter's notebook, a pencil, and a manual of shorthand.

He stared at these three items. "Say," he exclaimed, "you aren't studying that stuff?"

"What's wrong with that? You said I ought to, once."

He remembered vaguely what he had once said in an idle moment. "You taking a course or something?"

"Every morning," she said. "I've got to be in Russell Street at half-past nine. Half-past nine—for me. I have to get up before seven!"

He grinned. "Say, that's bad. What are you doing it for?"

"Something to do. I got fed up with harrowing the dung."

"How long have you been doing this?"

"Three days. I'm getting awfully good at it. I can make a squiggle now with anyone."

"Do you know what it means when you've made it?"

"Not yet," she admitted. She took a drink of brandy. "That's rather advanced work."

"Are you taking typing, too?"

She nodded. "And bookkeeping. All the lot."

He glanced at her in wonder. "You'll be quite a secretary by the time you're through."

"Next year," she said. "I'll be able to get a good job next year."

"Are many other people doing it?" he asked. "You go to a school, or something?"

She nodded. "There are more there than I'd thought there'd be. I think it's about half the usual number. There were hardly any pupils just after the war and they sacked most of the teachers. Now the numbers are going up and they've had to take them on again."

"More people are doing it now?"

"Mostly teen-agers," she told him. "I feel like a grandmother amongst them. I think their people got tired of having them at home and made them go to work." She paused. "It's the same at the university," she said. "There are many more enrollments now than there were a few months ago."

"I'd never have thought it would work out that way," he remarked.

"It's dull just living at home," she said. "They meet all their friends at the Shop."

He offered her another drink but she refused it, and they went in to lunch. "Have you heard about John Osborne and his car?" she asked.

He laughed. "I sure have. He showed it to me. I'd say he's showing it to everybody that will come and look at it. It's a mighty nice car."

"He's absolutely mad," she said. "He'll kill himself on it."

He sipped his cold consommé. "So what? So long as he doesn't kill himself before we start off on this cruise. He's having lots of fun."

"When are you starting off on the cruise?" she asked.

"I suppose we'll be starting about a week from now."

"Is it going to be very dangerous?" she asked quietly.

There was a momentary pause. "Why, no," he said. "What made you think that?"

"I spoke to Mary Holmes over the telephone yesterday. She seemed a bit worried over something Peter told her."

"About this cruise?"

"Not directly," she replied. "At least, I don't think so. More like making his will or something."

"That's always a good thing to do," he observed. "Everybody ought to make a will, every married man, that is."

The grilled steaks came. "Tell me, is it dangerous?" she asked again.

He shook his head. "It's quite a long cruise. We shall be away nearly two months, and nearly half of that submerged. But it's not more dangerous than any other operation would be up in northern waters." He paused. "It's always tricky to go nosing around in waters where there may have been a nuclear explosion," he said. "Especially submerged. You never really know what you may run into. Big changes in the sea bed. You may tangle with a sunken ship you didn't know was there. You've got to go in carefully and watch your step. But no, I wouldn't say it's dangerous."

"Come back safely, Dwight," she said softly.

He grinned. "Sure we'll come back safely. We've been ordered to. The admiral wants his submarine back."

She sat back and laughed. "You're impossible! As soon as I get sentimental you just—you just prick it like a toy balloon."

"I guess I'm not the sentimental type," he said. "That's what Sharon says."

"Does she?"

"Sure. She gets quite cross with me."

"I can't say that I'm surprised," she observed. "I'm very sorry for her."

They finished lunch, left the restaurant, and walked to the National Gallery to see the current exhibition of religious pictures. They were all oil paintings, mostly in a modernistic style. They walked around the gallery set aside for the forty paintings in the exhibition, the girl interested, the naval officer frankly uncomprehending. Neither of them had much to say about the green Crucifixions or the pink Nativities; the five or six paintings dealing with religious aspects of the war stirred them to controversy. They paused before the prizewinner, the sorrowing Christ on a background of the destruction of a great city. "I think that one's got something," she said. "For once I believe that I'd agree with the judges."

He said, "I hate it like hell."

"What don't you like about it?"

He stared at it. "Everything. To me it's just phony. No pilot in his senses would be flying as low as that with thermonuclear bombs going off all around. He'd get burned up."

She said, "It's got good composition and good colouring."

"Oh, sure," he replied. "But the subject's phony."

"In what way?"

"If that's meant to be the R.C.A. building, he's put Brooklyn Bridge on the New Jersey side, and the Empire State in the middle of Central Park."

She glanced at the catalogue. "It doesn't say that it's New York."

"Wherever it's meant to be, it's phony," he replied. "It couldn't have looked like that." He paused. "Too dramatic." He turned away, and looked around him with distaste. "I don't like any part of it," he said.

"Don't you see anything of the religious angle here?" she asked. It was funny to her, because he went to church a lot and she had thought this exhibition would appeal to him.

He took her arm. "I'm not a religious man," he said. "That's my fault, not the artists'. They see things differently than me."

They turned from the exhibition. "Are you interested in paintings?" she asked. "Or are they just a bore?"

"They're not a bore," he said. "I like them when they're full of color and don't try to teach you anything. There's a painter called Renoir, isn't there?"

She nodded. "They've got some Renoirs here. Would you like to see them?"

They went and found the French art, and he stood for some time before a painting of a river and a tree-shaded street beside it, with white houses and shops, very French and very colorful. "That's the kind of picture I like," he said. "I've got a lot of time for that." They strolled around the galleries for a time, chatting and looking at the pictures. Then she had to go; her mother was unwell and she had promised to be home in time to get the tea. He took her to the station on the tram.

In the rush of people at the entrance she turned to him. "Thanks for the lunch," she said, "and for the afternoon. I hope the other pictures made up for the religious ones."

He laughed. "They certainly did. I'd like to go back there again and see more of them. But as for religion, that's just not my line."

"You go to church regularly," she said.

"Oh well, that's different," he replied.

She could not argue it with him, nor would she have attempted to in that crowd. She said, "Will we be able to meet again before you go?"

"I'll be busy in the daytime, most days," he said. "We might take in a movie one evening, but we'd have to make it soon. We'll be sailing as soon as the work gets completed, and it's going well right now."

They arranged to meet for dinner on the following Tuesday, and she waved good-bye to him and vanished in the crowd. There was nothing of urgency to take him back to the dockyard, and there was still an hour left before the shops shut. He went out into the streets again and walked along the pavements looking at the shopwindows. Presently he came to a sports store, hesitated for a moment, and went in.

In the fishing department he said to the assistant, "I want a spinning outfit, a rod and a reel and a nylon line."

"Certainly, sir," said the assistant. "For yourself?" The American shook his head. "This is a present for a boy ten years old," he said. "His first rod. I'd like something good quality, but pretty small and light. You got anything in Fiberglas?"

The assistant shook his head. "I'm afraid we're right out of those at the moment." He reached down a rod from the rack. "This is a very good little rod in steel."

"How would that stand up in sea water, for rusting? He lives by the sea, and you know what kids are."

"They stand up all right," the assistant said. "We sell a lot of these for sea fishing." He reached for reels while Dwight examined the rod and tested it in his hand. "We have these plastic reels for sea fishing, or I can give you a multiplying reel in stainless steel. They're the better job, of course, but they come out a good deal more expensive."

Dwight examined them. "I think I'll take the multiplier,"

He chose the line, and the assistant wrapped the three articles together in a parcel. "Makes a nice present for a boy," he observed.

"Sure," said Dwight. "He'll have a lot of fun with that."

He paid and took the parcel, and went through into that portion of the store that sold children's bicycles and scooters. He said to the girl, "Have you got a Pogo stick?"

"A Pogo stick? I don't think so. I'll ask the manager."

The manager came to him. "I'm afraid we're right out of Pogo sticks. There hasn't been a great deal of demand for them recently, and we sold the last only a few days ago."

"Will you be getting any more in?"

"I put through an order for a dozen. I don't know when they'll arrive. Things are getting just a bit disorganized, you know. It was for a present, I suppose?" The commander nodded. "I wanted it for a little girl of six."

"We have these scooters. They make a nice present for a little girl that age."

He shook his head. "She's got a scooter."

"We have these children's bicycles, too."

Too bulky and too awkward, but he did not say so. "No, it's a Pogo stick I really want. I think I'll shop around, and maybe come back if I can't get one."

"You might try McEwen's," said the man helpfully. "They might have one left."

He went out and tried McEwen's, but they, too, were out of Pogo sticks. He tried another shop with similar results; Pogo sticks, it seemed, were off the market. The more frustration he encountered, the more it seemed to him that a Pogo stick was what he really wanted, and that nothing else would do. He wandered into Collins Street looking for another toy shop, but here he was out of the toy shop district and in a region of more expensive merchandise.

In the last of the shopping hour he paused before a jeweller's window. It was a shop of good quality; he stood for a time looking in at the windows. Emeralds and diamonds would be best. Emeralds went magnificently with her dark hair.

He went into the shop. "I was thinking of a bracelet," he said to the young man in the black morning coat. "Emeralds and diamonds, perhaps. Emeralds, anyway. The lady's dark, and she likes to wear green. You got anything like that?"

The man went to the safe, and came back with three bracelets which he laid on a black velvet pad. "We have these, sir," he said. "What sort of price had you in mind?"

"I wouldn't know," said the commander. "I want a nice bracelet."

The assistant picked one up. "We have this, which is forty guineas, or this one which is sixty-five guineas. They are very attractive, I think."

"What's that one, there?"

The man picked it up. "That is much more expensive, sir. It's a very beautiful piece." He examined the tiny tag. "That one is two hundred and twenty-five guineas."

It glowed on the black velvet. Dwight picked it up and examined it. The man had spoken the truth when he had said it was a lovely piece. She had nothing like it in her jewel box. He knew that she would love it.

"Would that be English or Australian work?" he asked.

The man shook his head. "This came originally from Cartier's, in Paris. It came to us from the estate of a lady in Toorak. It's in quite new condition, as you see. Usually we find that the clasp needs attention, but this didn't even need that. It is in quite perfect order."

He could picture her delight in it. "I'll take that," he said. "I'll have to pay you with a cheque. I'll call in and pick it up tomorrow or the next day."

He wrote the cheque and took his receipt Turning away, he stopped, and turned back to the man. "One thing," he said. "You wouldn't happen to know where I could buy a Pogo stick, a present for a little girl? Seems they're kind of scarce around here just at present."

"I'm afraid I can't, sir," said the man. "I think the only thing to do would be to try all the toy shops in turn."

The shops were closing and there was no time that night to do any more. He took his parcel back with him to Williamstown, and when he reached the carrier he went down into the submarine and laid it along the back of his berth, where it was inconspicuous. Two days later, when he got his bracelet, he took that down into the submarine also and locked it away in the steel cupboard that housed the confidential books.

That day a Mrs. Hector Fraser took a broken silver cream jug to the jeweller's to have the handle silver-soldered. Walking down the street that afternoon she encountered Moira Davidson, whom she had known from a child. She stopped and asked after her mother. Then she said, "My dear, you know Commander Towers, the American, don't you?"

The girl said, "Yes. I know him quite well. He spent a week-end out with us the other day."

"Do you think he's crazy? Perhaps all Americans are crazy. I don't know."

The girl smiled. "No crazier than all the rest of us, these days. What's he been up to?"

"He's been trying to buy a Pogo stick in Simmonds'."

Moira was suddenly alert. "A Pogo stick?"

"My dear, in Simmonds' of all places. As if they'd sell Pogo sticks there! It seems he went in and bought the most beautiful bracelet and paid some fabulous price for it. That wouldn't be for you by any chance?"

"I haven't heard about it. It sounds very unlike him."

"Ah well, you never know with these men. Perhaps he'll spring it on you one day as a surprise."

"But what about the Pogo stick?"

"Well, then when he'd bought the bracelet he asked Mr. Thompson, the fair-haired one, the nice young man—he asked him if he knew where he could buy a Pogo stick. He said he wanted it for a present for a little girl."

"What's wrong with that?" Miss Davidson asked quietly. "It would make a very good present for a little girl of the right age."

"I suppose it would. But it seems such a funny thing for the captain of a submarine to want to buy. In Simmonds' of all places."

The girl said, "He's probably courting a rich widow with a little girl. The bracelet for the mother and the Pogo stick for the daughter. What's wrong with that?"

"Nothing," said Mrs. Fraser, "only we all thought that he was courting you."

"That's just where you've been wrong," the girl said equably. "It's me that's been courting him." She turned away. "I must get along. It's been so nice seeing you.

I'll tell Mummy."

She walked on down the street, but the matter of the Pogo stick stayed in her mind. She went so far that afternoon as to inquire into the condition of the Pogo stick market, and found it to be depressed. If Dwight wanted a Pogo stick, he was evidently going to have some difficulty in getting one.

Everyone was going a bit mad these days, of course —Peter and Mary Holmes with their garden, her father with his farm programme, John Osborne with his racing motorcar, Sir Douglas Froude with the club port, and now Dwight Towers with his Pogo stick. Herself also, possibly, with Dwight Towers. All with an eccentricity that verged on madness, born of the times they lived in.

She wanted to help him, wanted to help him very much indeed, and yet she knew she must approach this very cautiously. When she got home that evening she went to the lumber room and pulled out her old Pogo stick and rubbed the dirt off it with a duster. The wooden handle might be sandpapered and revarnished by a skilled craftsman and possibly it might appear as new, though wet had made dark stains in the wood. Rust had eaten deeply into the metal parts, however, and at one point the metal step was rusted through. No amount of paint could ever make that part of it look new, and her own childhood was still close enough to raise in her distaste at the thought of a secondhand toy. That wasn't the answer.

She met him on Tuesday evening for the movie, as they had arranged. Over dinner she asked him how the submarine was getting on. "Not too badly," he told her. "They're giving us a second electrolytic oxygen regeneration outfit to work in parallel with the one we've got. I'd say that work might be finished by tomorrow night, and then we'll run a test on Thursday. We might get away from here by the end of the week."

"Is that very important?"

He smiled. "We shall have to run submerged for quite a while. I wouldn't like to run out of air, and have to surface in the radioactive area or suffocate."

"Is this a sort of spare set, then?"

He nodded. "We were lucky to get it. They had it over in the naval stores, in Fremantle."

He was absent-minded that evening. He was pleasant and courteous to her, but she felt all the time that he was thinking of other things. She tried several times during dinner to secure his interest, but failed. It was the same in the movie theatre; he went through all the motions of enjoying it and giving her a good time, but there was no life in the performance. She told herself that she could hardly expect it to be otherwise, with a cruise like that ahead of him.

After the show they walked down the empty streets towards the station. As they neared it she stopped at the dark entrance to an arcade, where they could talk quietly. "Stop here a minute, Dwight," she said, "I want to ask you something."

"Sure," he said kindly. "Go ahead."

"You're worried over something, aren't you?"

"Not really. I'm afraid I've been bad company tonight."

"Is it about the submarine?"

"Why no, honey. I told you, there's nothing dangerous in that. It's just another job."

"It's not about a Pogo stick, is it?"

He stared at her in amazement in the semidarkness. "Say, how did you get to hear about that?"

She laughed gently. "I have my spies. What did you get for Junior?"

"A fishing rod." There was a pause, and then he said, "I suppose you think I'm nuts."

She shook her head. "I don't Did you get a Pogo stick?"

"No. Seems like they're completely out of stock."

"I know." They stood in silence for a moment. "I had a look at mine," she said. "You can have that if it's any good to you. But it's awfully old, and the metal parts are rusted through. It works still, but I don't think it could ever be made into a very nice present."

He nodded. "I noticed that. I think we'll have to let it go, honey. If I get time before we sail, I'll come up here and shop around for something else."

She said, "I'm quite sure it must be possible to get a Pogo stick. They must have been made somewhere here in Melbourne. In Australia, anyway. The trouble is to get one in the time."

"Leave it," he said. "It was just a crazy idea I had. It's not important."

112

"It is important," she said. "It's important to me." She raised her head. "I can get one for you by the time you come back," she said. "I'll do that, even if I have to get it made. I know that isn't quite what you want. But would that do?"

"That's mighty kind of you," he said huskily. "I could tell her you were bringing it along with you."

"I could do that," she said. "But anyway, I'll have it with me when we meet again."

"You might have to bring it a long way," he said.

"Don't worry, Dwight. I'll have it with me when we meet."

In the dark alcove he took her in his arms and kissed her. "That's for the promise," he said softly, "and for everything else. Sharon wouldn't mind me doing this. It's from us both."

## Chapter Six

Twenty-five days later, *U.S.S. Scorpion* was approaching the first objective of her cruise. It was ten days since she had submerged thirty degrees south of the equator. She had made her landfall at San Nicolas Island off Los Angeles and had given the city a wide berth, troubled about unknown minefields. She had set a course outside Santa Rosa and had closed the coast to the west of Santa Barbara; from there she had followed it northwards cruising at periscope depth about two miles offshore. She had ventured cautiously into Monterey Bay and had inspected the fishing port, seeing no sign of life on shore and learning very little. Radioactivity was uniformly high, so that they judged it prudent to keep the hull submerged.

They inspected San Francisco from five miles outside the Golden Gate. All they learned was that the bridge was down. The supporting tower at the south end seemed to have been overthrown. The houses visible from the sea around Golden Gate Park had suffered much from fire and blast; it did not look as if any of them were habitable. They saw no evidence of any human life, and the radiation level made it seem improbable that life could still exist in that vicinity.

They stayed there for some hours, taking photographs through the periscope and making such a survey as was possible. They went back southwards as far as Half Moon Bay and closed the coast to within half a mile, surfacing for a time and calling through the loud hailer. The houses here did not appear to be much damaged, but there was no sign of any life on shore. They stayed in the vicinity till dusk, and then set course towards the north, rounding Point Reyes and going on three or four miles offshore, following the coast.

Since crossing the equator it had been their habit to surface once in every watch to get the maximum antenna height, and to listen for the radio transmission from Seattle. They had heard it once, in latitude five north; it had

113

gone on for about forty minutes, a random, meaningless transmission, and then had stopped. They had not heard it since. That night, somewhere off Fort Bragg, they surfaced in a stiff northwesterly wind and a rising sea, and directly they switched on the direction finder they heard it again. This time they were able to pinpoint it fairly accurately.

Dwight bent over the navigation table with Lieutenant Sunderstrom as he plotted the bearing. "Santa Maria," he said. "Looks like you were right."

They stood listening to the meaningless jumble coming out of the speaker. "It's fortuitous," the lieutenant said at last. "That's not someone keying, even somebody that doesn't know about radio. That's something that's just happening."

"Sounds like it." He stood listening. "There's power there," he said. "Where there's power there's people."

"It's not absolutely necessary," the lieutenant said.

"Hydroelectric," Dwight said. "I know it. But hell, those turbines won't run two years without maintenance."

"You wouldn't think so. Some of them are mighty good machinery."

Dwight grunted, and turned back to the charts. "I'll aim to be off Cape Flattery at dawn. We'll go on as we're going now and get a fix around midday, and adjust speed then. If it looks all right from there, I'll take her in, periscope depth, so we can blow tanks if we hit anything that shouldn't be there. Maybe we'll be able to go right up to Santa Maria. Maybe we won't. You ready to go on shore if we do?"

"Sure," said the lieutenant, "I'd kind of like to get out of the ship for a while."

Dwight smiled. They had been submerged now for eleven days, and though health was still good they were all suffering from nervous tension. "Let's keep our fingers crossed," he said, "and hope we can make it."

"You know something?" said the lieutenant. "If we can't get through the strait, maybe I could make it overland." He pulled out a chart. "If we got in to Grays Harbor I could get on shore at Hoquiam or Aberdeen, This road runs right through to Bremerton and Santa Maria."

"It's a hundred miles."

"I could probably pick up a car, and gas."

The captain shook his head. Two hundred miles in a light radiation suit, driving a hot car with hot gas over hot country was not practical. "You've only got a two hours' air supply," he said. "I know you could take extra cylinders. But it's not practical. We'd lose you, one way or another. It's not that important, anyway." They submerged again, and carried on upon the course. When they surfaced four hours later the transmission had stopped.

They carried on towards the north all the next day, most of the time at periscope depth. The morale of his crew was now becoming important to the captain. The close confinement was telling on them; no broadcast entertainment had been available for a long time, and the recordings they could play over the speakers had long grown stale. To stimulate their minds and give them something to talk about he gave free access to the periscope to anyone who cared to use it, though there was little to look at. This rocky and somewhat uninteresting coast was their home country and the sight of a cafe with a Buick parked outside it was enough to set them talking and revive starved minds.

At midnight they surfaced according to their routine, off the mouth of the Columbia River. Lieutenant Benson was coming to relieve Lieutenant Commander Farrell. The lieutenant commander raised the periscope from the well and put his face to it, swinging it around. Then he turned quickly to the other officer. "Say, go and call the captain. Lights on shore, thirty to forty degrees on the starboard bow."

In a minute or two they were all looking through the periscope in turn and studying the chart, Peter Holmes and John Osborne with them. Dwight bent over the chart with his executive officer. "On the Washington side of the entrance," he said. "They'll be around these places Long Beach and Ilwaco. There's nothing in the State of Oregon."

From behind him, Lieutenant Sunderstrom said, "Hydroelectric."

"I guess so. If there's lights it would explain a lot." He turned to the scientist. "What's the outside radiation level, Mr. Osborne?"

"Thirty in the red, sir."

The captain nodded. Much too high for life to be maintained, though not immediately lethal; there had been little change in the last five or six days. He went to the periscope himself and stood there for a long time. He did not care to take his vessel closer to the shore, at night. "Okay," he said at last. "We'll carry on the way we're going now. Log it, Mr. Benson."

He went back to bed. Tomorrow would be an anxious, trying day; he must get his sleep. In the privacy of his little curtained cabin he unlocked the safe that held the confidential books and took out the bracelet; it glowed in the synthetic light. She would love it. He put it carefully in the breast pocket of his uniform suit. Then he went to bed again, his hand upon the fishing rod, and slept.

They surfaced again at four in the morning, just before dawn, a little to the north of Grays Harbor. No lights were visible on shore, but as there were no towns and few roads in the district that evidence was inconclusive. They went down to periscope depth and carried on. When Dwight came to the control room at six o'clock the day was bright through the periscope and the crew off duty were taking turns to look at the desolate shore. He went to breakfast and then stood smoking at the chart table, studying the minefield chart that he already knew so well, and the well-remembered entrance to the Juan de Fuca Strait At seven forty-five his executive officer reported that Cape Flattery was abeam. The captain stubbed out his cigarette. "Okay," he said. "Take her in, Commander. Course is zero seven five. Fifteen knots."

The hum of the motors dropped to a lower note for the first time in three weeks; within the hull the relative silence was almost oppressive. All morning they made their way southeastwards down the strait between Canada and the United States, taking continuous bearings through the periscope, keeping a running plot at the chart table and altering course many times. They saw little change on shore, except in one place on Vancouver Island near Jordan River where a huge area on the southern slopes of Mount Valentine seemed to have been burned and blasted. They judged this area to be no less than seven miles long and five miles wide; in it no vegetation seemed to grow although the surface of the ground seemed undisturbed. "I'd say that's an air burst," the captain said, turning from the periscope. "Perhaps a guided missile got one there."

As they approached more populous districts there were always one or two men waiting to look through the periscope as soon as the officers relinquished it Soon after midday they were off Port Townsend and turning southwards into Puget Sound. They went on, leaving Whidbey Island on the port hand, and in the early afternoon they came to the mainland at the little town of Edmonds, fifteen miles north of the centre of Seattle. They were well past the mine defences by that time. From the sea the place seemed quite undamaged, but the radiation level was still high.

The captain stood studying it through the periscope. If the Geiger counter was correct no life could exist there for more than a few days, and yet it all looked so normal in the spring sunlight that he felt there must be people there. There did not seem to be glass broken in the windows, even, save for a pane here and there. He turned from the periscope. "Left ten, seven knots," he said. "We'll close the shore here, and lie off the jetty, and hail for a while."

He relinquished the command to his executive, and ordered the loud hailer to be tested and made ready. Lieutenant Commander Farrell brought the vessel to the surface and took her in, and they lay to a hundred yards from the boat jetty, watching the shore.

The chief of the boat touched the executive officer on the shoulder. "Be all right for Swain to have a look, sir?" he inquired. "This is his home town." Yeoman First Class Ralph Swain was a radar operator.

"Oh, sure."

He stepped aside, and the yeoman went to the periscope. He stood there for a long while, and then raised his head. "Ken Puglia's got his drugstore open," he said. "The door's open and the shades are up. But he's left his neon sign on. It's not like Ken to leave that burning in the daytime."

The chief asked, "See anybody moving around, Ralph?"

The radar operator bent to the eyepieces again. "No. There's a window broken in Mrs. Sullivan's house, up at the top."

He stood looking for three or four long minutes, till the executive officer touched him on the shoulder and took the periscope. He stood back in the control room.

The chief said, "See your own house, Ralphie?"

"No. You just can't see that from the sea. It's up Rainier Avenue, past the Safeway." He fidgeted irritably. "I don't see anything different," he said. "It all looks just the same."

Lieutenant Benson took the microphone and began hailing the shore. He said, "This is U.S. Submarine *Scorpion* calling Edmonds. U.S. Submarine *Scorpion* calling Edmonds. If anybody is listening, will you please come to the waterfront, to the jetty at the end of Main Street. U.S. Submarine calling Edmonds."

The yeoman left the control room and went forward. Dwight Towers came to the periscope, detached another sailor from it, and stood looking at the shore. The town sloped upwards from the waterfront giving a good view of the street and the houses. He stood back after a while. "There doesn't seem to be much wrong on shore," he said. "You'd think with Boeing as the target all this area would have been well plastered." Farrell said, "The defences here were mighty strong. All the guided missiles in the book."

"That's so. But they got through to San Francisco."

"It doesn't look as though they ever got through here." He paused. "There was that air burst, way back in the strait."

Dwight nodded. "See that neon sign that's still alight, over the drugstore?" He paused. "We'll go on calling here for quite a while—say, half an hour."

"Okay, sir."

The captain stood back from the periscope and the executive officer took it, and issued a couple of orders to keep the ship in position. At the microphone the lieutenant went on calling; Dwight lit a cigarette and leaned back on the chart table. Presently he stubbed out the cigarette and glanced at the clock.

From forward there was the clang of a steel hatch; he started , and looked round. It was followed a moment later by another, and then footsteps on the deck above them. There were steps running down the alley, and Lieutenant Hirsch appeared in the control room. "Swain got out through the escape hatch, sir," he said. "He's out on deck now!"

Dwight bit his lip. "Escape hatch closed?"

"Yes, sir. I checked that."

The captain turned to the chief of the boat. "Station a guard on the escape hatches forward and aft."

There was a splash in the water beside the hull as Mortimer ran off. Dwight said to Farrell, "See if you can see what he's doing."

The executive dropped the periscope down and put it to maximum depression, sweeping around. The captain said to Hirsch, "Why didn't somebody stop him?"

"I guess he did it too quick. He came from aft and sat down, kind of biting his nails. Nobody paid him much attention. I was in the forward torpedo flat, so I didn't see. First they knew, he was in the escape trunk with the door shut, and the outer hatch open to the air. Nobody cared to chase out there after him."

Dwight nodded. "Sure. Get the trunk blown through and then go in and see the outer hatch is properly secure."

From the periscope Farrell said, "I can see him now. He's swimming for the jetty."

Dwight stooped almost to the deck and saw the swimmer. He stood up and spoke to Lieutenant Benson at the microphone. The lieutenant touched the volume control and said, "Yeoman Swain, hear this." The swimmer paused and trod water. "The captain's orders are that you return immediately to the ship. If you come back at once he will take you on board again and take a chance on the contamination. You are to come back on board right now."

From the speaker above the navigation table they all heard the reply, "You go and get stuffed!"

A faint smile flickered on the captain's face. He bent again to the periscope and watched the man swim to the shore, watched him clamber up the ladder at the jetty. Presently he stood erect. "Well, that's it," he remarked. He turned to John Osborne by his side. "How long would you say he'll last?"

"He'll feel nothing for a time," said the scientist. "He'll probably be vomiting tomorrow night. After that—well, it's just anybody's guess, sir. It depends upon the constitution of the individual."

"Three days? A week?"

"I should think so. I shouldn't think it could be longer, at this radiation level."

"And we'd be safe to take him back—till when?"

"I've got no experience. But after a few hours everything that he evacuates would be contaminated. We couldn't guarantee the safety of the ship's company if he should be seriously ill on board."

Dwight raised the periscope and put his eyes to it. The man was still visible walking up the street in his wet clothes. They saw him pause at the door of the drugstore and look in; then he turned a comer and was lost to sight. The captain said, "Well, he doesn't seem to have any intention of coming back." He turned over the periscope to his executive. "Secure that loud hailer. The course is for Santa Maria, in the middle of the channel. Ten knots."

There was dead silence in the submarine, broken only by the helm orders, the low murmur of the turbines, and the intermittent whizzing of the steering engine. Dwight Towers went heavily to his cabin, and Peter Holmes followed him. He said, "You're not going to try to get him back, sir? I could go on shore in a radiation suit."

Dwight glanced at his liaison officer. "That's a nice offer, Commander, but I won't accept it. I thought of that myself. Say we put an officer on shore with a couple of men to go fetch him. First we've got to find him. Maybe we'd be stuck off here four or five hours, and then not know if we'd be risking everybody in the ship by taking him back in with us. Maybe he'll have eaten contaminated food, or drunk contaminated water. . ." He paused. "There's another thing. On this mission we shall be submerged and living on tinned air for twenty-seven days, maybe twenty-eight Some of us will be in pretty bad shape by then. You tell me on the last day if you'd like it to be four or five hours longer because we wasted that much time on Yeoman Swain."

Peter said, "Very good, sir. I just thought I'd like to make the offer."

"Sure. I appreciate that. We'll be coming back past here tonight or else maybe soon after dawn tomorrow. We'll stop a little while and hail him then."

The captain went back to the control room and stood by die executive officer, taking alternate glances through the periscope with him. They went close to the entrance to the Lake Washington Canal, scanning the shore, rounded Fort Lawton, and stood in to the naval dock and the commercial docks in Elliott Bay, in the heart of the city.

The city was undamaged. A minesweeper lay at the Naval Receiving Station, and five or six freighters lay in the commercial docks. Most of the window glass was still in place in the high buildings at the centre of the city. They did not go very close in, fearing underwater obstructions, but so far as they could see conditions through the periscope, there seemed to be nothing wrong with the city at all, except that there were no people there. Many electric lights and neon signs were burning still.

At the periscope Lieutenant Commander Farrell said to his captain, "It was a good defensive proposition, sir—better than San Francisco. The land in the Olympic Penninsula reaches way out to the west, over a hundred miles."

"I know it," said the captain. "They had a lot of guided missiles out there, like a screen."

There was nothing there to stay for, and they went out of the bay and turned southwest for Santa Maria Island; already they could see the great antenna towers. Dwight called Lieutenant Sunderstrom to his cabin. "You all set to go?"

"Everything's all ready," said the radio officer. "I just got to jump into the suit."

"Okay. Your job's half done before you start, because we know now that there's still electric power. And we're pretty darned near certain there's no life, although we don't know that for sure. It's a sixty-four thousand dollars to a sausage you'll find a reason for the radio that's just an accident of some sort. If it was just to find out what kind of an accident makes those signals, I wouldn't risk the ship and I wouldn't risk you. Got that?"

"I got that, sir."

"Well now, hear this. You've got air for two hours in the cylinders. I want you back decontaminated and in the hull in an hour and a half. You won't have a watch. I'll keep the time for you from here. I'll sound the siren every quarter of an hour. One blast when you've been gone a quarter of an hour, two blasts half an hour, and so on. When you hear four blasts you start winding up whatever you may be doing. At five blasts you drop everything, whatever it may be, and come right back. Before six blasts you must be back and decontaminating in the escape trunk. Is that all clear?"

"Quite clear, sir."

"Okay. I don't want this mission completed particularly now. I want you back on board safe. For two bits I wouldn't send you at all, because we know now most all of what you'll find, but I told the admiral we'd put somebody on shore to investigate. I don't want you to go taking undue risks. I'd rather have you back on board, even if we don't find out the whole story of what makes these signals. The only thing would justify you taking any risk would be if you find any signs of life on shore."

"I get that, sir."

"No souvenirs from shore. The only thing to come back in the hull is you, stark naked."

"Okay, sir."

The captain went back into the control room, and the radio officer went forward. The submarine nosed her way forward with the hull just awash, feeling her way to Santa Maria at a slow speed in the bright sunlight of the spring afternoon, ready to stop engines immediately and blow tanks if she hit any obstruction. They went very cautiously, and it was about five o'clock in the afternoon when she finally lay to off the jetty of the island, in six fathoms of water.

Dwight went forward, and found Lieutenant Sunderstrom sitting in the radiation suit complete but for the helmet and the pack of oxygen bottles, smoking a cigarette. "Okay, fella," he said. "Off you go."

The young man stubbed out his cigarette and stood while a couple of men adjusted the helmet and the harness of the pack. He tested the air, glanced at the pressure gauge, elevated one thumb, and climbed into the escape trunk, closing the door behind him.

Out on deck he stretched and breathed deeply, relishing the sunlight and the escape from the hull. Then he raised a hatch of the superstructure and pulled out the dinghy pack, stripped off the plastic sealing strips, unfolded the dinghy, and pressed the lever of the air bottle that inflated it. He tied the painter and lowered the rubber boat into the water, took the paddle and led the boat aft to the steps beside the conning tower. He clambered down into it, and pushed off from the submarine.

The boat was awkward to manoeuvre with the single paddle, and it took him ten minutes to reach the jetty. He made it fast and clambered up the ladder; as he began to walk towards the shore he heard one blast from the siren of the submarine. He turned and waved, and walked on.

He came to a group of grey painted buildings, stores of some kind. There was a weatherproof electric switch upon an outside wall; he went to it and turned it, and a lamp above his head lit up. He turned it off again, and went on.

He came to a latrine. He paused, then crossed the road, and looked in. A body in khaki gabardine lay half in and half out of one of the compartments, much decomposed. It was no more than he had expected to see, but the sight was sobering. He left it, and went on up the road.

The communications school lay over on the right, in buildings by itself. This was the part of the installation that he knew, but that was not what he had come to see. The coding office lay to the left, and near the coding office the main transmitting office would almost certainly be located.

He entered the brick building that was the coding office, and stood in the hallway trying the doors. Every door was locked except for two that led into the toilets. He did not go in there.

He went out and looked around. A transformer station with a complex of wires and insulators attracted his attention, and he followed the wiring to another two-storey, wooden office building. As he approached he heard the hum of an electrical machine running, and at the same moment the siren of the submarine sounded two blasts.

When they had died away he heard the hum again, and followed it to a powerhouse. The converter that was running was not very large; he judged it to be about fifty kilowatts. On the switchboard the needles of the instruments stood steady, but one indicating temperature stood in a red sector of the dial. The machine itself was running with a faint grating noise beneath the quiet hum. He thought it would not last very much longer.

He left the powerhouse and went into the office building. Here all the doors were unlocked, some of them open. The rooms on the ground floor appeared to be executive offices; here papers and signals lay strewn about the floor like dead leaves, blown by the wind. In one room a casement window was entirely missing and there was much water damage. He crossed this room and looked out of the window; the casement window frame lay on the ground below, blown from its hinges.

He went upstairs, and found the main transmitting room. There were two transmitting desks, each with a towering metal frame of grey radio equipment in front of it. One of these sets was dead and silent, the instruments all at zero.

The other set stood by the window, and here the casement had been blown from its hinges and lay across the desk. One end of the window frame projected outside the building and teetered gently in the light breeze. One of the upper corners rested on an overturned Coke bottle on the desk. The transmitting key lay underneath the frame that rested unstably above it, teetering a little in the wind.

He reached out and touched it with his gloved hand. The frame rocked on the transmitting key, and the needle of a milliammeter upon the set flipped upwards. He released the frame, and the needle fell back. There was one of *U.S.S. Scorpion's* missions completed, something that they had come ten thousand miles to see, that had absorbed so much effort and attention in Australia, on the other side of the world.

He lifted the window frame from the transmitting desk and set it down carefully on the floor; the woodwork was not damaged and it could be repaired and put back in its place quite easily. Then he sat down at the desk and with gloved hand upon the key began transmitting in English and in clear.

He sent, "Santa Maria sending. *U.S.S. Scorpion* reporting. No life here. Closing down." He went on repeating this message over and over again, and while he was doing so the siren blew three blasts.

As he sat there, his mind only half occupied with the mechanical repetition of the signal that he knew was almost certainly being monitored in Australia, his eyes roamed around the transmitting office. There was a carton of American cigarettes with only two packs removed that he longed for, but the captain's orders had been very definite. There were one or two bottles of Coke. On a window sill there was a pile of copies of The Saturday Evening Post.

He finished transmitting when he judged he had been at it for twenty minutes. In the three final repetitions he added the words, "Lieutenant Sunderstrom sending. All well on board. Proceeding northwards to Alaska." Finally he sent, "Closing down the station now, and switching off."

He took his hand from the key and leaned back in the chair. Gee, these tubes and chokes, this milliammeter and that rotary converter down below— they'd done a mighty job. Nearly two years without any maintenance or replacement, and still functioning as well as ever! He stood up, inspected the set, and turned off three switches. Then he walked round to the back and opened a panel and looked for the name of the manufacturer on the tubes; he would have liked to send them a testimonial.

He glanced again at the carton of Lucky Strikes, but the captain was right, of course; they would be hot and it might well be death to smoke them. He left them with regret, and went downstairs. He went to the powerhouse where the converter was running, inspected the switchboard carefully, and tripped two switches. The note of the machine sank progressively in a diminuendo; he stood watching it till finally it came to rest. It had done a swell job and it would be good as ever when the bearings had been overhauled. He could not have borne to leave it running till it cracked up.

The siren blew four blasts while he was there, and his work now was over. He had still a quarter of an hour. There was everything here to be explored and nothing to be gained by doing so. In the living quarters he knew he would find bodies like the one that he had found in the latrine; he did not want to see them. In the coding room, if he broke down a door, there might be papers that would interest historians in Australia, but he could not know which they would be, and anyway the captain had forbidden him to take anything on board.

He went back and up the stairs into the transmitting office. He had a few minutes left for his own use, and he went straight to the pile of copies of The Saturday Evening Post. As he had suspected, there were three numbers issued after *Scorpion* had left Pearl Harbor before the outbreak of the war, that he had not seen and that no one in the ship had seen. He leafed them through avidly. They contained the three concluding instalments of the serial, The Lady and the Lumberjack. He sat down to read.

The siren blew five blasts and roused him before he was halfway through the first instalment. He must go. He hesitated for a moment, and then rolled up the three magazines and tucked them under his arm. The dinghy and his radiation suit would be hot and must be left in the locker on the outer casing of the submarine to be washed by the sea water; he could roll up these hot magazines in the deflated dinghy and perhaps they would survive, perhaps they could be decontaminated and dried out and read when they got back to the safe southern latitudes. He left the office, closing the door carefully behind him, and made his way towards the jetty.

The officers' mess stood facing the Sound, a little way from the jetty. He had not noticed it particularly on landing, but now something about it attracted his attention and he deviated fifty yards towards it. The building had a deep verandah, facing the view. He saw now that there was a party going on there. Five men in khaki gabardine sat with two women in easy chairs around a table; in the light breeze he saw the flutter of a summer frock. On the table there were highball and old-fashioned glasses.

For a moment he was deceived, and went quickly closer. Then he stopped in horror, for the party had been going on for over a year. He broke away, and turned, and went back to die jetty, only anxious now to get back into the close confinement and the warmth of fellowship and the security of the submarine.

On deck he deflated and stowed the dinghy, wrapping up his magazines in the folds. Then he stripped quickly, put the helmet and the clothing into the locker, slammed the hatch down and secured it, and got down into the escape trunk, turning on the shower. Five minutes later he emerged into the humid stuffiness of the submarine.

John Osborne was waiting at the entrance to the trunk to run a Geiger counter over him and pass him as clean, and a minute later he was standing with a towel round his waist making his report to Dwight Towers in his cabin, the executive officer and the liaison officer beside him. "We got your signals on the radio here," the captain said. "I don't just know if they'll have got them in Australia—it's daylight all the way. It's around eleven in the morning there. What would you say?"

"I'd say they'd have got them," the radio officer replied. "It's autumn there, and not too many electric storms."

The captain dismissed him to get dressed, and turned to his executive. "We'll stay right here tonight," he said. "It's seven o'clock, and dark before we reach the minefields." With no lights he could depend upon he did not dare to risk the navigation through the minefields of the Juan de Fuca Strait during the hours of darkness. "We're out of the tide here. Sunrise is around zero four fifteen—that's twelve noon, Greenwich. We'll get under way then."

They stayed that night in the calm waters of the harbour just off Santa Maria Island, watching the shore lights through the periscope. At dawn they got under way on a reverse course, and immediately ran aground upon a mud bank. The tide was ebbing and within a couple of hours of low water; even so there should have been a fathom of water underneath their keel according to the chart. They blew tanks to surface, and got off with ears tingling from the pressure reduction in the hull, reviling the Survey, and tried again to get away, twice, with the same result Finally they settled down to wait irritably for the tide, and at about nine o'clock in the morning they got out into the main channel and set course northwards for the open sea.

At twenty minutes past ten Lieutenant Hirsch at the periscope said suddenly, "Boat ahead, under way." The executive jumped to the eyepieces, looked for a moment, and said, "Go call the captain." When Dwight came he said, "Outboard motorboat ahead, sir. About three miles. One person in it."

"Alive?"

"I guess so. The boat's under way."

Dwight took the periscope and stood looking for a long time. Then he stood back from it. "I'd say that's Yeoman Swain," he said quietly. "Whoever it is, he's fishing. I'd say he's got an outboard motorboat, and gas for it, and he's gone fishing."

The executive stared at him. "Well, what do you know?"

The captain stood in thought for a moment. "Go on and close the boat, and lie close up," he said. "I'll have a talk with him."

There was silence in the submarine, broken only by the orders from the executive. Presently he stopped engines and reported that the boat was close aboard. Dwight took the long lead of the microphone and went to the periscope. He said, "This is the captain speaking. Good morning, Ralphie. How are you doing?"

From the speaker they all heard the response. "I'm doing fine, Cap."

"Got any fish yet?"

In the boat the yeoman held up a salmon to the periscope. "I got one." And then he said, "Hold on a minute, Cap—you're getting across my line." In the submarine Dwight grinned, and said, "He's reeling in."

Lieutenant Commander Farrell asked, "Shall I give her a touch ahead?"

"No—hold everything. He's getting it clear now." They waited while the fisherman secured his tackle. Then he said, "Say, Cap, I guess you think me a heel, jumping ship like that."

Dwight said, "That's all right, fella. I know how it was. I'm not going to take you on board again, though. I've got the rest of the ship's company to think about."

"Sure, Cap, I know that. I'm hot and getting hotter every minute, I suppose."

"How do you feel right now?"

"Okay so far. Would you ask Mr. Osborne for me how long I'll go on that way?"

"He thinks you'll go for a day or so, and then you'll get sick."

From the boat the fisherman said, "Well, it's a mighty nice day to have for the last one. Wouldn't it be hell if it was raining?"

Dwight laughed. "That's the way to take it. Tell me, what are things like on shore?"

"Everybody's dead here, Cap—but I guess you know that. I went home. Dad and Mom were dead in bed—I'd say they took something. I went around to see the girl, and she was dead. It was a mistake, going there. No dogs or cats or birds, or anything alive—I guess they're all dead, too. Apart from that, everything is pretty much the way it always was. I'm sorry about jumping ship, Cap, but I'm glad to be home." He paused. "I got my own car and gas for it, and I got my own boat and my own outboard motor and my own fishing gear. And it's a fine, sunny day. I'd rather have it this way, in my own home town, than have it in September in Australia."

"Sure, fella. I know how you feel. Is there anything you want right now, that we can put out on the deck for you? We're on our way, and we shan't be coming back."

"You got any of those knockout pills on board, that you take when it gets bad? The cyanide?"

"I haven't got those, Ralphie. I'll put an automatic out on deck if you want it."

The fisherman shook his head. "I got my own gun. I'll take a look around the pharmacy when I get on shore—maybe there's something there. But I guess the gun would be the best."

"Is there anything else you want?"

"Thanks, Cap, but I got everything I want on shore. Without a dime to pay, either. Just tell the boys on board hullo for me."

"I'll do that, fella. We'll be going on now. Good fishing."

"Thanks, Cap. It's been pretty good under you, and I'm sorry I jumped ship."

"Okay. Now just watch the suck of the propellers as I go ahead."

He turned to the executive. "Take the con, Commander. Go ahead, and then on course, ten knots."

That evening Mary Holmes rang Moira at her home. It was a pouring wet evening in late autumn, the wind whistling around the house at Harkaway. "Darling," she said, "there's been a wireless signal from them. They're all well."

The girl gasped, for this was totally unexpected. "However did they get a signal through?"

"Commander Peterson just rang me up. It came through on the mystery station that they went to find out about. Lieutenant Sunderstorm was sending and he said they were all well. Isn't it splendid?"

The relief was so intense that for a moment the girl felt faint. "It's marvellous," she whispered. "Tell me, can they get a message back to them?"

"I don't think so. Sunderstrom said that he was closing down the station, and there wasn't anyone alive there."

"Oh. . . ." The girl was silent. "Well, I suppose we'll just have to be patient."

"Not really. Just something I wanted to tell Dwight. But it'll have to wait."

"Darling! You don't mean . . ."

"No, I don't."

"Are you feeling all right, dear?"

"I'm feeling much better than I was five minutes ago." She paused. "How are you getting on, and how's Jennifer?"

"She's fine. We're all right, except it's raining all the time. Can't you come over sometime? It's an age since we met."

The girl said, "I could come down one evening after work, and go up again next day."

"Darling! That would be wonderful!"

She arrived at Falmouth station two nights later, and set herself to walk two miles up the hill in a misty drizzle. In the little flat Mary was waiting to welcome her with a bright fire in the lounge. She changed her shoes, helped Mary bathe the baby and put her down, and then they got the supper. Later they sat together on the floor before the fire.

The girl asked, "When do you think they'll be back?"

"Peter said that they'd be back about the fourteenth of June." She reached out for a calender upon the desk behind her. "Three more weeks—just over. I've been crossing off the days."

"Do you think they're up to time at this place— wherever they sent the wireless signal from?"

"I don't know. I ought to have asked Commander Peterson that. I wonder if it would be all right to ring him up tomorrow and ask?"

"I shouldn't think he'd mind."

"I think I'll do that. Peter says this is his last job for the navy, he'll be unemployed after they come back. I was wondering if we couldn't get away in June or July and have a holiday. It's so piggy here in the winter— nothing but rain and gales."

The girl lit a cigarette. "Where would you go to?"

"Somewhere where it's warm. Queensland or somewhere. It's such an awful bore not having the car.

We'd have to take Jennifer by train, I suppose."

Moira blew a long cloud of smoke. "I shouldn't think Queensland would be very easy."

"Because of the sickness? It's so far away."

"They've got it at Maryborough," the girl said. That's only just north of Brisbane."

But there are plenty of warm places to go to without going right up there, aren't there?"

"I should think there would be. But it's coming down south pretty steadily."

Mary twisted round and glanced at her. "Tell me, do you really think it's going to come here?"

"I think I do."

"You mean, we're all going to die of it? Like the men say?"

"I suppose so."

Mary twisted round and pulled a catalogue of garden flowers down from a muddle of papers on the settee. "I went to Wilson's today and bought a hundred daffodils," she said. "Bulbs. King Alfreds—these ones." She showed the picture. "I'm going to put them in that comer by the wall, where Peter took out the tree. It's sheltered there. But I suppose if we're all going to die that's silly."

"No sillier than me starting in to learn shorthand and typing," the girl said drily. "I think we're all going a bit mad, if you ask me. When do daffodils come up?"

"They should be flowering by the end of August," Mary said. "Of course, they won't be much this year, but they should be lovely next year and the year after. They sort of multiply, you know."

"Well, of course it's sensible to put them in. You'll see them anyway, and you'll sort of feel you've done something."

127

Mary looked at her gratefully. "Well, that's what I think. I mean, I couldn't bear to—to just stop doing things and do nothing. You might as well die now and get it over."

Moira nodded. "If what they say is right, we're none of us going to have time to do all that we planned to do. But we can keep on doing it as long as we can." They sat on the hearthrug, Mary playing with the poker and the wood fire. Presently she said, "I forgot to ask you if you'd like a brandy or something. There's a bottle in the cupboard, and I think there's some soda."

The girl shook her head. "Not for me. I'm quite happy."

"Really?"

"Really."

"Have you reformed, or something?"

"Or something," said the girl. "I never tip it up at home. Only when I'm out at parties, or with men. With men particularly. Matter of fact, I'm even getting tired of that, now."

"It's not men, is it, dear? Not now. It's Dwight Towers."

"Yes," the girl said. "It's Dwight Towers."

"Don't you ever want to get married? I mean, even if we are all dying next September."

The girl stared into the fire. "I wanted to get married," she said quietly. "I wanted to have everything you've got. But I shan't have it now."

"Couldn't you marry Dwight?"

The girl shook her head. "I don't think so."

"I'm sure he likes you."

"Yes," she said. "He likes me all right."

"Has he ever kissed you?"

"Yes," she said again. "He kissed me once."

"I'm sure he'd marry you."

The girl shook her head again. "He wouldn't ever do that. You see, he's married already. He's got a wife and two children in America."

Mary stared at her. "Darling, he can't have. They must be dead."

"He doesn't think so," she said wearily. "He thinks he's going home to meet them, next September. In his own home town, at Mystic." She paused. "We're all going a bit mad in our own way," she said. "That's his way."

"You mean, he really thinks his wife is still alive?"

"I don't know if he thinks that or not. No, I don't think he does. He thinks he's going to be dead next September, but he thinks he's going home to them, to Sharon and Dwight Junior and Helen. He's been buying presents for them."

Mary sat trying to understand. "But if he thinks like that, why did he kiss you?"

"Because I said I'd help him with the presents." Mary got to her feet. "I'm going to have a drink," she said firmly. "I think you'd better have one, too." And when that was adjusted and they were sitting with glasses in their hands, she asked curiously, "It must be funny, being jealous of someone that's dead?"

The girl took a drink from her glass and sat staring at the fire. "I'm not jealous of her," she said at last. "I don't think so. Her name is Sharon, like in the Bible. I want to meet her. She must be a very wonderful person, I think. You see, he's such a practical man."

"Don't you want to marry him?"

The girl sat for a long time in silence. "I don't know," she said at last. "I don't know if I do or not. If it wasn't for all this ... I'd play every dirty trick in the book to get him away from her. I don't think I'll ever be happy with anyone else. But then, there's not much time left now to be happy with anyone."

"There's three or four months, anyway," said Mary. "I saw a motto once, one of those things you hang on the wall to inspire you. It said, 'Don't worry—it may never happen.' "

"I think this is going to happen all right," Moira remarked. She picked up the poker and began playing with it. "If it was for a lifetime it'd be different," she said. "It'd be worth doing her dirt if it meant having Dwight for good, and children, and a home, and a full life. I'd go through anything if I could see a chance of that. But to do her dirt just for three months' pleasure and nothing at the end of it—well, that's another thing. I may be a loose woman, but I don't know that I'm all that loose." She looked up, smiling. "Anyway, I don't believe that I could do it in the time. I think he'd take a lot of prising away from her."

"Oh dear," said Mary. "Things are difficult, aren't they?"

"Couldn't be worse," Moira agreed. "I think I'll probably die an old maid."

"It doesn't make sense. But nothing seems to make sense, these days. Peter..." She stopped.

"What about Peter?" the girl asked curiously.

"I don't know. It was just horrible, and crazy." She shifted restlessly.

"What was? Tell me."

"Did you ever murder anybody?"

"Me? Not yet. I've often wanted to. Country telephone girls, mostly."

"This was serious. It's a frightful sin to murder anybody, isn't it? I mean, you'd go to Hell."

"I don't know. I suppose you would. Who do you want to murder?"

The mother said dully, "Peter told me I might have to murder Jennifer." A tear formed and trickled down her cheek.

129

The girl leaned forward impulsively and touched her hand. "Darling, that can't be right! You must have got it wrong."

She shook her head. "It's not wrong," she sobbed. "It's right enough. He told me I might have to do it, and he showed me how." She burst into a torrent of tears.

Moira took her in her arms and soothed her, and gradually the story came out. At first the girl could not believe the words she heard, but later she was not so sure. Finally they went together to the bathroom and looked at the red boxes in the cabinet. "I've heard something about all this," she said seriously. "I never knew that it had got so far. . . One craziness was piled on to another.

"I couldn't do it alone," the mother whispered. "However bad she was, I couldn't do it. If Peter isn't here ... if anything happens to *Scorpion* . . . will you come and help me, Moira? Please?"

"Of course I will," the girl said gently. "Of course I'll come and help. But Peter will be here. They're coming back all right. Dwight's that kind of a man." She produced a little screwed up ball of handkerchief, and gave it to Mary. "Dry up, and let's make a cup of tea. I'll go and put the kettle on."

They had a cup of tea before the dying fire.

Eighteen days later *U.S.S. Scorpion* surfaced in clean air in latitude thirty-one degrees south, near Norfolk Island. At the entrance to the Tasman Sea in winter the weather was bleak and the sea rough, the low deck swept by every wave. It was only possible to allow the crew up to the bridge deck eight at a time; they crept up, white faced and trembling, to huddle in oilskins in the driving rain and spray. Dwight kept the submarine hove-to head into the wind for most of the day till everyone had had his allotted half-hour in the fresh air, but few of the men stayed on the bridge so long.

Their resistance to the cold and wet conditions on the bridge was low, but at least he had brought them all back alive, with the exception of Yeoman Swain. All were white faced and anaemic after thirty-one days' confinement within the hull, and he had three cases of intense depression rendering those men unreliable for duty. He had had one bad fright when Lieutenant Brody had developed all the symptoms of acute appendicitis; with John Osborne helping him he had read up all the procedure for the operation and prepared to do it on the wardroom table. However the symptoms had subsided and the patient was now resting comfortably in his berth; Peter Holmes had taken over all his duties and the captain now hoped that he might last out until they docked at Williamstown in five days' time. Peter Holmes was as normal as anyone on board. John Osborne was nervous and irritable though still efficient; he talked incessantly of his Ferrari.

They had disproved the Jorgensen effect. They had ventured slowly into the Gulf of Alaska using their underwater mine detector as a defense against floating icebergs till they had reached latitude fifty-eight north in the vicinity of Kodiak. The ice was thicker near the land and they had not

130

approached it; up there the radiation level was still lethal and little different to that they had experienced in the Seattle district. There seemed to be no point in risking the vessel in those waters any longer than was necessary; they took their readings and set course a little to the east of south till they found warmer water and less chance of ice, and then southwest towards Hawaii and Pearl Harbor.

At Pearl Harbor they had learned practically nothing. They had cruised right into the harbour and up to the dock that they had sailed from before the outbreak of the war. Psychologically this was relatively easy for them, because Dwight had ascertained before the cruise commenced that none of the ship's company had had their homes in Honolulu or had any close ties with the Islands. He could have put an officer on shore in a radiation suit as he had done at Santa Maria and he debated for some days with Peter Holmes before he reached the Islands whether he should do so, but they could think of nothing to be gained by such an expedition. When Lieutenant Sunderstorm had had time on his hands at Santa Maria all that he had found to do had been to read The Saturday Evening Post, and they could think of little more useful that an officer on shore could do at Pearl Harbor. The radiation level was much as it had been at Seattle; they noted and listed the many ships in the harbour, the considerable destruction on the shore, and left That day, hove-to at the entrance to the Tasman Sea, they were within easy radio communication with Australia. They raised the radio mast and made a signal reporting their position and their estimated time of arrival back at Williamstown. They got a signal in reply asking for their state of health, and Dwight answered in a fairly lengthy message that he worded with some difficulty in regard to Yeoman Swain. A few routine messages came through then dealing with weather forecasts, fueling requirements, and engineering work required when they docked, and in the middle of the morning came a more important one.

It bore a dateline three days previous. It read,

From: Commanding Officer, U.S. Naval Forces, Brisbane.

To: Commander Dwight L. Towers, *U.S.S. Scorpion.*

Subject: Assumption of additional duties.

1.      On the retirement of the present Commanding Officer, U.S. Naval Forces, at this date you will immediately and henceforth assume the duty of Commanding Officer, U.S. Naval Forces, in all areas. You will use your discretion as to the disposition of these forces, and you will terminate or continue their employment under Australian command as you think fit.

2.      Guess this makes you an admiral if you want to be one. Goodbye and good luck. Jerry Shaw.

3.      Copy to First Naval Member, Royal Australian Navy.

Dwight read this in his cabin with an expressionless face. Then, since a copy had already gone to the Australians, he sent for his liaison officer. When Peter came he handed him the signal without a word.

The lieutenant commander read it. "Congratulations, sir," he said quietly.

"I suppose so . . . said the captain. And then he said, "I suppose this means that Brisbane's out now."

Brisbane was two hundred and fifty miles in latitude to the north of their position then. Peter nodded, his mind on the radiation figures. "It was pretty bad still yesterday afternoon."

"I thought he might have left his ship and come down south," the captain said.

"They couldn't move at all?"

"No fuel oil," Dwight said. "They had to stop all services in the ships. The tanks were bone dry."

"I should have thought that he'd have come to Melbourne. After all, the Supreme Commander of the U.S. Navy...."

Dwight smiled, a little wryly. "That doesn't mean a thing, not now. No, the real point is that he was captain of his ship and the ship couldn't move. He wouldn't want to run out on his ship's company." There was no more to be said, and he dismissed his liaison officer. He drafted a short signal in acknowledgment and gave it to the signals officer for transmission via Melbourne, with a copy for the First Naval Member. Presently the yeoman came to him and laid a signal on his desk.

Your 12/05663.

Regret no communications are now possible with Brisbane.

The captain nodded. "Okay," he said. "Let it go."

## Chapter Seven

Peter Holmes reported to the second Naval Member the day after they returned to Williams-town. The admiral motioned to him to sit down. "I met Commander Towers for a few minutes last night, Lieutenant Commander," he said. "You seem to have got on well with him."

"I'm glad to hear that, sir."

"Yes. Now I suppose you want to know about a continuation of your appointment."

Peter said diffidently, "In a way. I take it that the general situation is the same? I mean, there's only two or three months left to go?"

The admiral nodded. "That seems to be correct You told me when I saw you last that you would prefer to be on shore in these last months."

"I should." He hesitated. "I've got to think a bit about my wife."

"Of course." He offered the young man a cigarette, and lit one himself. "*Scorpion* is going into dry dock for hull reconditioning," he said. "I suppose you know that."

132

"Yes, sir. The captain was anxious to have that done. I saw the Third Naval Member's office about it this morning."

"Normally that might take about three weeks. It may take longer under present conditions. Would you like to stay on with her as liaison officer while that work is going on?" He paused. "Commander Towers has asked for you to continue in the appointment for the time being."

"Could I live at home, down at Falmouth? It takes me about an hour and three quarters to get to the dockyard."

"You'd better take that up with Commander Towers. I don't suppose you'll find that he has any objection. It's not as if the ship was in commission. I understand he's giving leave to most of the ship's company. I don't suppose your duties would be very arduous, but you would be a help to him in dealing with the dockyard."

"I'd like to carry on with him, sir, subject to living at home. But if the ship is programmed for another cruise, I'd like you to replace me. I don't think I could undertake another seagoing appointment." He hesitated. "I don't like saying that."

The admiral smiled. "That's all right, Lieutenant Commander. I'll keep that in mind. Come back and see me if you want to be relieved." He rose to his feet, terminating the interview. "Everything all right at home?"

"Quite all right. Housekeeping seems to be more difficult than when I went away, and it's all becoming a bit of a battle for my wife, with the baby to look after."

"I know it is. And I'm afraid it's not going to get any easier."

That morning Moira Davidson rang up Dwight Towers in the aircraft carrier at lunch time. "Morning, Dwight," she said. "They tell me that I've got to congratulate you."

"Who told you that?" he asked.

"Mary Holmes."

"You can congratulate me if you like," he said a little heavily. "But I'd just as soon you didn't."

"All right," she said, "I won't. Dwight, how are you? Yourself?"

"I'm okay," he said. "Got a bit of a letdown today, but I'm okay." In fact, everything that he had done since they had come back to the aircraft carrier had been an effort; he had slept badly and was infinitely tired.

"Are you very busy?"

"I should be," he said. "But I don't know—nothing seems to get done and the more nothing gets done the more there is to do."

This was a different Dwight from the one that she had grown accustomed to. "You sound as if you're getting ill," she said severely.

"I'm not getting ill, honey," he said a little irritably. "It's just that there's some things to do and everybody off on leave. We've been away so long at sea we've just forgotten what work is."

"I think you ought to take some leave yourself," she said. "Could you come out to Harkaway for a bit?"

He thought for a moment. "That's mighty nice of you. I couldn't do that for a while. We're putting *Scorpion* into dry dock tomorrow."

"Let Peter Holmes do that for you."

"I couldn't do that, honey. Uncle Sam wouldn't like it." She forebore to say that Uncle Sam would never know. "After you've done that, the ship'll be in dockyard hands, won't she?"

"Say, you know a lot about the navy."

"I know I do. I'm a beautiful spy, Mata Hari, femme fatale, worming secrets out of innocent naval officers over a double brandy. She will be in dockyard hands, won't she?"

"You're very right."

"Well then, you can chuck everything else on Peter Holmes and get away on leave. What time are you putting her in dock?"

"Ten o'clock tomorrow morning. We'll probably be through by midday."

"Come out and spend a little time at Harkaway with us, tomorrow afternoon. It's perishing cold up there. The wind just whistles round the house. It rains most of the time, and you can't go out without gumboots. Walking beside the bullock and the pasture harrows is the coldest job known to man— to woman, anyway.

Come out and try it. After a few days with us you'll be just longing to get back and fug it in your submarine." He laughed. "Say, you're making it sound really attractive."

"I know I am. Will you come out tomorrow afternoon?"

It would be a relief to relax, to forget his burdens for a day or two. "I think I could," he said. "I'll have to shuffle things around a little, but I think I could." She arranged to meet him the next afternoon at four o'clock in the Australia Hotel. When she did so she was concerned at his appearance; he greeted her cheerfully and seemed glad to see her, but he had gone a yellowish colour beneath his tan, and in unguarded moments he was depressed. She frowned at the sight of him. "You're looking like something that the cat brought in and didn't want," she told him. "Are you all right?" She took his hand and felt it. "You're hot. You've got a temperature!"

He withdrew his hand. "I'm okay," he said "What'll you have to drink?"

"You'll have a double whisky and about twenty grains of quinine," she said. "A double whisky, anyway. I'll see about the quinine when we get home. You ought to be in bed!"

It was pleasant to be fussed over, and relax. "Double brandy for you?" he asked.

"Small one for me, double for you," she said. "You ought to be ashamed of yourself, going about like this. You're probably spreading germs all over the place. Have you seen a doctor?"

He ordered the drinks. "There's no doctor in the dockyard now. *Scorpion* is the only ship that's operational, and she's in dockyard hands. They took the last naval surgeon away while we were on the cruise."

"You have got a temperature, haven't you?"

"I might have just a little one," he said. "Perhaps I might have a cold coming on."

"I'd say perhaps you might. Drink up that whisky while I telephone Daddy."

"What for?"

"To meet us with the buggy at the station. I told them we'd walk up the hill, but I'm not going to have you doing that You might die on my hands, and then I'd have a job explaining to the coroner. It might even make a diplomatic incident."

"Who with honey?"

"The United States. It's not so good to kill the Supreme Commander of the U.S. Naval Forces."

He said wearily, "I guess the United States is me, right now. I'm thinking of running for President."

"Well, think about it while I go and telephone Mummy."

In the little telephone booth, she said, "I think he's got flu, Mummy. He's frightfully tired, for one thing. He'll have to go to bed directly we get home. Could you light a fire in his room, and put a hot-water bag in the bed? And, Mummy, ring up Dr. Fletcher and ask if he could possibly come round this evening. I shouldn't think it's anything but flu, but he has been in the radioactive area for over a month, and he hasn't seen a doctor since he got back. Tell Dr. Fletcher who he is. He's rather an important person now, you know."

"What train will you be catching, dear?"

She glanced at her wrist. "We'll catch the four-forty. Look, Mummy, it's going to be perishing cold in the buggy. Ask Daddy to bring down a couple of rugs."

She went back to the bar.

"Drink up and come along," she said. "We've got to catch the four-forty."

135

He went with her obediently. A couple of hours later he was in a bedroom with a blazing log fire, creeping into a warm bed as he shook with a light fever. He lay there infinitely grateful while the shakes subsided, glad to relax and lie staring at the ceiling, listening to the patter of the rain outside. Presently his grazier host brought him a hot whisky and lemon and asked what he wanted to eat, which was nothing.

At about eight o'clock there was the sound of a horse outside, and voices in the rain. Presently the doctor came to him; he had discarded his wet coat, but his jodhpurs and riding boots were dark with rain and steamed a little as he stood by the fire. He was a man of about thirty-five or forty, cheerful and competent.

"Say, Doctor," said the patient, "I'm really sorry they brought you out here on a night like this. There's not a thing wrong with me that a day or two in bed won't cure."

The doctor smiled. "I'm glad to come out to meet you," he said. He took the American's wrist and felt the pulse. "I understand you've been up in the radioactive area."

"Why, yes. But we didn't get exposed."

"You were inside the hull of the submarine all the time?"

"All the time. We had a guy from the C.S.I.R.O. poking Geiger counters at us every day. It's not that doctor."

"Have you had any vomiting, or diarrhoea?"

"None at all. Nor did any of the ship's company."

The doctor put a thermometer into his mouth, and stood feeling his pulse. Presently he withdrew the thermometer. "A hundred and two," he said. "You'd better stay in bed for a bit. How long were you at sea?"

"Fifty-three days."

"And how long submerged?"

"More than half of it."

"Are you very tired?"

The captain thought for a moment. "I might be," he admitted.

"I should say you might. You'd better stay in bed till that temperature goes down, and one full day after that. I'll look in and see you again in a couple of days' time. I think you've only got a dose of flu—there's quite a lot of it about. You'd better not go back to work for at least a week after you get up, and then you ought to take some leave. Can you do that?"

"I'll have to think about it."

They talked a little of the cruise and of conditions at Seattle and in Queensland. Finally the doctor said, "I'll probably look in tomorrow afternoon with one or two things you'd better take. I've got to go to Dandenong; my partner's operating at the hospital and I'm giving the anaesthetic for him. I'll pick up the stuff there and look in on my way home."

"Is it a serious operation?"

"Not too bad. Woman with a growth upon the stomach. She'll be better with it out. Give her a few more years of useful life, anyway."

He went away, and outside the window Dwight heard the backing and curvetting of the horse as the rider got into the saddle, and heard the doctor swear. Then he listened to the diminuendo of the hoofs as they trotted away down the drive in the heavy rain. Presently his door opened, and the girl came in.

"Well," she said, "you've got to stay in bed tomorrow, anyway." She moved to the fire and threw a couple of logs on. "He's nice, isn't he?"

"He's nuts," said the commander.

"Why? Because he's making you stay in bed?"

"Not that. He's operating on a woman at the hospital tomorrow so that she'll have some years of useful life ahead of her."

She laughed. "He would. I've never met anyone so conscientious." She paused. "Daddy's going to make another dam next summer. He's been talking about it for some time, but now he says he's really going to do it. He rang up a chap who has a bulldozer today and booked him to come in as soon as the ground gets hard."

"When will that be?"

"About Christmas time. It really hurts him to see all this rain running away to waste. This place gets pretty dry in the summer."

She took his empty glass from the table by his bed. "Like another hot drink?"

He shook his head. "Not now, honey. I'm fine."

"Like anything to eat?"

He shook his head.

"Like another hot-water bag?"

He shook his head. "I'm fine."

She went away, but in a few minutes she was back again, and this time she carried a long paper parcel in her hand, a parcel with a bulge at the bottom. "I'll leave this with you, and you can look at it all night." She put it in a comer of the room, but he raised himself on one elbow. "What's that?" he asked.

She laughed. "I'll give you three guesses and you can see which one's right in the morning."

"I want to see now."

"Tomorrow."

"No—now."

She took the parcel and brought it to him in the bed, and stood watching as he tore off the paper. The Supreme Commander of the U.S. Naval Forces was really just a little boy, she thought.

The Pogo stick lay on the bedclothes in his hands, shining and new. The wooden handle was brightly varnished, the metal step gleaming in red enamel. On the wooden handle was painted in neat red lettering the words HELEN TOWERS.

"Say," he said huskily, "that's a dandy. I never saw one with the name on it and all. She's going to love that." He raised his eyes. "Where did you get it, honey?"

"I found the place that makes them, out at Elsternwick," she said. "They aren't making any more, but they made one for me."

"I don't know what to say," he muttered. "Now I've got something for everyone."

She gathered up the torn brown paper. "That's all right," she said casually. "It was fun finding it. Shall I put it in the corner?"

He shook his head. "Leave it right here."

She nodded, and moved towards the door. "I'll turn this top light out. Don't stay up too long. Sure you've got everything you want?"

"Sure, honey," he said. "I've got everything now."

"Good night," she said.

She closed the door behind her. He lay for some time in the firelight thinking of Sharon and of Helen, of bright summer days and tall ships at Mystic, of Helen leaping on the Pogo stick on the swept sidewalk with the piles of snow on either hand, of this girl and her kindness. Presently he drifted into sleep, one hand upon the Pogo stick beside him.

Peter Holmes lunched with John Osborne at the United Services Club next day. "I rang the ship this morning," said the scientist. "I wanted to get hold of Dwight to show him the draft report before I get it typed. They told me that he's staying out at Harkaway with Moira's people."

Peter nodded. "He's got the flu. Moira rang me up last night to tell me that I wouldn't see him for a week, or longer if she's got anything to do with it."

The scientist was concerned. "I can't hold it so long as that. Jorgensen's got wind of our findings already, and he's saying that we can't have done our job properly. I'll have to get it to the typist by tomorrow at the latest."

"I'll look it over if you like, and we might be able to get hold of the exec, though he's away on leave. But Dwight ought to see it before it goes out. Why don't you give Moira a ring and take it out to him at Harkaway?"

"Would she be there? I thought she was in Melbourne every day, doing shorthand and typing."

"Don't be so daft. Of course she's there."

The scientist brightened. "I might run it out to him this afternoon in the Ferrari."

"Your juice won't last out if you're going to use it for trips like that. There's a perfectly good train."

"This is official business, naval business," said John Osborne. "One's entitled to draw on Naval stores." He bent towards Peter and lowered his voice. "You know that aircraft carrier, the *Sydney*? She's got about three thousand gallons of my ether-alcohol mixture in one of her tanks. They used it for getting reluctant piston-engined aircraft off the deck at full boost."

"You can't touch that!" said Peter, shocked.

"Can't I? This is naval business, and there's going to be a whole lot more."

"Well, don't tell me about it. Would a Morris Minor run on it?"

"You'd have to experiment a bit with the carburetion, and you'd have to raise the compression. Take the gasket out and fit a bit of thin sheet copper, with cement. It's worth trying."

"Can you run that thing of yours upon the road, safely?"

"Oh, yes," said the scientist. "There's not much else upon the road to hit, except a tram. And people, of course. I always carry a spare set of plugs because she oils up if you run her under about three thousand."

"What's she doing at three thousand revs?"

"Oh well, you wouldn't put her in top gear. She'd be doing about a hundred, or a bit more than that. Sin does about forty-five in first at those revs. She gets away with a bit of a rush, of course; you want a couple of hundred yards of empty road ahead of you. I generally push her out of the mews into Elizabeth Street and wait till there's a gap between the trams."

He did so that afternoon directly after lunch, with Peter Holmes helping him to push. He wedged the attaché case containing the draft report down beside the seat and climbed in, fastened the safety belt and adjusted his crash helmet before an admiring crowd. Peter said quietly, "For God's sake don't go and kill anybody."

"They're all going to be dead in a couple of months' time anyway," said the scientist. "So am I, and so are you. I'm going to have a bit of fun with this thing first."

A tram passed and he tried the cold engine with the self-starter, but it failed to catch. Another tram came by; when that was gone a dozen willing helpers pushed the racing car until the engine caught and she shot out of their hands like a rocket with an ear-splitting crash from the exhaust, a screech of tires, a smell of burnt rubber, and a cloud of smoke. The Ferrari had no horn and no need for one because she could be heard coming a couple of miles away; more important to John Osborne was the fact that she had no lights at all, and it was dark by five o'clock- If he was to get out to Harkaway, do his business, and be back in daylight he must step on it.

He weaved around the tram at fifty, skidded round into Lonsdale Street, and settled in his seat as he shot through the city at about seventy miles an hour. Cars on the road at that time were a rarity and he had little trouble in the city streets but for the trams; the crowds parted to let him through. In the suburbs it was different; children had grown accustomed to playing in the empty roads and had no notion of getting out of the way; he had to brake hard on a number of occasions and go by with engine roaring as he slipped the clutch, agonizing over the possibility of damage, consoling himself with the thought that the clutch was built to take it in a race.

He got to Harkaway in twenty-three minutes having averaged seventy-two miles an hour over the course without once getting into top. He drew up at the homestead in a roaring skid around the flowerbeds and killed the motor; the grazier with his wife and daughter came out suddenly and watched him as he unbuttoned his crash hat and got out stiffly, "I came to see Dwight Towers," he said. "They told me he was here."

"He's trying to get some sleep," Moira said severely. "That's a loathsome car, John. What does she do?"

"About two hundred, I think. I want to see him—on business. I've got a few things here that he's got to look over before it gets typed. It's got to be typed tomorrow, at the latest."

"Oh well, I don't suppose he's sleeping now."

She led the way into the spare bedroom. Dwight was awake and sitting up in bed. "I guessed it must be you," he said. "Killed anybody yet?"

"Not yet," said the scientist. "I'm hoping to be the first. I'd hate to spend the last days of my life in prison. I've had enough of that in the last two months." He undid his attaché case and explained his errand.

Dwight took the report and read it through, asking a question now and then. "I kind of wish we'd left that radio station operational, the way it was," he said once. "Maybe we'd have heard a little more from Yeoman Swain."

"It was a good long way from him."

"He had his outboard motorboat. He might have stopped off one day when he was tired of fishing, and sent a message."

"I don't think he'd have lasted long enough for that, sir. I'd have given him three days, at the very outside." The captain nodded. "I don't suppose he'd have wanted to be bothered with it, anyway. I wouldn't, if the fish were taking well, and it was my last day." He read on, asking a question now and then. At the end he said, "That's okay. You'd better take out that last paragraph, about me and the ship."

"I'd prefer to leave it in, sir."

"And I'd prefer you take it out. I don't like things like that said about what was just a normal operation in the line of duty."

The scientist put his pencil through it. "As you like."

"You got that Ferrari here?"

"I came out in it."

"Sure. I heard you. Can I see it from the window?"

"Yes. It's just outside."

The captain got out of bed and stood in his pyjamas at the window. "That's the hell of a car," he said. "What are you going to do with it?"

"Race it. There's not much time left so they're starting the racing season earlier than usual. They don't usually begin before about October, because of the wet roads. They're having little races all the winter, though. As a matter of fact I raced it twice before I went away."

The captain got back into bed. "So you said. I never raced a car like that. I never even drove one. What's it like in a race?"

"You get scared stiff. Then directly it's over you want to go on and do it again."

"Have you ever done this before?"

The scientist shook his head. "I've never had the money, or the time. It's what I've wanted to do all my life."

"Is that the way you're going to make it, in the end?"

There was a pause. "It's what I'd like to do," John Osborne said. "Rather than die in a sick muck, or take those pills. The only thing is, I'd hate to smash up the Ferrari. She's such a lovely bit of work. I don't think I could bring myself to do that willingly."

Dwight grinned. "Maybe you won't have to do it willingly, not if you go racing at two hundred per on wet roads."

"Well, that's what I've been thinking, too. I don't know that I'd mind that happening, any time from now on."

The captain nodded. Then he said, "There's no chance now of it slowing up and giving us a break, is there?"

John Osborne shook his head. "Absolutely none. There's not the slightest indication—if anything it seems to be coming a little faster. That's probably associated with the reduced area of the earth's surface as it moves down from the equator; it seems to be accelerating a little now in terms of latitude. The end of August seems to be the time."

The captain nodded. "Well, it's nice to know. It can't be too soon for me."

"Will you be taking *Scorpion* to sea again?"

"I've got no orders. She'll be operational again at the beginning of July. I'm planning to keep her under the Australian command up till the end. Whether I'll have a crew to make her operational—well, that's another thing again. Most of the boys have got girl friends in Melbourne here, about a

141

quarter of them married. Whether they'll feel allergic to another cruise is anybody's guess. I'd say they will."

There was a pause. "I kind of envy you having that Ferrari," he said quietly. "I'll be worrying and working right up till the end."

"I don't see that there's any need for you to do that," the scientist said. "You ought to take some leave. See a bit of Australia."

The American grinned. "There's not much left of it to see."

"That's true. There's the mountain parts, of course. They're all skiing like mad up at Mount Buller and at Hotham. Do you ski?"

"I used to, but not for ten years or so. I wouldn't like to break a leg and get stuck in bed up till the end." He paused. "Say," he said. "Don't people go trout fishing up in those mountains?"

John Osborne nodded. "The fishing's quite good."

"Do they have a season, or can you fish all year round?"

"You can fish for perch in Eildon Weir all year round. They take a spinner, trolling from a boat. But there's good trout fishing in all the little rivers up there." He smiled faintly. "There's a close season for trout. It doesn't open till September the first."

There was a momentary pause. "That's running it kind of fine," Dwight said at last. "I certainly would like a day or two trout fishing, but from what you say we might be busy just around that time."

"I shouldn't think it would make any odds if you went up a fortnight early, this year."

"I wouldn't like to do a thing like that," the American said seriously. "In the States—yes. But when you're in a foreign country, I think a fellow should stick by the rules."

Time was going on, John Osborne had no lights on the Ferrari and no capacity to go much slower than fifty miles an hour. He gathered his papers together and put them in the attaché case, said good-bye to Dwight Towers, and left him to get upon the road back to the city. In the lounge he met Moira. "How did you think he was?" she asked.

"He's all right," the scientist said. "Only a bat or two flying round the belfry."

She frowned a little; this wasn't the Pogo stick. "What about?"

"He wants a couple of days' trout fishing before we all go home," her cousin said. "But he won't go before the season opens, and that's not until September the first."

She stood in silence for a moment. "Well, what of it? He's keeping the law, anyway. More than you are, with that disgusting car. Where do you get the petrol for it?"

"It doesn't run on petrol," he replied. "It runs on something out of a test tube."

"Smells like it," she said. She watched him as he levered himself down into the seat and adjusted his crash helmet, as the engine crackled spitefully into life, as he shot off down the drive leaving great wheel ruts on the flower bed.

A fortnight later, in the Pastoral Club, Mr. Allan Sykes walked into the little smoking room for a drink at twenty minutes past twelve. Lunch was not served till one o'clock so he was the first in the room; he helped himself to a gin and stood alone, considering his problem. Mr. Sykes was the director of the State Fisheries and Game Department, a man who liked to run his businesses upon sound lines regardless of political expediency. The perplexities of the time had now invaded his routine, and he was a troubled man.

Sir Douglas Froude came into the room. Mr. Sykes, watching him, thought that he was walking very badly and that his red face was redder than ever. He said, "Good morning, Douglas, I'm in the book."

"Oh, thank you, thank you," said the old man. "I'll take a Spanish sherry with you." He poured it with a trembling hand. "You know," he said, "I think the Wine Committee must be absolutely crazy. We've got over four hundred bottles of magnificent dry sherry, Ruy de Lopez, 1947, and they seem to be prepared to let it stand there in the cellars. They said the members wouldn't drink it because of the price. I told them, I said—give it away, if you can't sell it. But don't just leave it there. So now it's the same price as the Australian." He paused. "Let me pour you a glass, Alan. It's in the most beautiful condition."

"I'll have one later. Tell me, didn't I hear you say once that Bill Davidson was a relation of yours?"

The old man nodded shakily. "Relation, or connection. Connection, I think. His mother married my . . . married my— No, I forget. I don't seem to remember things like I used to."

"Do you know his daughter Moira?"

"A nice girl, but she drinks too much. Still, she does it on brandy they tell me, so that makes a difference."

"She's been making some trouble for me."

"Eh?"

"She's been to the Minister, and he sent her to me with a note. She wants us to open the trout season early this year, or nobody will get any trout fishing. The Minister thinks it would be a good thing to do. I suppose he's looking to the next election."

"Open the trout season early? You mean, before September the first?"

"That's the suggestion."

"A very bad suggestion, if I may say so. The fish won't have finished spawning, and if they have they'll be in very poor condition. You could ruin

143

the fishing for years, doing a thing like that. When does he want to open the season?"

"He suggests August the tenth." He paused. "It's that girl, that relation of yours, who's at the bottom of this thing. I don't believe it would ever have entered his head but for her."

"I think it's a terrible proposal. Quite irresponsible. I'm sure I don't know what the world's coming to... "

As member after member came into the room the debate continued and more joined in the discussion. Mr. Sykes found that the general opinion was in favour of the change in date. "After all," said one, "they'll go and fish in August if they can get there and the weather's fine, whether you like it or not. And you can't find them or send them to jail because there won't be time to bring the case on. May as well give a reasonable date, and make a virtue of necessity. Of course," he added conscientiously, "it'd be for this year only."

A leading eye surgeon remarked, "I think it's a very good idea. If the fish are poor we don't have to take them; we can always put them back. Unless the season should be very early they won't take a fly; we'll have to use a spinner. But I'm in favour of it, all the same. When I go, I'd like it to be on a sunny day on the bank of the Delatite with a rod in my hand." Somebody said, "Like the man they lost from the American submarine."

"Yes, just like that I think that fellow had the right idea."

Mr. Sykes, having taken a cross section of the most influential opinion of the city, went back to his office with an easier mind, rang up his Minister, and that afternoon drafted an announcement to be broadcast on the radio that would constitute one of those swift changes of policy to meet the needs of the time, easy to make in a small, highly educated country and very characteristic of Australia. Dwight Towers heard it that evening in the echoing, empty wardroom of *H.M.A.S. Sydney*, and marvelled, not connecting it in the least with his own conversation with the scientist a few days before. Immediately he began making plans to try out Junior's rod. Transport was going to be the difficulty, but difficulties were there to be overcome by the Supreme Commander of the U.S. Naval Forces.

In what was left of Australia that year a relief of tension came soon after midwinter. By the beginning of July, when Broken Hill and Perth went out, few people in Melbourne were doing any more work than they wanted to. The electricity supply continued uninterrupted, as did the supply of the essential foodstuffs, but fuel for fires and little luxuries now had to be schemed and sought for by a people who had little else to do. As the weeks went by the population became noticeably more sober; there were still riotous parties, still drunks sleeping in the gutter, but far fewer than there had been earlier. And, like harbingers of the coming spring, one by one motorcars started to appear on the deserted roads.

It was difficult at first to say where they came from or where they got the petrol, for each case on investigation proved to be exceptional. Peter

Holmes' landlord turned up in a Holden one day to remove firewood from the trees that had been felled, explaining awkwardly that he had retained a little of the precious fluid for cleaning clothes. A cousin in the Royal Australian Air Force came to visit them from Laverton Aerodrome driving an M.G., explaining that he had saved the petrol but there didn't seem to be much sense in saving it any longer; this was clearly nonsense, because Bill never saved anything. An engineer who worked at the Shell refinery at Corio said that he had managed to buy a little petrol on the black market in Fitzroy but very properly refused to name the scoundrel who had sold it. Like a sponge squeezed by the pressure of circumstances, Australia began to drip a little petrol, and as the weeks went on towards August the drip became a trickle.

Peter Holmes took a can with him to Melbourne one day and visited John Osborne. That evening he heard die engine of his Morris Minor for the first time in two years, clouds of black smoke emerging from the exhaust till he stopped the engine and took out the jets and hammered them a little smaller. Then he drove her out upon the road, with Mary, delighted, at his side and Jennifer upon her knee. "It's just like having one's first car all over again!" she exclaimed. "Peter, it's wonderful! Can you get any more, do you think?"

"We saved this petrol," he told her. "We saved it up. We've got a few more tins buried in the garden, but we're not telling anybody how much."

"Not even Moira?"

"Lord, no. Her last of all." He paused. "Tires are the snag now. I don't know what we're going to do about those."

Next day he drove to Williamstown, in at the dockyard gates, and parked the Morris on the quayside by the practically deserted aircraft carrier. In the evening he drove home again.

His duties at the dockyard were now merely nominal. Work upon the submarine was going very slowly, and his presence was required upon the job no more than two days in each week, which fitted in well with the requirements of his little car. Dwight Towers was there most days in the morning, but he, too, had become mobile. The First Naval Member had sent for him one morning and, with poker face, had declared that it was only fitting that the Supreme Commander of the U.S. Naval Force should have transport at his disposal, and Dwight had found himself presented with a grey painted Chevrolet with Leading Seaman Edgar as the driver. He used it principally for going to She club for lunch or driving out to Harkaway to walk beside the bullock as they spread the dung, while the leading seaman shovelled silage.

The last part of July was a very pleasant time for most people. The weather was seasonally bad with high winds and plenty of rain and a temperature down in the low forties, but men and women cast off the restraints that long had galled them. The weekly wage packet became of little value or importance; if you went into the works on Friday you would probably get it whether you had worked or not, and when you had it there was little you could do with it. In the butcher's shop the cash desk would accept money thrust at them but didn't grieve much if it wasn't, and if the meat was there you took it If it wasn't, you just went and looked for somewhere where there was some. There was all day to do it in.

On the high mountains the skiers skied weekdays and week-ends alike. In their little garden, Mary and Peter Holmes laid out the new beds and built a fence around the vegetable garden, planting a passion fruit vine to climb all over it. They had never had so much time for gardening before, or made such progress. "It's going to be beautiful," she said contentedly. "It's going to be the prettiest garden of its size in Falmouth."

In the city mews John Osborne worked on the Ferrari with a small team of enthusiasts to help him. The Australian Grand Prix at that time was the premier motor race of the Southern Hemisphere, and it had been decided to advance the date of the race that year from November to August the 17th. On previous occasions the race had been held at Melbourne in the Albert Park, roughly corresponding to Central Park in New York or Hyde Park in London. The organizing club would have liked to race for the last time in Albert Park but the difficulties proved to be insuperable. It was clear from the outset that there would be a shortage of marshals and a shortage of labour to provide the most elementary safety precautions for the crowd of a hundred and fifty thousand people who might well be expected to attend. Nobody worried very much about the prospect of a car spinning off the course and killing a few spectators, or the prospect of permission to use the park for racing in future years being withheld. It seemed unlikely, however, that there would be sufficient marshals ever to get the crowds off the road and away from the path of the oncoming cars, and, unusual though the times might be, few of the drivers were prepared to drive straight into a crowd of onlookers at a hundred and twenty miles an hour. Racing motorcars are frail at those speeds, and a collision even with one person would put the car out of the race. It was decided regretfully that it was impracticable to run the Australian Grand Prix in Albert Park, and that the race would have to take place at the track at Tooradin.

The race in this way became a race for racing drivers only; in the prevailing difficulties of transport not very many spectators could be expected to drive forty miles out of the city to see it. Rather unexpectedly, it attracted an enormous entry of drivers. Everybody in Victoria and southern New South Wales who owned a fast car, new or old, seemed to have entered for the last Australian Grand Prix, and the total of entries came to about two hundred and eighty cars. So many cars could not be raced together with any justice to the faster cars, and for two week-ends previous to the great day eliminating heats were held in the various classes. These heats were drawn by ballot, so that John Osborne found himself competing with a three-litre Maserati piloted by Jerry Collins, a couple of Jaguars, a Thunderbird, two Bugattis, three vintage Bentleys, and a terrifying concoction of a Lotus chassis powered by a blown Gipsy Queen aeroengine of about three hundred horsepower and little forward

146

view, built and raced by a young air mechanic called Sam Bailey and reputed to be very fast.

In view of the distance from the city there was only a small crowd of people disposed around the three-mile course. Dwight Towers drove down in the official Chevrolet, picking up Moira Davidson and Peter and Mary Holmes upon the way. On that day there were five classes of heats, commencing with the smallest cars, each race being of fifty miles. Before the first race was over the organizers had put in a hurried call to Melbourne for two more ambulances, the two already allocated to the meeting being busy.

For one thing, the track was wet with rain, although it was not actually raining at the time of the first race. Six Lotus competed with eight Coopers and five M.G.'s, one of which was piloted by a girl, Miss Fay Gordon. The track was about three miles in length. A long straight with the pits in the middle led with a slight sinuosity to a left-hand turn of wide radius but 180° in extent enclosing a sheet of water; this was called Lake Bend. Next came Haystack Comer, a right-hand turn of about 120° fairly sharp, and this led to The Safety Pin, a sharp left-hand hairpin with rather a blind turn on top of a little mound, so that you went up and came down again. The back straight was sinuous and fast with a left-hand bend at the end of it leading down a steep hill to a very sharp right-hand comer, called The Slide. From there a long fast left-hand bend led back to the finishing straight.

From the start of the first heat it was evident that the racing was to be unusual. The race started with a scream that indicated that the drivers intended to show no mercy to their engines, their competitors, or themselves. Miraculously the cars all came round on the first lap, but after that the troubles started. An M.G. spun on Haystack Comer, left the road and found itself careering through the low scrub on the rough ground away from the circuit. The driver trod on it and swung his car round without stopping and regained the road. A Cooper coming up behind swerved to avoid collision with the M.G., spun on the wet road, and was hit fair and square amidships by another Cooper coming up behind. The first driver was killed instantaneously and both cars piled up into a heap by the roadside, the second driver being flung clear with a broken collarbone and internal injuries. The M.G. driver, passing on the next time round, wondered quickly as he took the comer what had happened to cause that crash.

On the fifth lap a Lotus overtook Fay Gordon at the end of the finishing straight and spun on the wet road of Lake Bend, thirty yards in front of her. Another Lotus was passing on her right; the only escape for her was to go left. She left the track at ninety-five miles an hour, crossed the short strip of land before the lake in a desperate effort to turn right and so back to the track, broadsided in the scrub, and rolled over into the water. When the great cloud of spray subsided, her M.G. was upside down ten yards from the shore, the bottom of the rear wheels just above the surface. It was half an hour before the wading helpers managed to right the little car and get the body out.

On the thirteenth lap three cars tangled at The Slide and burned. Two of the drivers were only slightly injured and managed to extract the third with both legs broken before the fire took hold. Of nineteen starters seven finished the race, the first two qualifying to run in the Grand Prix.

As the chequered flag fell for the winner, John Osborne lit a cigarette. "Fun and games," he said. His race was the last of the day.

Peter said thoughtfully, "They're certainly racing to win. . . ."

"Well, of course," said the scientist. "It's racing as it ought to be. If you buy it, you've got nothing to lose."

"Except to smash up the Ferrari."

John Osborne nodded. "I'd be very sorry to do that."

A little rain began to fall on them, wetting the track again. Dwight Towers stood a little way apart with Moira. "Get into the car, honey," he said. "You'll get wet."

She did not move. "They can't go on in this rain, can they?" she asked. "Not after all these accidents?"

"I wouldn't know," he said. "I'd say they might After all, it's the same for everybody. They don't have to go so fast they spin. And if they wait for a dry day this time of year they might wait, well, longer than they've got."

"But it's awful," she objected. "Two people killed in the first race and about seven injured. They can't go on. It's like the Roman gladiators, or something."

He stood in silence for a moment in the rain. "Not quite like that," he said at last. "There isn't any audience. They don't have to do it." He looked around. "Apart from the drivers and their crews, I don't suppose there's five hundred people here. They haven't taken any money at a gate. They're doing it because they like to do it, honey."

"I don't believe they do."

He smiled. "You go up to John Osborne and suggest he scratch his Ferrari and go home." She was silent. "Come on in the car and I'll pour you a brandy and soda."

"A very little one, Dwight," she said. "If I'm going to watch this, I'll watch it sober."

The next two heats produced nine crashed, four ambulance cases, but only one death, the driver of the bottom Austin-Healy in a pile up of four cars at The Safety Pin. The rain had eased to a fine, misty drizzle that did nothing to damp the spirits of the competitors. John Osborne had left his friends before the last race, and he was now in the paddock sitting in the Ferrari and warming it up, his pit crew around him. Presently he was satisfied and got out of the car, and stood talking and smoking with some of the other drivers. Don Harrison, the driver of a Jaguar, had a glass of whisky in his hand and a couple of bottles with more glasses on an upturned box beside him; he offered John a drink, but he refused it.

"I've got nothing to give away on you muggers," he said, grinning. Although he had what was probably the fastest car on the circuit, he had almost the least experience of any of the drivers. He still raced the Ferrari with the three broad bands of tape across the back that indicated a novice driver; he was still very conscious that he did not know by instinct when he was about to spin. A spin always caught him unawares and came as a surprise. If he had known it, all the drivers were alike on these wet roads; none of them had much experience of driving under such conditions and his consciousness of inexperience was perhaps a better protection than their confidence.

When his crew pushed the Ferrari out on to the grid, he found himself placed on the second line, in front of him the Maserati, the two Jaguars, and the Gipsy-Lotus, beside him the Thunderbird. He settled himself into his seat revving his engines to warm up, fastening his safety belt, making his crash helmet and his goggles comfortable upon his head. In his mind was the thought—This is where I get killed. Better than vomiting to death in a sick misery in less than a month's time. Better to drive like hell and go out doing what he wanted to. The big steering wheel was a delight to handle, the crack of the Ferrari's exhaust music to his ears. He turned and grinned at his pit crew in unalloyed pleasure, and then fixed his eyes upon the starter.

When the flag dropped he made a good start and got away well, weaving ahead of the Gipsy-Lotus as he changed up into third and outdistancing the Thunder-bird. He went into Lake Bend hard on the heels of the two Jaguars, but driving cautiously on the wet road with seventeen laps to go. Time enough to take chances in the last five laps. He stayed with the Jaguars past Haystack Comer, past The Safety Pin and cautiously put his foot down on the sinuous back straight. Not hard enough, apparently, for with a roar and a crackle the Gipsy-Lotus passed him on the right, showering him with water, Sam Bailey driving like a madman.

He slowed a little, while he wiped his goggles, and followed on behind. The Gipsy-Lotus was wandering all over the road, harnessed only by the immensely quick reaction time of its young driver. John Osborne, watching, sensed disaster round it like an aura; better follow on at a safe distance for a while and see what happened. He shot a quick glance at the mirror, the Thunderbird was fifty yards behind, with the Maserati overtaking it. There was time to take it easy down The Slide, but after that he must step on it.

On entering the straight at the end of the first lap he saw that the Gipsy-Lotus had taken one of the Jaguars. He passed the pits at about a hundred and sixty miles an hour making up upon the second Jaguar; with a car between him and the Gipsy-Lotus he felt safer. A glance in the mirror as he braked before Lake Bend showed that he had drawn well away from the two cars behind; if he could do that, he could hold the fourth position for a lap or two and still go carefully upon the comers.

149

He did so till the sixth lap. By that time the Gipsy-Lotus was in the lead and the first four cars had lapped one of the Bentleys. As he accelerated away from The Slide he glanced in his mirror and in a momentary glimpse saw what appeared to be a most colossal mix-up at the comer. The Maserati and the Bentley seemed to be tangled broadside on across the road, and the Thunderbird was flying through the air. He could not look again. Ahead of him, in the lead, the Gipsy-Lotus was trying to lap one of the Bugattis by synchronizing its desperate swerves at a hundred and forty miles an hour to the manoeuvre necessary for passing, and failing to do so. The two Jaguars were holding back at a discreet distance.

When he came round again to The Slide he saw that the shambles at the comer had involved two cars only; the Thunderbird lay inverted fifty yards from the track and the Bentley stood with its rear end crushed and a great pool of petrol on the road. The Maserati was apparently still racing. He passed on, and as he entered his eighth lap it began to rain quite heavily. It was time to step on it.

So thought the leaders, for on that lap the Gipsy-Lotus was passed by one of the Jaguars taking advantage of Sam Bailey's evident nervousness of his unstable car upon a comer. Both leaders now lapped a Bugatti, and a Bentley immediately after. The second Jaguar went to pass them on Haystack Comer with John Osborne close behind. What happened then was very, very swift. The Bugatti spun upon the comer and was hit by the Bentley, which was deflected into the path of the oncoming Jaguar, which rolled over twice and finished right side up by the roadside without a driver. John Osborne had no time to stop and little to avoid; the Ferrari hit the Bugatti a glancing blow at about seventy miles an hour and came to a standstill by the roadside with a buckled near side front wheel.

John Osborne was shaken, but unhurt. Don Harrison, the driver of the Jaguar who had offered him a drink before the race, was dying of multiple injuries in the scrub; he had been thrown from his car as it rolled and had then been run over by the Bentley. The scientist hesitated for a moment but there were people about; he tried the Ferrari. The engine started and the car moved forward, but the buckled wheel scrooped against the frame. He was out of the race, and out of the Grand Prix, and with a sick heart he waited till the Gipsy-Lotus weaved by and then crossed the track to see if he could help the dying driver.

While he was standing there, helpless, the Gipsy-Lotus passed again.

He stood there in the steady rain for several seconds before it struck him that there had been no other cars between the two transits of the Gypsy-Lotus. When it did so, he made a dash for the Ferrari. If in fact there was only one car left in the race he still had a chance for the Grand Prix; if he could struggle round the track to the pits he might yet change the wheel and get the second place. He toured on slowly, wrestling with the steering, while the rain ran down his neck and the Gipsy-Lotus passed a third time. The tire burst at

The Slide, where about six cars seemed to be tangled in a heap, and he went on the rim, and reached the pits as the Lotus passed again.

The wheel change took his pit crew about thirty seconds, and a quick inspection showed little damage apart from panelling. He was off again several laps behind, and now one of the Bugattis detached itself from the chaos around The Slide and joined in. It was never a threat, however, and John Osborne toured around the course discreetly to win second place in the heat and a start in the Grand Prix. Of the eleven starters in the heat eight had failed to complete the course and three drivers had been killed.

He swung his Ferrari into the paddock and stopped the engine, while his pit crew and his friends crowded round to congratulate him. He hardly heard them; his fingers were trembling with shock and the release of strain. He had only one thought in his mind, to get the Ferrari back to Melbourne and take down the front end; all was not well with the steering though he had managed to complete the course. Something was strained or broken; she had pulled heavily towards the left in the concluding stages of the race.

Between the friends crowding round he saw the upturned box where Don Harrison had parked his Jaguar, the glasses, the two whisky bottles. "God," he said to no one in particular, "I'll have that drink with Don now." He got out of the car and walked unsteadily to the box; one of the bottles was still nearly full. He poured a generous measure with a very little water, and then he saw Sam Bailey standing by the Gipsy-Lotus. He poured another drink and took it over to the winner, pushing through the crowd. "I'm having this on Don," he said. "You'd better have one, too."

The young man took it, nodded, and drank. "How did you come off?" he asked. "I saw you'd tangled."

"Got round for a wheel change," said the scientist thickly. "She's steering like a drunken pig. Like a bloody Gipsy-Lotus."

"My car steers all right," the other said nonchalantly. "Trouble is, she won't stay steered. You driving back to town?"

"If she'll make it."

"I'd pinch Don's transporter. He's not going to need it."

The scientist stared at him. "That's an idea. . . The dead driver had brought his Jaguar to the race on an old truck to avoid destroying tune by running on the road. The truck was standing not far from them in the paddock, unattended.

"I should nip in quick, before someone else gets it."

John Osborne downed his whisky, shot back to his car, and galvanized his pit crew of enthusiasts with the new idea. Together they mustered willing hands to help and pushed the Ferrari up the steel ramps on to the tray body, lashing her down with ropes. Then he looked round uncertainly. A marshal passed and he stopped him. "Are there any of Don Harrison's crew about?"

"I think they're all over with the crash. I know his wife's down there."

He had been minded to drive off in the transporter with the Ferrari because Don would never need it again, nor would his Jaguar. To leave his pit crew and his wife without transport back to town, however, was another thing.

He left the paddock and started to walk down the track towards the Haystack, with Eddie Brooks, one of his pit crew, beside him. He saw a little group standing by the wreckage of the cars in the rain, one of them a woman. He had intended to talk to Don's pit crew, but when he saw the wife was dry-eyed he changed his mind, and went to speak to her.

"I was the driver of the Ferrari," he said. "I'm very sorry that this happened, Mrs. Harrison."

She inclined her head. "You come up and bumped into them right at the end," she said. "It wasn't anything to do with you."

"I know. But I'm very sorry."

"Nothing for you to be sorry about," she said heavily. "He got it the way he wanted it to be. None of this being sick and all the rest of it. Maybe if he hadn't had that whisky ... I dunno. He got it the way he wanted it to be. You one of his cobbers?"

"Not really. He offered me a drink before the race, but I didn't take it. I've just had it now."

"You have? Well, good on you. That's the way Don would have wanted it. Is there any left?"

He hesitated. "There was when I left the paddock. Sam Bailey had a go at it, and I did. Maybe the boys have finished up the bottles."

She looked up at him. "Say, what do you want? His car? They say it isn't any good."

He glanced at the wrecked Jaguar. "I shouldn't think it is. No, what I wanted to do was to put my car on his transporter and get it back to town. The steering's had it, but I'll get her right for the Grand Prix."

"You got a place, didn't you? Well, it's Don's transporter but he'd rather have it work with cars that go than work with wrecks. All right, chum, you take it." He was a little taken aback. "Where shall I return it to?"

"I won't be using it. You take it."

He thought of offering money but rejected the idea; the time was past for that. "That's very kind of you," he said. "It's going to make a big difference to me, having the use of that transporter."

"Fine," she said. "You go right ahead and win that Grand Prix. Any parts you need from that—" She indicated the wrecked Jaguar—"you take them, too."

"How are you getting back to town?" he asked. "Me? I'll wait and go with Don in the ambulance. But they say there's another load of hospital cases for each car to go first, so it'll probably be around midnight before we get away."

There seemed to be nothing more that he could do for her. "Can I take some of the pit crew back?"

She nodded, and spoke to a fat, balding man of fifty. He detached two youngsters to go back with John. "Alfie here, he'll stay with me and see this all squared up," she said dully. "You go right ahead, mister, and win that Grand Prix."

He went a little way aside and talked to Eddie Brooks, standing in the rain. "Tires are the same size as ours. Wheels are different, but if we took the hubs as well . . . That Maserati's crashed up by The Slide. We might have a look at that one, too. I believe that's got a lot of the same front-end parts as we have. ..."

They walked back to their newly acquired transporter and drove it back in the half-light to Haystack Corner, and commenced the somewhat ghoulish task of stripping the dead bodies of the wrecked cars of anything that might be serviceable to the Ferrari. It was dark before they finished and they drove back to Melbourne in the rain.

## Chapter Eight

In Mary Holmes' garden the first narcissus bloomed on the first day of August, the day the radio announced, with studied objectivity, cases of radiation sickness in Adelaide and *Sydney*. The news did not trouble her particularly; all news was bad, like wage demands, strikes, or war, and the wise person paid no attention to it. What was important was that it was a bright, sunny day; her first narcissus were in bloom, and the daffodils behind them were already showing flower buds. "They're going to be a picture," she said happily to Peter. "There are so many of them. Do you think some of the bulbs can have sent up two shoots?"

"I shouldn't think so," he replied. "I don't think they do that. They split in two and make another bulb or something."

She nodded. "We'll have to dig them up in the autumn, after they die down, and separate them. Then we'll get a lot more and put them along here. They're going to look marvellous in a year or two." She paused in thought. "We'll be able to pick some then, and have them in the house."

One thing troubled her upon that perfect day, that Jennifer was cutting her first tooth, and was hot and fractious. Mary had a book called Baby's First Year which told her that this was normal, and nothing to worry about, but she was troubled all the same. "I mean," she said, "they don't know everything, the people who write these books. And all babies aren't the same, anyway. She oughtn't to keep crying like this, ought she? Do you think we ought to get in Dr. Halloran?"

"I shouldn't think so," Peter said. "She's chewing her rusk all right."

"She's so hot, the poor little lamb." She picked up the baby from her cot and started patting it on the back across her shoulder; the baby had

153

intended that, and stopped yelling. Peter felt that he could almost hear the silence. "I think she's probably all right," he said. "Just wants a bit of company." He felt he couldn't stand much more of it, after a restless night with the child crying all the time and Mary getting in and out of bed to soothe it. "Look, dear," he said, "I'm terribly sorry, but I've got to go up to the Navy Department. I've got a date in the Third Naval Members office at eleven forty-five."

"What about the doctor, though? Don't you think he ought to see her?"

"I wouldn't worry him. The book says she may be upset for a couple of days. Well, she's been going on for thirty-six hours now." By God, she has, he thought.

"It might be something different—not teeth at all. Cancer, or something. After all, she can't tell us where the pain is. . . ."

"Leave it till I get back," he said. "I should be back here around four o'clock, or five at the latest. Let's see how she is then."

"All right," she said reluctantly.

He took the petrol cans and put them in the car, and drove out on the road, glad to be out of it. He had no appointment in the Navy Department that morning but there would be no harm in looking in on them if, indeed, there was anybody in the office. *Scorpion* was out of dry dock and back alongside the aircraft carrier waiting for orders that might never come; he could go and have a look at her and, as a minor side issue, fill up his petrol tank and cans.

On that fine morning there was no one in the Third Naval Member's office save for one Wran writer, prim, and spectacled and conscientious. She said that she was expecting Commander Mason on board any minute now. Peter said he might look in again, and went down to his car, and drove to Williamstown. He parked beside the aircraft carrier and walked up the gangway with his cans in hand, accepting the salute of the officer of the day. "Morning," he said. "Is Commander Towers about?"

"I think he's down in *Scorpion*, sir."

"And I want some juice."

"Very good, sir. If you leave the cans here... Fill the tank as well?"

"If you would." He went on through the cold, echoing, empty ship and down the gangplank to the submarine. Dwight Towers came up to the bridge deck as he stepped on board. Peter saluted him formally. "Morning, sir," he said. "I came over to see what's doing, and to get some juice."

"Plenty of juice," said the American. "Not much doing. I wouldn't say there would be now, not ever again. You haven't any news for me?"

Peter shook his head. "I looked in at the Navy Department just now. There didn't seem to be anyone there, except one Wran."

"I had better luck than you. I found a lieutenant there yesterday. . . . Kind of running down."

154

"There's not so long to run now, anyway." They leaned on the bridge rail; he glanced at the captain. "You heard about Adelaide and *Sydney*?"

Dwight nodded. "Sure. First it was months, and then it got to be weeks, and now I'd say it's getting down to days. How long are they figuring on now?"

"I haven't heard. I wanted to get into touch with John Osborne today and get the latest gen."

"You won't find him in the office. He'll be working on that car. Say, that was quite a race."

Peter nodded. "Are you going down to see the next one—the Grand Prix itself? That's the last race ever, as I understand it. It's really going to be something."

"Well, I don't know. Moira didn't like the last one so much. I think women look at things differently.

Like boxing or wrestling." He paused. "You driving back to Melbourne now?"

"I was—unless you want me for anything, sir?"

"I don't want you. There's nothing to do here. I'll thumb a ride to town with you, if I may. My Leading Seaman Edgar hasn't shown up with the car today; I suppose he's running down, too. If you can wait ten minutes while I change this uniform I'll be with you." Forty minutes later they were talking to John Osborne in the garage in the mews. The Ferrari hung with its nose lifted high on chain blocks to the roof, its front end and steering dismantled. John was in an overall working on it with one mechanic; he had got it all so spotlessly clean that his hands were hardly dirty. "It's very lucky we got those parts off the Maserati," he said seriously. "One of these wishbones was bent all to hell. But the forgings are the same; we've had to bore out a bit and fit new bushes. I wouldn't have liked to race her if we'd had to heat the old one and bend it straight. I mean, you never know what's going to happen after a repair like that."

"I'd say you don't know what's going to happen anyway in this kind of racing," said Dwight "When is the Grand Prix to be?"

"I'm having a bit of a row with them over that," said the scientist. "They've got it down for Saturday fortnight, the 17th, but I think that's too late. I think we ought to run it on Saturday week, the 10th."

"Getting kind of close, is it?"

"Well, I think so. After all, they've got definite cases in Canberra now."

"I hadn't heard of that. The radio said Adelaide and *Sydney*."

"The radio's always about three days late. They don't want to create alarm and despondency until they've got to. But there's a suspect case in Albury today."

"In Albury? That's only about two hundred miles north."

"I know. I think Saturday fortnight is going to be too late."

Peter asked, "How long do you think we've got then, John?"

The scientist glanced at him. "I've got it now. You've got it, we've all got it. This door, this spanner—everything's getting touched with radioactive dust The air we breathe, the water that we drink, the lettuce in the salad, even the bacon and eggs. It's getting down now to the tolerance of the individual. Some people with less tolerance than others could quite easily be showing symptoms in a fortnight's time. Maybe sooner." He paused. "I think it's crazy to put off an important race like the Grand Prix till Saturday fortnight. We're having a meeting of the Committee this afternoon and I'm going to tell them so. We can't have a decent race if half the drivers have got diarrhoea and vomiting. It just means that the Grand Prix might be won by the chap with the best tolerance to radioactivity. Well, that's not what we're racing for!"

"I suppose that's so," said Dwight. He left them in the garage, for he had a date to lunch with Moira Davidson. John Osborne suggested lunch at the Pastoral Club, and presently he wiped his hands on a clean piece of rag, took off his overall, locked the garage, and they drove up through the city to the club.

As they went, Peter asked, "How's your uncle getting on?"

"He's made a big hole in the port, him and his cobbers," the scientist said. "He's not quite so good, of course. We'll probably see him at lunch; he comes in most days now. Of course, it's made a difference to him now that he can come in in his car."

"Where does he get his petrol from?"

"God knows. The army, probably. Where does anybody get his petrol from these days?" He paused. "I think he'll stay the course, but I wouldn't bank on it. The port'll probably give him longer than most of us."

"The port?"

The other nodded. "Alcohol, taken internally, seems to increase the tolerance to radioactivity. Didn't you know that?"

"You mean, if you get pickled you last longer?"

"A few days. With Uncle Douglas it's a toss-up which'll kill him first. Last week I thought the port was winning, but when I saw him yesterday he looked pretty good."

They parked the car and went into the club. They found Sir Douglas Froude sitting in the garden room, for the wind was cold. A glass of sherry was on the table by him and he was talking to two old friends. He made an effort to get to his feet when he saw them, but abandoned it at John's request. "Don't get about so well as I used to, once," he said. "Come, pull a chair up, and have some of this sherry. We're down to about fifty bottles now of the Amontillado. Push that bell." John Osborne did so, and they drew up chairs. "How are you feeling now, sir?"

"So-so, so-so. That doctor was probably right. He said that if I went back to my old habits I shouldn't last longer than a few months, and I shan't. But nor will he, and nor will you." He chuckled. "I hear you won that motor race that you were going in for."

"I didn't win it—I was second. It means I've got a place in the Grand Prix."

"Well, don't go and kill yourself. Although, I'm sure, it doesn't seem to matter very much if you do. Tell me, somebody was saying that they've got it in Cape Town. Do you think that's true?"

His nephew nodded. "That's true enough. They've had it for some days. We're still in radio communication, though."

"So they've got it before us?"

"That's true."

"That means that all of Africa is out, or will be out, before we get it here?"

John Osborne grinned. "It's going to be a pretty near thing. It looks as though all Africa might be gone in a week or so." He paused. "It seems to go quite quickly at the end, so far as we can ascertain. It's a bit difficult, because when more than half the people in a place are dead the communications usually go out and then you don't quite know what's happening. All services are usually stopped by then, and food supplies. The last half seem to go quite quickly. . . . But as I say, we don't really know what does happen, in the end."

"Well, I think that's a good thing," the general said robustly. "We'll find out soon enough." He paused. "So all of Africa is out. I've had some good times there, back in the days before the First War, when I was a subaltern. But I never did like that apartheid. ... Does that mean that we're going to be the last?"

"Not quite," his nephew said. "We're going to be the last major city. They've got cases now in Buenos Aires and Montevideo, and they've got a case or two in Auckland. After we're gone Tasmania may last another fortnight, and the South Island of New Zealand. The last of all to die will be the Indians in Tierra del Fuego."

"The Antarctic?"

The scientist shook his head. "There's nobody there now, so far as we know." He smiled. "Of course, that's not the end of life upon the earth. You mustn't think that. There'll be life here in Melbourne long after we've gone."

They stared at him. "What life?" Peter asked.

He grinned broadly. "The rabbit. That's the most resistant animal we know about."

The general pushed himself upright in his chair, his face suffused with anger. "You mean to say the rabbit's going to live longer than we do?"

"That's right. About a year longer. It's got about twice the resistance that we've got. There'll be rabbits running about Australia and eating all the feed next year."

"You're telling me the bloody rabbit's going to put it across us, after all? They'll be alive and kicking when we're all dead?"

John Osborne nodded. "Dogs will outlive us. Mice will last a lot longer, but not so long as rabbits. So far as we can see, the rabbit has them all licked—he'll be the last." He paused. "They'll all go in the end, of course. There'll be nothing left alive here by the end of the next year."

The general sank back in his chair. "The rabbit! After all we've done, and all we've spent in fighting him—to know he's going to win out in the end!" He turned to Peter. "Just press that bell beside you. I'm going to have a brandy and soda before going in to lunch. We'd all better have a brandy and soda after that."

In the restaurant Moira Davidson and Dwight settled at a table in a corner, and ordered lunch. Then she said, "What's troubling you, Dwight?"

He took up a fork and played with it. "Not very much."

"Tell me."

He raised his head. "I've got another ship in my command—U.S.S. Swordfish at Montevideo. It's getting hot around those parts right now. I radioed the captain three days ago asking him if he thought it practical to leave and sail his vessel over here."

"What did he say?"

"He said it wasn't. Shore associations, he called them. What he meant was girls, same as *Scorpion*. Said he'd try and come if there was a compelling reason but he'd be leaving half his crew behind." He raised his head. "There'd be no point in coming that way," he told her. "He wouldn't be operational."

"Did you tell him to stay there?"

He hesitated. "Yes," he said at last. "I ordered him to take Swordfish out beyond the twelve-mile limit and sink her on the high seas, in deep water." He stared at the prongs of the fork. "I dunno if I did the right thing or not," he said. "I thought that was what fie Navy Department would want me to do—not to leave a ship like that, full of classified gear, kicking around in another country. Even if there wasn't anybody there." He glanced at her. "So now the U.S. Navy's been reduced again," he said. "From two ships down to one."

They sat in silence for a minute. "Is that what you're going to do with *Scorpion*?" she asked at last.

"I think so. I'd have liked to take her back to the United States, but it wouldn't be practical. Too many shore associations, like he said."

Their lunch came. "Dwight," she said when the waiter had departed. "I had an idea."

"What's that, honey?"

158

"They're opening the trout fishing early this year, on Saturday week. I was wondering if you'd like to take me up into the mountains for the week-end." She smiled faintly. "For the fishing, Dwight—fishing to fish. Not for anything else. It's lovely up by Jamieson." He hesitated for a moment. "That's the day that John Osborne thinks they'll be running the Grand Prix."

She nodded. "So I thought. Would you rather see that?"

He shook his head. "Would you?"

"No. I don't want to see any more people get killed. We're going to see enough of that in a week or two."

"I feel that way about it, too. I don't want to see that race, and maybe see John get killed. I'd rather go fishing." He glanced at her and met her eyes. "There's just one thing, honey. I wouldn't want to go if it was going to mean that you'd get hurt."

"I shan't get hurt," she said. "Not in the way you mean."

He stared across the crowded restaurant. "I'm going home quite soon," he said. "I've been away a long time, but it's nearly over now. You know the way it is. I've got a wife at home I love, and I've played straight with her the two years that I've been away. I wouldn't want to spoil that now, these last few days."

"I know," she said. "I've known that all the time." She was silent for a minute, and then she said, "You've been very good for me, Dwight. I don't know what would have happened if you hadn't come along. I suppose half a loaf is better than no bread, when you're starving."

He wrinkled his brows. "I didn't get that, honey."

"It doesn't matter. I wouldn't want to start a smutty love affair when I'm dying in a week or ten days' time. I've got some standards, too—now, anyway."

He smiled at her. "We could try out Junior's rod. . . ."

"That's what I thought you'd want to do. I've got a little fly rod I could bring, but I'm no good."

"Got any flies and leaders?"

"We call them casts. I'm not quite sure. I'll have to look around and see what I can find at home."

"We'd go by car, would we? How far is it?"

"I think we'd want petrol for about five hundred miles. But you don't have to worry about that. I asked Daddy if I might borrow the Customline. He's got it out and running, and he's got nearly a hundred gallons of petrol tucked away in the hay shed behind the hay." He smiled again. "You think of everything. Say, where would we stay?"

"I think at the hotel," she said. "It's only a small country place, but I think it's the best bet. I could borrow a cottage, but it wouldn't have been slept in for two years, and we'd spend all our time in housekeeping. I'll ring up and make a booking at the hotel. For two rooms," she said.

"Okay. I'll have to chase that Leading Seaman Edgar and see if I can use my car without taking him along. I'm not just sure if I'm allowed to drive myself."

"That's not terribly important now, is it? I mean, you could just take it and drive it."

He shook his head. "I wouldn't want to do that."

"But, Dwight, why not? I mean, it doesn't matter —we can go in the Customline. But if that car's been put at your disposal, you can use it, surely. We're all going to be dead in a fortnight's time. Then nobody will be using it."

"I know. . ." he said. "It's just that I'd like to do things right, up till the end. If there's an order I'll obey it. That's the way I was trained, honey, and I'm not changing now. If it's against the rules for an officer to take a service car and drive it up into the mountains for a week-end with a girl, then I'll not do it. There'll be no alcoholic liquor on board *Scorpion*, not even in the last five minutes." He smiled. "That's the way it is, so let me buy you another drink."

"I can see that it will have to be the Customline. You're a very difficult man—I'm glad I'm not a sailor serving under you. No, I won't have a drink, thanks, Dwight. I've got my first test this afternoon."

"Your first test?"

She nodded. "I've got to try and take dictation at fifty words a minute. You've got to be able to do that and type it out without more than three mistakes in shorthand and three in typing. It's very difficult"

"I'd say it might be. You're getting to be quite a shorthand typist."

She smiled faintly. "Not at fifty words a minute. You have to be able to do a hundred and twenty if you're ever going to be any good." She raised her head. "I'd like to come and see you in America one day," she said. "I want to meet Sharon—if she'd want to meet me."

"She'll want to meet you," he said, "I'd say she's kind of grateful to you now, already."

She smiled faintly. "I don't know. Women are funny about men. ... If I came to Mystic, would there be a shorthand typing school where I could finish off my course?"

He thought for a minute. "Not in Mystic itself," he said. "There's plenty of good business colleges in New London. That's only about fifteen miles away."

"I'll just come for an afternoon," she said thoughtfully. "I want to see Helen jumping round upon that Pogo stick. But after that, I think I'd better come back here."

"Sharon would be very disappointed if you did that, honey. She'd want you to stay."

"That's what you think. I shall want a bit of convincing on that point"

He said, "I think things may be kind of different by that time."

She nodded slowly. "Possibly. I'd like to think they would be. Anyway, we'll find out pretty soon." She glanced at her wrist watch. "I must go, Dwight, or I'll be late for my test." She gathered up her gloves and her bag. "Look, I'll tell Daddy that we'd like to take the Customline and about thirty gallons of petrol."

He hesitated. "I'll find out about my car. I don't like taking your father's car away for all that time, with all that gas."

"He won't be using it," she said. "He's had it on the road for a fortnight, but I think he's only used twice. There's so much that he wants to see done on the farm while there's still time."

"What's he working on now?"

"The fence along the wood—the one in the forty acre. He's digging postholes to put up a new one. It's about twenty chains long. That's going to mean digging nearly a hundred holes."

"There's not so much to do at Williamstown. I could come out and lend a hand, if he'd like that."

She nodded. "I'll tell him. Give you a ring tonight, about eight o'clock?"

"Fine," he said. He escorted her to the door. "Good luck with the test."

He had no engagement for that afternoon. He stood in the street outside the restaurant after she had left him, completely at a loose end. Inactivity was unusual for him, and irksome. At Williamstown there was absolutely nothing for him to do; the aircraft carrier was dead and his ship all but dead. Although he had received no orders, he knew that now she would never cruise again; for one thing, with South America and South Africa out, there was now nowhere much for them to cruise to, unless it were New Zealand. He had given half of his ship's company leave, each half alternating a week at a time; of the other half he kept only about ten men on duty for maintenance and cleaning in the submarine, permitting the rest daily leave on shore. No signals now arrived for him to deal with; once a week he signed a few stores requisitions as a matter of form, though the stores they needed were supplied from dockyard sources with a disregard of paper work. He would not admit it, but he knew that his ship's working life was over, as his own was. He had nothing to replace it.

He thought of going to the Pastoral Club, and abandoned the idea; there would be no occupation for him there. He turned and walked towards the motor district of the town where he would find John Osborne working on his car; there might be work there of the sort that interested him. He must be back at Williamstown in time to receive Moira's call at about eight o'clock; that was his next appointment. He would go out next day and help her father with that fence, and he looked forward to the labour and the occupation.

On his way downtown he stopped at a sports shop and asked for flies and casts. "I'm sorry, sir," the man said. "Not a cast in the place, and not a fly. I've got a few hooks left, if you can tie your own. Sold clean out of everything the last few days, on account of the season opening, and there won't be any more coming in now, either. Well, as I said to the wife, it's kind of satisfactory. Get the stock down to a minimum before the end. It's how the accountants would like to see it, though I don't suppose they'll take much interest in it now. It's a queer turnout."

He walked on through the city. In the motor district there were still cars in the windows, still motor mowers, but the windows were dirty and the stores closed, the stock inside covered in dust and dirt. The streets were dirty now and littered with paper and spoilt vegetables; it was evidently some days since the street cleaners had operated. The trams still ran, but the whole city was becoming foul and beginning to smell; it reminded the American of an oriental city in the making. It was raining a little and the skies were grey; in one or two places the street drains were choked, and great pools stood across the road.

He came to the mews and to the open garage door. John Osborne was working with two others, and Peter Holmes was there, his uniform coat off, washing strange, nameless parts of the Ferrari in a bath of kerosene, more valuable at that time than mercury. There was an atmosphere of cheerful activity in the garage that warmed his heart.

"I thought we might see you," said the scientist. "Come for a job?"

"Sure," said Dwight. "This city gives me a pain. You got anything I can do?"

"Yes. Help Bill Adams fit new tires on every wheel you can find." He indicated a stack of brand-new racing tires; there seemed to be wire wheels everywhere.

Dwight took his coat off thankfully. "You've got a lot of wheels."

"Eleven, I think. We got the ones off the Maserati —they're the same as ours. I want a new tire on every wheel we've got. Bill works for Goodyear and he knows the way they go, but he needs somebody to help."

The American, rolling up his sleeves, turned to Peter. "He got you working, too?"

The naval officer nodded. "I'll have to go before very long. Jennifer's teething, and been crying for two bloody days. I told Mary I was sorry I'd got to go on board today, but I'd be back by five."

Dwight smiled. "Left her to hold the baby."

Peter nodded. "I got her a garden rake and a bottle of dillwater. But I must be back by five."

162

He left half an hour later, and got into his little car, and drove off down the road to Falmouth. He got back to his flat on time, and found Mary in the lounge, the house miraculously quiet. "How's Jennifer?" he asked.

She put her finger to her lips. "She's sleeping," she whispered. "She went off after dinner, and she hasn't woken up since."

He went towards the bedroom, and she followed him. "Don't wake her," she whispered.

"Not on your life," he whispered back. He stood looking down at the child, sleeping quietly. "I don't think she's got cancer," he remarked.

They went back into the lounge, closing the door quietly behind them, and he gave her his presents. "I've got dillwater," she said, "—masses of it, and anyway she doesn't have it now. You're about three months out of date. The rake's lovely. It's just what we want for getting all the leaves and twigs up off the lawn. I was trying to pick them up by hand yesterday, but it breaks your back."

They got short drinks, and presently she said, "Peter, now that we've got petrol, couldn't we have a motor mower?"

"They cost quite a bit," he objected, almost automatically.

"That doesn't matter so much now, does it? And with the summer coming on, it would, be a help. I know we've not got very much lawn to mow, but it's an awful chore with the hand mower, and you may be away at sea again. If we had a very little motor mower that I could start myself. Or an electric one. Doris Haynes has an electric one, and it's no trouble to start at all."

"She's cut its cord in two at least three times, and each time she does that she dam nearly electrocutes herself."

"You don't have to do that if you're careful. I think it would be a lovely thing to have."

She lived in the dream world of unreality, or else she would not admit reality; he did not know. In any case, he loved her as she was. It might never be used, but it would give her pleasure to have it. "I'll see if I can find one next time I go up to town," he said. "I know there are plenty of motor mowers, but I'm not just sure about an electric one." He thought for a moment. "I'm afraid the electric ones may all be gone.

People would have bought them when there wasn't any petrol."

She said, "A little motor one would do, Peter. I mean, you could show me how to start it."

He nodded. "They're not much trouble, really."

"Another thing we ought to have," she said, "is a garden seat. You know—one that you can leave outside all winter, and sit on whenever it's a nice fine day. I was thinking, how nice it would be if we had a garden seat in that sheltered comer just by the arbutus. I think we'd use it an awful lot next summer. Probably use it all the year round, too."

163

He nodded. "Not a bad idea." It would never be used next summer, but let that go. Transport would be a difficulty; the only way he could transport a garden seat with the Morris Minor would be by putting it on the roof, and that might scratch the enamel unless he padded it very well. "We'll get the motor mower first, and then see what the bank looks like."

He drove her up to Melbourne the next day to look for a motor mower; they went with Jennifer in her carrying basket on the back seat. It was some weeks since she had been in the city, and its aspect startled and distressed her. "Peter," she said, "what's the matter with everything? It's all so dirty, and it smells horrid."

"I suppose the street cleaners have stopped working," he observed.

"But why should they do that? Why aren't they working? Is there a strike or something?"

"Everything's just slowing down," he said. "After all, I'm not working."

"That's different," she said. "You're in the navy." He laughed. "No, what I mean is, you go to sea for months and months, and then you go on leave. Street cleaners don't do that. They go on all the time. At least, they ought to."

He could not elucidate it any further for her, and they drove on to the big hardware store. It had only a few customers, and very few assistants. They left the baby in the car and went through to the gardening department, and searched some time for an assistant. "Motor mowers?" he said. "You'll find a few in the next hall, through that archway. Look them over and see if what you want is there."

They did so, and picked a little twelve-inch mower. Peter looked at the price tag, picked up the mower, and went to find the assistant. "I'll take this one," he said.

"Okay," said the man. "Good little mower, that" He grinned sardonically. "Last you a lifetime."

"Forty-seven pounds ten," said Peter. "Can I pay by cheque?"

"Pay by orange peel for all I care," the man said. "We're closing down tonight."

The naval officer went over to a table and wrote his cheque; Mary was left talking to the salesman. "Why are you closing down?" she asked. "Aren't people buying things?"

He laughed shortly. "Oh—they come in and they buy. Not much to sell them now. But I'm not going on right up till the end, same with all the staff. We had a meeting yesterday, and then we told the management. After all, there's only about a fortnight left to go.

They're closing down tonight."

Peter came back and handed his cheque to the salesman. "Okeydoke," the man said. "I don't know if they'll ever pay it in without a staff up in the
164

office. Maybe I'd better give you a receipt in case they get on to your tail next year. . . ." He scribbled a receipt and turned to another customer.

Mary shivered. "Peter, let's get out of this and go home. It's horrid here, and everything smells."

"Don't you want to stay up here for lunch?" He had thought she would enjoy the little outing.

She shook her head. "I'd rather go home now, and have lunch there."

They drove in silence out of the city and down to the bright little seaside town that was their home. Back in their apartment on the hill she regained a little of her poise; here were the familiar things she was accustomed to, the cleanness that was her pride, the carefully tended little garden, the clean wide view out over the bay. Here was security.

After lunch, smoking before they did the washing up, she said, "I don't think I want to go to Melbourne again, Peter."

He smiled. "Getting a bit piggy, isn't it?"

"It's horrible," she said vehemently. "Everything shut up, and dirty, and stinking. It's as if the end of the world had come already."

"It's pretty close, you know," he said.

She was silent for a moment. "I know; that's what you've been telling me all along." She raised her eyes to his. "How far off is it, Peter?"

"About a fortnight," he said. "It doesn't happen with a click, you know. People start getting ill, but not all on the same day, of course. Some people are more resistant than others."

"But everybody gets it, don't they?" she asked in a low tone. "I mean, in the end."

He nodded. "Everybody gets it, in the end."

"How much difference is there in people? I mean, when they get it?"

He shook his head. "I don't really know. I think everybody would have got it in three weeks."

"Three weeks from now, or three weeks after the first case?"

"Three weeks after the first case, I mean," he said. "But I don't really know." He paused. "It's possible to get it slightly and get over it," he said. "But then you get it again ten days or a fortnight later."

She said, "There's no guarantee, then, that you and I would get it at the same time? Or Jennifer? We might any of us get it, any time?"

He nodded. "That's the way it is. We've just got to take it as it comes. After all, it's what we've always had to face, only we've never faced it, because we're young. Jennifer might always have died first, of the three of us, or I might have died before you. There's nothing much that's new about it."

"I suppose not," she said. "I did hope it all might happen on one day."

165

He took her hand. "It may quite well do so," he said. "But—we'd be lucky." He kissed her. "Let's do the washing up." His eye fell on the lawn mower. "We can mow the lawn this afternoon."

"The grass is all wet," she said sadly. "It'll make it rusty."

"Then we'll dry it in front of the fire in the lounge," he promised her. "I won't let it get rusty."

Dwight Towers spent the week-end with the Davidsons at Harkaway, working from dawn till dusk each day on the construction of the fences. The hard physical work was a relief from all his tensions, but he found his host to be a worried man. Someone had told him about the resistance of the rabbit to radioactive infection. The rabbit did not worry him a great deal, for Harkaway had always been remarkably free from rabbits, but the relative immunity of the furred animals raised questions in regard to his beef cattle, and to these he had found no answer.

He unburdened himself one evening to the American. "I never thought of it," he said. "I mean, I assumed the Aberdeen Angus, they'd die at the same time as us. But now it looks as though they'll last a good while longer. How much longer they'll last—that I can't find out. Apparently there's been no research done on it. But as it is, of course, I'm feeding out both hay and silage, and up here we go on feeding out until the end of September in an average year—about half a bale of hay a beast each day. I find you have to do that if you're going to keep them prime. Well, I can't see how to do it if there's going to be no one here. It really is a problem."

"What would happen if you opened the hay barn to them, and let them take it as they want it?"

"I thought of that, but they'd never get the bales undone. If they did, they'd trample most of it underfoot and spoil it." He paused. "I've been puzzling to think out if there isn't some way we could do it with a time clock and an electric fence. . . . But any way you look at it, it means putting out a month's supply of hay into the open paddock, in the rain. I don't know what to do. . . "

He got up. "Let me get you a whisky."

"Thank you—a small one." The American reverted to the problem of the hay. "It certainly is difficult. You can't even write to the papers and find out what anybody else is doing."

He stayed with the Davidsons until the Tuesday morning, and then went back to Williamstown. At the dockyard his command was beginning to disintegrate, in spite of everything that the executive and the chief of the boat had been able to do. Two men had not returned from leave and one was reported to have been killed in a street brawl at Geelong, but there was no confirmation. There were eleven cases of men drunk on return from leave waiting for his jurisdiction and he found these very difficult to deal with. Restriction of leave when there was no work to do aboard and only about a fortnight left to go did not seem to be the answer. He left the culprits confined in the brig of the aircraft carrier while they sobered up and while he thought about it; then he had them lined up before him on the quarter deck.

"You men can't have it both ways," he told them. "We've none of us got long to go now, you or me. As of today, you're members of the ship's company of *U.S.S. Scorpion*, and that's the last ship of the U.S. Navy in commission. You can stay as part of the ship's company, or you can get a dishonorable discharge."

He paused. "Any man coming aboard drunk or late from leave, from this time on, will get discharged next day. And when I say discharged, I mean dishonorable discharge, and I mean it quick. I'll strip the uniform off you right there and then and put you outside the dockyard gates as a civilian in your shorts, and you can freeze and rot in Williamstown for all the U.S. Navy cares. Hear that, and think it over. Dismissed." He got one case next day, and turned the man outside the dockyard gates in shirt and underpants to fend for himself. He had no more trouble of that sort.

He left the dockyard early on the Friday morning in the Chevrolet driven by his leading seaman, and went to the garage in the mews off Elizabeth Street in the city. He found John Osborne working on the Ferrari, as he had expected; the car stood roadworthy and gleaming, to all appearances ready to race there and then. Dwight said, "Say, I just called in as I was passing by to say I'm sorry that I won't be there to see you win tomorrow. I've got another date up in the mountains, going fishing."

The scientist nodded. "Moira told me. Catch a lot of fish. I don't think there'll be many people there this time except competitors and doctors."

"I'd have thought there would be, for the Grand Prix."

"It may be the last week-end in full health for a lot of people. They've got other things they want to do."

"Peter Holmes—he'll be there?"

John Osborne shook his head. "He's going to spend it gardening." He hesitated. "I oughtn't to be going really."

"You don't have a garden."

The scientist smiled wryly. "No, but I've got an old mother, and she's got a Pekinese. She's just woken up to the fact that little Ming's going to outlive her by several months, and now she's worried stiff what's going to happen to him. . . ." He paused. "It's the hell of a time, this. I'll be glad when it's all over."

"End of the month, still?"

"Sooner than that for most of us." He said something in a low tone, and added, "Keep that under your hat. It's going to be tomorrow afternoon for me."

"I hope that's not true," said the American. "I kind of want to see you get that cup."

The scientist glanced lovingly at the car. "She's fast enough," he said. "She'd win it if she had a decent driver. But it's me that's the weak link."

"I'll keep my fingers crossed for you."

"Okay. Bring me back a fish."

The American left the mews and went back to his car, wondering if he would see the scientist again. He said to his leading seaman, "Now drive out to Mr. Davidson's farm at Harkaway, near Berwick. Where you've taken me once before."

He sat in the back seat of the car fingering the little rod as they drove out into the suburbs, looking at the streets and houses that they passed in the grey light of the winter day. Very soon, perhaps in a month's time, there would be no one here, no living creatures but the cats and dogs that had been granted a short reprieve. Soon they too would be gone; summers and winters would pass by and these houses and these streets would know them. Presently, as time passed, the radioactivity would pass also; with a cobalt half-life of about five years these streets and houses would be habitable again in twenty years at the latest, and probably sooner than that. The human race was to be wiped out and the world made clean again for wiser occupants without undue delay. Well, probably that made sense.

He got to Harkaway in the middle of the morning; the Ford was in the yard, the boot full of petrol cans. Moira was ready for him, a little suitcase stowed on the back seat with a good deal of fishing gear. "I thought we'd get away before lunch and have sandwiches on the road," she said. "The days are pretty short."

"Suits me," he said. "You got sandwiches?"

She nodded. "And beer."

"Say, you think of everything." He turned to the grazier. "I feel kind of mean taking your car like this," he said. "I could take the Chev, if you'd rather."

Mr. Davidson shook his head. "We went into Melbourne yesterday. I don't think we'll be going again. It's too depressing."

The American nodded. "Getting kind of dirty."

"Yes. No, you take the Ford. There's a lot of petrol might as well be used up, and I don't suppose that I'll be needing it again. There's too much to do here."

Dwight transferred his gear into the Ford and sent his leading seaman back to the dockyard with the Chev. "I don't suppose he'll go there," he said reflectively as the car moved off. "Still, we go through the motions."

They got into the Ford. Moira said, "You drive."

"No," he replied. "You'd better drive. I don't know the way, and maybe I'd go hitting something on the wrong side of the road."

"It's two years since I drove," she said. "But it's your neck." They got in and she found first gear after a little exploration, and they moved off down the drive.

It pleased her to be driving again, pleased her very much indeed. The acceleration of the car gave her a sense of freedom, of escape from the restraints of her daily life. They went by side roads through the Dandenong mountains spattered with guest houses and residences and stopped for lunch not far from Lilydale beside a rippling stream. The day had cleared up and it was now sunny, with white clouds against a bright blue sky.

They eyed the stream professionally as they ate their sandwiches. "It's muddy kind of water," said Dwight "I suppose that's because it's early in the year."

"I think so," the girl said. "Daddy said it would be too muddy for fly fishing. He said you might do all right with a spinner, but he advised me to kick about upon the bank until I found a worm and dab about with that."

The American laughed. "I'd say there's some sense in that, if the aim is to catch fish. I'll stick to a spinner for a time, at any rate, because I want to see that this rod handles right."

"I'd like to catch one fish," the girl said a little wistfully. "Even if it's such a dud one that we put it back. I think I'll try with worm unless the water's a lot clearer up at Jamieson."

"It might be clearer high up in the mountains, with the melting snow."

She turned to him. "Do fish live longer than we're going to? Like dogs?"

He shook his head. "I wouldn't know, honey."

They drove on to War hurt on and took the long, winding road up through the forests to the heights. They emerged a couple of hours later on the high ground at Matlock; here there was snow upon the road and on the wooded mountains all around; the world looked cold and bleak. They dropped down into a valley to the little town of Woods Point and then up over another watershed. From there a twenty mile run through the undulating, pleasant valley of the Goulburn brought them to the Jamieson Hotel just before dusk.

The American found the hotel to be a straggling collection of somewhat tumble-down single-storey wooden buildings, some of which dated from the earliest settlement of the state. It was well that they had booked rooms, for the place was crowded with fishermen. More cars were parked outside it than ever in the palmiest days of peacetime; inside, the bar was doing a roaring trade. They found the landlady with some difficulty, her face aglow with excitement As she showed them their rooms, small and inconvenient and badly furnished, she said, "Isn't this lovely, having all you fishermen here again? You can't think what's it's been like the last two years, with practically no one coming here except on pack horse trips. But this is just like old times. Have you got a towel of your own? Oh well, I'll see if I can find one for you. But we're so full. She dashed off in a flurry of pleasure.

The American looked after her. "Well," he said, "she's having a good time, anyway. Come on, honey, and I'll buy you a drink."

They went to the crowded barroom, with a boarded, sagging ceiling, a huge fire of logs in the grate, a number of chromium-plated chairs and tables, and a seething mass of people.

"What'll I get you, honey?"

"Brandy," she shouted above the din. "There's only one thing to do here tonight, Dwight."

He grinned, and forced his way through the crowd towards the bar. He came back in a few minutes, struggling, with a brandy and a whisky. They looked around for chairs, and found two at a table where two earnest men in shirt sleeves were sorting tackle. They looked up and nodded as Dwight and Moira joined them. "Fish for breakfast," said one.

"Getting up early?" asked Dwight.

The other glanced at him. "Going to bed late. The season opens at midnight."

He was interested. "You're going out then?"

"If it's not actually snowing. Best time to fish." He held up a huge white fly tied on a small hook. "That's what I use. That's what gets them. Put a shot or two on it, and sink it down, and then cast well across. Never fails."

"It does with me," his companion said. "I like a little frog. You get alongside a pool you know about two in the morning with a little frog and put the hook just through the skin on his back and cast him across and let him swim about. . . . That's what I do. You going out tonight?"

Dwight glanced at the girl, and smiled. "I guess not," he said. "We just fish around in daylight—we're not in your class. We don't catch much."

The other nodded. "I used to be like that. Look at the birds and the river and the sun upon the ripples, and not care much what you caught. I do that sometimes. But then I got to this night fishing, and that's really something." He glanced at the American. "There's a ruddy great monster of a fish in a pool down just below the bend that I've been trying to get for the last two years. I had him on a frog the year before last, and he took out most of my line and then broke me. And then I had him on again last year, on a sort of doodlebug in the late evening, and he broke me again—brand-new, o.x. nylon. He's twelve pounds if he's an ounce. I'm going to get him this time if I've got to stay up all of every night until the end."

The American leaned back to talk to Moira. "You want to go out at two in the morning?"

She laughed. "I'll want to go to bed. You go if you'd like to."

He shook his head. "I'm not that kind of fisherman."

"Just the drinking kind," she said. "I'll toss you who goes and battles for the next drink."

"I'll get you another," he said.

She shook her head. "Just stay where you are and learn something about fishing. I'll get you one."

She struggled through the crowd to the bar carrying the glasses, and came back presently to the table by the fireside. Dwight got up to meet her, and as he did so his sports jacket fell open. She handed him the glass and said accusingly, "You've got a button off your pull-over!"

He glanced down. "I know. It came off on the way up here."

"Have you got the button?"

He nodded. "I found it on the floor of the car."

"You'd better give it to me with the pull-over tonight, and I'll sew it on for you."

"It doesn't matter," he said.

"Of course it matters." She smiled softly. "I can't send you back to Sharon looking like that"

"She wouldn't mind, honey...."

"No, but I should. Give it to me tonight, and I'll give it back to you in the morning."

He gave it to her at the door of her bedroom at about eleven o'clock that night. They had spent most of the evening smoking and drinking with the crowd, keenly anticipating the next day's sport, discussing whether to fish the lake or the streams. They had decided to try it on the Jamieson River, having no boat. The girl took the garment from him and said, "Thanks for bringing me up here, Dwight. It's been a lovely evening, and it's going to be a lovely day tomorrow." He stood uncertain. "You really mean that, honey? You're not going to be hurt?"

She laughed. "I'm not going to be hurt, Dwight. I know you're a married man. Go to bed. I'll Have this for you in the morning."

"Okay." He turned and listened to the noise and snatches of songs still coming from the bar. "They're having themselves a real good time," he said. "I still can't realize it's never going to happen again, not after this week-end."

"It may do, somehow," she said. "On another plane, or something. Anyway, let's have fun and catch fish tomorrow. They say it's going to be a fine day."

He grinned. "Think it ever rains, on that other plane?"

"I don't know," she said. "We'll find out soon enough."

"Got to get some water in the rivers, somehow," he said thoughtfully. "Otherwise there wouldn't be much fishing. . . ." He turned away. "Good night, Moira. Let's have a swell time tomorrow, anyway."

171

She closed her door, and stood for a few moments bolding the pull-over to her. Dwight was as he was, a married man whose heart was in Connecticut with his wife and children; it would never be with her. If she had had more time things might have been different, but it would have taken many years. Five years, at least, she thought, until the memories of Sharon and of Junior and of Helen had begun to fade; then he would have turned to her, and she could have given him another family, and made him happy again. Five years were not granted to her; it would be five days, more likely. A tear trickled down beside her nose and she wiped it away irritably; self-pity was a stupid thing, or was it the brandy? The light from the one fifteen-watt bulb high in the ceiling of her dark little bedroom was too dim for sewing buttons on. She threw off her clothes, put on her pyjamas, and went to bed, the pullover on the pillow by her head. In the end she slept. They went out next day after breakfast to fish the Jamieson not far from the hotel. The river was high and the water clouded; she dabbled her flies amateurishly in the quick water and did no good, but Dwight caught a two-pounder with the spinning tackle in the middle of the morning and she helped him to land it with the net. She wanted him to go on and catch another, but having proved the rod and tackle he was now more interested in helping her to catch something. About noon one of the fishermen that they had sat with at the bar came walking down the bank, studying the water and not fishing. He stopped to speak to them.

"Nice fish," he said, looking at Dwight's catch. "Get him on the fly?"

The American shook his head. "On the spinner. We're trying with the fly now. Did you do any good last night?"

"I got five," the man said. "Biggest about six pounds. I got sleepy about three in the morning and turned it in. Only just got out of bed. You won't do much good with fly, not in this water." He produced a plastic box and poked about in it with his forefinger. "Look, try this."

He gave them a tiny fly spoon, a little bit of plated metal about the size of a sixpence ornamented with one hook. "Try that in the pool where the quick water runs out. They should come for that, on a day like this."

They thanked him, and Dwight tied it on the cast for her. At first she could not get it out; it felt like a ton of lead on the end of her rod and fell in the water at her feet. Presently she got the knack of it, and managed to put it into the fast water at the head of the pool. On the fifth or sixth successful cast there was a sudden pluck at the line, the rod bent, and the reel sang as the line ran out. She gasped. "I believe I've got one, Dwight"

"Sure, you've got one," he said. "Keep the rod upright, honey. Move down a bit this way." The fish broke surface in a leap. "Nice fish," he said. "Keep a tight line, but let him run if he really wants to go. Take it easy, and he's all yours."

Five minutes later she got the exhausted fish in to the bank at her feet, and he netted it for her. He killed it with a quick blow on a stone, and they

172

admired her catch. "Pound and a half," he said. "Maybe a little bigger." He extracted the little spoon carefully from its mouth. "Now catch another one."

"It's not so big as yours," she said, but she was bursting with pride.

"The next one will be. Have another go at it." But it was close to lunchtime, and she decided to wait till the afternoon. They walked back to the hotel proudly carrying their spoils and had a glass of beer before lunch, talking over their catch with the other anglers.

They went out again in the middle of the afternoon to the same stretch of river and again she caught a fish, a two-pounder this time, while Dwight caught two smaller fish, one of which he put back. Towards evening they rested before going back to the hotel, pleasantly tired and content with the day's work, the fish laid out beside them. They sat against a boulder by the river, enjoying the last of the sunlight before it sank behind the hill, smoking cigarettes. It was growing chilly, but they were reluctant to leave the murmur of the river.

A sudden thought struck her. "Dwight," she said. "That motor race must be over by this time."

He stared at her. "Holy smoke! I meant to listen to it on the radio. I forgot all about it."

"So did I," she said. There was a pause, and then she said, "I wish we'd listened. I'm feeling a bit selfish."

"We couldn't have done anything, honey."

"I know. But—I don't know. I do hope John's all right."

"The news comes on at seven," he said. "We could listen then."

"I'd like to know," she said. She looked around her at the calm, rippling water, the long shadows, the golden evening light. "This is such a lovely place," she said. "Can you believe—really believe—that we shan't see it again?"

"I'm going home," he said quietly. "This is a grand country, and I've liked it here. But it's not my country, and now I'm going back to my own place, to my own folks. I like it in Australia well enough, but all the same I'm glad to be going home at last, home to Connecticut." He turned to her. "I shan't see this again, because I'm going home."

"Will you tell Sharon about me?" she asked.

"Sure," he said. "Maybe she knows already."

She stared down at the pebbles at her feet. "What will you tell her?"

"Lots of things," he said quietly. "I'll tell her that you turned what might have been a bad time for me into a good time. I'll tell her that you did that although you knew, right from the start, that there was nothing in it for you. I'll tell her it's because of you I've come back to her like I used to be, and not a drunken bum. I'll tell her that you've made it easy for me to stay faithful to her, and what it's cost you."

She got up from the stone. "Let's go back to the hotel," she said. "You'll be lucky if she believes a quarter of all that."

He got up with her. "I don't think so," he said. "I think she'll believe it all, because it's true."

They walked back to the hotel carrying their fish. When they had cleaned up they met again in the hotel bar for a drink before tea; they ate quickly in order to be back at the radio before the news. It came on presently, mostly concerned with sport; as they sat tense the announcer said, The Australian Grand Prix was run today at Tooradin and was won by Mr. John Osborne, driving a Ferrari. The second place . . .

The girl exclaimed, "Oh Dwight, he did it!" They sat forward to listen.

The race was marred by the large number of accidents and casualties. Of the eighteen starters only three finished the race of eighty laps, six of the drivers being killed outright in accidents and many more removed to hospital with more or less severe injuries. The winner, Mr. John Osborne, drove cautiously for the first half of the race and at the fortieth lap was three laps behind the leading car, driven by Mr. Sam Bailey. Shortly after-wards Mr. Bailey crashed at the comer known as The Slide, and from that point onwards the Ferrari put on speed. At the sixtieth lap the Ferrari was in the lead, the field by that time being reduced to five cars, and thereafter Mr. Osborne was never seriously challenged. On the sixty-fifth lap he put up a record for course, lapping at 97.83 miles an hour, a remarkable achievement for this circuit Thereafter Mr. Osborne reduced speed in response to signals from his pit, and finished the race at an average speed of 89.61 miles an hour. Mr. Osborne is an official of the C.S.I.R.O.; he has no connection with the motor industry and races as an amateur.

Later they stood on the verandah of the hotel for a few minutes before bed, looking out at the black line of the hills, the starry night. "I'm glad John got what he wanted," the girl said. "I mean, he wanted it so much. It must kind of round things off for him."

The American beside her nodded. "I'd say things are rounding off for all of us right now."

"I know. There's not much time. Dwight, I think I'd like to go home tomorrow. We've had a lovely day up here and caught some fish. But there's so much to do, and now so little time to do it in."

"Sure, honey," he said. "I was thinking that myself.

You glad we came, though?"

She nodded. "I've been very happy, Dwight, all day. I don't know why—not just catching fish. I feel like John must feel—as if I've won a victory over something. But I don't know what."

He smiled. "Don't try and analyze it," he said. "Just take it, and be thankful. I've been happy, too. But I'd agree with you, we should get home tomorrow. Things will be happening down there."

"Bad things?" she asked.

He nodded in the darkness by her side. "I didn't want to spoil the trip for you," he said. "But John Osborne told me yesterday before we came away they got several cases of this radiation sickness in Melbourne, as of Thursday night. I'd say there'd be a good many more by now."

## Chapter Nine

On the Tuesday morning Peter Holmes went to Melbourne in his little car. Dwight Towers had telephoned to him to meet him at ten forty-five in the anteroom to the office of the First Naval Member. The radio that morning announced for the first time the incidence of radiation sickness in the city, and Mary Holmes had been concerned about him going there. "Do be careful, Peter," she said. "I mean, about all this infection. Do you think you ought to go?"

He could not bring himself to tell her again that the infection was there around them, in their pleasant little flat; either she did not or she would not understand. "I'll have to go," he said. "I won't stay longer than I've absolutely got to."

"Don't stay up to lunch," she said. "I'm sure it's healthier down here."

"I'll come straight home," he said.

A thought struck her. "I know," she said. "Take those formalin lozenges with you that we got for my cough, and suck one now and then. They're awfully good for all kinds of infection. They're so antiseptic."

It would set her mind at ease if he did so. "That's not a bad idea," he said.

He drove up to the city deep in thought. It was no longer a matter of days now; it was coming down to hours. He did not know what this conference with the First Naval Member was to be about, but it was very evident that it would be one of the last naval duties of his career. When he drove back again that afternoon his service life would probably be over, as his physical life soon would be.

He parked his car and went into the Navy Department. There was practically no one in the building; he walked up to the anteroom and there he found Dwight Towers in uniform, and alone. His captain said cheerfully, "Hi, fella."

Peter said, "Good morning, sir." He glanced around; the secretary's desk was locked, the room empty. "Hasn't Lieutenant Commander Torrens shown up?"

"Not that I know of. I'd say he's taking the day off."

175

The door into the admiral's office opened, and Sir David Hartman stood there. The smiling, rubicund face was more serious and drawn than Peter had remembered. He said, "Come in, gentlemen. My secretary isn't here today."

They went in, and were given seats before the desk. The American said, "I don't know if what I have to say concerns Lieutenant Commander Holmes or not. It may involve a few liaison duties with the dockyard. Would you prefer he wait outside, sir?"

"I shouldn't think so," said the admiral. "If it will shorten our business, let him stay. What is it you want, Commander?"

Dwight hesitated for a moment, choosing his words. "It seems that I'm the senior executive officer of the U.S. Navy now," he said. "I never thought I'd rise so high as that, but that's the way it is. You'll excuse me if I don't put this in the right form or language, sir. But I have to tell you that I'm taking my ship out of your command."

The admiral nodded slowly. "Very good, Commander. Do you wish to leave Australian territorial waters, or to stay here as our guest?"

"I'll be taking my ship outside territorial waters," the commander said. "I can't just say when I'll be leaving, but probably before the week-end."

The admiral nodded. He turned to Peter. "Give any necessary instructions in regard to victualling and towage to the dockyard," he said. "Commander Towers is to be given every facility."

"Very good, sir."

The American said, "I don't just know what to suggest about payments, sir. You must forgive me, but I have no training in these matters."

The admiral smiled thinly. "I don't know that it would do us much good if you had, Commander. I think we can leave those to the usual routine. All countersigned indents and requisitions are costed here and are presented to the Naval Attach^ at your embassy in Canberra, and forwarded by him to Washington for eventual settlement I don't think you need worry over that side of it."

Dwight said, "I can just cast off and go?"

"That's right Do you expect to be returning to Australian waters?"

The American shook his head. "No, sir. I'm taking my ship out in Bass Strait to sink her."

Peter had expected that but the imminence and the practical negotiation of the matter came with a shock; somehow this was the sort of thing that did not happen. He wanted for a moment to ask if Dwight required a tug to go out with the submarine to bring back the crew, and then abandoned the question. If the Americans wanted a tug to give them a day or two more life they would ask for it, but he did not think they would. Better the sea than death by sickness and diarrhoea homeless in a strange land.

The admiral said, "I should probably do the same, in your shoes. . . . Well, it only remains to thank you for your co-operation, Commander. And to wish you luck. If there's anything you need before you go don't hesitate to ask for it—or just take it." A sudden spasm of pain twisted his face and he gripped a pencil on the desk before him. Then he relaxed a little, and got up from the desk. "Excuse me," he said. "I'll have to leave you for a minute."

He left them hurriedly, and the door closed behind him. The captain and the liaison officer had stood up at his sudden departure; they remained standing, and glanced at each other. "This is it," said the American.

Peter said in a low tone, "Do you suppose that's what's happened to the secretary?"

"I'd think so."

They stood in silence for a minute or two, staring out of the window. "Victualling," Peter said at last "There's nothing much in *Scorpion*. Is the exec getting out a list of what you'll need, sir?"

Dwight shook his head. "We shan't need anything," he said. "I'm only taking her down the bay and just outside the territorial limit"

The liaison officer asked the question that he had wanted to ask before. "Shall I lay on a tug to sail with you and bring the crew back?"

Dwight said, "That won't be necessary."

They stood in silence for another ten minutes. Finally the admiral reappeared, grey faced. "Very good of you to wait," he said. "I've been a bit unwell...." He did not resume his seat, but remained standing by the desk. "This is the end of a long association, Captain," he said. "We British have always enjoyed working with Americans, especially upon the sea. We've had cause to be grateful to you very many times, and in return I think we've taught you something out of our experience. This is the end of it." He stood in thought for a minute, and then he held out his hand, smiling. "All I can do now is to say good-bye."

Dwight took his hand. "It certainly has been good, working under you, sir," he said. "I'm speaking for the whole ship's company when I say that, as well as for myself."

They left the office and walked down through the desolate, empty building to the courtyard. Peter said, "Well, what happens now, sir? Would you like me to come down to the dockyard?"

The captain shook his head. "I'd say that you can consider yourself to be relieved of duty," he said. "I won't need you any more down there."

"If there's anything that I can do, I'll come very gladly."

"No. If I should find I need anything from you, I'll ring your home. But that's where your place is now, fella."

This, then, was the end of their fellowship. "When will you be sailing?" Peter asked.

177

"I wouldn't know exactly," the American said. "I've got seven cases in the crew, as of this morning. I guess we'll stick around a day or two, and sail maybe on Saturday."

"Are many going with you?"

"Ten Eleven, with myself."

Peter glanced at him. "Are you all right, so far?"

Dwight smiled. "I thought I was, but now I don't just know. I won't be taking any lunch today." He paused. "How are you feeling?"

"I'm all right. So is Mary—I think."

Dwight turned towards the cars. "You get back to her, right now. There's nothing now for you to stay here for."

"Will I see you again, sir?"

"I don't think you will," said the captain. "I'm going home now, home to Mystic in Connecticut, and glad to go."

There was nothing more for them to say or do. They shook hands, got into their cars, and drove off on their separate ways.

In the old-fashioned, two-storey brick house in Malvern, John Osborne stood by his mother's bed. He was not unwell, but the old lady had fallen sick upon the Sunday morning, the day after he had won the Grand Prix. He had managed to get a doctor for her on Monday but there was nothing he could do, and he had not come again. The daily maid had not turned up, and the scientist was now doing everything for his sick mother.

She opened her eyes for the first time in a quarter of an hour. "John," she said. "This is what they said would happen, isn't it?"

"I think so, Mum," he said gently. "It's going to happen to me, too."

"Did Dr. Hamilton say that was what it was? I can't remember."

"That's what he told me, Mum. I don't think he'll be coming here again. He said he was getting it himself."

There was a long silence. "How long will it take me to die, John?"

"I don't know," he said. "It might be a week."

"How absurd," said the old lady. "Much too long."

She closed her eyes again. He took a basin to the bathroom, washed it out, and brought it back into the bedroom. She opened her eyes again. "Where is Ming?" she asked.

"I put him out in the garden," he said. "He seemed to want to go."

"I am so terribly sorry about him," she muttered. "He'll be so dreadfully lonely, without any of us here."

"He'll be all right, Mum," her son said, though without much confidence. "There'll be all the other dogs for him to play with."

She did not pursue the subject, but she said, "I'll be quite all right now, dear. You go on and do whatever you have to do."

178

He hesitated. "I think I ought to look in at the office," he said. "I'll be back before lunch. What would you like for lunch?"

She closed her eyes again. "Is there any milk?"

"There's a pint in the frig," he said. "I'll see if I can get some more. It's not too easy, though. There wasn't any yesterday."

"Ming ought to have a little," she said. "It's so good for him. There should be three tins of rabbit in the larder. Open one of those for his dinner, and put the rest in the frig. He's so fond of rabbit. Don't bother about lunch for me till you come back. If I'm feeling like it I might have a cup of cornflour."

"Sure you'll be all right if I go out?" he asked.

"Quite sure," she said. She held out her arms. "Give me a kiss before you go."

He kissed the limp old cheeks, and she lay back in bed, smiling at him.

He left the house and went down to the office. There was nobody there, but on his desk there was the daily report of radioactive infection. Attached to it was a note from his secretary. She said that she was feeling very unwell, and probably would not be coming to the office again. She thanked him for his kindness to her, congratulated him upon the motor race, and said how much she had enjoyed working for him.

He laid the note aside and took up the report. It said that in Melbourne about fifty per cent of the population appeared to be affected. Seven cases were reported from Hobart in Tasmania, and three from Christchurch in New Zealand. The report, probably the last that he would see, was much shorter than usual.

He walked through the empty offices, picking up a paper here and there and glancing at them. This phase of his life was coming to an end, with all the others. He did not stay very long, for the thought of his mother was heavy on him. He went out and made his way towards his home by one of the occasional, crowded trams still running in the streets. It had a driver, but no conductor; the days of paying fares were over. He spoke to the driver. The man said, "I'll go on driving this here bloody tram till I get sick, cock. Then I'll drive it to the Kew depot and go home. That's where I live, see? I been driving trams for thirty-seven years, rain or shine, and I'm not stopping now."

In Malvern he got off the tram and commenced his search for milk. He found it to be hopeless; what there was had been reserved for babies by the dairy. He went home empty-handed to his mother.

He entered the house and released the Pekinese from the garden, thinking that his mother would like to see him. He went upstairs to her bedroom, the dog hopping up the stairs before him.

In the bedroom he found his mother lying on her back with her eyes closed, the bed very neat and tidy. He moved a little closer and touched her hand, but she was dead. On the table by her side was a glass of water, a pencilled note, and one of the little red cartons, open, with the empty vial beside it. He had not known that she had that.

He picked up the note. It read,

My dear son,

It's quite absurd that I should spoil the last days of your life by hanging on to mine, since it is such a burden to me now. Don't bother about my funeral. Just close the door and leave me in my own bed, in my own room, with my own things all around me. I shall be quite all right

Do whatever you think best for little Ming. I am so very, very sorry for him, but I can do nothing.

I am so very glad you won your race.

My very dearest love.

Mother

A few tears trickled down his cheeks, but only a few. Mum had always been right, all his life, and now she was right again. He left the room and went down to the drawing room, thinking deeply. He was not yet ill himself, but now it could only be a matter of hours. The dog followed him; he sat down and took it on his lap, caressing the silky ears.

Presently he got up, put the little dog in the garden, and went out to the chemist at the corner. There was a girl behind the counter still, surprisingly; she gave him one of the red cartons. "Everybody's after these," she said smiling. "We're doing quite a lot of business in them."

He smiled back at her. "I like mine chocolate-coated."

"So do I," she said. "But I don't think they make them like that I'm going to take mine with an icecream soda."

He smiled again, and left her at the counter. He went back to the house, released the Pekinese from the garden, and began to prepare a dinner for him in the kitchen. He opened one of the tins of rabbit and warmed it a little in the oven, and mixed with it four capsules of Nembutal. Then he put it down before the little dog, who attacked it greedily, and made his basket comfortable for him before the stove.

He went out to the telephone in the hall and rang up the club, and booked a bedroom for a week. Then he went to his own room and began to pack a suitcase.

Half an hour later he came down to the kitchen; the Pekinese was in his basket, very drowsy. The scientist read the directions on the carton carefully and gave him the injection; he hardly felt the prick.

When he was satisfied that the little dog was dead he carried him upstairs in the basket and laid it on the floor beside his mother's bed.

Then he left the house.

Tuesday night was a disturbed night for the Holmes. The baby began crying at about two in the morning, and it cried almost incessantly till dawn. There was little sleep for the young father or mother. At about seven o'clock it vomited.

Outside it was raining and cold. They faced each other in the grey light, weary and unwell themselves. Mary said, "Peter—you don't think this is it, do you?"

"I don't know," he replied. "But I should think it might be. Everybody seems to be getting it."

She passed a hand across her brow, wearily. "I thought we'd be all right, out here in the country."

He did not know what he could say to comfort her, and so he said, "If I put the kettle on, would you like a cup of tea?"

She crossed to the cot again, and looked down at the baby; she was quiet for the moment. He said again, "What about a cup of tea?"

It would be good for him, she thought; he had been up for most of the night. She forced a smile. "That'd be lovely."

He went through to the kitchen to put the kettle on. She was feeling terrible, and now she wanted to be sick. It was being up all night, of course, and the worry over Jennifer. Peter was busy in the kitchen; she could go quietly to the bathroom without him knowing. She was often sick, but this time he might think it was something else, and get worried.

In the kitchen there was a stale smell, or seemed to be. Peter Holmes filled the kettle at the tap, and plugged it in; he switched on and saw with some relief the indicator light come on that showed the current was flowing. One of these days the juice would fail, and then they would be in real trouble.

The kitchen was intolerably stuffy; he threw open the window. He was hot, and then suddenly cold again, and then he knew that he was going to be sick. He went quietly to the bathroom, but the door was locked; Mary must be in there. No point in alarming her; he went out of the back door in the rain and vomited in a secluded comer behind the garage.

He stayed there for some time. When he came back he was white and shaken, but feeling more normal. The kettle was boiling and he made the tea, and put two cups on a tray, and took it to their bedroom. Mary was there, bending over the cot He said, "I've got the tea."

She did not turn, afraid her face might betray her. She said, "Oh, thanks. Pour it out; I'll be there in a minute." She did not feel that she could touch a cup of tea, but it would do him good.

He poured out the two cups and sat on the edge of the bed, sipping his; the hot liquid seemed to calm his stomach. He said presently, "Come on and have your tea, dear. It's getting cold."

She came a little reluctantly; perhaps she could manage it. She glanced at him, and his dressing gown was soaking wet with rain. She exclaimed, "Peter, you're all wet! Have you been outside?"

He glanced at his sleeve; he had forgotten that. "I had to go outside," he said.

"Whatever for?"

He could not keep up a dissimulation. "I've just been sick," he said. "I don't suppose it's anything."

"Oh, Peter! So have I."

They stared at each other in silence for a minute. Then she said dully, "It must be those meat pies we had for supper. Did you notice anything about them?" He shook his head. "Tasted all right to me. Besides, Jennifer didn't have any meat pie."

She said, "Peter. Do you think this is it?"

He took her hand. "It's what everybody else is getting," he said. "We wouldn't be immune."

"No," she said thoughtfully. "No. I suppose we wouldn't." She raised her eyes to his. "This is the end of it, is it? I mean, we just go on now getting sicker till we die?"

"I think that's the form," he said. He smiled at her. "I've never done it before, but they say that's what happens."

She left him and went through to the lounge; he hesitated for a moment and then followed her. He found her standing by the French window looking out into the garden that she loved so much, now grey and wintry and windswept. "I'm so sorry that we never got that garden seat," she said irrelevantly. "It would have been lovely just there, just beside that bit of wall."

"I could have a stab at getting one today," he said.

She turned to him. "Not if you're ill."

"I'll see how I'm feeling later on," he said. "Better to be doing something than sit still and think how miserable you are."

She smiled. "I'm feeling better now, I think. Could you eat any breakfast?"

"Well, I don't know," he said. "I don't know that I'm feeling quite so good as all that. What have you got?"

"We've got three pints of milk," she said. "Can we get any more?"

"I think so. I could take the car for it."

"What about some cornflakes, then? It says they're full of glucose on the packet. That's good for when you're being sick, isn't it?"

He nodded. "I think I'll have a shower," he said. "X might feel better after that."

He did so; when he came out to their bedroom she was in the kitchen busy with the breakfast. To his amazement he heard her singing, singing a cheerful little song that inquired who'd been polishing the sun. He stepped into the kitchen. "You sound cheerful," he remarked.

She came to him. "It's such a relief," she said, and now he saw she had been crying a little as she sang. He wiped her tears away, puzzled, as he held her in his arms.

"I've been so terribly worried," she sobbed. "But now it's going to be all right."

Nothing was further from right, he thought but he did not say so. "What's been worrying you?" he asked gently.

"People get this thing at different times," she said. "That's what they say. Some people can get it as much as a fortnight later than others. I might have got it first and had to leave you, or Jennifer, or you might have got it and left us alone. It's been such a nightmare...."

She raised her eyes to his, smiling through her tears. "But now we've got it all together, on the same day. Aren't we lucky?"

On the Friday Peter Holmes drove up to Melbourne in his little car, ostensibly to try and find a garden seat. He went quickly because he could not be away from home too long. He wanted to find John Osborne and to find him without delay; he tried the garage in the mews first, but that was locked; then he tried the C.S.I.R.O. offices. Finally he found him in his bedroom at the Pastoral Club; he was looking weak and ill.

Peter said, "John, I'm sorry to worry you. How are you feeling?"

"I've got it," said the scientist "I've had it two days. Haven't you?"

"That's what I wanted to see you about" Peter said. "Our doctor's dead, I think—at any rate, he isn't functioning. Look, John, Mary and J both started giving at both ends on Tuesday. She's pretty bad. But on Thursday, yesterday, I began picking up. I didn't tell her, but I'm feeling as fit as a flea now, and bloody hungry. I stopped at a cafe on the way up and had breakfast —bacon and fried eggs and all the trimmings, and I'm still hungry. I believe I'm getting well. Look—can that happen?"

The scientist shook his head. "Not permanently. You can recover for a bit, but then you get it again."

"How long is a bit?"

"You might get ten days. Then you'll get it again. I don't think there's a second recovery. Tell me, is Mary very bad?"

"She's not too good. I'll have to get back to her pretty soon."

"She's in bed, is she?"

Peter shook his head. "She came down to Falmouth with me this morning to buy moth balls."

"To buy what?"

"Moth balls. Napthalene—you know." He hesitated. "It's what she wanted," he said. "I left her putting all our clothes away to keep the moths out of them. She can do that in between the spasms, and she wants to do it" He reverted to the subject he had come for. "Look, John. I take it that I get a week or ten days' health, but there's no chance for me at all after that?"

"Not a hope, old boy," the scientist said. "Nobody survives this thing. It makes a clean sweep."

"Well, that's nice to know," said Peter. "No good hanging on to any illusions. Tell me, is there anything that I can do for you? I'll have to beat it back to Mary in a minute."

The scientist shook his head. "I'm just about through. I've got one or two things that I've got to do today, but then I think I'll finish it."

Peter knew he had responsibilities at home. "How's your mother?"

"She's dead," the scientist said briefly. "I'm living here now."

Peter nodded, but the thought of Mary filled his mind. "I'll have to go," he said. "Good luck old man."

The scientist smiled weakly. "Be seeing you," he replied.

When the naval officer had gone he got up from the bed and went along the passage. He returned half an hour later a good deal weaker, his lip curling with disgust at his vile body. Whatever he had to do must be done today; tomorrow he would be incapable.

He dressed carefully, and went downstairs. He looked into the garden room; there was a fire burning in the grate and his uncle sitting there alone, a glass of sherry by his side. He glanced up, and said, "Good morning, John. How did you sleep?"

The scientist said briefly, "Very badly. I'm getting pretty sick."

The old man raised his flushed, rubicund face in concern. "My dear boy, I'm sorry to hear that. Everybody seems to be sick now. Do you know, I had to go down to the kitchen and cook my breakfast for myself?

Imagine that, in a club like this!"

He had been living there for three days, since the death of the sister who had kept house for him at Macedon. "However, Collins the hall porter has come in now, and he's going to cook us some lunch. You'll be lunching here today?"

John Osborne knew that he would not be lunching anywhere. "I'm sorry I can't today, Uncle. I've got to go out."

"Oh, what a pity. I was hoping that you'd be here to help us out with the port. We're on the last bin now—I think about fifty bottles. It should just see us through."

"How are you feeling yourself, Uncle?"

"Never better, my boy, never better. I felt a little unsteady after dinner last night, but really, I think that was the Burgundy. I don't think Burgundy mixes very well with other wines. In France, in the old days, if you drank Burgundy you drank it from a pint pot or the French equivalent, and you drank nothing else all evening. But I came in here and had a quiet brandy and soda with a little ice in it, and by the time I went upstairs I was quite myself again. No, I had a very good night."

The scientist wondered how long the immunity from radioactive disease conferred by alcohol would last. So far as he was aware no research had yet been done upon that subject; here was an opportunity, but there was now nobody to do it. "I'm sorry I can't stay to lunch," he said. "But I'll see you tonight, perhaps."

"I shall be here, my boy, I shall be here. Tom Fotherington was in last night for dinner, and he said that he'd be coming in this morning, but he hasn't shown up. I hope he isn't ill."

John Osborne left the club and walked down the tree-lined street in a dream. The Ferrari was urgently in need of his attention and he must go there; after that he could relax. He passed the open door of a chemist's shop and hesitated for a moment; then he went in. The shop was unattended and deserted. In the middle of the floor was an open packing case full of the little red cartons, and a heap of these had been piled untidily upon the counter between the cough medicines and the lipsticks. He picked up one and put it in his pocket, and went on his way.

When he pushed back the sliding doors of the mews garage the Ferrari stood facing him in the middle of the floor, just as he had left it, ready for instant use. It had come through the Grand Prix unscratched, in bandbox condition. It was a glorious possession to him still, the more so since the race. He was now feeling too ill to drive it and he might never drive it again, but he felt that he would never be too ill to touch it and to handle it and work on it. He hung his jacket on a nail, and started.

First of all, the wheels must be jacked up and bricks arranged under the wishbones to bring the tires clear of the floor. The effort of manoeuvring the heavy jack and working it and carrying the bricks upset him again. There was no toilet in the garage but there was a dirty yard behind, littered with the black, oily junk of ancient and forgotten motorcars. He retired there and presently came back to work, weaker than ever now, more resolute to finish the job that day.

He finished jacking up the wheels before the next attack struck him. He opened a cock to drain the water from the cooling system, and then he had to go out to the yard again. Never mind, the work was easy now. He detached the terminals from the battery and greased the connections. Then he took out each of the six sparking plugs and filled the cylinders with oil, and screwed the plugs back finger tight.

He rested then against the car; she would be all right now. The spasm shook him, and again he had to go out to the yard. When he came back evening was drawing near and the light was fading. There was no more to be done to preserve the car he loved so well, but he stayed by it, reluctant to leave it and afraid that another spasm might strike him before he reached the club.

For the last time he would sit in the driving seat and handle the controls. His crash helmet and goggles were in the seat; he put the helmet on and snugged it down upon his head, and hung the goggles round his neck beneath his chin. Then he climbed into the seat and settled down behind the wheel.

It was comfortable there, far more so than the club would be. The wheel beneath his hands was comforting, the three small dials grouped around the huge rev counter were familiar friends. This car had won for him the race that was the climax of his life. Why trouble to go further?

He took the red carton from his pocket, took the tablets from the vial, and threw the carton on the ground. No point in going on; this was the way he'd like to have it.

He took the tablets in his mouth, and swallowed them with an effort.

Peter Holmes left the club and drove down to the hardware store in Elizabeth Street where he had bought the motor mower. It was untenanted and empty of people, but somebody had broken in a door and it had been partially looted in that anyone who wanted anything had just walked in to take it. It was dim inside, for all the electricity had been turned off at the main. The garden department was on the second floor; he climbed the stairs and found the garden seats he had remembered. He selected a fairly light one with a brightly coloured detachable cushion that he thought would please Mary and would also serve to pad the roof of his car. With great effort he dragged the seat down two flights of stairs to the pavement outside the shop, and went back for the cushion and some rope. He found a hank of clothesline on a counter. Outside he heaved the seat up on the roof of the Morris Minor and lashed it in place with many ties of rope attached to all parts of the car. Then he set off for home.

He was still ravenously hungry, and feeling very well. He had not told Mary anything of his recovery, and he did not intend to do so now; it would only upset her, confident as she now was that they were all going together. He stopped on the way home at the same cafe that he had breakfasted at, kept by a beery couple who appeared to be enjoying remarkably good health. They were serving hot roast beef for lunch; he had two platefuls of that and followed it up with a considerable portion of hot jam roly-poly. Then as an afterthought he got them to make him an enormous parcel of beef sandwiches; he could leave those in the boot of the car where Mary would not know about them, so that he could go out in the evening and have a quiet little meal unknown to her.

He got back to his little flat in the early afternoon; he left the garden seat on top of the car and went into the house. He found Mary lying on the bed, half dressed, with an eiderdown over her; the house seemed cold and damp. He sat down on the bed beside her. "How are you feeling now?" he asked.

"Awful," she said. "Peter, I'm so worried about Jennifer. I can't get her to take anything at all, and she's messing all the time." She added some details.

He crossed the room and looked at the baby in the cot. It looked thin and weak, as Mary did herself. It seemed to him that both were very ill.

She asked, "Peter—how are you feeling yourself?"

"Not too good," he said. "I was sick twice on the way up and once on the way down. As for the other end, I've just been running all the time."

She laid her hand upon his arm. "You oughtn't to have gone. . . ."

He smiled down at her. "I got you a garden seat, anyway."

Her face lightened a little. "You did? Where is it?"

"On the car," he said. "You lie down and keep warm. I'm going to light the fire and make the house cosy. After that I'll get the seat down off the car and you can see it."

"I can't lie down," she said wearily. "Jennifer needs changing."

"I'll see to that, first of all," he said. He led her gently to the bed. "Lie down and keep warm."

An hour later he had a blazing fire in their sitting room, and the garden seat was set up by the wall where she wanted it to be. She came to look at it from the French window, with the brightly coloured cushion on the seat. "It's lovely," she said. "It's exactly what we needed for that comer. It's going to be awfully nice to sit there, on a summer evening. . . ." The winter afternoon was drawing in, and a fine rain was falling. "Peter, now that I've seen it, would you bring the cushion in and put it in the verandah? Or, better, bring it in here till it's dry. I do want to keep it nice for the summer."

He did so, and they brought the baby's cot into the warmer room. She said, "Peter, do you want anything to eat? There's plenty of milk, if you could take that." He shook his head. "I couldn't eat a thing," he said. "How about you?"

She shook her head.

"If I mixed you a hot brandy and lemon?" he suggested. "Could you manage that?"

She thought for a moment. "I could try." She wrapped her dressing gown around her. "I'm so cold. . . "

The fire was roaring in the grate. "I'll go out and get some more wood," he said. "Then I'll get you a hot drink." He went out to the woodpile in the gathering darkness, and took the opportunity to open the boot of the car and eat three beef sandwiches. He came back presently to the living room with a basket of wood, and found her standing by the cot. "You've been so long," she said. "Whatever were you doing?"

187

"I had a bit of trouble," he told her. "Must be the meat pies again."

Her face softened. "Poor old Peter. We're all of us in trouble. . . ." She stooped over the cot, and stroked the baby's forehead; she lay inert now, too weak apparently to cry. "Peter, I believe she's dying. . . ."

He put his arm around her shoulder. "So am I," he said quietly, "and so are you. We've none of us got very long to go. I've got the kettle here. Let's have that drink."

He led her from the cot to the warmth of the huge fire that he had made. She sat down on the floor before it and he gave her the hot drink of brandy and water with a little lemon squeezed in it. She sat sipping it and staring into the fire, and it made her feel a little better. He mixed one for himself, and they sat in silence for a few minutes.

Presently she said, "Peter, why did all this happen to us? Was it because Russia and China started fighting each other?"

He nodded. "That's about the size of it," he said. "But there was more to it than that. America and England and Russia started bombing for destruction first. The whole thing started with Albania."

"But we didn't have anything to do with it all, did we—here in Australia?"

"We gave England moral support," he told her. "I don't think we had time to give her any other kind. The whole thing was over in a month."

"Couldn't anyone have stopped it?"

"I don't know. . . . Some kinds of silliness you just can't stop," he said. "I mean, if a couple of hundred million people all decide that their national honour requires them to drop cobalt bombs upon their neighbour, well, there's not much that you or I can do about it. The only possible hope would have been to educate them out of their silliness."

"But how could you have done that, Peter? I mean, they'd all left school."

"Newspapers," he said. "You could have done something with newspapers. We didn't do it. No nation did, because we were ill too silly. We liked our newspapers with pictures of beach girls and headlines about cases of indecent assault, and no government was wise enough to stop us having them that way. But something might have been done with newspapers, if we'd been wise enough."

She did not fully comprehend his reasoning. "I'm glad we haven't got newspapers now," she said. "It's been much nicer without them."

A spasm shook her, and he helped her to the bathroom. While she was in there he came back to the sitting room and stood looking at his baby. It was in a bad way, and there was nothing he could do to help it; he doubted now if it would live through the night. Mary was in a bad way, too, though not quite so bad as that. The only one of them who was healthy was himself, and that he must not show.

The thought of living on after Mary appalled him. He could not stay in the flat; in the few days that would be left to him he would have nowhere to go, nothing to do. The thought crossed his mind that if *Scorpion* were still in Williamstown he might go with Dwight Towers and have it at sea, the sea that had been his life's work. But why do that? He didn't want the extra time that some strange quirk of his metabolism had given to him. He wanted to stay with his fam-fly.

She called him from the bathroom, and he went to help her. He brought her back to the great fire that he had made; she was cold and trembling. He gave her another hot brandy and water, and covered her with the eiderdown around her shoulders. She sat holding the glass in both hands to still the tremors that were shaking her.

Presently she said, "Peter, how is Jennifer?"

He got up and crossed to the cot, and then came back to her. "She's quiet now," he said. "I think she's much the same."

"How are you, yourself?" she asked.

"Awful," he said. He stopped by her, and took her hand. "I think you're worse than I am," he told her, for she must know that. "I think I may be a day or so behind you, but not more. Perhaps that's because I'm physically stronger."

She nodded slowly. Then she said, "There's no hope at all, is there? For any of us?

He shook his head. "Nobody gets over this one, dear."

She said, "I don't believe I'll be able to get to the bathroom tomorrow. Peter dear, I think I'd like to have it tonight, and take Jennifer with me. Would you think that beastly?"

He kissed her. "I think it's sensible," he said. "I'll come too."

She said weakly, "You're not so ill as we are."

"I shall be tomorrow," he said. "It's no good going on."

She pressed his hand. "What do we do, Peter?"

He thought for a moment "I'll go and fill the hot-water bags and put them in the bed," he said. "Then you put on a clean nightie and go to bed and keep warm. I'll bring Jennifer in there. Then I'll shut up the house and bring you a hot drink, and we'll have it in bed, together, with the pill."

"Remember to turn off the electricity at the main," she said. "I mean, mice can chew through a cable and set the house on fire."

"I'll do that," he said.

She looked up at him with tears in her eyes. "Will you do what has to be done for Jennifer?"

He stroked her hair. "Don't worry," he said gently. "I'll do that."

He filled the hot-water bags and put them in the bed, tidying it and making it look fresh as he did so. Then he helped her into the bedroom. He went into the kitchen and put the kettle on for the last time, and while it boiled he read the directions on the three red cartons again very carefully.

He filled a thermos jug with the boiling water, and put it neatly on a tray with the two glasses, the brandy, and half a lemon, and took it into the bedroom. Then he wheeled the cot back and put it by the bedside. Mary was in bed looking clean and fresh; she sat up weakly as he wheeled the cot to her.

He said, "Shall I pick her up?" He thought that she might like to hold the baby for a little.

She shook her head. "She's too ill." She sat looking down at the child for a minute, and then lay back wearily. "I'd rather think about her like she was, when we were all well. Give her the thing, Peter, and let's get this over."

She was right, he thought; it was better to do things quickly and not agonize about them. He gave the baby the injection in the arm. Then he undressed himself and put on clean pyjamas, turned out all the lights in the flat except their bedside light, put up the fire screen in the sitting room, and lit a candle that they kept in case of a blackout of the electricity. He put that on the table by their bed and turned off the current at the main.

He got into bed with Mary, mixed the drinks, and took the tablets out of the red cartons. "I've had a lovely time since we got married," she said quietly. "Thank you for everything, Peter."

He drew her to him and kissed her. "I've had a grand time, too," he said. "Let's end on that."

They put the tablets in their mouths, and drank.

That evening Dwight Towers rang up Moira Davidson at Harkaway. He doubted when he dialled if he would get through, or if he did, whether there would be an answer from the other end. But the automatic telephone was still functioning, and Moira answered him almost at once.

"Say," he said, "I wasn't sure I'd get an answer. How are things with you, honey?"

"Bad," she said. "I think "Mummy and Daddy are just about through."

"And you?"

"I'm just about through, too, Dwight How are you?"

"I'd say I'm much the same," he said. "I rang to say good-bye for the time being, honey. We're taking *Scorpion* out tomorrow morning to sink her."

"You won't be coming back?" she asked.

"No, honey. We shan't be coming back. We've just got this last job to do, and then we've finished." He paused. "I called to say thank you for the last six months," he said. "It's meant a lot to me, having you near."

"It's meant a lot to me, too," she said. "Dwight, if I can make it, may I come and see you off?"

He hesitated for a moment. "Sure," he said. "We can't wait, though. The men are pretty weak right now, and they'll be weaker by tomorrow."

190

"What time are you leaving?"

"'We're casting off at eight o'clock," he said. "As soon as it's full daylight"

She said, "I'll be there."

He gave her messages for her father and her mother, and then rang off. She went through to their bedroom, where they were lying in their twin beds, both of them sicker than she was, and gave them the messages. She told them what she wanted to do. "I'll be back by dinnertime," she said.

Her mother said, "You must go and say good-bye to him, dearie. He's been such a good friend for you. But if we're not here when you come back, you must understand."

She sat down on her mother's bed. "As bad as that, Mummy?"

"I'm afraid so, dear. And Daddy's worse than me today. But we've got everything we need, in case it gets too bad."

From his bed her father said weakly, "Is it raining?"

"Not at the moment, Daddy."

"Would you go out and open the stockyard gate into the lane, Moira? All the other gates are open, but they must be able to get at the hay."

"I'll do that right away, Daddy. Is there anything else I can do?"

He closed his eyes. "Give Dwight my regards. I wish he'd been able to marry you."

"So do I," she said. "But he's the kind of man who doesn't switch so easily as that."

She went out into the night and opened the gate and checked that all the other gates in the stockyard were open; the beasts were nowhere to be seen. She went back into the house and told her father what she had done; he seemed relieved. There was nothing that they wanted; she kissed them both good night and went to bed herself, setting her little alarm clock for five o'clock in case she slept.

She slept very little. In the course of the night she visited the bathroom four times, and drank half a bottle of brandy, the only thing she seemed to be able to keep down. She got up when the alarm went off and had a hot shower, which refreshed her, and dressed in the red shirt and slacks that she had worn when she had met Dwight first of all, so many months ago. She made her face up with some care and put on an overcoat. Then she opened the door of her parents' room quietly and looked in, shading the light of an electric torch between her fingers. Her father seemed to be asleep, but her mother smiled at her from the bed; they, too, had been up and down most of the night. She went in quietly and kissed her mother, and then went, closing the door softly behind her.

She took a fresh bottle of brandy from the larder and went out to the car, and started it, and drove off on the road to Melbourne. Near Oakleigh she stopped on the deserted road in the first grey light of dawn, and took a swig out of the bottle, and went on.

She drove through the deserted city and out along the drab, industrial road to Williamstown. She came to the dockyard at about a quarter past seven; there was no guard at the open gates and she drove straight in to the quay, beside which lay the aircraft carrier. There was no sentry on the gangway, no officer of the day to challenge her. She walked into the ship trying to remember how she had gone when Dwight had showed her the submarine, and presently she ran into an American rating who directed her to the steel port in the ship's side from which the gangway led down to the submarine.

She stopped a man who was going down to the vessel. "If you see Captain Towers, would you ask him if he could come up and have a word with me?" she said.

"Sure, lady," he replied. "I'll tell him right away," and presently Dwight came in view, and came up the gangway to her.

He was looking very ill, she thought, as they all were. He took her hands regardless of the onlookers. "It was nice of you to come to say good-bye," he said. "How are things at home, honey?"

"Very bad," she said. "Daddy and Mummy will be finishing quite soon, and I think I shall, too. This is the end of it for all of us, today." She hesitated, and then said, "Dwight, I want to ask something."

"What's that, honey?"

"May I come with you, in the submarine?" She paused, and then she said, "I don't believe that I'll have anything at home to go back to. Daddy said I could just park the Customline in the street and leave it. He won't be using it again. May I come with you?" He stood silent for so long that she knew the answer would be no. "I've been asked the same thing by four men this morning," he said. "I've refused them all, because Uncle Sam wouldn't like it. I've run this vessel in the navy way right through, and I'm running her that way up till the end. I can't take you, honey. We'll each have to take this on our own."

"That's all right," she said dully. She looked up at him. "You've got your presents with you?"

"Sure," he said. "I've got those, thanks to you."

"Tell Sharon about me," she said. "We've nothing to conceal."

He touched her arm. "You're wearing the same outfit that you wore first time we met."

She smiled faintly. "Keep him occupied—don't give him time to think about things, or perhaps he'll start crying. Have I done my job right, Dwight?"

"Very right indeed," he said. He took her in his arms and kissed her, and she clung to him for a minute.

Then she freed herself. "Don't let's prolong the agony," she said. "We've said everything there is to say. What time are you leaving?

192

"Very soon," he said. "We'll be casting off in about five minutes."

"What time will you be sinking her?" she asked.

He thought for a moment. "Thirty miles down the bay, and then twelve miles out. Forty-two sea miles. I shan't waste any time. Say two hours and ten minutes after we cast off from here."

She nodded slowly. "I'll be thinking of you." And then she said, "Go now, Dwight. Maybe I'll see you in Connecticut one day."

He drew her near to kiss her again, but she refused him. "No—go on now." In her mind she phrased the words, "Or I'll be the one that starts crying." He nodded slowly, and said, "Thanks for everything," and then he turned and went away down the gangway to the submarine.

There were two or three women now standing at the head of the gangway with her. There were apparently no men aboard the carrier to run the gangway in. She watched as Dwight appeared on the bridge from the interior of the submarine and took the con, watched as the lower end of the gangway was released, as the lines were singled up. She saw the stem line and the spring cast off, watched as Dwight spoke into the voice pipe, watched the water swirl beneath her stem as the propellers ran slow ahead and the stem swung out. It began to rain a little from the grey sky. The bow line and spring were cast off and men coiled them down and slammed the steel hatch of the superstructure shut as the submarine went slow astern in a great arc away from the carrier. Then they all vanished down below, and only Dwight with one other was left on the bridge. He lifted his hand in salutation to her, and she lifted hers to him, her eyes blurred with tears, and the low hull of the vessel swung away around Point Gellibrand and vanished in the murk.

With the other women, she turned away from the steel port. "There's nothing now to go on living for," she said.

One of the women replied, "Well, you won't have to, ducks."

She smiled faintly, and glanced at her watch. It showed three minutes past eight. At about ten minutes past ten Dwight would be going home, home to the Connecticut village that he loved so well. There was nothing now for her in her own home; if she went back to Harkaway she would find nothing there now but the cattle and sad memories. She could not go with Dwight because of naval discipline, and that she understood. Yet she could be very near him when he started home, only about twelve miles away. If then she turned up by his side with a grin on her face, perhaps he would take her with him, and she could see Helen hopping round upon the Pogo stick.

She hurried out through the dim, echoing caverns of the dead aircraft carrier, and found the gangway, and went down on to the quay to her big car. There was plenty of petrol in the tank; she had filled it up from the cans hidden behind the hay the previous day. She got into it and opened her bag; the red carton was still there. She uncorked the bottle of brandy and took a long swallow of the neat liquor; it was good, that stuff, because she hadn't had to go since she left home. Then she started the car and swung it round upon the quay, and drove out of the dockyard, and on through minor roads and suburbs till she found the highway to Geelong.

Once on the highway she trod on it, and went flying down the unobstructed road at seventy miles an hour in the direction of Geelong, a bareheaded, white-faced girl in a bright crimson costume, slightly intoxicated, driving a big car at speed. She passed Laverton with its big aerodrome, Werribee with its experimental farm, and went flying southwards down the deserted road. Somewhere before Corio a spasm shook her suddenly, so that she had to stop and retire into the bushes; she came out a quarter of an hour later, white as a sheet, and took a long drink of her brandy.

Then she went on, fast as ever. She passed the grammar school away on the left and came to shabby, industrial Corio, and so to Geelong, dominated by its cathedral. In the great tower the bells were ringing for some service. She slowed a little to pass through the city but there was nothing on the road except deserted cars at the roadside. She only saw three people, all of them men.

Out of Geelong upon the fourteen miles of road to Barwon Heads and to the sea. As she passed the flooded common she felt her strength was leaving her, but there was now not far to go. A quarter of an hour later she swung right into the great avenue of macrocarpa that was the main street of the little town. At the end she turned left away from the golf links and the little house where so many happy hours of childhood had been spent, knowing now that she would never see it again. She turned right at the bridge at about twenty minutes to ten and passed through the empty caravan park up on to the headland. The sea lay before her, grey and rough with great rollers coming in from the south on to the rocky beach below.

The ocean was empty and grey beneath the overcast, but away to the east there was a break in the clouds and a shaft of light striking down on to the waters. She parked across the road in full view of the sea, got out of her car, took another drink from her bottle, and scanned the horizon for the submarine. Then as she turned towards the lighthouse on Point Lonsdale and the entrance to Port Phillip Bay she saw the low grey shape appear, barely five miles away and heading southwards from the Heads.

She could not see detail but she knew that Dwight was there upon the bridge, taking his ship out on her last cruise. She knew he could not see her and he could not know that she was watching, but she waved to him. Then she got back into the car because the wind was raw and chilly from south polar regions, and she was feeling very ill, and she could watch him just as well when sitting down in shelter.

She sat there dumbly watching as the low grey shape went forward to the mist on the horizon, holding the bottle on her knee. This was the end of it, the very, very end.

Presently she could see the submarine no longer; it had vanished in the mist. She looked at her little wrist watch; it showed one minute past ten.

194

Her childhood religion came back to her in those last minutes; one ought to do something about that, she thought. A little alcoholically she murmured the Lord's Prayer.

Then she took out the red carton from her bag, and opened the vial, and held the tablets in her hand. Another spasm shook her, and she smiled faintly. "Foxed you this time," she said.

She took the cork out of the bottle. It was ten past ten. She said earnestly, "Dwight, if you're on your way already, wait for me."

Then she put the tablets in her mouth and swallowed them down with a mouthful of brandy, sitting behind the wheel of her big car.

Made in the USA
Monee, IL
10 January 2020

20117102R00107

# Battle of Wills

er Wills

Items should be returned on or before the last date shown below. Items not already requested by other borrowers may be renewed in person, in writing or by telephone. To renew, please quote the number on the barcode label. To renew online a PIN is required.
This can be requested at your local library.
Renew online @ www.dublincitypubliclibraries.ie
Fines charged for overdue items will include postage incurred in recovery. Damage to or loss of items will be charged to the borrower.

First published in 2012 by
Mentor Books Ltd.
43 Furze Road,
Sandyford Industrial Estate,
Dublin 18.
Republic of Ireland

Tel. +353 1 295 2112/3     Fax. +353 1 295 2114
e-mail: admin@mentorbooks.ie
www.mentorbooks.ie

A catalogue record for this book is available
from the British Library

ISBN: 978-1-906623-89-0

Cover by Mentor Books
Editing, typesetting and design by Mentor Books

Printed in Ireland by Colorman Ltd.

# Contents

# Terminology

**Testator**: The person who has made a will.

**Witnesses**: A lawful will must be signed by two witnesses who are not beneficiaries of the will.

**Executor/Executrix**: The man or woman named in the will whose duty it is to carry out the wishes expressed in the will.

**Estate**: The estimate value of the assets belonging to the deceased. This includes property and possessions and is not to be taken as a cash amount.

**Probate**: The process by which the assets are identified and valued and the executors given power by the courts to distribute the assets belonging to the deceased.

**Beneficiaries**: Those who benefit from a will.

**Codicil**: An amendment to a will which is written after the original will has been executed. If the codicil is properly executed and witnessed, it overrides the original will as it is taken to be the person's final wishes.

**Caveat**: A legal move by which someone who is dissatisfied with the terms of the will or the activities of the executors can inform the courts that they wish to make a legal challenge. By 'entering a caveat' they can prevent the distribution of the estate until a judge has ruled on the issues involved

**Intestate**: Someone who has not left a will dies 'intestate'.

*The author has no legal training and this book is not to be taken as a guide to making or contesting a will.*

# Acknowledgements

To Danny McCarthy of Mentor Books for his continued support and editor Una Whelan for all her help and support.

To the many reporters, whose by-lines are in most cases now forgotten (and in some cases were never there in the first place), but all are acknowledged for their diligence and flair in covering various legal cases mentioned in this book.

To the staff of the Probate Office for their courtesy.

Most of the sources in various chapters are acknowledged but Anne Kelly's fine paper 'The Lane bequest: A British-Irish cultural conflict revisited' published in the *Journal of the History of Collections* was of tremendous help in writing the chapter 'Hail and Farewell' and is well worth mentioning again.

Liam Collins
September 2012

# Introduction

'What survives of us is love,' concluded the poet Philip Larkin. Many families, however, end up with less romantic concerns when it comes to the last will and testament of a loved one.

The will is the story of a person's life – in more than just pure financial terms. How they decide to divide their worldly possessions often tells its own tale and sometimes reveals the tragic divisions that befall families and friends.

It often casts a light on how some people, especially those with money, find an almost obsessive pleasure in agonising during their lifetime about what will happen to their worldly wealth once they are gone. As if it makes any difference – to them, at any rate!

It matters to some people, however, those who are lucky to get what they want from 'the Will' and those who are disappointed and decide to do something about it.

Families often find the last will and testament of a 'loved one' worth fighting over, especially if there is the accumulated loot of a lifetime in business, or a valuable portfolio of property, paintings or other possessions, at stake. In the case of Hugh Lane, it wasn't a family, but two nations, Ireland and Britain, that battled for decades over the disputed ownership of the fabulous art collection he left behind.

Wills have a way of haunting the living, bringing happiness to some, disappointment to others and, sometimes, discord to family and friends of the deceased. This may even be the outcome intended by some people when drawing up their will: a lonely and, it seems, insecure businessman and art collector wrote 31 different wills in the last years of his life; a wealthy aristocrat used his final will as a weapon to punish his son, while an airline tycoon showed his sensitive side by remembering a wronged ex-girlfriend with a fortune that would leave her comfortable for life.

These are among the stories that reach from the dark past to influence the future.

Making a last will and testament is often regarded as the final flourish of one's life, but actually a person's will is not about the dying or the dead – it is about the living, which is why it is such a crucial and, at times, cruel, document.

For most people a will is about disposing of their assets in a fair and honourable way. For the elderly, it is about dividing their accumulated wealth among their children; for younger people it can be a way of assigning guardianship of young children to the person they think is best prepared for that responsibility, should tragedy suddenly strike them down. Usually it is all a rather straightforward business.

It wasn't always like that, however. Former taoiseach Charles Haughey was known for many things in his lifetime and is remembered now mostly for the bad. In conversation with the journalist Cathal O'Shannon before he died, however, he recalled 'doing the State' some service with initiatives like free travel for old people, the tax incentive for artists and writers, the International Financial Services Centre and turning the rundown UCD building in Merrion Street into an office fit for a taoiseach. As far as he was personally concerned, though, the most important piece of legislation he introduced was the 1965 Succession Act, which was passed while he was Minister for Justice.

Prior to this, a person could leave whatever they had to whomever they liked. Which seemed fair enough up to a point. But it meant a husband could effectively leave his wife destitute and homeless by not including her in his will.

In those days the man owned virtually everything and the wife, who possibly stayed at home looking after a family, or even ran a business or a farm, could be disinherited at the stroke of a pen.

Haughey told Cathal O'Shannon that the Catholic hierarchy had 'begged' him to change the law. Old farmers were dying and leaving their money and sometimes their farms to have Masses said for their immortal souls, without making any provision for their living wives and children.

Now when a person making the will is married their options are limited by the 1965 legislation, which ensures that half a spouse's estate goes by law to the remaining spouse if there are no children, and one-third if there are. It also makes provision that all the children must be treated equally in a will, unless expressly stated otherwise.

Section 117 states that parents should provide for their children 'as a just and prudent parent would'. This has been interpreted to mean that, unless there is a good reason, a parent can not disinherit or significantly disfavour a child in the division of an estate.

When Sir John Prichard-Jones the wealthy owner of Allenswood House near Lucan in County Dublin was making his will, which originally was worth €19,721,763, he left everything to his wife Helen. In the event that she died before him, the bulk of his estate was left to his daughter Susan, and in the event that she too had died, to his nephew Richard Prichard-Jones.

Inserted in the will, dated 13 January 2006, was a special clause which stated: 'I declare that I have made proper provision for my son David in accordance with my means during the course of my life, and have discharged any moral duty I may be deemed to owe my said son pursuant to the provisions of Section 117 of the Succession Act, 1965.'

In other words, David Prichard-Jones was disinherited.

Sir John also invoked a clause, often stated in contentious wills, that if any party challenged the terms of the will they would be automatically entitled to nothing.

In a legal test in July 2012, Judge Roderick Murphy decided that an elderly County Kildare publican, Mrs Mary Boyle of The Square, Kildare, 'failed in her moral duty' when she left the family pub and a dwelling house to one of her sons, Jarlath, and nothing to her other son, Walter.

The judge decided that leaving everything to one son was contrary to Section 117 of the 1965 Succession Act and ruled that Walter Boyle was entitled to €315,000 to be funded from his brother Jarlath's share of their mother's estate.

Divorce has been a complicating factor when writing a will, particularly when multiple families are involved. Not only is the inheritance diluted, but how it is distributed among the children of two or more marriages can become a major issue.

In the case of the wealthy businessman Brian Rhatigan, this was complicated further by the fact that he had an aversion to paying tax, and much of his fortune, which it is believed ran into tens of millions, was held in complex offshore trusts which were not included in his will. Although he had a lover and two additional children, his wife Odilla, from whom he was not officially separated or divorced, believes the will had been structured in such a way as to deny her her rightful share of his estate.

So what then do we leave behind us? The accumulated value of what a person leaves behind in their last will and testament can often be a misleading guide to the life they led and in this respect the poet Philip Larkin is correct. People who have lived nondescript lives accumulating wealth can leave behind a fortune, while artists, writers and lovers of life often burn up whatever worldly wealth comes their way.

Wander through any cemetery or country churchyard and you will see everything from the ornamental crosses to the crooked stones that commemorate the dead. Some may come with a flourish of words, an apt quotation and the dates that mark the milestones of life and death. But often, within a generation or two, the lives thus commemorated have turned to dust, just like the corpse in the coffin beneath the soil.

Not so with a will. These documents, whether in the National Archives or the Probate Office, contain some record of how the deceased lived their lives. From the will it is often possible to piece together some important aspects of their lives and their interests.

Until recently the public also had access to the deceased's Schedule of Assets, an important source of information for historians which gave a valuation of major assets such as property, art and investments. But in a High Court direction issued by the President of the High Court Richard Johnson on 25 May 2009 this document can now only be inspected by direct beneficiaries of the will.

A will does not give any sort of complete guide to a person's life, but it may go some way towards giving a broad outline of their life story.

In the case of the famous New York Tammany Hall chief, 'Boss' Croker, the documents evoke the actual drama of his passing and the looming family dispute over his fortune, which lasted for nearly a decade and was fought in Dublin, New York and Florida. Even the slightly soiled envelope containing the legal papers breathes life into the story that caused a world sensation in its day.

Then there is the thorny subject of what happens when someone kills their partner, wife or husband. Although under Irish law the killer is not meant to benefit from the estate, there is a lack of clarity in Irish legislation in this area which hasn't gone unnoticed:

'There should be legislation in place which prescribes the destination of co-owned property in the event of the unlawful killing of one of the co-owners by another co-owner,' said Judge Mary Laffoy in her summation of the case of Eamonn Lillis who killed his wife Celine Cawley.

Similarly, the brother and sister of murdered publican Tom Nevin are continuing a long-running legal action to prevent the entire inheritance from Jack White's pub near Brittas Bay, County Wicklow, going to his widow, Catherine Nevin the woman convicted of his murder.

Double killer John Gallagher spent 12 years in the Central Mental Hospital in Dundrum for the murder of his girlfriend and her mother before absconding in 2000. After 12 years on the run, he returned to the facility in 2012 and has since been released. Some family members believe his move is linked to the fortune left by his father, a wealthy salvage and scrap dealer, Josie Gallagher, in Lifford, County Donegal. Gallagher gave himself up after letters of administration in his father's estate were granted by the Probate Office to a member of the deeply divided family. Now that he is no longer a fugitive from justice he stands to inherit part of his father's estate.

And so these stories tell tales of discord and strife, of human tragedy and weakness, of greed and disappointment and, occasionally, of redemption.

The last will and testament is as one lawyer put it, something that 'reaches from beyond the grave' to touch those who are left behind . . . and not always for the best.

# Chapter 1

## *A Golden Promise*

---

She had noticed for several months now that there was something different about her husband, Brian. After 30 years of marriage you get to sense such things and she was a shrewd judge of character.

Ever since he had taken on a young and rather beautiful personal trainer her husband, Brian Rhatigan, seemed to have a lot of meetings that lasted well into the night.

Up to then he had a predictable routine. He often worked late into the evening, but he would always come home, have his dinner in the family mansion near Foxrock, County Dublin and then sit down to watch the 9 o'clock news. It was his ritual and his wife, Odilla, was comfortable with it.

But lately he was staying out much later and when he did come home he wasn't in the mood to eat. He would tell Odilla he had taken some associates to dinner, or he had grabbed something on the way home and sat in the Bentley eating his takeaway.

She asked him a couple of times if he was having an affair. He laughed and denied it.

But when he didn't come home on St Valentine's night she started going through his pockets and found a sheaf of receipts, most of them from expensive restaurants around Dublin, the kind of places he always shunned when she asked to be taken out for dinner.

At that moment Odilla Rhatigan knew that while she was roaming around their Foxrock mansion waiting for Brian to come home her husband was dining at a 'table for two' with his lover and personal trainer Rachel Kiely.

Life as they knew it was about to change for ever.

❧ • ☙

It was a standing joke between the multimillionaire property developer Brian Rhatigan and his solicitor Sharon Scally that the only asset he personally owned was a stylish gold watch and a set of golf clubs.

On 15 February 2005 Rhatigan and the financial controller of one of his myriad companies, Paddy O'Sullivan, arrived at the offices of Amorys solicitors in Sandyford, County Dublin to discuss drawing up a new will. Rhatigan had drawn up an earlier will, supposedly dated 21 November 1989, but that was about to be overtaken and was subsequently destroyed.

But then, so had the life he had once led.

In a couple of years his life had changed radically and dramatically. His wife and the mother of their three grown-up children, Odilla, had thrown him out of the house after she discovered he was having an affair. He had moved into a luxurious new mansion with his new partner, Rachel Kiely and by now they had one infant child and another on the way.

Tragically, his 20-year-old son, who bore his name, had, in the meantime, committed suicide.

Along the leafy lanes of Foxrock where the Rhatigans had once been one of the village's best-known couples, old friends could only watch in wonder at the sudden and dramatic transformation of their lives.

But there was another and altogether more practical reason for Brian Rhatigan's desire to 'set his house in order'.

The developer and builder, who had played rugby into his forties and was a dynamic figure in Dublin's business circles, was now in an advanced stage of motor neurone disease, a debilitating illness that simply shuts the body down, bit by bit, relentlessly attacking and destroying the nervous system. And with each new challenge the quality of his life deteriorated.

Although he was fighting it every step of the way, spending long nights on the computer investigating new methods of treating the disease and travelling to China and other far-flung destinations in search of alternative therapies that would slow down the debilitating effects of the illness, Brian Rhatigan wasn't stupid. He knew that, bar a miracle, he was fighting a losing battle for his life.

By the time he arrived in the offices of Amorys solicitors that February morning he had already lost the power of speech and was communicating through an appliance called a DynaWrite. But as he and Sharon Scally knew each other very well from conducting business together over the years he also used signs like nods and 'thumbs up' to indicate whether he agreed or disagreed with suggestions.

'I had every reason to think that Mr Rhatigan was thinking straight and thinking true,' said Ms Scally later.

When they sat down at the desk, solicitor Sharon Scally, like the good lawyer she was, told him if he wished to make a will they had to discuss his assets. Rhatigan looked at her across the desk and pointed to the gold watch on his wrist. She got it, it was the joke between them, but it was also a code word for his solicitor to stop asking questions.

During their business relationship, which had lasted for almost 30 years, whenever she asked him to set out on paper what he owned, he pointed to the watch and told her: 'I never owned any asset either legally or beneficially apart from a small number of personal items, including a gold Audemars Piguet watch and a set of golf clubs.'

Now the solicitor, whose task it was to draw up his last will and testament, was being placed in a very difficult position.

As the meeting proceeded they talked about a couple of properties known as the Kildare Units, which were a cluster of industrial buildings he owned near Celbridge, a number of life policies and a certain amount of cash that was due to him, tragically, from the estate of his 20-year-old son Brian, who had killed himself.

'There won't be very much,' said Paddy O'Sullivan. Brian Rhatigan nodded in agreement.

By 'very much' he meant that it would not seem a lot for the 'wheeler-dealer' who had been among Dublin's best-known businessmen for nearly 40 years and, among other things, owned an entire block called Plaza 4 in the Dublin financial district, the IFSC.

Scally could immediately see the problem that was going to arise. Brian Rhatigan was one of the biggest property developers in Ireland for many years, although he was not very well known outside his own circle, staying away from the social scene and avoiding the glare of the media. His wife Odilla, from whom he had never formally separated, and his family had the 'expectation', as a judge would later put it, 'that there was going to be a very substantial amount of money' in the will.

To solve the conundrum it would be necessary to send for Mr Charles Haccius, a barrister and tax expert who specialised in offshore trusts, particularly those based in Cyprus. Perhaps he could unravel the tangled web of mysterious and highly secret offshore trusts in Guernsey, the Isle of Man and Cyprus where it is believed Brian Rhatigan's treasure was buried.

And none was more mysterious than the aptly named 'Golden Promise Trust'.

❧ • ❧

Brian Rhatigan was born in County Kildare on 7 January 1945. He was a promising rugby player with Old Belvedere, joining the club as a young man and playing on the senior team in the early part of his career. He was a 'nice guy' according to club mates and after the first flush of youth passed he never lost his enthusiasm for the game. He played prop forward on the junior teams well into his forties and was well known around the club which had boasted such famous internationals as Tony O'Reilly.

A few years after leaving school he and his brother Tony (Anthony), who was two years younger, decided to go into house-building together. With his earnings he pursued another lifelong interest, car rallying, and was known to be a competitive and dashing figure around Dublin at the time. A poignant photograph of himself and his son Brian with their 1963 Mercedes Benz 220SE captures the family bond that held them together.

He first met promising young model Odilla, who was two years younger than him, when she was 17, and five years later, in 1969, they were married. By then he was already involved in a development that would make his name, and his fortune.

Brian Rhatigan started the building company Rhatigan Holdings with Tony and two friends, Max and Noel McMullan of the Maxol oil-importing family. They had good business credentials and, it was later said, Brian Rhatigan also had the proper political connections in Fianna Fáil as well. Their opportunity came from an unlikely source.

Castletown House in Celbridge, County Kildare, probably the most magnificent Palladian mansion in Ireland, had by the sixties fallen on hard times. Home of the famous 'Speaker' Connolly in the eighteenth century, it had eventually passed through the generations to the Connolly-Carew family who virtually abandoned the vast mansion while using the estate for their extensive equestrian business.

It was bought in 1965 by a British property developer called Major Willson who sold off the contents at auction the following year and decided to break up the estate. The youthful Brian Rhatigan masterminded the purchase of several hundred acres of parkland on the outskirts of the estate for a housing development. At the time, houses in established suburbs of Dublin like Mount Merrion on the south side and Malahide on the north side were too expensive and Castletown was the ideal place for ambitious young executives who could drive in and out of the city in their company cars on relatively empty roads.

Rhatigan may not even have needed his political connections to obtain the planning permission that would be unthinkable today. The Rhatigan company, Castletown Homes began building what over the next few years would turn into 500 houses in various housing estates in the grounds of the mansion.

Luckily for Ireland's Georgian heritage, the aristocratic Desmond Guinness who lived at nearby Leixlip Castle called to look at Castletown one day and found the main door open to the elements and the house sadly dilapidated.

Concerned about the future of the great house he managed to buy the mansion and 120 acres before further destruction ruined it completely.

Through another company called Janus Holdings, the Rhatigan/McMullan consortium held on to several hundred acres of land to the rear of the house. In a complex deal which involved handing over 130 acres of the estate to Kildare County Council, they got permission to build a technology park on a 98-acre site to the rear of Castletown House. However, the planning permission was overturned after objections by An Taisce and Rhatigan was embroiled in various planning rows in the years that followed. But by the time he had finished Castletown Brian Rhatigan was a significant and wealthy Dublin developer.

He and his bride Odilla built a mansion on a private avenue on Brennanstown Road which, although officially called Cabinteely, is much closer to leafy Foxrock village in south County Dublin. Still very much in love, they called their new mansion 'Bri-Odi' – a combination of their first names – and Brian liked the name so much that he called one of his many development companies Bri Odi Holdings Ltd.

The money he made enabled him and Odilla to have what, on the surface at least, looked like the idyllic life of a prosperous Foxrock business couple. They had three children, Odilla, David and Brian Jnr, known in the family as 'Budsy'.

As well as having an insatiable thirst for business he continued to pursue his interest in sport, playing rugby and indulging his passion for motor rallying and skiing.

Rhatigan liked to buy sites cheap and wait for the market to lift, or for a blue chip client to come along with a guaranteed profit. He bought a site on the seafront in Dun Laoghaire for £60,000 in 1972 and waited until the early 1990s for what Frank McDonald in his book *The Destruction of Dublin* said was 'a good fairy to make their dreams come true'.

The 'good fairy' in this case was the State fisheries board BIM, which decided to decentralise and move all of five miles from Dublin city centre to Dun Laoghaire. The 'politically well-connected' Brian Rhatigan, it is said, prevailed on the then Minister for Fisheries Brian Lenihan Snr to avail of his offer of a seafront site – netting a profit running into millions.

Rhatigan was so successful in those heady days of development that he attracted the attention of the controversial British property company Slater Walker, who raised £5 million to go into a joint venture with him in a series of property developments around Dublin. It didn't end well, but it was the British rather than Rhatigan who lost out on the deal.

He also bought the Scotch House, a pub on the Dublin quays and a favourite watering hole of Myles na gCopaleen, demolishing it and replacing it with what Frank McDonald calls 'a hideous mock Georgian office, replete with aluminium sash windows and multi-level Mansard roof'. Brian Rhatigan wasn't into the aesthetics of architecture; he was consumed with fitting as much as he could squeeze into the space he owned and maximising his rent roll and his profits.

Despite the ups and downs of the property market, Rhatigan survived and prospered. He made money in the good times and, unlike those who tried to follow in his footsteps, he never over-extended himself. He had enough to keep ticking over during the bad times and, when the boom returned, he had development sites 'bought on the cheap' ready to roll.

Yet there were financial pressures. Odilla was asked 'to pledge' the family home in 1997 when Rhatigan decided to invest in a block of the new IFSC, known as Plaza 4 in the Custom House Plaza scheme. It was a gamble because he didn't have a tenant, but it was a speculative investment that would prove highly profitable when foreign banks took leases in the building, which was later sold at a considerable profit.

For most of their 30 years of marriage he and Odilla seemed to be happy. They kept to the 'Foxrock set', playing tennis, dining occasionally with friends but keeping far from the limelight. Apart from the secluded mansion and the Bentley he didn't live an ostentatious life.

Then in 1998 Brian Rhatigan, perhaps needing a change, or possibly feeling that he was letting himself go to seed, decided he needed to be leaner and fitter. He no longer had the regime of rugby training so he decided to use some of his accumulated wealth to employ his own personal trainer and, as it turned out, the one he selected just happened to be young, fit and good looking.

'He started to change almost immediately,' Odilla would later claim. 'From a man who was home almost every night for his meal, suddenly it was always: "I'm meeting this architect", and he would disappear. Then I started finding receipts from restaurants.'

The most upsetting were the ones she found for 14 February after he rang to say that he had an urgent meeting and wouldn't be home that night. It was Valentine's night, after all. So she started searching his pockets and what she found indicated to Odilla that her husband was having an affair.

Only later did she discover that, instead of spending Valentine's night with her, he had wined and dined his new mistress, gym instructor Rachel Kiely who, at the age of 30, was 23 years younger than him.

Odilla challenged him three times about having an affair. Each time he denied that he had a lover. But by then she knew he was lying.

'You just know these things. My husband was married to his work, he didn't socialise, he didn't come home until nine in the evening and then all he wanted to do was have his meal and watch a bit of telly, the news and go to bed.

'He was never a party animal. From the age of 22 he didn't drink, he gave up smoking, he just hated going out when we were kids. Night clubs – he hated them . . . absolutely hated it.' Hers, she said, was 'a lonely life'.

She asked him to leave. Within days Brian Rhatigan and his mistress were sharing a flat in Sandymount, Dublin 4, and to add 'insult to injury' he went public with his new relationship, escorting Miss Kiely to various functions. They were even photographed together in the social columns of a well-known women's magazine, something he had previously avoided while with Odilla.

Brian Rhatigan later bought 'Chantilly', a millionaire's retreat in Rathmichael in the foothills of the Dublin Mountains. Approached by a long gravel driveway, the 'exquisite property' with two guest apartments came with grounds that incorporated 'walkways, terraces and arbours', while inside there was opulent living accommodation as well as a modern gym and a heated indoor swimming pool complex.

Rhatigan had it renovated to the highest standard for his lover and they moved into their luxurious new home in early December 1999, throwing a lavish Christmas party for all the friends who had sided with him or stayed neutral during his messy parting from his wife.

When they broke up Brian Rhatigan told Odilla that she would 'get half' of his estate when he died. But life was changing dramatically for Brian Rhatigan. In early 2001 he began to display symptoms of what would later be diagnosed as motor neurone disease.

Rachel was pregnant with their first child in February 2003 when tragedy struck two months later: his son and namesake Brian, took his own life.

Odilla said later that due to her husband's illness and her son's suicide she had not pursued either a legal separation, or a divorce. She had the family mansion in Foxrock and she was paid €1,800 a week in maintenance. She also had a holiday home in Spain, which she said she bought with an inheritance of her own, and while she was there in the summer the maintenance payments were made via an offshore trust.

Not everything went smoothly, however, and after Brian Rhatigan lost a lot of money on a property development in Paris her payments came to a halt for a time. Odilla Rhatigan demanded a meeting with her husband in her solicitor's office to discuss her financial situation.

Brian Rhatigan claimed he was a 'consultant' earning €30,000 a year through York Securities Ltd, a company which provided 'project management services' to the various companies and developments in which he had an interest. Her solicitor, John O'Connor, began to laugh. 'How can you pay your wife €70,000 a year and drive a Bentley?' he asked, witheringly.

On 6 April 2005 a second meeting took place to draw up a will for Brian Rhatigan. He was now so ill that it was decided the meeting would take place at the country estate he and Rachel Kiely shared in Rathmichael.

He had converted the two guest apartments which were in an enclosed yard beside the main house into a suite of offices and had moved his business there from Baggot Street to make it easier for him to conduct his affairs.

The meeting was again attended by his aide Paddy O'Sullivan and his solicitor Sharon Scally of Amorys. This time the well-known barrister and tax expert Mr Charles Haccius who had been a long-time confidant of Rhatigan was also present.

It had already been decided that Odilla would get what she was entitled to under the 1965 Succession Act, which was one-third of his estate and the house 'Bri-Odi'.

The first issue at the meeting, which went on for a considerable time, was the size of the estate that would be covered in the will 'and the potential disappointment on the part of family members if it was small'.

Sharon Scally had previously been told by Brian Rhatigan that he did not have 'any connection, on the face of it' to the Cyprus-based Golden Promise Trust. Charles Haccius emphasised the point, saying that Mr Rhatigan hadn't created the trust and was not a beneficiary of it. Haccius, who had once lived in Lucan, County Dublin but was now living outside Ireland, added that any legal proceedings to break the trust would have to be taken in Cyprus and it was 'unlikely' that the integrity or secrecy of the trust could be challenged because of Cypriot law. Rhatigan nodded in agreement.

The will, which had an estimated value of between €3 million and €3.5 million, included the Kildare Units which were to go to his surviving children, Odilla and David. There was also money and a number of life insurance policies held by Allied Irish Banks which would make up the rest of the estate.

They then came to what provisions would be made for Rachel Kiely. At the time, their infant daughter Sophie was four months old and Rachel was pregnant with their second child (a daughter, Isabelle, born in December 2005). It was decided that she would get €200,000 in cash. Brian Rhatigan also made it clear that she was to stay in 'Chantilly'.

At this point Sharon Scally pointed out that the house was owned by a company called Unit 33 Nominees Ltd, incorporated in the Isle of Man and beneficially owned by the Golden Promise Trust. So she asked, if Mr Rhatigan and Ms Kiely were 'tenants' of the house, rather than the owners, what would her rights be and how could she remain in the house after his death? Mr Haccius said he would 'look into it'.

Sharon Scally then asked if she was drawing up the will on the basis that 'Chantilly' was not to be part of it, and that she was not to concern herself that Sophie and soon-to-be-born Isabelle, were not being catered for in the will. Rhatigan, through his voice box, communicated that such was the case.

The draft will also included a bequest of €47,815 to each of his four grandchildren, Odilla, Brian and twins Matthew and Katie, the children of his daughter Odilla Gilson, which was the threshold for a legacy which would not carry any tax implications.

His brother and business partner, Tony, was left a sum of €13,000. His younger brother Francis, also prominent in the Dublin construction business as a long-time director of the Construction Industry Federation and a director of Ellier Developments, was left €13,000. His sisters Margaret and Una were each left bequests with an additional provision of €65,000 to be put towards the purchase of a house.

There was also a lengthy discussion about Mr Rhatigan's desire to leave €100,000 to the Third World charity, Goal, plus €30,000 to another charity.

The residue of the estate was then to be divided between Rachel Kiely and Brian Rhatigan's children, although what share each would get was not spelled out.

Mr Rhatigan decided finally that Sharon Scally and an old acquaintance, Dan O'Donoghue, would be his executors. The meeting broke up with a decision that Ms Scally would prepare a draft will along the lines discussed at the meeting which was then to be copied and sent to Brian Rhatigan and his financial advisor, Charles Haccius, for approval.

However, Sharon Scally, mindful of her duties to her client, took the will, in draft form, back to Brian Rhatigan five days later and when he approved it she sent it to Mr Haccius. Mr Rhatigan then went on a holiday to France for a number of weeks.

On 13 May 2005, the four of them assembled for another meeting to finalise the details of the will. It was held in Amorys' offices and went on for six hours, with a break for lunch.

Charles Haccius had drafted two clauses for inclusion in the will. The first was to give the 'trustees of the draft will' power to make a claim to a beneficial interest in the Rhatigan family home 'Bri-Odi' which was now occupied by Odilla Rhatigan. However Mr Rhatigan made it clear that the house should go to Odilla and this proposal would not be included in the will.

The second lengthy clause was to make provision for any 'windfall' that might arise for the estate from any of the trusts associated with Mr Rhatigan.

At the heart of Brian Rhatigan's finances was a series of offshore trusts. These included the Dolphin Trust established in Guernsey in 1984; the Golden Promise Trust set up in Cyprus in 1999 and the Doni Trust established in the Isle of Man in 2002. By their very nature offshore trusts are highly secretive and difficult to unravel, even for those who set them up. For tax reasons, once these trusts are established, power is vested in the trustees and the person who established the trust no longer has any legal say in how they are conducted, although after their death, it is up to the trustees to abide by a letter of wishes which the owner of the trust leaves with their legal and financial advisors. After a specified period after the death of the person who established the trust, the funds are distributed according to the letter of wishes.

At the end of the meeting everything was read out carefully and explained to Mr Rhatigan. As they went through the document they stopped at the various clauses asking him if he wished to change any of the provisions or make any further comments. Mr Rhatigan was apparently satisfied that everything was in order.

There was only one further complication. The golden rule of a will under the Succession Act is that it should be made by a person who is of 'sound disposing mind'. Normally it is presumed that the person making the will knows what they are doing, but in a case like Rhatigan's where someone is suffering from a serious, almost certainly terminal illness or from a stroke or any other serious ailment, the onus then shifts to the person making the will to prove that they are of 'sound mind' at the time it is executed.

It was time to send for Timothy Lynch, professor of neurology.

ॐ • ॐ

'The tragedy underlying this case is that the deceased who, on the evidence, was clearly a robust, congenial, generous man, who played rugby until he was forty and continued to participate in sports such as skiing and motor rallying, started displaying symptoms around 2001 which ultimately led to a diagnosis of motor neurone disease,' said Judge Mary Laffoy when she came to adjudicate on the last will and testament of Brian Rhatigan.

When his faculties first began to deteriorate and he noticed that there was something seriously wrong with his health Brian Rhatigan had, as another consultant put it, 'done the rounds'. He had seen several doctors and experts in Dublin, he had been to a consultant in London for a further opinion and then spent three weeks in the Mayo Clinic in the United States of America, where it was confirmed that he was suffering from an incurable condition, motor neurone disease.

He had then travelled to Shanghai, China, to consult at a clinic specialising in alternative medicine in the hope of finding a cure.

By the time he came back to Ireland he had been 'focused on it' looking up the Internet for information about the disease, seeking out medications that might slow it up and regularly questioned his consultant about 'antioxidant medication'.

When he was first referred to Professor Timothy Lynch by Dr Raymond Murphy he had also had 'ongoing discussions' about gene therapy and stem cell therapy treatments. Brian Rhatigan was a competitive man and he didn't want to die. He brought up the subject at every meeting, hoping that there was some breakthrough on the horizon that might save his life.

Now, five days after the meeting at which his last will and testament were drafted, Brian Rhatigan signed a letter which was faxed by his secretary Liz Scanlon to Professor Lynch, consultant neurologist at the Dublin Neurology Institute at the Mater Hospital and at Beaumont Hospital and professor of neurology at University College Dublin.

'I am about to sign my will and I shall be pleased if you will let me have a letter confirming that I am mentis compus [sic] so that I can file the same.'

The following morning Professor Lynch replied by fax. Headed 'To whom it may concern' it said that he had assessed Mr Rhatigan on 22 October 2004, 19 January 2005 and 20 April 2005.

Mr Rhatigan, he said, was suffering from a neurodegenerative condition. 'This has resulted in balance difficulty, Parkinsonism, progressive speech loss (he is mute at this time), swallowing difficulty, muscle wasting suggestive of motor neurone disease and, furthermore, some cognitive difficulties. The cognitive difficulties are characterised by frontal lobe executive dysfunction including slowness in thought process, some deficits in mental flexibility and sequential thinking. Mr Rhatigan's condition is called progressive supernuclear palsy/corticobasal degeneration and motor neurone disease. This is a very rare disorder and is caused by degeneration of specific regions of the brain and, less so, the spinal cord.

'In my opinion Mr Rhatigan is capable of making a will and testament. His neurodegenerative conditions predominately affects his motor, speech and swallowing and less so his mental and cognitive abilities.'

After she received the medical report Liz Scanlon rang Sharon Scally at Amorys and told her that Brian Rhatigan would call to her office that afternoon. When he arrived, Ms Scally read the draft will to Mr Rhatigan. They made only one change, apart from correcting a number of typographical errors: he wanted to take out the bequest to the unnamed charity. When the corrections were made the will was read by Ms Scally and another solicitor at Amorys, Ms Sheila O'Neill. Sharon Scally then left the room.

The will, which ran to 23 pages, was signed on 19 May 2005 in the presence of Ms O'Neill and the other witness, a trainee solicitor at the firm called Elaine Cahill.

Sharon Scally then came back into the room and just before they concluded their business she asked Brian Rhatigan if he had any burial wishes. He became upset at the questions, and left without answering it.

But the following day he sent her documents indicating that he owned two grave plots in Shanganagh Cemetery in south Dublin and wished to be buried beside his late son Brian.

It was the end of one saga, and the beginning of another.

When he died at the age of 61 on 7 February 2006, a little over six months after making his last will and testament, it was quite clear that as well as a lot of money in offshore trusts and other assets, Brian Rhatigan had left behind two deeply divided families.

He was also leaving behind a Revenue Commissioners investigation into his offshore activities, including a revelation in the Moriarty Tribunal that he had funds on deposit with College Trustees in the Channel Islands which placed them with Ansbacher in the Cayman Islands.

The day after his death the newspapers carried two death notices. One was from his wife Odilla Rhatigan and his children David and Odilla, the other, directly under it, was from Rachel Kiely and their two daughters Sophie and Isabelle. Both said he died 'at home after a long illness'.

In April 2008 Mr Dan O'Donoghue, co-executor of the will, died, leaving the sole responsibility of establishing probate with Sharon Scally.

In October 2008 the Inland Revenue Affidavit disclosed a net estate valued at €6,358,168 – however this included a sum of €3.3 million from the sale of 'Chantilly' Brian Rhatigan's love nest in Rathmichael, which his solicitor argued was not part of his will as it was not his property.

The matter was further complicated by a report compiled by the accountancy firm Deloitte which concluded that Mr Rhatigan's estate could be liable for €18 million arising from the Revenue Commissioners investigation into his offshore accounts and his involvement in the Ansbacher scheme.

Certainly Odilla Rhatigan was growing increasingly unhappy as Ms Scally moved towards completing probate on the will. She was particularly 'pained' that she was getting the minimum one-third share of the estate she was entitled to under law and not the half share she said she had been promised when she separated from her husband.

On 20 November 2008 a 'caveat' or warning that the will would be challenged, was entered in the Probate Office in Dublin by Odilla Rhatigan and her two surviving children, David and Odilla.

Sharon Scally lodged a Statement of Claim in the High Court in Dublin on 3 January 2009, seeking to overturn the caveat and have the will of Brian Rhatigan 'proved in solemn form of law as the last will and testament'.

On 15 January 2009 Odilla Rhatigan, as defendant, delivered a defence and counterclaim to those proceedings.

The two women have been locked in legal combat every since.

When the case Scally v Rhatigan was called in the High Court on Thursday, 7 October 2010, Sharon Scally was seeking a judgement to prove the will, which she had drawn up on behalf of Brian Rhatigan.

Odilla Rhatigan declared that after the breakdown of her marriage she had not pursued a judicial separation or divorce on the basis that her husband had promised her half of his estate. She argued that the will should be worth at least €6.3 million which was the value put on it by the Revenue Commissioners and not the €3.3 million value put on it by her husband's solicitor, Sharon Scally.

Odilla Rhattigan also said that after their verbal settlement agreement Brian Rhatigan had put 'significant assets' into settlements and trusts for the purpose of defeating her legal right to her share of the estate under the Succession Act of 1965. She also claimed that 'Chantilly' had been sold and the proceeds were held in trust for Rachel Kiely and her two children. And, she argued, solicitor Sharon Scally had 'a conflict of interest' in drawing up the will and also acting as sole executor, following the death of the joint executor Dan O'Donoghue.

As his daughter Odilla admitted, Brian Rhatigan throughout his lifetime was determined to pay the bare minimum of taxes liable to the Irish State. Like a lot of businessmen of his ilk he went to endless trouble to avoid paying tax, developing an obsession which led him to put money into an Ansbacher account and establish a variety of discretionary trusts in Guernsey, the Isle of Man and Cyprus.

But what Rhatigan and others like him didn't realise was that in their obsessive search for tax havens they were actually creating huge difficulty for their heirs.

Apart from the legal minefield the family were in, the people he claimed to have loved the most were now clearly in danger of being left with a tax bill of €18 million.

Perhaps the tangled web of Mr Rhatigan's business dealings is best illustrated by what happened to 'Chantilly' the home in Rathmichael, County Dublin, he shared with Rachel Kiely and their children during his lifetime.

The house was purchased originally in the name of a company called Unit 33 Nominees Ltd with the aid of a loan from the developers' favourite bank, Anglo Irish Bank.

On 10 March 2006 Golden Promise Holdings Ltd, a Cypriot registered company which was, apparently, a trustee of the Golden Promise Trust, applied to Doni Ltd, the trustee of the Doni Trust, for a loan of €2,757,000 and requested that €1,757,219, would be lodged to an account of Golden Promise Holdings Ltd at Anglo Irish Bank.

'It is a condition that in making this payment on our behalf in the sum of €1,757,219.30 to Anglo . . . that the bank will release its mortgage/charge over the house and premises known as 'Chantilly', Ballybride Road, Shankill, County Dublin which is owned by our subsidiary company, Unit 33 Nominees Ltd.'

By the time it came to be sold there was no mortgage on 'Chantilly' and it is believed that the €3.3 million sale price was paid to the original company which purchased the house, Unit 33 Nominees Ltd, part of the Golden Promise Trust.

But who got the money?

When it was put to her that the ultimate beneficiary of the €3.3 million was Brian Rhatigan's mistress Rachel Kiely, the solicitor and executor of the will Ms Scally said she could not say.

'The distinct impression I got from Ms Kiely's evidence during her cross-examination was that she is the beneficiary of the proceeds of the sale of 'Chantilly',' said Judge Mary Laffoy later.

When Sharon Scally discovered that Brian Rhatigan was the beneficial owner of the Doni Trust she included the €2,757,000 loan which was used to purchase 'Chantilly' as an asset in the Revenue Commissioners affidavit. This explains the bulk of the increase in the value of the estate from the €3.5 million to the

€6.3 million shown in that affidavit.

However, Ms Scally said that the loan may not be recoverable from the Golden Promise Trust.

'What is significant is that a lot more was going on in relation to assets associated with the deceased at the time than the mere drafting and execution of the will,' said Judge Laffoy. 'It is difficult to accept that the deceased was not the instigator of what was happening in relation to assets with which he was associated, but which, apparently, were not in his name and were not to be dealt with in his will.'

In Scally v Rhatigan the High Court judge Mary Laffoy was asked to determine three things:

1. Whether the will was executed in accordance with the formalities required by Section 78 of the Succession Act, 1965.
2. Whether the deceased knew and approved the contents of the will.
3. Whether, at the time of executing the will, the deceased was of sound disposing mind and had capacity to make a valid will.

'On the basis of the evidence, the deceased's business affairs were a very "tangled web" and I use that expression fully conscious of its provenance in Scott's 'Marmion' and its implications in that context,' said Judge Mary Laffoy. 'It is not possible and, in any event, it is unnecessary, to disentangle the labyrinthine network of offshore trusts, corporations, property developments and investments in which the deceased would appear to have had an involvement at this juncture.'

In her judgement delivered on 21 December 2010 the judge conceded that 'much more was going on behind the scenes' in relation to Mr Rhatigan's assets 'than was reflected in the will'.

Judge Laffoy also found that Brian Rhatigan's 'objective' was to limit his will to the Kildare Units, life policies, cash and what was coming to him from the estate of his son.

'It may well be that the deceased was deliberately limiting the assets which would pass on his death under the will so as to exclude the defendant [his wife

Odilla] as well as, perhaps, the Revenue Commissioners from recourse to other assets in respect of which he had power of disposition.

'The deceased also clearly recognised that he had a duty to make provision for Ms Kiely and the infants. It would appear that the deceased decided that such a provision would be made primarily out of assets other than the assets which were in his name and would pass under the will on his death.'

The judge decided that Brian Rhatigan had made calm and rational decisions about disposing of his assets and there was no evidence of 'insane delusion' or 'disorder of the mind' in the way he exercised his powers.

'It may be that the deceased was motivated by improper considerations,' said the judge but 'despite the severe physical disability' he was of sound mind when he made his will.

Judge Laffoy found that the will was made in accordance with the 1965 Succession Act and Brian Rhatigan knew and approved the will.

Following this judgement a second legal action was undertaken in which the terms of the will were challenged by Odilla Rhatigan on the basis that substantial assets had been 'hidden' and she was entitled to a half share of her late husband's estate, including money in offshore trusts established by her late husband.

Odilla Gilson, Mr Rhatigan's daughter, giving evidence, said that she knew nothing about her father's tax affairs, but she believed he would try to pay the least tax that was legally possible. She said her father had told her that she and her brother were beneficiaries of trusts he had created and he also told her he had created these trusts to safeguard his money and put it out of her mother's reach. She believed that was unfair to her mother, but admitted she didn't tell her as she didn't want to upset her.

Odilla Rhatigan Snr said she knew her husband had offshore trusts and had expected that she and her children would benefit from them 'like every other normal family who had trusts'.

A month after her husband died, Paddy O'Sullivan, her husband's 'right-hand man' came to her and asked her not to block the proceeds of the sale of the Kildare Units. She only agreed after he told her the money was going 'out of the country' and she would be able to avail of at least some of the proceeds.

Sharon Scally said that she knew nothing about Brian Rhatigan's offshore financial activities. 'I was not privy to discussions between Mr Rhatigan and the trustees of the Golden Promise Trust, so I have no idea what was in the Golden Promise Trust,' she said, denying that she had any 'conflict of interest' in drawing up Mr Rhatigan's will.

'I have racked my brain and reflected on this issue at length and I cannot see what information I could possibly have with regard to the function I exercised in relation to those companies. I have never worked for the Golden Promise Trust.

'If there were assets from outside that should have been brought in, they would swell the estate for everyone's benefit,' she said. She also said she was 'appalled' at the hostility shown to her by lawyers acting in the case.

'It has been aggressive and gratuitously hostile. I have been attacked at every conceivable opportunity . . . it has probably been my most stressful and distressing case in 35 years of practice.'

What was not taken into account in the probate documents, pointed out Judge Mary Laffoy, was the 'indebtedness' of the deceased to the Revenue Commissioners. 'As a consequence, the net value of the deceased to the Revenue Commissioners is unknown.'

To date nobody has yet been able to say just how much Brian Rhatigan did leave behind in the 'tangled web'.

And it isn't over yet.

Odilla Rhatigan's solicitor John O'Connor has since taken out letters of administration on the estate of Brian Rhatigan, which indicates that the widow is not yet ready to accept that her husband's offshore fortune is gone. What the Revenue Commissioners are doing to reclaim what could be €18 million in unpaid tax owed by Mr Rhatigan's estate is unknown at this time.

The 'tangled web' of Brian Rhatigan's financial affairs appears to be as long-running as his rugby career.

# Chapter 2

## *Celine's Will*

A little over six months after her daughter Georgia May was born on 24 November 1992, Celine Cawley sat down to do what any sensible 30-year-old mother should – she made her will.

The glamorous businesswoman had been a model, an aspiring film actress with a small part in a Bond movie, and had 'hung out' with the young tennis star John McEnroe.

Earlier in 1992, Celine had established a film company Toytown Films. Her husband, Eamonn Lillis, who had his own graphic design business, was a joint shareholder in the film company and her elder brother Christopher was also a director of the firm. But it was Celine's business and, in the years that followed, she would turn it into an enterprise generating more than €1 million in cash a year.

The daughter of a prominent Dublin solicitor, Celine (pronounced Saleen) was probably far more conscious the day she was making her will of what would happen to her daughter Georgia May should anything happen to herself and her husband, rather than the distribution of her wealth, which didn't amount to a lot at the time.

The document itself, drawn up in her father's law office in Hatch Street, Dublin and dated 7 June 1993, is a typical professionally drawn-up will, dispassionate in tone and containing no hint of the marital discord and terrible violence that would eventually afflict the Lillis family many years later.

The will was witnessed by her father James Cawley, and his daughter, Celine's younger sister, Susanna, who was also a solicitor practising in her father's firm and who lived in the family home, Coillrua, Baily, Howth, County Dublin.

The first page of it reads as follows:

> I hereby revoke all former Will and Testamentary Dispositions made by me at any time heretofore.
>
> I appoint my husband Eamonn Lillis to be my executor of this my will.
>
> 1.    I give, devise and bequeath all property, which I shall die seized or possessed of, to my husband Eamonn for his own use absolutely and I appoint him my Residuary Legatee.
>
> 2.    Should my husband predecease me or if he does not survive me by 30 days then the following provisions shall apply.
>
> (a)    I appoint Christopher Cawley of 1 Thormamby Grove, Howth, County Dublin and Susanna Cawley of Coillrua, Baily, Howth, County Dublin (hereinafter referred to as 'my Trustees') to be my executors and trustees and appoint them trustees for the purposes of the Settled Land Acts 1882 to 1890, the Conveyancing and Law of Property Acts 1881 to 1911, and Section 57 of the Succession Act, 1965.
>
> (b)    I appoint Christopher Cawley and Sorca Cawley, both of 1 Thormamby Grove, Howth, County Dublin, Guardians of my daughter Georgia May and any other children of my marriage.

Sorca Cawley was married to Celine's brother Christopher.

The rest of the will, which runs to five pages, goes on in the usual legal vein dealing with the rather mundane matter of distributing her assets.

And of course it would probably never have come into the public domain if Celine Cawley hadn't met a tragic and brutal end 15 years later.

By the time that happened Celine Cawley had moved to a trophy home, 'Rowan Hill' on Windgate Road in Howth, her baby daughter Georgia May was a 16-year-old teenager, and her husband Eamonn Lillis was having a passionate affair with a masseuse who worked in a beauty salon in the nearby village of Howth.

Celine Cawley was born on 19 June 1962 into a professional upper-class family. Her father, James Cawley, counted the newspaper magnate and rugby player Tony O'Reilly among his wide circle of friends. He was also involved professionally in the entertainment business and acted as a consultant to film companies investing in Ireland. Another client was the famous Barings Bank of London, which was owned by the Ravelstoke family who kept a home on Lambay Island off the north Dublin coast.

Celine's mother Brenda, was a stay-at-home housewife who looked after the family's then home at Ardcarrick in Portmarnock, where they lived in some splendour next door to the well-known television personality and businessman, Eamonn Andrews, best known as the presenter of the hit television series *This Is Your Life*. James Cawley also had a close relationship with the McEnroe family and some of the family stayed with the Cawleys at their Portmarnock home when the young John McEnroe was cutting a swathe through the stuffy Centre Court at Wimbledon.

Celine was the glamorous member of the family. She went to school in nearby Malahide before being sent to boarding school in Rathnew, County Wicklow. Young and beautiful she began her career in the world of modelling, doing work for well-known designers and photo shoots for magazines, including an edition of *Vogue*.

She got a small part in the 1985 James Bond film *A View to a Kill* with Roger Moore, whom her father had met through his business dealings. But fame in modelling and film was to prove fleeting for Celine. When the initial glamour faded, the clients and the parts dried up and she went to work in an advertising agency, where the lure of the big time was always just around the corner, the lunches were long and there was usually a party or opening to attend.

It was at one such event, the annual advertising awards week in Kinsale, County Cork that her future took what seemed to be a turn for the better.

☙ • ❧

Eamonn Lillis, the son of a captain in the Irish Army, who came from Wainsfort

Park in Terenure, south Dublin was born on 3 March 1957. After attending Terenure College and later University College Dublin, he trained as a graphic designer, although he would sometimes describe himself as an 'art director'. He had his own graphic design business called Powerhouse, operated with his partner from Glenageary in south Dublin.

In 1990 he went to the annual advertising awards 'bash' in Kinsale, at which the industry parties late into the night and makes a series of awards for the best advertisements of the year amid a great deal of backslapping and bonhomie. The Irish football manager Jack Charlton was that year's celebrity guest and in his honour there was an international soccer match arranged between the Irish advertising agencies and their foreign guests. Celine Cawley was one of the organisers, and Lillis got to know her as he badgered the committee for a place on the Irish team. They soon discovered that as well as advertising they had another shared interest – dogs, German Shepherds in particular.

Back in Dublin they dated and at the age of 29 Celine Cawley married the 34-year-old Eamonn Lillis in the Church of the Assumption in Howth, County Dublin in July 1991. They were a carefree couple, moving into their new home at Seaview Terrace, but determined to start a family as soon as possible. Their only daughter Georgia May was born on 24 November 1992.

Shortly before her marriage the advertising agency she worked for went bust and Celine decided that there was an opening for a film production company specialising in making high-end television advertising.

Her company Toytown Films was incorporated on 4 February 1992 and based in Windmill Lane in Dublin city centre, a creative hub that housed recording studios used by U2 and a film business established by James Morris who was in the early stages of establishing a television company that would eventually become TV3.

Ambitious, hard working and well known in the industry, her production company soon became the firm of choice when it came to filming advertisements. Her client list included blue-chip advertising agencies producing commercials for the likes of Kellogg's, the National Lottery, Coca-Cola, Volkswagen, McDonald's, Carlsberg and many others.

It was hard work but highly profitable and Celine Cawley relished the business. Like her father she had a driving ambition to be the best at what she did.

The couple celebrated the millennium by buying 'Rowan Hill', a spacious five-bedroomed split-level mansion behind security gates on Windgate Road on fashionable Howth Hill. Set on almost an acre of private grounds with a hot tub in the garden and stabling for two horses, it was a private idyll with views over the Irish Sea. It was registered in their joint names as full owners on 16 February 2000 and was mortgage-free after the property crash.

On 25 January 2002 they bought an investment property at Tramway Court in nearby Sutton, it too being mortgage-free.

They also bought a sprawling villa in the village of Hossegor in southwest France. At one time it was valued at around €800,000.

By 2007 Toytown Films had a turnover of over €1million and retained profits of over €270,000. With the success of his wife's business, Eamonn Lillis had gradually scaled back his own graphic design work. Although he was a director of Toytown Films, in many ways Lillis was a gentleman of leisure, dabbling in film production when he was needed, but mainly looking after the house and their daughter. Certainly when it came to making the business decisions for Toytown Films Celine was the boss.

Georgia May attended the nearby Sutton Park School, which boasted the highest fees of any non-boarding secondary school in the country while Celine kept a horse in stables at Ashbourne and was planning to get another to keep at the end of the garden in Howth. But all was not quite what it seemed in the idyllic family life.

After the birth of their daughter, Celine Cawley and Eamonn Lillis's lifestyle changed, subtly at first but, without either of them noticing it, permanently. They lived together, worked together, brought up their daughter together, but no longer shared a marital bed. Celine was a troublesome sleeper, snoring and kicking out in her sleep and because of film commitments often worked irregular hours, rising early for filming. They began sleeping in separate rooms. Georgia May as an infant slept with her mother but after a couple of years moved into her own room. Celine and Eamonn, however, never resumed the normal arrangements of a married couple.

She slept in the upstairs master bedroom which had a balcony and views out over Howth Hill, while his bedroom was one of the four downstairs bedrooms. It was a lifestyle that seemed to suit both of them and later a witness, who was never identified, would tell gardaí that it was a 'sexless marriage'.

For all that, Eamonn Lillis seems to have been a caring husband and father. He often rose early, especially when his wife wasn't working, and brought her and their daughter breakfast in bed. Sometimes he got in beside Celine and they had 'a kiss and a cuddle' before he left to take their German Shepherd dogs for their early morning walk.

By 2008, like most other businesses, Toytown Films was suffering from the collapse of the Irish economy and the advertising industry in particular. The company still had healthy cash reserves but profits had slipped and she was beginning to get jittery about the future of the business. On occasions she was heard telling Eamonn that he had to start 'getting out there' to search for work and pull his weight, instead of sitting back and playing the role of stay-at-home dad to their daughter, who by now didn't need permanent minding.

But something else was going on behind her back: her husband was having an affair right under her nose.

❧ • ☙

Jean Treacy from Nenagh, County Tipperary came from a family of five children. She grew up in the town where her father was a well-known musician and local historian. She went to St Mary's school before leaving after the Junior Cert to complete her education in St Joseph's College in Borrisoleigh, about 12 miles away. She spent a number of years working as a lifeguard in Nenagh Leisure Centre before getting a job in marketing.

Around 2005 she decided on a change of career and took a course in the well-known Galligan School of Beauty where she trained as a beauty therapist. Later she was described as 'curvaceous, fit but not especially thin' by one observant onlooker.

On 1 August 2006 she got a job at Howth Haven, a beauty parlour in the fishing village patronised by a wealthy upper-middle class clientele who came regularly each week for beauty treatments and massage.

Celine Cawley, who had suffered from a bad back for many years, went to Howth Haven for a massage and other treatments, and was so pleased with the service there that she encouraged her husband to do the same, recommending Jean Treacy as the therapist to visit.

He started attending regularly in mid-2008, going most Fridays for a deep-tissue massage. He would pull up outside the salon in one of the couple's two cars, usually in the black Mercedes ML jeep with darkened windows, which he used when Celine permitted. As Jean Treacy gave him a back, neck and shoulder massage, Lillis, who was a good story teller with literary ambitions, would tell her about his dogs. Being a dog lover, she listened avidly.

She began to 'fancy' him and even told a work colleague about her 'crush' on her unusual customer. Then one Friday in October as he was dressing to leave she told him she would love to see the dogs. He invited her out to his car and when she sat into the passenger seat, leaving the door open, he took out his iPod and showed her pictures of the three dogs.

'The rapport between us was different that day,' she said.

The next Friday he told her he had a 'tightness' to the front of his shoulder and he turned over so that she could massage the area concerned. The two of them were looking directly into each other's eyes for the first time.

During face-to-face massage a client usually closes their eyes, Jean Treacy said later, but he stared directly at her, making her feel slightly uncomfortable at first.

'What are you thinking?' she asked.

'Nothing,' he replied.

'What are you thinking . . . honestly?' she asked again.

He didn't say anything.

She put his hand on her 'racing' pulse and told him, 'That's what I'm thinking about.' Then she walked out of the treatment room.

The following Friday the atmosphere was sexually charged and they kissed for the first time.

Before Eamonn Lillis left the beauty parlour they exchanged telephone numbers and so began a torrid affair that would consume their lives for the next eight weeks until their clandestine romance was overtaken by the calamitous events on the decking of the Cawley / Lillis home on 15 December that year.

In the meantime they fell into each other's arms with a shocking intensity. After their first sexual encounter, Eamonn Lillis bought two mobile phones, so that each could deceive their partner, he his wife Celine, Jean Treacy, her fiancé Keith.

Throughout the day, and sometimes late into the night, they would text each other, exchanging little love notes and arranging their sexual encounters. These took place, mostly, in the blacked-out Mercedes ML in car parks overlooking scenic outposts in Howth, in quiet corners of shopping centre car parks and in remote corners of stately homes like Howth Castle and Malahide Castle where unwitting families passed by on their way to the children's playgrounds.

In one two-week period, the 52-year-old Lillis and 32-year-old Treacy exchanged 200 text messages and 90 phone calls – many of them made while Celine Cawley was off scouting for work for the film company, or late at night while he was alone in his bedroom in Rowan Hill.

Neither his wife nor his daughter had any inkling of the affair.

As they went deeper and deeper, the way lovers do, Lillis began to discuss his marriage with Jean Treacy. She told him she thought 'they [Lillis and Celine] looked very good together' but Lillis told her that he was unhappy. When he had told his wife how he felt she told him they would just have to 'work on it'. Oddly, Jean Treacy seemed to relish this and together they worked on what they called a 'resolution list' of things he could do to make his marriage better.

Jean Treacy was engaged to be married herself, although no date was set for the wedding, and so she didn't want to be the catalyst for the break-up of her lover's marriage.

Was she in love with Eamonn Lillis?

'At the time I thought I was, but it was more infatuation than anything. It came and went,' she said.

Before going to bed on 14 December Lillis and Treacy had been texting and, unusually for them, had decided to meet in central Dublin the following day. It was a meeting that would never take place. Events were hurtling towards disaster.

Eamonn Lillis got up early on the morning of Monday, 15 December 2008. He had a shower and when he came down to the kitchen Celine had made breakfast. Then he dropped his daughter Georgia May off at Sutton Park School where she was a fifth-year pupil. He had a chat that morning with the vice principal, who was an old classmate of his from UCD. He got back into his car and went to the shop at the Howth Summit where he picked up a copy of *The Irish Times*.

Back at Rowan Hill he sat in the kitchen reading the sports pages before doing a few domestic chores and feeding the cats. He could hear the pump going so he assumed that Celine was in the shower.

He got out the leads for the dogs and set off for their first walk of the day, down Windgate Road, before turning into a little used laneway. As he ambled along for 20 minutes – one of the dogs was old and slow – he was thinking about getting some holly to decorate the house for Christmas.

When he got home he filled the dogs' bowls with water and moved the rubbish, which had been left at the front door, to the side garden where the bins were kept. It was now about 9.20am and when he went into the kitchen Celine was at the sink dressed in a grey top and tracksuit bottoms and wearing rubber gloves as she cleaned some ice-trays from the fridge.

She asked him if he wanted a cup of tea and he said 'in a minute' as he put on black rubber gloves and prepared to go out to collect the dogshit strewn around the decking surrounding the house.

As he was going out she asked if he had put meal worms in the bird box for the robin that inhabited the garden. He said he had forgotten and she said she had asked him three days before.

'That's bloody typical,' she remarked.

He told her to 'feck off', he said later.

Suddenly that little spark seemed to set off an explosion. The mild, almost casual, exchange between the couple turned into a vicious argument about

41

their financial state and the state of the family. Lillis said that Celine asked him sarcastically why he wasn't out there trying to get business and he told her she was being unfair. She said he didn't care for her, or for their daughter.

He hit back. 'You're only interested in your own image – in being superwoman,' he replied, telling her she was forgetting all the work that he did around the house, keeping the place looking good.

'I don't do bins,' he claims she said.

They had edged out of the kitchen and onto the deck as the verbal argument continued.

According to Lillis, Celine slipped during this heated exchange. Then he saw her picking herself up off the ground with a brick in her hand. He presumed she had slipped on it and with her other hand she was rubbing the back of her head.

'Are you all right?' he says he asked her.

'What do you care?' he claims she replied.

As they began screaming at each other again they tussled for the brick which ended up in Lillis's hand.

'I went up to her, shoved the brick at her and said, "Why don't you shove this where the sun don't shine?"'

According to Lillis, she took the brick and as he jabbed her on the shoulder she took a swipe at him and caught him a glancing blow on the side of the face. He pushed her back towards the sliding doors and tried to grab the brick, but his glove came off and, with it, one of his fingernails.

'I was extremely angry. I pushed her again, quite hard, against the corner of the living room window. She let out an almighty scream.'

The scream was heard by a neighbour at 9.35am, fixing the time Celine was attacked.

'She pushed around me. I grabbed her by the shoulder. I was trying to get the brick off her. She caught me with the brick again. I grabbed her right wrist and pushed her hand over her right shoulder. The brick was in her hand.

'We did a half-turn and ended up on the decking. I lost my balance so she lost her balance because I was pushing her. She was lying on the ground, on the flat of her back. I was on my knees, half across her.

'I went to get up. She grabbed my hand and bit my finger. She wouldn't let go. She was twisting her head from side to side biting the little finger of my right hand.

'I hit her on the forehead to stop her moving. I screamed at her. It was extremely painful,' said Lillis later.

Finally he got up and threw the brick away.

'I was stunned, I didn't know what to say,' he said.

After the intensity of the row he said that Celine seemed quiet and dazed, but not for a moment did he think she was seriously hurt.

He said he cradled her head in his lap and the blood from her head wound soaked into his jeans.

According to him she sat up and he asked her what they should tell Georgia May about what happened. He suggested that they should say that the house had been burgled, which was something that had happened before. He brought out some kitchen paper for her to hold against her bloodied head and asked again, 'Are you all right?' 'Yeah, yeah, fuck off and leave me alone, go away, go away,' he said she replied.

Eamonn Lillis said he then went back into the house and began the cover up. He went into the bathroom and washed himself in the sink, before going into his bedroom to change his clothes.

His jeans and V-neck sweater were too bloodstained to wash so he put them in a bin bag along with his socks, boxer shorts and the black rubber gloves. He put his T-shirt and his black Y3 boots in the wardrobe and put his watch which also had blood on it on the bedroom locker. He put on new clothes and a different watch.

Then he took the black plastic bag and some camera equipment, which needed to 'disappear' if the robbery story was to stand up, and put them in a small suitcase which he hid under Georgia May's old toys and some books, in the attic.

In all it took about 10 to 12 minutes he said. He then went out to the decking and called Celine, but she didn't answer. He knelt beside her but could get no response. He tried her pulse but didn't know whether there was anything there. So he rang 999.

When the emergency services and gardaí arrived they took charge and he waited in the background acting the 'shocked' victim of a robbery gone wrong.

'I saw them picking her up and bringing her to the ambulance. I presumed she was okay. I presumed that if someone was dead they were not moved,' he said later. But at Beaumount Hospital Celine Cawley was pronounced dead.

When the house was calm again detectives asked what happened to his wife. Eamonn Lillis didn't tell them the truth about the row. Instead, he told them the invented story of the burglary, including the dramatic details of how he grappled with the intruder who eventually fled.

It was a good story; Eamon Lillis knew how to tell them. But how he hoped to get away with it is a mystery. Lillis must have read enough thrillers and seen enough television programmes to know that when you stuff your bloodied clothes in the wardrobe and hide things in the attic the detectives are going to find them.

But he stuck with the story, even when Chris Cawley and his wife Sorca took him and Georgia May into their own home to comfort them and help him recover from the shock and trauma of the brutal 'break-in' that morning.

In further interviews with gardaí he described graphically how, when he came home from walking the dog that morning, he had found a man wearing a balaclava in the house and the two of them had grappled with each other, resulting in scratches on his face and the loss of his fingernail. The attacker had run off and he then found his wife and rushed to call the ambulance and gardaí.

Sceptical detectives listened to his story, even pretending to go along with it publicly. In the following 48 hours there were searches along the route where he said the attacker had made his escape. Initially, suspicions centred on a local vagrant who lived rough but did odd-jobs for home owners to get a bit of cash. It quickly emerged, however, that most local people knew this man to be perfectly harmless.

Things were moving fast; detectives searched the house and found the black refuse sack full of bloodstained clothes. The bloodstains matched the blood profile of Celine Cawley.

The search team then uncovered a brick concealed in a tea towel near the dining room. They also trawled through his phone records and found a lot of traffic that led to his mistress rather than his wife.

Eamonn Lillis's story was quickly unravelling.

But Eamonn Lillis loved to tell stories and when his former lover Jean Treacy had too much to drink and phoned him one night, they met up whereupon he told her another version of events, drawing her into the murder case that gardaí were assembling as they prepared to bring him to justice.

Finally, he was arrested and charged with the murder of his wife. It was another terrible shock to the Cawley family. Lillis's futile cover-up had added to the trauma they had to endure. Not only had he killed Celine, but he had involved them all, including his daughter Georgia May, in a web of deceit.

The dramatic 16-day murder trial of Eamonn Lillis took place in the Central Criminal Court in Dublin, presided over by Judge Barry White, in mid-January, 2010. It was one of those cases that had all the ingredients of a classic film, a wealthy woman once beautiful but who no longer had her looks, a supposedly downtrodden husband having a passionate love affair with a much younger femme fatale, and finally, a dramatic life and death struggle at their home in one of Dublin's most sought-after suburbs.

Eamonn Lillis and his lover Jean Treacy gave evidence of the events leading up to Celine Cawley's death on 15 December 2008. Their every word was dramatically reported in the media where there was an almost insatiable appetite for details of the trial.

The deputy state pathologist Dr Michael Curtis told the court that Celine died from a combination of three head wounds and restricted oxygen due to obesity and an enlarged heart. In his evidence he said that Celine was struck on the head, which caused her to fall to the ground on the decking surrounding the house, where she was hit twice more. She was left lying on the deck bleeding profusely from the head and, in the position she was in, she would have been unable to breathe properly and became starved of oxygen. This would have led to intolerable pressure on her heart.

45

Dr Curtis said he had been told by a garda that Celine was found lying on her front. However the garda who told him this was never identified, or called as a witness. The ambulance crew who were first on the scene said that Celine was lying on her side. This would have caused her great difficulty, said Dr Curtis, because she was so overweight.

Dr Curtis doubted Mr Lillis's evidence that somehow Celine had bounced 'like a beach ball' after he first struck her. He said that humans did not 'bounce' and the head injuries were not in the right place to have been inflicted by a fall. The pathologist said that it was likely that if Celine Cawley had received medical attention earlier she might have survived.

Convicted of manslaughter by a jury on 29 January, Eamonn Lillis was sentenced a week later on 5 February 2010. Judge Barry White said that Lillis was 'self-serving' and his protestations of remorse for the events of that cold December morning 'rang hollow'. The appropriate sentence for Eamonn Lillis for killing his wife should be 10 years in prison, said the judge. But because of the media intrusion in the case, which the judge said was, among other things, an 'affront to the human dignity' of Eamonn Lillis and because he had already served three weeks in custody, he would impose a prison sentence of six years and 11 months.

Lillis did not appeal the sentence.

In addition to the media intrusion, members of the Cawley family believed a distorted portrait of Celine had emerged from the case. During a series of interviews with gardaí prior to being charged with murder, it was put to Lillis that his wife was a 'dominant' woman, a 'bully' who had treated him as a 'lapdog' and as a result of this he had suddenly snapped and killed her.

This image was reinforced by Jean Treacy, who gave evidence that while they were sitting in the Mercedes ML together, Celine Cawley had called her husband on his mobile phone and demanded that he come home with the car 'now' and that her tone of voice was 'particularly bad'.

According to legal sources, following his manslaughter conviction Lillis dramatically agreed to 'step aside' as sole executor of his wife's will at 6pm on a Friday – when legal proceedings were due the following Monday morning by

Celine's family to force him to do so.

The legal renunciation in which he 'expressly renounced his right to probate of the will of the deceased' he was still determined to cling to as much as he possibly could of Celine Cawley's estate and the assets jointly held with her.

He acknowledged that he was not entitled to any assets held by his wife in her sole name – but it didn't mean he was giving up what he believed to be his rightful inheritance.

According to documents lodged in the Probate Office in Dublin on 24 March 2010 – just weeks after the trial and sentencing – letters of administration on her estate were granted to Susanna Cawley of Naas, County Kildare and Christopher Cawley of Howth, County Dublin, the dead woman's sister and brother.

The papers reveal that the net value of Celine Cawley's estate was put at €1,059,988.

The value of the house in Howth, Rowan Hill, was put at €1.1 million, but because of what one valuer described as its 'unfortunate history', it was reduced to between €750,000 and €800,000 for valuation purposes. The property at Tramway Court was valued at €220,000.

Celine Cawley's will included the value of the two Irish properties, two financial bonds in joint names which were valued at €45,000 and two joint bank accounts, one in Permanent TSB and the other in Bank of Ireland which had a credit balance of €24,000 before Celine's death. However, by the time the will came to probate, one of these accounts was 'diminished' while the other was in the red – meaning the money had been used by Eamonn Lillis between the time of his wife's death and the administration of the estate.

There was also the 'winding up' of Toytown Films. It was put into voluntary liquidation with assets of €809,572, but when fees and other payments were made this came out at €754,511. Lillis as a 50 per cent shareholder was entitled to half the amount, with the other half share going to his wife's estate.

It was initially believed that because of the 1965 Succession Act Lillis was legally barred from inheriting his wife's estate. According to subsection (1) of Section 120:

A sane person who has been guilty of the murder, attempted murder or manslaughter of another shall be precluded from taking any share in the estate of that other, except a share arising under a will made after the act constituting the offence.

Sub-section (5) reads:

Any share which a person is precluded from taking under this section shall be distributed as if that person had died before the deceased.

This statute was 'hardly worth the paper on which it was written', a source close to the Cawley family claimed, after they had spent a fortune on legal fees fighting the case.

On 15 June 2010 Christopher and Susanna Cawley issued a 'special summons' before the High Court to exclude Lillis from benefiting from his wife's estate. Two days later Georgia May Cawley, a minor, was 'joined' in the proceedings against her father.

They argued that the estate of the deceased should be distributed as if Eamonn Lillis were already dead, meaning that he could not inherit anything and that all of the estate, including property in their joint names such as the family home, should pass in its entirety to his daughter Georgia May.

In affidavits submitted to the court Lillis argued that he was, as a spouse and the person named in the will, entitled to inherit his wife's entire estate. His justification was brazen – he hadn't intended to kill his wife that morning in December 2008.

He had been in contact with his daughter Georgia May since being found guilty, and she with him.

'Our daughter is in regular telephone contact with me. She keeps me up-to-date on her life. She shares successes such as passing her driving test with me . . . she has visited me in prison,' he insisted.

She was also aware of his plans to return to Rowan Hill once his sentence was served and to resume family life together.

In response, Georgia May said in an affidavit that she had visited him once in prison to 'get some answers' about her mother's death, but none had been forthcoming. She said she totally supported her uncle and aunt in their legal attempt to have her mother's will treated as if her husband were already dead.

Georgia May's response was simple and to the point. 'I would rather stick pins in my own eyes' than share the family home with him on his release from prison.

In full it read: 'I am a strong person and know my own mind. My mother was 46 years of age when she died. The defendant [Lillis] was 51 years of age. Given that females have a longer life expectancy it is likely she would have survived him.

'I'm the only child of my mother. It is unlikely she would have had any further children. It is likely she would have left all of her estate to me.

'The defendant appears to suggest he is the real victim of this crime and not my mother and myself. It is a bit late and a bit rich for my dad to complain now of the effect of his crime on him.

'I visited my father in prison only once. I do not wish to have any contact from the defendant when he is released from prison.

'To put it as strongly as I can, I would rather stick pins in my own eyes than have the defendant return to within six miles of Rowan Hill.

'I will have to live my life without my mother's company, care, friendship, love and advice. Every milestone in my life will be blighted by her absence.

'I no longer feel I have any duty towards him after all he has put me through. My dad has lied to me concerning the circumstances surrounding my mother's death and I wanted answers and I got none.

'The consequences of my dad's crime in causing my mother's death have been devastating.'

It was signed 'Georgia May Cawley'.

The Cawleys argued that Celine was five years younger than her husband and, being a woman it was a 'matter of probability' she would have survived the defendant had he not killed her. Therefore, if he got half their joint assets he would 'in effect, be benefiting from his crime'.

They also argued that 'because of the act of the defendant' the value of Rowan Hill was diminished and he should be held responsible for that, and be penalised by having that value taken out of anything he might get from the estate.

Originally, Lillis had counter argued that he was entitled to be the sole beneficiary of the joint assets in the estate. Even when the Cawleys conceded, in an open letter dated 17 May 2011, to 'resolve the matter', that he might be entitled to a half share in the joint assets, he still insisted that he was entitled to inherit the entire estate.

It was only 'late in the day' when the matter went to hearing that 'it was conceded on behalf of the defendant that he was not solely beneficially entitled to the joint assets', only to a half share in their joint assets, with the other half going to the estate of the deceased Celine Cawley and, ultimately, their daughter Georgia May.

He argued, according to Judge Mary Laffoy's summing up, that: 'Those rights were property rights which enjoyed the protection of Article 40 of the Constitution. The defendant cannot be penalised further by being excluded from his property rights, which he enjoyed for eight or nine years, by being forced to forfeit them.'

It continued: 'He [Lillis's legal advisor] stressed that the defendant is entitled to an undivided moiety or half share of the joint assets. He also submitted that to make an adjustment on the basis of the alleged diminution of the value of Rowan Hill would constitute a penalty on the defendant, and he made the point that, in any event, property valuations fluctuate from day to day.'

The judge said she had to make a decision 'which is highly technical, rather than an exercise of discretion by the court'.

After considering the law in such matters in various jurisdictions, Judge Laffoy continued: 'In making that concession [that he was only entitled to half the joint estate], the defendant [Lillis], through his counsel, properly, if belatedly, acknowledged that the law, as a matter of public policy, will not permit him to obtain a benefit or enforce a right resulting from the crime he committed against the deceased.'

The judge concluded that, depending on circumstances, whichever of them died first, either Celine Cawley or Eamonn Lillis, could expect to become sole owner of the properties and assets involved – so that giving him his half share could not be seen as 'conferring a benefit on the defendant as a result of the crime he had committed'.

'On the other hand, if the court were to hold that the defendant on that day held, and continues to hold, the entire interest in the joint assets on trust for the estate of the deceased solely, the court would effectively be interfering with the defendant's existing right in the joint assets. In the absence of legislation empowering the court to so interfere with the defendant's existing rights at the date of the deceased's death, in my view the court has no power or jurisdiction to do so.'

She said the law was about the distribution of property owned by the deceased person, and not 'distribution of property in which an unworthy potential successor has rights'.

She said it was not possible to say who would have become sole owner of the joint properties 'if those tragic events had not occurred'.

Judge Laffoy held that, in the absence of legislation, Eamonn Lillis was entitled to a half share in the joint assets he held with his wife Celine Cawley, the other half belonging to her estate, ultimately to her daughter.

The Cawleys, Chris, Susanna and Georgia May, emphasised to the court that they wanted 'finality to be brought to the issues which had arisen'.

Judge Laffoy suggested that either Lillis could transfer his assets to the estate of Celine Cawley, for which he would get a half share, or they could sell the properties and divide the proceeds. Certainly this seems to have been the solution favoured by Celine Cawley's family, as Rowan Hill was put up for sale in March 2012, with sources indicating that it would be sold for €1 million.

Although the Cawley family were dismayed by the finding of the judge they felt let down by the legislation rather than the judicial system. They felt they were 'forced to concede' that Lillis could benefit from the homicide of their sister. Added to the 'emotional intensity' of going to court, Celine Cawley's executors knew enough about the system to know that if they challenged the judge's ruling there was a real danger that the legal costs would swallow up a huge part of the estate, diminishing what was due to Georgia May. As it was, they incurred what was described as a 'a substantial six figure sum' getting the legal issue clarified.

What the 'substantive issue' of the case clarified is that a killer can profit from their foul deed by remaining legally entitled to half the joint assets.

'The issues raised in these proceedings demonstrate that, ideally, there should be legislation in place which prescribes the destination of co-owned property in the event of the unlawful killing of one of the co-owners by another co-owner,' concluded Judge Laffoy in her judgement.

No such legislation is planned as yet.

The Cawleys felt that they received 'real' justice from a French judge when Lillis claimed entitlement to a half share in the family holiday villa in Hossegor, about 150 miles from Biarritz in southwest France. The judge in the case found that Lillis was 'unfit' to inherit anything from the sale of the villa – valued at one time between €750,000 and €800,000 – because he had killed his wife.

The Cawleys didn't have to actually go to court to have the issue decided, they just had to submit papers to the judge, who found that, unlike in Ireland, when a person acts violently against another person their rights are automatically reduced.

The judge found that Lillis was 'not worthy to succeed' in his claim to half the joint assets. The contrast between Irish and French law on the subject was described by one source as 'dramatic'.

The French judge also ordered Lillis to pay €1,000 compensation to his daughter Georgia May for putting her through the 'inconvenience' of the court proceedings, and a further €2,000 to Susanna and Chris Cawley, who had initiated the legal challenge in France to prevent him benefiting in any way from the sale of the holiday home.

It is estimated that although he killed his wife, Eamonn Lillis could be due a windfall of up to €850,000 in cash when he comes out of prison after serving his sentence, which could be cut to about four years given that he is a model prisoner and likely to receive a reduced sentence.

# Chapter 3

# *The Man Who Put the Figs into the Fig Rolls*

Between 8 June 1979 and 21 May 2004 the businessman and art collector Gordon Lambert, bachelor, made 31 different wills detailing the dispersal of his multimillion euro personal fortune. This did not include his valuable art collection, worth over €3 million, which had already been donated to the Irish Museum of Modern Art (IMMA) and his alma mater, Trinity College Dublin.

Born into a sporting Protestant family in Dublin, Charles Gordon Lambert rose to become managing director and chairman of W&R Jacob, the Dublin biscuit-making firm that was famous for its Fig Rolls and other products.

Unfortunately for the family he would become even better known after his death, on 27 January 2005, at the age of 86, for the acrimonious dispute that arose over his final will, which was drawn up in two parts – a will dated 21 August 2003 with a codicil, or amendment, added on 21 May 2004.

At stake in this dispute was the residue of his fortune, including at least €4.5 million from the sale of his art-filled bungalow in Rathfarnham, County Dublin. This was acquired by a businessman who paid €1.5 million over the auction reserve to secure the property at the height of the boom in April 2006.

The main beneficiary of the final will was Anthony 'Tony' Lyons, a former Press and Information Executive in RTÉ who had been given enduring power of attorney for the businessman's affairs on 17 November 1997. Mr Lambert had been suffering from Parkinson's disease for over 10 years by then. As Gordon Lambert would later tell members of his extended family: 'I chose Tony Lyons to be my attorney over six years ago because I trusted him to handle my affairs as my illness progressed. Tony has been a trusted friend for over 30 years and has made many sacrifices to ensure that I am cared for properly.'

Mr Lyons was first included as a beneficiary under Gordon Lambert's sixth will, dated 22 October 1985, when he was left the sum of £1,000. In successive wills this increased to £5,000, £12,000 and £25,000, with an additional £100,000 legacy added in 1997 that was to come out of the residue of the estate. This legacy from the residue was increased to €250,000 in a will dated 14 April 2002.

One of Mr Lambert's nephews, Mark Lambert, would later allege that Tony Lyons told him that 'there would be trouble' when the will was read.

How right he was.

In the final will and codicil, dated August 2003 and May 2004, Mr Gordon Lambert left a number of legacies to various organisations.

He started with a bequest of €50,000 to Tony Lyons and a friend from the artistic world, Catherine Marshall, to write a biography of 'different aspects' of his life: his work with Jacob's, his roles as a member of Seanad Éireann, the Junior Chamber International and the Arts Council of Northern Ireland. It would also be a history of the Lambert and Mitchell – his mother's maiden name – families 'and the many associations, economic and cultural, included in my career profile and many awards received by me during my lifetime, including the first ever lifetime award given by the Business to Arts.'

Catherine Marshall, who was then head of collections at the Irish Museum of Modern Art (IMMA), and a friend of Mr Lambert, was also left €50,000 in her own right, plus one-eighth of the residue of the estate, which eventually came to a grand total of about €400,000.

A further two-eighths of the residue (limited to a maximum value of €100,000) was divided equally among the family of his elder brother Noel Hamilton 'Ham' Lambert: his nephew Bruce Lambert, his niece Janette, nephew Mark and his wife Hedda, and Ham's grandchildren Ben, Jessica, Mayla, Molly, Daniel and Louis.

Another two-eighths of the residue (up to a maximum value of €100,000) went to the family of his late brother Thomas, nieces Valerie Rohan, June Lambert, and his brother's grandchildren, Catriona and David.

His friend Anthony Lyons inherited €250,000 and the proceeds of an investment account with Northern Rock plus three-eighths of the residue of Gordon Lambert's estate, which eventually amounted to an estimated €3.8 million in total, making him the major beneficiary of the last will and testament of Gordon Lambert.

It was clear from the will that this was the way Gordon Lambert wanted it, because the will stipulated that if Anthony Lyons died before him his share would not go to members of the extended Lambert family, but was to be transferred to the Modern Art Trustees, the trustees of his collection of paintings and sculptures.

As he was in the process of drawing up what turned out to be his final will, one of Mr Lambert's advisors at the legal firm of McCann Fitzgerald, solicitor Susan O'Connell, 'adverted to concerns that the will might be challenged'.

A note on the solicitor's file regarding a meeting at Mr Lambert's home on 19 February 2003 to begin work on the will, said that if his brother 'Ham and/or his family' were unhappy with the latest changes that he intended to make they might challenge it on the grounds that he 'lacked testamentary capacity', meaning he wasn't sufficiently mentally fit to decide these matters himself.

According to the file note, 'They might also allege that GL [Gordon Lambert] was under the influence of Tony [Lyons] but SO'C [Susan O'Connell] said she was certain that this was not the case, as GL was a man of his own mind.'

Despite this, the final will led to a High Court action in which the well-known actor and nephew of the deceased, Mark Lambert of Rathdown Park, Greystones, County Wickow and his cousin, Gordon Lambert's niece and godchild, June Lambert, of Pembroke Lane, Dublin 4, challenged the final will.

They did so even though Clause 8 of the will stated: 'I direct that if any beneficiary of this my will seeks to question, challenge, disagree with or take legal action of any kind whatsoever against my estate in respect of my will, that person will be automatically disinherited.'

Their legal action was against Anthony Lyons of Beaumont Avenue, Churchtown, County Dublin, Gordon Lambert's long-time friend and neighbour, and the other executors of the will, Olive Beaumont of Heytesbury Lane, Ballsbridge, Dublin 4, a friend, and Catherine Marshall of Kevin Street, Dublin.

However, the case when it came to court was solely against Mr Lyons, who by then had moved from his home at Whitebarn Road, close to Mr Lambert's home at Hillside Drive.

The Lambert cousins claimed that Gordon Lambert's final will was 'extracted under duress and the undue influence' of Mr Anthony Lyons. They asked instead that the High Court admit a will made by Mr Lambert on 14 April 2002, under which Mr Anthony Lyons would have been entitled to a legacy of €26,000 and €200,000 from the residue of the estate.

Under this will the bulk of Mr Lambert's fortune would then have been distributed among his extended family and other beneficiaries without the cap of €100,000 which was put on the family's half share of the 'residue' of the estate in the final will.

✦ • ✦

Charles Gordon Lambert was born on 9 April 1918, the youngest of four sons of a Dublin upper middle-class Protestant family. His father JH (Bob) Lambert was a well-known veterinary surgeon in the city and a distinguished Irish international cricketer. His mother, Nora Mitchell, a major influence on his life, came from the Mitchell wine-importing family who have been operating in Dublin for generations, in Grafton Street, Kildare Street and most recently in the International Financial Services Centre.

His elder brother Noel Hamilton, 'Ham', who followed his father's profession as a veterinary surgeon was an outstanding Irish rugby international, cricketer and later referee. He had two other brothers, Thomas and Drummond, who were already deceased at the time of these events.

The family grew up in an idyllic home, 'Berehaven' set on three-quarters of an acre on Castle Park (later renamed Hillside Drive) in Rathfarnham, their next door neighbour being Jefferson Smurfit, founder of the packaging company that bore his name, and behind the house was the Castle Golf Club.

The Lambert brothers attended Sandford Park School in Ranelagh before being sent off to the British public school Rossall in Lancashire, a popular destination for the sons of Church of Ireland clergymen and professional people. He would later say his abiding memory of school was the cold baths on a winter morning. 'Sometimes you had to break the ice,' he recalled.

After public school he made leisurely progress through Trinity College Dublin where he graduated with an Honours BComm distinction. None of his family attended the conferring.

'He believes that his happy family background – with endless talk of sport at the dinner table – engendered in him a lifelong feeling of goodwill towards people and enabled him to give people the benefit of the doubt,' wrote one profile writer years later when Gordon Lambert was at the height of his powers.

His mother put his name down for the accountancy firm of Stokes Brothers & Pim where he became a trainee accountant. He was working for the firm as a junior accountant when he was sent to audit the books of the Quaker biscuit makers, W&R Jacob, in 1944. It was to be the turning point in his life. He never left, spending the rest of his working life with the firm. He went on to become chief accountant, marketing director and in 1971 he was appointed managing director of Jacob's. After the acquisition of its main competitor Boland's and a number of other smaller manufacturers, Jacob's was renamed Irish Biscuits and employed more than 3,000 people at its various facilities, which included its headquarters in Bishop Street in central Dublin before the entire operation was moved to a new facility in Tallaght.

At an early stage in life, he later admitted, he felt there was something lacking in his personal development and, according to one observer, he chose to fill the void with art.

'Gordon Lambert has not married,' a profile of him in *The Irish Times* noted as late as 1986, the year he retired, where he talked about his personal life and how he had cared for his elderly parents until the time of their death.

Because he was the youngest son he stayed in the family home, which eventually became his own, and was left with the burden of looking after his infirm mother for the last 10 years of her life, including the three painful months leading up to her death. It was an experience that left a lasting impression on him. 'I don't regret it,' he explained to the reporter, 'but it did deter one from marriage.'

More importantly, as would transpire in later life, it also fuelled a deep insecurity that would come back to haunt him in his own old age. He constantly sought reassurance that he would not be put into a home and he ended up distrusting the motives of his own family, eventually banishing them from his presence in the belief that they were trying to have him put into a home.

If business made him money, art was his consuming passion. As a single man who had inherited the family home, which he estimated cost €160,000 a year to run between housekeepers, gardeners, helpers and entertainment, he had plenty of money to acquire the things he liked.

The artist Cecil King got him interested in modern art, taking him around the salons of Paris. Gordon Lambert and his advisor David Hendricks took pride in discovering new talent and buying their work early, before it became expensive and widely sought after. In this way he amassed a huge collection of paintings, drawings, posters and sculptures which filled his home and garden in Rathfarnham.

He was not interested in popular painters, preferring to spend his money on what the artist Sean Keating would famously call 'rubbish' at the opening of the Rosc exhibition in Dublin in the early 1970s, a breakthrough in the marketing of modern art in Ireland in which Gordon Lambert played a leading role. Lambert was more interested in work by Victor Vasarely, described as one of the most important painters of the twentieth century, Picasso, Miro and others, whose works he collected before the price of their work became prohibitive. He also knew and bought work by Irish painters such as Patrick Scott, Barrie Cooke, Louis le Brocquy, Robert Ballagh and many others as he trawled through the auction houses and gallery openings. In time he was rewarded with an appointment to the Seanad, where he did not make as great a mark as his benefactor Jack Lynch might have hoped, being described by one colleague as 'an unwilling passenger on the ship of state'.

He was one of the few non-Americans to be appointed to the board of the prestigious New York Museum of Modern Art in recognition of his work in collecting and promoting international artists. He also initiated the Jacob's Television Awards in 1962, an event which is fondly remembered for recognising the talents of some of the stars of Irish radio and television and the first 'celebrity' event in the city. Lambert and his public relations executive, the famous Frankie Byrne, even boasted of providing wheelchairs to get some of the more inebriated guests from the event to their cars.

Gordon Lambert retired in 1986 and immediately set about deciding the future of more than 300 pieces of artwork which he had collected. This brought him into regular contact with his niece June Lambert, who had a degree in fine art and was a founding director of his foundation, the Gordon Lambert Trust. He also encountered Catherine Marshall, an art historian and head of collections with the Irish Museum of Modern Art, where he intended to donate much of his collection, and she became a good friend and confidante.

He was later diagnosed with Parkinson's disease, a debilitating condition which attacks the central nervous system. He executed an 'enduring power of attorney' in favour of his friend Tony Lyons on 17 November 1997, although this was not formally registered until 12 January 2003, two years before he died.

Anthony Lyons, born in 1934, was the son of a shopkeeper from Castlebar, County Mayo. He left home at the age of 17 and started his working life in the accounts department of Roscommon County Council, where he was appointed the first local government county cashier. He later moved to Dublin where he took an interest in the theatre and worked as a freelance journalist, mainly with *The Irish Press*, while studying for a degree in Arts and Commerce. He successfully applied to be put on a panel of announcers and newsreaders for Radio Éireann with the likes of Jim Sherwin, Mike Murphy and the late Maurice O'Doherty. In 1965 he was appointed Information Officer at RTÉ and later Press and Information Executive. It was through that connection that he first met Gordon Lambert, when Frankie Byrne, public relations officer for Jacob's, asked him to help with the script for that year's awards show. By chance, his first cousin Una Cunnane was then Gordon Lambert's personal assistant.

Lyons believed that his new friend was what he called a public relations 'creation'. With the help of Frankie Byrne – who had a long running affair with Frank Hall, one of the early RTÉ 'stars' – Gordon Lambert had 'created an image of himself as a patron of the arts as well as a businessman'. Lambert, in turn, was fascinated by Lyons's theories on the art of public relations. The two men, according to an acquaintance, 'bounced off each other and had so much in common'.

They had a shared interest in art, dogs and gardening. Gordon Lambert bought one of Mr Lyons's paintings, which he hung in his home and, while Mr Lyons had bred champion Yorkshire Terriers and planted an impressive garden, Mr Lambert had what was described as 'an army of ancient retainers' to carry out such tasks.

Tony Lyons was working as an editor on a programme called *Access* when he decided to take early retirement from RTÉ at the age of 52 in 1986 – coincidentally the same year that Gordon Lambert retired. His widowed sister was terminally ill with cancer at the time and he went over to England and cared for her until her death.

Lambert made Tony Lyons executor of his will on 22 June 1997, and would include him in 12 subsequent wills with the same role. A year later he gave him 'enduring power of attorney'.

Enduring power of attorney is a serious and onerous commitment which bestowed on Anthony Lyons the legal right to act with authority and take decisions regarding almost every aspect of Gordon Lambert's life when he fell ill. It is also supervised by the High Court. In a document signed by both of them on 21 November 1997 Mr Lambert agreed that Mr Lyons could make decisions on the following:

> Where I should live;
> With whom I should live;
> Whom I should see and not see;

What training or rehabilitation I should get;

My diet and dress;

Inspection of my personal papers;

Housing, social services and other benefits for me.

This was accompanied by a number of documents, one of which was a letter from Mr Lyons saying he understood what was required of him, including 'limited power to use the donor's property to benefit persons other than the donor and my obligation to keep adequate accounts in relation to the management and disposal of the donor's property for production to the High Court if required.'

Also included was a Letter of Wishes (dated 13/04/02 and signed Charles Gordon Lambert) and headed, To My Attorney: 'It is my wish that if I require nursing care because of my illness that such nursing care be administered in my home. It is not my wish, if I become incapacitated, to reside in a nursing home and it is only if medical treatment in a hospital is required that I should be moved from my home.' For taking on these duties Tony Lyons was to be get 'out of pocket' expenses.

The two men lived about 5 minutes' walk away from each other in Rathfarnham and as he grew older and his illness developed Gordon Lambert began to depend more and more on Tony to be a personal assistant, a carer and a 'gatekeeper' in his hour of need, especially after Lambert stopped driving in the year 2000.

He would phone Tony Lyons in the morning and ask him what he was doing that day. If he was going to a garden centre, as he frequently did, they would go together and have lunch afterwards.

In his final will Lambert would describe Lyons as 'an acquaintance of over 30 years whose steadfast care and attention in my progressive illness has enabled me to live a life of mobility, good humour and close association with my trusted friends. In my direst need he has never failed me.'

'I didn't realise I was in his will at all,' Anthony Lyons would later declare. 'I don't have an interest in other people's money, I always earned my own.'

By mid-2002 the Parkinson's became so severe that Gordon Lambert was hallucinating. He would ring Anthony Lyons late at night, saying there were people outside climbing the walls or there was a white van waiting to take him away. On another occasion he believed that the IRA were about to kidnap him; it had happened to tycoons like Ben Dunne and Don Tidey, so it may not have been as far-fetched as it seems.

'He was used to having people work for him all his life and he expected me to do things,' said Tony Lyons, meaning that when he got a call he had to drop everything and go over to Lambert's house.

But Gordon Lambert clearly valued their friendship above everything else. 'Even in my worse moments, Tony always has the ability to make me laugh,' he told his solicitor on one occasion.

On Wednesday, 25 September 2002 at about 7am, Tony Lyons was going to buy his newspapers, as he habitually did, when he saw that the front door of Gordon Lambert's house was open, although the security chain was still in place. He rang the bell and called and when there was no response he burst open the door and found Mr Lambert lying on the floor outside the bathroom, where he had been all night. After he got him into bed he rang Mr Lambert's elder brother Ham to tell him what had happened.

The keys were missing and Mr Lyons presumed they were stolen. As he was responsible for the house, he rang a locksmith and later that morning when he went back to the house Ham and his wife Jean were in the study with Gordon. It appears that Gordon had, inadvertently or otherwise, given a copy of his latest will to his brother, who, after reading it, was furious. It appears that Ham Lambert believed his wife Jean 'hadn't been left enough' in the will and he became extremely agitated, striding up and down the living room in a foul temper demanding it to be changed.

Once the lock was replaced, Tony Lyons gave a copy of the key to Ham Lambert, keeping another copy for himself.

The next day Ham Lambert phoned Mr Lyons, speaking to him in a 'domineering' manner and insisted that changes must be made to the will or 'Jean will be so annoyed that she won't even go to Gordon's funeral'. Mr Lyons told Ham that the will was between Gordon and his solicitor and he had no say in it at all. He hadn't read it and didn't know anything about it.

Two days later on the evening of Friday, 27 September 2002, Ham Lambert telephoned Tony Lyons and asked him if he was sure he couldn't change the will. Mr Lyons would later say that Ham 'ranted and raved' when he was told it was a matter between Gordon and his solicitors. Ham Lambert said he had already phoned the solicitors in McCann Fitzgerald, but they were not returning his calls and 'obviously don't want to speak to me'.

Later that night Gordon Lambert phoned Tony Lyons, who had to go over to his house four times in order to persuade him to go to bed, which he did about midnight.

The following morning, Saturday, as he was going for his papers, Tony Lyons passed Gordon Lambert's house and got a feeling that everything was not in order. When he went in he found Gordon lying on the floor again. He had been like that all night and couldn't reach the phone to ring for help. Lyons dragged him along the landing and got him into bed and turned on the electric blanket and the heat in the house. After making sure that he was comfortable he left, telling Gordon to go to sleep and he would call later.

He came back about two hours later and found Ham Lambert was in the living room. Tony Lyons said that Ham Lambert had said his brother would have to be 'put away' and that he was 'mad'. Tony Lyons said that he had specific instructions from Gordon Lambert that he was not to be removed from his home.

A little while later Janette Lambert, Ham's daughter, arrived. Tony Lyons said that while they were whispering the phone rang and when he answered it a woman's voice said: 'This is John of God Hospital here. We can't take that man in unless two doctors certify he is insane.'

Tony Lyons put the phone down, but he was now very alarmed. He said he realised that his enduring power of attorney was being completely ignored by members of the extended Lambert family.

Just then the doorbell went and two men in uniform asked whether there was an accident. Tony Lyons said there had not been an accident, but he said Jeanette

Lambert put her hand over his mouth and said: 'No, you don't live here, you don't know what's happened. He had a bad fall. He will have to go to hospital.'

Tony Lyons said Gordon Lambert was taken from the bedroom and brought to the waiting ambulance, which then sped off. He didn't go out because he was so shocked at the speed of the events that were taking place. Then he remembered that he had instructions from Gordon that if anything ever happened to him he was to take possession of a black metal box which he kept under his chair in the study.

As he was putting the box into his briefcase he said he saw Ham Lambert crouching behind the settee. He said Ham took some leatherette boxes containing gold cufflinks and tie pins and also a little camera and put them in his pocket. He told Ham that they were Gordon's things and that no one should touch them as he was responsible for everything in the house.

That afternoon Jean Lambert rang him to say that Gordon was in St James's Hospital but she couldn't do anything further for him and she was going on a holiday with her daughter the following day.

Later that evening when he went to St James's with Olive Beaumont, one of the other executors of Mr Lambert's will, they found Gordon still lying on a trolley and deeply agitated. He wasn't seen by a doctor until 10pm that night. The diagnosis was that he was dehydrated, which resulted in his hallucinating.

When Tony Lyons got home he returned a message left on his phone by June Lambert and they had 'a battle' in which, he alleged, she screamed down the phone at him. He told her he knew she had been fighting with her uncle 'for ages' and she should stop the hypocrisy and the crying.

The following Monday when Tony Lyons called to the nursing station at the hospital he was told by the duty sister that she could not deal with him, as Mr Lambert's niece June Lambert was there and had said that she was the next of kin. The staff, therefore, had been told only to deal with her. Gordon Lambert's then solicitor at McCann Fitzgerald, Patricia Rickard-Clarke, had to come to the hospital and give him a paper confirming that he had enduring power of attorney for Gordon Lambert.

He said he never saw June Lambert at the hospital again and he went in every day and gave Gordon Lambert his post and took instructions on what should be done about his personal affairs.

Although he was due to be discharged on 8 December, Gordon was becoming institutionalised and afraid. He finally came home on 15 December, 2002. Mr Lyons had arranged a home care team to look after him round the clock.

On 19 December Ham and Jean Lambert called with a Christmas present of home-made soup and a cyclamen plant.

According to Tony Lyons, Gordon Lambert did not hear again from any of the family until after Christmas and none of them either called or rang to inquire about their uncle's health or welfare.

Gordon Lambert's carer wanted to spend Christmas with her family and so Tony Lyons took him to his home for the day, where they ate Christmas dinner together. He said later that he wasn't disappointed by the family ignoring Gordon over Christmas, but Mr Lambert was, and made it known to his solicitors.

On 27 December Ham called to request a meeting with his brother, alone. But when Tony Lyons asked Gordon if he wanted to see his brother, he replied 'no'. Ham called his brother directly on 30 December, and he made two further calls on 1 January, two calls on the 3rd , a call on the 4th and two calls on the 5th, all requesting a private meeting with Gordon.

On 8 January Tony Lyons received a phone call from Ham accusing him of stopping him from seeing his brother. It was the first time he was accused of this and he said that when Ham continued to phone him and became aggressive and hostile he stopped taking his calls.

Tony Lyons decided to write to Ham in his capacity as attorney, asking him to stop pressuring his brother, who needed rest and recuperation: 'I have been aware for quite some time that you have been making inappropriate remarks about me,' he wrote. 'I am satisfied that I have acted with complete propriety in this situation and have dealt honestly and fairly with you. You, in turn, have turned what should have been conversations about Gordon's health into confrontations and interrogations. I have found you ill-mannered, devious and excessively arrogant, while seemingly being unable or unwilling to accept the reality of Gordon's illness.

'I would remind you that Gordon has never asked his family to care for or look after him. He is fully aware of his condition and lives with it bravely every day. Back in 1997 he made legal arrangements for his future care. These are now in place and he has told his medical team that he is perfectly happy with the arrangements. The last thing Gordon needs, in his condition, is pressure. So please respect his wishes.

'Encouraged by his doctors, who have told him it is his life, his home, his estate, not theirs, not mine, not yours, Gordon is now in control of his life and making decisions that suit him and are best for him.'

Tony Lyons also phoned solicitors McCann Fitzgerald's around this time and is recorded as telling them: 'I think he wants to change his will. His speech isn't very good; he thinks he wants to change his will.'

In a letter dated 22 January 2003 Gordon Lambert's solicitors wrote to his brother Ham telling them that 'he does not wish to receive family visits at present'.

When he was well enough Gordon Lambert circulated through his solicitors a letter dated 22 March 2003 to his relatives, including in it a series of bullet points which set out reasons why he no longer wanted to be associated with members of his family, citing that they wanted to put him in a home or institution.

This was followed by another letter in which Susan O'Connell, who had taken over from Patricia Rickard-Clarke as his solicitor, clarified in detail to a solicitor from Matheson Ormsby Prentice acting for June and Valerie Lambert, the reasons why he didn't want to see him.

Among the points made in the letter were the incident involving Ham's wife Jean and her dissatisfaction with what was left to her in his will; that he had spent 11 weeks in St James's and it was four weeks before he received a visit from any of Ham's family; and that 'pressure' from the family was not good for his health.

'Gordon is aware that some family members have suggested to a number of people that it is Tony Lyons who is preventing Gordon from seeing his family. Gordon has asked me to refute this absolutely. He himself has made all decisions as to who he sees and doesn't see. Gordon chose Tony as his attorney because he trusted him to handle his affairs and personal care. Gordon has stated that Tony has been a huge support and a great friend to him over the last 30 years and, in particular, over the last nine months. Gordon would like his family to respect his decision to appoint Tony as his attorney,' said the letter.

Susan O'Connell suggested that as a first step towards reconciliation with his brother he might think about setting up a meeting with Ham. Gordon, however, said he would first 'ask Tony' whether he was willing to accept an apology if Ham was willing to make one. She said that was a good idea, but he should not discuss the contents of his will with Ham, although he could, if he wished, say he would exclude Ham and his family from the will if Ham did not apologise to Tony.

The solicitor said that the difficulty was caused by Ham, who had behaved badly, and had not tried to 'mend the bridges' between the brothers.

The older brother was unwilling to admit he was wrong, and would not accept that he could not speak to Gordon again for the rest of his life. Ham was also having difficulty in his personal life; his wife Jean, who had been ill for some time, died. This led to further problems as Gordon Lambert felt annoyed with his executor Olive Beaumont who he said 'let the side down' by attending her funeral.

Ham's son, Mark Lambert, who admitted that he saw 'relatively little of his own parents' then wrote to his uncle Gordon from Stratford-On-Avon in December 2003, in response to what had by now become known in the family as the 'banning' letter.

'The facts you have sent make awful and disappointing reading. I am very saddened by the overall impression that you feel under siege and even threatened . . . I can also understand the trauma and hurt you went through in going to hospital and the isolation you suffered while you were there . . .

'They [Ham and Jean] were both concerned about you and we felt responsible for looking after you. That I can honestly vouch for. We also felt concern for Tony who I know and repeat myself that they constantly praise for his caring and loyalty to you. I saw this in relation to the traumatic events of your admission to hospital . . . I am not sure what anyone would have done under the immediate circumstances.

'The result of their action of calling ambulances was clearly horrid ... Mum's behaviour was also out of character, as she was for at least a year cross and sometimes more cross with [other members of the family]. I know she also said some terrible things to Tony and one phone call which may be hard to forgive. This seems to be the crux. Shakespeare in one of his tragedies had a character say that 'time is out of joint'. Mum knew that she was dying ... This merely explains but doesn't condone her behaviour any more than Dad's sometimes childish behaviour as he gets increasingly frail and frustrated at his indisposition. All I can say is that I don't expect you to forgive Dad and Mum all of a sudden, but I would beg you above all else to allow Dad to talk to you. I have seen how upset and confused he is by not being able to see you and I would hope he would say sorry about some of the things you have said he has said and done ...

'I want Tony's position to be appreciated and respected and whatever apologies be made to you and him. There must never again be any mention of wills or inheritance, but only respect and family pride.'

He said his sole desire in writing the letter to his uncle was 'reconciliation'.

June Lambert said she was also very hurt by the letter of 22 January 2003 which effectively banned members of the family from seeing their uncle. She was Gordon's godchild and had emigrated to Australia, but came back to Ireland in 1986 and studied for a master's degree in fine arts and later in business studies. She said she had a good and loving relationship with her uncle and saw him frequently when she was in the country.

He had given her a valuable parcel of shares in Mitchell's, the wine business, which he had inherited from his mother. She had also replaced him as a director of the firm and he 'trusted and loved' her enough, she said, to make her a founding trustee of the Gordon Lambert Trust which held his art collection. She had at one time also been an executor of his will and had been 'at his beck and call' attending functions with him socially, as well as hosting functions in his own house over the years.

However, Gordon Lambert would later tell her: 'I am extremely angry and upset about the way the family have acted towards Tony, who has proved my trust in him and without whom I would not be able to enjoy the quality of life and peace of mind I now enjoy.

'I am adamant that if the family do not acknowledge the unselfish help and support Tony has provided to me, and apologise to him for the accusations they have made against him, I do not wish to meet with any of them in the future.'

Influenced by the events that had taken place at the end of 2002 and early 2003, Gordon Lambert planned yet another will. Beginning with a meeting with Susan O'Connell at his home on 19 February 2003, he began to work on what turned out to be his final will and testament.

In the presence of Ms O'Connell and another solicitor from McCann Fitzgerald, Cormac Brennan, he spoke about the ongoing disagreement which he had with his brother Ham. Many other aspects of his personal life were also discussed at a series of meetings regarding the will.

At one of them Susan O'Connell mentioned that as the deposit interest rate was very low at the time that Gordon Lambert might consider investing a proportion of his liquid assets, up to 30 per cent, in shares which might provide a better rate of return.

Wise man that he was Mr Lambert said he would consider this, but feared losing money; there were numerous people he knew who had invested in the stock market and lost, he said.

In any event Gordon Lambert made the necessary changes to his will, drawing up the new document which effectively capped the legacies to the nieces, nephews and grandchildren of his brothers, Ham and Thomas, at €200,000.

Dr Tim Gleeson, who attended him at the request of his solicitors, found that he was of sound mind at the time.

What hadn't really been taken into account in the new calculation of the value of Gordon Lambert's estate was the booming state of the Dublin property market. The Schedule of Assets dated 1 August 2003 valued his house at Hillside Drive, Rathfarnham at €680,000, although Susan O'Connell believed it was worth about €1 million at the time. As a result it was estimated that his will would come out at €1,272,000 when it went to probate.

It was well wide of the mark.

In an affidavit signed towards the end of that year Gordon Lambert's solicitor Susan O'Connell made it clear that Gordon Lambert's wish was to be left alone by his family.

'Mr Lambert expressed his wish to me that Mr Lyons should continue to look after his affairs going forward. He was particularly anxious to ensure that Mr Lyons would have full powers to make his personal care decisions as he trusted Mr Lyons to have regard to his wishes. He did not want his family as his next of kin to be making any such decisions. Therefore no attempt was made to revoke his enduring power of attorney, notwithstanding Mr Lambert's improved physical and mental state.'

She also declared: 'Mr Lambert instructed me that due to the deterioration in the relationship he had with his family, he also wished to impose a maximum value of €100,000 on each of the shares of the residue of his estate to be divided among family members under his will' and she was satisfied he 'fully understood the effect of these changes to his will'.

Gordon Lambert went into hospital again on 3 January 2005. June Lambert and Tony Lyons kept in contact by phone during his illness.

She later claimed that Tony Lyons told her that her uncle had repeatedly asked to change his will again and although he could no longer talk he had spelled out on an alphabet board the words: 'They are all using me, I must change my will.' Mr Lyons denied he ever said such a thing and no further changes were ever made.

On the morning of 27 January 2005 Tony Lyons visited Gordon Lambert in hospital and knew that he hadn't long to live. His carer Anita Delaney was with him all that day. Later that evening she telephoned Tony Lyons when he was at a meeting with Eoin McGonigal, the chairman of the Irish Museum of Modern Art, to tell him that Gordon had died.

Tony Lyons phoned June Lambert to tell her the news. She would later allege that he told her she was 'not to organise his funeral and not to take the limelight'. Mr Lyons denies this ever happened. He told her that Gordon Lambert had left written instructions that he wanted no public announcement of his death before a small private funeral was held. A memorial service was to be organised later in the Museum of Modern Art in the Royal Hospital, Kilmainham.

But it being Dublin 'word got out' and Tony Lyons realised that if he was to succeed in honouring his friend's wishes he would have to 'move quickly'. He arranged the funeral for the following day, Saturday.

Mark Lambert said later that the funeral was a small family affair, which he believed was 'sad and rather pathetic as a tribute to his uncle'.

Some time later when members of the family visited Gordon's home at Hillside Drive, his father Ham saw a chair that he liked and took it. He said his father was also interested in a sepia photograph of his grandparents' wedding and told Tony Lyons, who was 'very polite', that it was one of the things he would like. Mr Lyons said it would be 'awkward' as it was part of the estate but that he could come back and discuss it at another time. Mark Lambert said later he didn't know what happened to the photograph.

Mark was interested in a painting by Robert Ballagh and bid for it at an auction of his uncle's property but wasn't successful in securing it.

When Gordon Lambert's death notice appeared in *The Irish Times* on 30 January 2005 the well-known businessman, art collector and philanthropist had already been buried, 'according to his wishes'.

As the executors of the will began the process of converting his assets into cash it turned out none his advisors had properly estimated the value of his residence. Situated behind granite piers and set back from the road it wasn't a terribly imposing property, but it was set on almost an acre of gardens and backed on to the Castle Golf Club. A publican paid €4.5 million for the house, which was later demolished and rebuilt.

It would lead to a bitter struggle over the will of Charles Gordon Lambert in the High Court that would involve much pain and torment for all involved.

❦ • ❦

A grant of probate was issued in respect of Gordon Lambert's will on 7 March 2007 but was withdrawn eight days later when a plenary summons was put before the High Court.

Mark Lambert and his cousin June Lambert claimed that their uncle was 'reliant' on Tony Lyons who, they claimed, had threatened Gordon Lambert that he would 'resign his power of attorney' unless he cut off communications with the Lambert family, and in this way the family were prevented from seeing him from 2002 onwards.

Mark Lambert, a well-known Abbey actor who had parts opposite Cate Blanchett in the movie *Veronica Guerin* and the television dramatisation *Bloody Sunday* as well as roles in programmes like *Cracker* and *The Young Ones*, said he and members of the family had a very good relationship with Gordon Lambert until he was admitted to St James's Hospital in September 2002.

The following day he said he got a phone call from Anthony Lyons.

'I received a tirade of abuse in which he said he was going to sue my sister and my father [Ham, who was then 93]. He said Ham was a thief and trying to put Gordon into a mental institution and that he was after Gordon's money.'

Mark Lambert said he believed Anthony Lyons's undue influence was responsible for the cap of €200,000 put on benefits to Gordon Lambert's nephews and nieces in the will and the addition of Clause 8, the condition that anyone who challenged the will would be disinherited.

'The first named defendant [Anthony Lyons] so overbore the will of the testator [Gordon Lambert] that the testator was in fear of him,' the Lamberts said in their Statement of Claim, adding that Mr Lyons had 'abused his position and power so as to apply duress and undue influence on the deceased in the disposition of his estate.'

In a further claim they said that in the days before his death Gordon Lambert wanted to alter his will, replacing Catherine Marshall as his executor with June Lambert, 'but due to the unavailability of a solicitor, the amendments were not and could not be made.'

James Gilhooly SC, acting for Mark and June Lambert in the High Court action that followed said that Anthony Lyons's share of the residue of the estate rose from €146,000 in 2002 to €1,484,500 in August 2003. But when the house was sold in 2007 for €4.5 million it meant that Mr Lyons's share of the proceeds was approximately €3.6 million.

'If there was undue influence, Mr Lyons benefits to a very substantial extent,' he said.

Gordon Lambert's tearful cleaning lady, Pauline Slater, told the High Court that the businessman and art collector had died exactly in the manner that he did not want to – alone, without friends or family. She said that while she was his cleaner if ever he contacted a member of the Lambert family Anthony Lyons would get 'very annoyed' and wouldn't speak to him, sometimes for weeks on end. She said that Gordon Lambert found this very hurtful.

She also visited him once when he was gravely ill in hospital, but on her second visit she was denied entrance and told everything had to go through Mr Lyons. At the time, Mr Lambert was in an isolation ward and no visitors of any kind were allowed. In cross-examination Frank Callinan SC for Anthony Lyons accused her of 'bragging' and being 'invasive, intrusive and utterly irresponsible' to her former employer.

'I will never regret going to see that man as long as I live,' retorted the feisty cleaner.

'Have you anything else you wish to add . . . out of spite?' asked Mr Callinan as she finished giving her evidence.

However, his carer Anita Delaney, who was the only carer for Gordon Lambert from June 2003 until his death in 2005 and who lived at the house, said Gordon Lambert 'knew his own mind'. She said that Mr Lambert and Mr Lyons were 'very good friends' and that they 'bounced off each other'. They had a lot in common, such as gardening, television and dogs. Gordon Lambert, she said, could be quite demanding of Mr Lyons and other people and he would phone Lyons every night. He told her one night, 'if the family phone, don't put me through, I am busy,' but she had never received instructions from Tony Lyons to exclude them.

Tony Lyons, now aged 75, said he lived two minutes from Gordon Lambert who 'invited me to his home from time to time'.

'I didn't think I was in his social circle at all, but one day he phoned me and told me he had Parkinson's disease and was thinking of executing his will,' said Anthony Lyons, explaining how he was given enduring power of attorney

Gordon Lambert asked Mr Lyons to become involved in his daily life. Tony

Lyons said he told Gordon that the Lambert family would do that. At this point he said Gordon Lambert purportedly said: 'No, No. They would put me into a home.'

'I realised he was distancing himself from his family and I got the feeling he was quite afraid of them. He didn't want to be removed from his home,' said Tony Lyons. He said it was 'ridiculous' to say that he had Gordon Lambert locked away from his family and totally incorrect that he had given instructions to Mr Lambert's cleaner to report to him if any visitors called to the house. He also denied giving instructions that the family were not to be informed in the event of Gordon Lambert's death. 'Neither I nor Mr Lambert ever contemplated his death,' he said.

Until he was hospitalised, Anthony Lyons had very little to do with Gordon Lambert's social life. Lambert rarely drank, but occasionally he liked to have people round, or artists called to his house. Guests included the artist Louis le Brocquy and his wife Anne Madden, Dr Moore McCann, Catherine Marshall, Rita Childers, the wife of the late President, Erskine Childers, and some banking friends of Gordon Lambert. They also included a director of Adam's Auctioneers Brian Coyle, and the artist Robert Ballagh and his wife Betty.

Mr Lyons said that Gordon Lambert had three mobile phones and a landline all that time and was constantly on the phone to anybody he wished.

As regards enduring power of attorney he indicated that it was far more trouble than he ever anticipated. He said it was a pretty grim task and that his health had been damaged, his hearing was affected by stress, his garden had gone to seed, he was not able to show his dogs or to fulfil judging appointments at dog shows in England.

'I got you into this awful mess,' he said his friend would say, apologetically.

Edward Woods, who had been vicar of Rathfarnham since 1993, said he had never been refused access to Mr Lambert and Mr Lyons had never interfered in his visits. He recalled meeting him only once. He said that he could not recall speaking 'quite pointedly' of the thoughtlessness of others during his homily at Mr Lambert's funeral service.

June Lambert told the High Court that she and other family members were 'prevented' from seeing the will until 16 months after her uncle's death and they only initiated legal action after it was admitted to probate.

Patricia Rickard-Clarke, who was Mr Lambert's solicitor from 1983 to 2002 and dealt with 27 of the 31 wills, said that Mr Lambert was very diligent in his affairs and gave 'clear and well-thought out instructions' to her, but did not want his family involved. She did not believe he was 'unduly influenced' by Mr Lyons. Susan O'Connell, the solicitor who succeeded her as Mr Lambert's legal advisor and drew up his final will, said Mr Lambert was 'perfectly sharp' at the time and even though he suffered from Parkinson's disease he never became mentally incapable, he was just appreciative of what Anthony Lyons did for him.

As regards changing his will in the days leading up to his death, she told June Lambert in a letter dated 1 June 2005: 'I note from the records of your conversations during the weeks leading to Gordon's death that he was generally unable to speak and drifted in and out of consciousness. On that basis, and given the severity of Gordon's condition during that period, it would not have been possible for Gordon to have satisfied the test for testamentary capacity and instruct us in relation to any amendment of the will.'

After 13 days in the High Court, Judge Roderick Murphy summed up the case.

'Mark Lambert confirmed in cross-examination that he was not privy to what happened at the time in relation to the making of the will and, indeed, admitted that he had no evidence to support his claim other than his own belief and suspicions.' He added that 'belief and suspicion do not prove allegations.'

He said June Lambert had confirmed that she had last seen her uncle in December 2002, which was eight months before the execution of his last will and 17 months before he executed the codicil.

'The court is satisfied that June Lambert did not adduce any evidence of undue influence allegedly exercised by Mr Lyons in relation to the will or codicil,' said the judge. 'The issue of Mr Lambert indicating to Mr Lyons, shortly before Mr Lambert died, of changing his will is, in the view of the court, not relevant to the issue of undue influence in relation to his last will and codicil.'

'The court is satisfied from the evidence of Susan O'Connell that the testator knew and approved of the contents of his will. He initiated the request to change the will and gave instructions to Susan O'Connell in relation thereto. He had explained his instructions to cap certain legacies.'

The judge also found that the fact that Mr Lambert's home in Rathfarnham had far 'exceeded' the valuation put on it had no relevance to the case before him.

'Mr Lambert's central concern in his last will and codicil was the adequacy of his assets to meet all the legacies,' said the judge. What he hadn't taken into account in the 'detailed planning of the will' was the capacity of the Irish property boom to dramatically increase the value of his 'residuary' estate – the amount left over after all the legacies were paid out.

The court was, he said, satisfied as to the 'righteousness' of the transaction and he found that Anthony Lyons did not exercise duress or undue influence over Gordon Lambert or 'deprive him of his free will' in drawing up his last will dated 21 August 2003 and the codicil dated 21 May 2004 and would allow them to stand. Effectively, the decision made a multimillionaire of Anthony Lyons.

Noel Hamilton 'Ham' Lambert died in a nursing home on 10 October 2006, at the age of 96, before the commencement of the legal proceedings that would shine a searching spotlight on such solid, private, Protestant pillars of society. Ham's gravestone, in Schull, County Cork, bears the inscription 'A lovely man'.

# Chapter 4

# *The Last Will & Testament of Nuala O'Faolain*

Nuala O'Faolain was a well-known Irish journalist and author. Her father, who went under the pen-name Terry O'Sullivan, was a celebrated columnist with the *Evening Press* who, for many years, wrote 'Dubliners Diary'.

'Our father had been a big fish in a small pond because he was the first journalist in Dublin to write a daily social diary about the receptions and parties and formal events that happened around the town every night. His dapper, charming figure, usually wearing evening dress, had been welcome everywhere he went. Not so, my poor mother. She was a shy, lonely woman, the inefficient manageress of wherever we happened to be living, a bookworm who, when she added drinking to reading, could escape the reality of nine children and a husband she was in love with but could not trust,' Nuala O'Faolain wrote in her less well-known memoir *Almost There*.

Her earlier and highly successful account of her life *Are You Somebody? – The Accidental Memoir of a Dublin Woman* painted a graphic and searing portrait of neglect and her damaged childhood at the hands of her alcoholic mother and philandering father.

'From outside it seemed privileged but behind closed doors there was destitution and neglect,' said her friend Marian Finucane who made a documentary on the life and death of Nuala O'Faolain.

Their mother was a chronic alcoholic who went drinking in the Dollymount Inn in Clontarf in the early afternoon while her husband, who was originally Tom Phelan but was now universally known as Terry O'Sullivan, conducted an endless series of affairs, including one with his wife's sister, Maureen.

Sadly, it was his daughter Nuala's fate to do exactly as her father did, and she embarked on an endless series of sexual encounters few of which were affectionate or loving. She moved swiftly along leaving the men behind, including one who was stranded at the altar rails without so much as an explanation or a goodbye.

Although two of her brothers died of alcoholism, other members of the family did not look back on their childhood as harshly as their journalist sister, remembering a rather kind father and a hopeless mother.

'Terry O' as he was known in social circles around Dublin was a former army officer who had served with Douglas Gageby, the first editor of the *Sunday Press*. Gageby employed him to write a column. O'Sullivan, getting a hefty advance to go on a trip to America, repaid Gageby by not returning for months. He was sacked.

But when Gageby later became editor of the *Evening Press* he once more hired O'Sullivan to write 'Dubliners Diary', paying him a salary equivalent to his own. The column was a huge success and O'Sullivan was the best-known journalist with *The Irish Press* until Con Houlihan came into his own.

While her father was a stylish writer and probably the most successful journalist during the 1960s and 1970s, he was increasingly mocked in the business because of the 'plugs' he gave unashamedly to the businessmen and public relations executives who plied him with drink and presents on his nightly rounds of the posh hotels and restaurants where the receptions and parties about which he wrote were held. Terrified executives would await his arrival at the door of a reception with a bottle of Château Talbot, the only wine he would drink. It was said that if they didn't have this particular vintage he and his photographer would turn on their heels and he would order his chauffeur to drive on to another reception and ignore their event, thus ruining the evening for all concerned.

Old hands at the *Evening Press* said they would frequently arrive to work in the newspaper's Burgh Quay office early in the morning to find the 'dapper' diarist slumped over his typewriter sleeping off the effects of his nightly rounds on the Dublin social scene, where there was a strong belief that the more drink Terry O was plied with, the better the plug they would get in the following day's paper.

Nuala O'Faolain, who seemed to hero-worship her father, followed him into journalism after a brief stint teaching in University College Dublin. She became a talented reporter with the BBC and later with *The Irish Times*, where she too was employed by Douglas Gageby.

Her appetite for lovers, alcohol and self-examination led to a mental collapse after the death of her father. She was rescued from this despair by the columnist Nell McCafferty, which led the two women into a well-publicised 15-year lesbian affair. This ended bitterly, leading to an inconclusive debate in media and literary circles about whether Nuala O'Faolain was heterosexual or bisexual.

Nell McCafferty, who had declined to cooperate with the documentary into O'Faolain's life, later wrote to *The Irish Times* on the subject: 'Moral gatekeepers of the documentary wrongly ask if Nuala was bisexual. A trivial detail like gender would never have prevented Nuala from loving another. Nuala was sexual, I was irresistible. Readers, we loved each other.'

O'Faolain herself said on the subject: 'I was unable to bring a moral sense or even common sense to my dealings with the opposite sex – and my own sex.'

The broadcaster Gay Byrne put it a little more crudely when he introduced her on *The Late Late Show* television programme prior to the publication of *Are You Somebody*? 'Well Nuala, you have slept with a lot of men, haven't you?' he said, introducing the nervous writer as his guest that night. (Her sister would later reveal that when asked about the amount of lovers she chronicled in the book, she replied 'I didn't put in the half of them.')

However, the programme turned the book into an overnight literary success in Ireland and it was then taken up by an American publisher and topped *The New York Times* best-seller list for several weeks in 1997. This literary success led her to live between an apartment in New York, a holiday home in County Clare and a small red-brick artisan dwelling in Ringsend near Dublin city centre.

Her autobiography was followed by a novel, *My Dream of You*, which was also a major commercial success, justifying the $1 million advance from her publishers.

However her next literary work was rejected and she never spoke to her publisher again.

In New York she formed a relationship with an attorney, John Low-Beer, through a dating website. It was while in New York that she was diagnosed with terminal cancer.

On Saturday, 12 April 2008 Nuala O'Faolain went on her friend Marian Finucane's radio show on RTÉ to reveal that she was dying of cancer.

'Yeah, it must look as if I'm an awful divil for publicity altogether and, in a sense, since I wrote *Are You Somebody?* and it reached, what is truth to say, a huge response, I have in a sense put myself out there. And the interviews I gave back then 10 or 11 years ago are like one bookend in which I presented myself and lots of people didn't like me and lots of people did. But one way or another it was company for me who happens to be a childless middle-aged woman. Now I am actually dying and I have metastatic cancer in three different parts of my body. And, somehow or another, it helps me to set up the other bookend and to say to those people who were interested in me and did care about me to say to them 'well this is how it is for me now, for what its worth'.

It was a moving interview and it showed a courage and openness rare for a journalist, as many of whom, while quite willing to write about other people's lives and other people's tragedies, are reluctant to explore their own.

Nuala O'Faolain spent the last weeks of her life travelling. She went alone to Paris, and then visited Madrid and later Berlin with her friends Brian Sheehan and Luke Dodd, going to the opera, seeing the Pergamon Museum and the remains of the Berlin Wall.

A week before she died she went with the remaining members of her family to Sicily, an annual event she had funded since literary success had made her a wealthy woman.

Her last words were a telephone conversation with Marian Finucane. 'Goodbye, dear friend,' she said, the day before she died.

Nuala O'Faolain died on 9 May 2008 at the age of 68.

೫ • ೫

Just two days before she died Nuala O'Faolain made her last will and testament, signing it with a spindly weak signature and leaving an estate valued at €2,149,028.

According to the Schedule of Assets lodged in the Probate Office, she had €400,000 in cash in an account in Anglo Irish Bank; €262,000 in cash in AIB; property in Ireland and America valued at €725,000; €379,000 in insurance policies; €168,000 in an account with Goodbody stockbrokers and a number of other small assets.

Few journalists, especially those who led as colourful a life as Nuala O'Faolain, have left such a financial legacy. But perhaps conscious of the amount of money she was leaving, she spread the largesse far and wide, as her will testifies. It is peppered with bequests to friends she made during her lifetime and reads more like someone holding court at a dinner party than a last will and testament.

The beneficiaries included her lover, the lawyer John Low-Beer with whom she lived in New York; Noreen Hegarty, then editor of the *Sunday Tribune* newspaper who had employed her as a columnist; journalist Mary Rose Doorly and her writer husband Hugo Hamilton; Claire Duignan who worked with Nuala O'Faolain in RTÉ; the writers Polly Devlin and Colm Tóibín; broadcaster Marian Finucane and her husband John Clarke; *The Irish Times* journalist and friend Sean McConnell and her one-time lover Nell McCafferty. But possibly the main beneficiaries were her family, her remaining brother and sisters and nieces and nephews, as well as friends in Ireland and America.

This is the text of her last will and testament, dated 7 May 2008 and also Nuala O'Faolain's last literary work.

> This is the Last Will and Testament of me, Nuala O'Faolain of Bartra, County Clare, Ireland, and I hereby revoke all former wills and testamentary dispositions hitherto made by me.
>
> I appoint John Low-Beer, Attorney, New York City Law Department and my sister Noreen O'Faolain, Solicitor, to be the executors of this my will (herein called 'my executor').

1. I direct my executor to pay my just debts, funeral and testamentary expenses and that they take from my estate their appropriate professional fees for acting as executors of my estate.

2. I give and bequeath the following gifts:

   o €10,000 to Noreen and Frank Hegarty and their three children to get their sandwiches ready for the Dublin Mountains.

   o €20,000 to Fiona Green in happy memories.

   o €15,000 to David Birge with thanks for tireless daily help.

   o €10,000 to my old friend Daisy Hayes.

   o €5,000 to Tony and Gay Lalyea with great fondness.

   o €10,000 to the great Dr Michael Kelleher to be distributed at his discretion.

   o €10,000 to Mary Rose Doorly for imagination and wit and Hugo.

   o €3,000 to Claire Duignan for a bottle of something good.

   o €4,000 to Polly Devlin and Bruton Somerset, probably for shoes.

   o €4,000 to Naomi Eppel of San Francisco for the good times.

   o €15,000 to John and Marian Finucane Clarke for dinner my old friends.

   o €15,000 to Aideen Friel in loving bilingual memory.

   o €4,000 to Elaine Lafferty but if I die and Hillary Clinton becomes President of the USA we will re-discuss this.

   o €2,000 to brilliant Daphne Mekin.

   o €3,000 to Gervase and Zoe McCourt for exceptional thanks and good cheer.

   o €40,000 to Tim and Mairead Robinson with sincere love.

   o €5,000 to Susan Sultan of Great Barrington, Massachusetts, for treats for dogs and Susan.

   o €4,000 to Brigid and Andy Sanford Smith in loving memories of many pints.

- o €5,000 to Mary Grace Sandes of 152 Conception Street, San Nicholas, San Antonio, Philippines.

- o €5,000 to Colm Tóibín of 12 Upper Pembroke Street, Dublin and maybe to remember me in Cabourg.

- o €3,000 to Jim Weber, 21 Queen Victoria Street, Toronto, with love to you and all cats.

- o €5,000 to Bill Young of Wisconsin with loving thoughts of cats and dogs and Wisconsin.

- o €3,000 to Noel Murphy tax accountant with thanks for his exceptional helpfulness.

- o My blue carpet and brown sofa now in 12th Street New York to John Low-Beer.

- o Auntie Anne's tea set and my car to my sister Niamh O'Faolain and her fiancé Joe Mulvihill.

- o The four paintings by Alice Maher depicting the things her beloved mother used are a special gift to my beloved friend Sheridan Hay Jacobs.

3. I give and bequeath the whole of my investment in Le Premier 111 to the charity Friends in Ireland.

4. I give, devise and bequeath the whole of my right title and interest in the Lake Huntington property to John Low-Beer.

5. I give, devise and bequeath my house and furnishings at Bartra to my sisters Deirdre Brady and Noreen O'Faolain to hold as tenants in common on half share each.

6. I direct that my executor shall have discretion to distribute specific objects of my personal property as they think fit.

7. I direct that my executor sell and convert into cash all of my remaining property real and personal whatsoever and wheresoever situate.

8. I give, devise and bequeath the whole of the residue of my estate real and personal, whatsoever and wheresoever situate to be divided equally between the following people in equal share.

o My sister Grainne O'Broin

o My sister Deirdre Brady

o My brother Terry O'Faolain

o My sister Noreen O'Faolain

o My sister Marian O'Faolain

o My sister Niamh O'Faolain

o Luke Dodd

o Brian Sheehan

o Helen and John Browne

o Nell McCafferty.

o Sean McConnell

o Sheridan Hay Jacob

o John Low-Beer

o Anthony Glavin

In witness whereof I have hereunto set my hand this 7th day of May, 2008.
Nuala O'Faolain.

She also left a literary will, signed the previous month, on 19 April 2008.

I, the undersigned, Mme. Nuala O'Faolain, healthy in body and in spirit, bequeath to Madame Sabine Wespieser, the entirety of my moral rights as an author, and the author's copyright, in my published literary works and any works not yet published.

I leave to Madame Sabine Wespieser the mission of seeing that respect is paid to my name and my literary work.

Sabine Wespieser will equally have the task of presenting, publishing or editing my literary work whenever she judges the time to be opportune.

She will also have responsibility of taking any decisions to do with the exploitation and promotion of existing works.

Finally – she will supervise the conservation, the exploitation, the planning for the presentation of my literary works.

Moreover, my niece Mairead Brady, for her contribution in the diffusion of my works, shall receive 30 per cent from my authorship copyright generated by my literary works.

Sabine Wespieser shall therefore receive 70 per cent from my authorship copyright generated by my literary works.


Signed,

Nuala O'Faolain,

April 19th, 2008

# Chapter 5

## *The Boss and the Child Bride*

When Richard Welstead Croker, better known as 'Boss' Croker, sailed out of New York for the last time in late October 1921 bound for Ireland, he was leaving behind a city that he had helped to create and which, in return, had made him rich and famous on its graft and corruption.

With a beautiful young wife who claimed to be an American Indian princess 50 years younger than him, the 74-year-old Croker was leaving his luxurious townhouse off Fifth Avenue as he did every year to travel to Glencairn, his Irish baronial mansion in the foothills of the Dublin Mountains.

As the liner sailed down the Hudson River passing Ellis Island, the man who was known as 'The Master of Manhattan' was leaving the same harbour where as a child he had disembarked as one of the seething mass of poor Irish emigrant families washed up on the shores of the New World.

His was the classic emigrant story, the penniless son who used his fists and his brain to brawl his way to the very top and in the process made what was rapidly becoming the greatest city in the world his very own.

But it had come at a price.

Boss Croker wasn't just leaving behind the city that never sleeps, he was also leaving behind a broken family, the tragedy of two wayward sons who had died of drugs and fast cars, and what his biographer later described as 'a snarl of lawsuits in both America and Ireland' which had bedevilled his later years and would continue long after his death.

During his time as 'Boss' of Tammany Hall, the well-oiled centre of graft, bribery and corruption that had dominated New York politics for almost a half century, where he dispensed plunder and patronage to its favourite sons, he had amassed a fortune estimated at $8 million from the city.

But since his sudden marriage to a young woman of 'dubious' origins Boss Croker had been involved in a series of vicious court cases on both sides of the Atlantic as three of his four surviving children attempted to prevent his new wife from getting her hands on the spoils he had accumulated during his years running the city. A court in Dublin would later hear that the woman, now known as Bula E Croker, had been previously married and was a 'streetwalker' when she ensnared their wealthy father. First they tried to have him declared senile and unfit to take care of his own affairs, and when he retaliated by trying to break up the family trust funds the Croker family squabble descended into a poisonous personal vendetta.

When a friend asked him what he thought the outcome of these legal tangles would be Croker replied with his usual dry, perceptive humour: 'The lawyers'll get all the money.'

But he also knew that the loot he had acquired as 'Boss' of New York was a fortune worth fighting for. There were mansions and estates in Ireland and New York. There were two miles of prime beach-front real estate in Florida where the town of West Palm Beach was already attracting the multimillionaire retirees. And stashed away on both sides of the Atlantic were caseloads of cash that had come out of Tammany Hall and a massive portfolio of stocks and shares in some of America's most valuable corporations.

Boss Croker hadn't been stealing from the teeming masses of Irish emigrants on New York's West Side whose votes he controlled with an iron fist; he had been 'on the take' from the big corporations who wanted to get public contracts to build the power plants, the railroads, the skyscrapers and the other utilities that made New York the most exciting city in the world.

As New York grew and the firms that built it and serviced it made millions in profits, their corporate value soared, and so too did the wealth of 'The Master of Manhattan'.

And it all came because of his control of Tammany Hall, a renegade political organisation linked to the Democratic Party, but not controlled by it. Their headquarters was named with a certain amount of irony after an Indian chief who had once ruled the island of Manhattan. Its power came from the organisation of the uneducated Irish masses into a political force and the shrewd judgement, iron discipline and ruthless efficiency of the 'ward' bosses who had wrested control of the city from the professional political classes. They knew that they were probably unelectable themselves, but they had control over the voters and so they could put forward puppet candidates and then share out the plum jobs among themselves.

Under Croker it had become so powerful that one of its puppets became Mayor of New York and at one stage he came close to deciding who would become President of the United States.

Growing out of the slums of Hell's Kitchen and the Bowery, its headquarters was a grand false-fronted mansion on 14th Street in Harlem called 'The Wigwam'. The philosophy that dominated Tammany Hall was articulated not by Boss Croker, himself a man of few words, but by another Tammany chief, the more loquacious George Washington Plunkitt.

'Everybody is talkin' these days about Tammany growin' rich on graft, but nobody thinks of drawin' the distinction between honest graft and dishonest graft,' he said in all seriousness. 'There's all the difference in the world between the two. Yes, many of our men have grown rich on politics. I myself have made a big fortune out of the game, and I'm gettin' richer every day. But I've not gone in for dishonest graft (backmailin' saloon-keepers, disorderly people, etc.). There's an honest graft, and I'm an example of how it works. I might sum up the whole thing by sayin': I seen my opportunities and I took 'em.'

Boss Croker more then lived up to that philosophy.

In his later years Croker liked to spend his summers in Ireland where he was a familiar figure at The Curragh and Leopardstown racecourses. The rest of the year was spent either in New York or at his estate in West Palm Beach.

But in 1921 legal proceedings over trust funds and disputes with his sons, Richard Jnr and Howard, and the younger of his two daughters, Mrs Ethel C

White, kept him in America all through the summer. When he finally got away in late October the voyage was unusually stormy and he developed a heavy cold. To add to his woes, when the liner arrived at Queenstown (Cobh) the passengers couldn't disembark because of the War of Independence raging in Cork city and the party had to travel on to Liverpool and make their way via Holyhead to Dun Laoghaire. Exhausted and ill he finally arrived 'home' in Glencairn in late November a very sick man.

Boss Croker lived on until the final day of April 1922 when he died at Glencairn. He was buried in the grounds of the estate and the 'honorary' pallbearers at his funeral included Arthur Griffith, President of Dáil Éireann, Alfie Byrne the famous Lord Mayor of Dublin and Oliver St John Gogarty, the writer and doctor who was immortalised as Buck Mulligan in James Joyce's novel *Ulysses*.

If his life had been filled with drama his death was no different.

Boss Croker's second wife, Beulah Benton Edmondson, or Bula as she wanted to be known, was a 23-year-old circus performer when he married her in 1914, just two months after the death of his first wife. Within weeks of her husband's death Bula found herself at the centre of a bitter struggle for control of his vast wealth. Croker's children challenged his last will and testament in a celebrated court case in Dublin which went on for two weeks and was a sensation relayed around the world by newspaper correspondents.

Yet, according to the probate documents, his estate in Ireland, which included Glencairn, was worth just £150, his property in Florida, including almost 160 acres of West Palm Beach, was valued at a mere $2,885, and there were so many mortgages on his home in New York that they exceeded the value of the property, and the bank took it back.

The question was, where had all Boss Croker's millions gone?

❧ • ☙

Richard Boss Croker was born on 23 November 1841 into a prominent family from Clonakilty, County Cork. Despite his later rise to fame among the Catholic Irish masses in Manhattan, the Crokers were well-to-do Presbyterians who had originally come to Ireland as soldiers of fortune in the army of Oliver Cromwell.

His father, Eyre Coote Croker, was an army officer and veterinary surgeon who spent his inheritance and sailed to America in 1846 on board the *Henry Cay* with his wife, Florence, and their three sons and two daughters.

Richard Croker was eight years old when they arrived penniless in the tenements of New York. His father got a job as a 'horse doctor' and the family settled down to eking out a living in the New World. Richard was a poor student who left school at 13 to become an apprentice fitter, gradually working his way up to mechanic and getting a job in the Fire Department.

But there was always something different about Richard. He was determined to have his own way and he was a good boxer who wasn't averse to a bit of street fighting. It was a quality that soon came to the attention of Jimmy O'Brien, a ward boss for the Tammany Hall organisation then led by William H 'March' Tweed, the first 'Boss' whose organisation controlled the Democratic Party in New York City.

Like many young men with their eyes on greater things, Croker started at the bottom as what was called 'a repeater', a faithful party man who could be relied on to vote repeatedly for the favoured Tammany candidate in whatever election was underway. Because he was young and tough he was never challenged and soon made a name at this particular calling.

With the fall of Boss Tweed, convicted of a string of bribery and corruption charges in 1873, there was a split in the organisation. Croker's mentor Jimmy O'Brien, known as Jimmy 'the Famous', jumped ship for another Democratic Party faction, thinking that Tammany Hall could not survive the stink of corruption coming from its headquarters, The Wigwam.

He was wrong.

The next Boss of Tammany Hall, 'Honest' John Kelly, though hardly a man of virtue, just wasn't as venal and downright corrupt as his predecessor. He took Croker under his wing, rewarding him with the plum post of City Coroner which carried the princely stipend of $15,000 a year.

With his fine salary and good prospects, Richard Croker married Elizabeth

Fraser in 1873 and converted to Catholicism, which was also a sound political move. Although it wasn't to be a happy marriage the couple had six children, four sons, Richard Jnr, Hubert, Frank and Howard, and two daughters, Florence and Ethel.

In the meantime Croker began the long, arduous and dangerous assent to the leadership of Tammany Hall.

In 1874 it almost came to a dramatic halt when he came face to face with his old mentor turned political adversary, Jimmy 'the Famous' O'Brien who was running for Congress, while Croker was the main enforcer for his opponent, a millionaire businessman, Abram S. Hewitt, a puppet of Tammany Hall.

On election day O'Brien's chief tactic was to use his muscle, mainly a bruiser called Owney Geoghegan, and other thugs to beat up any known 'repeaters' of Tammany Hall who came near his patch on the West Side of New York City.

Just like the film *Gangs of New York,* it led to a street confrontation between the old hand O'Brien and the young pretender Croker.

'You are a damned loafer, and a God-damned loafer and a repeater,' said Jimmy O'Brien addressing Croker as the two gangs faced each other.

'And you are a damned thief,' replied Croker.

'You damned cur, I picked you off the gutter and now you're supporting a rich man like Hewitt against me for Congress,' said O'Brien with venom and with that both sides waded in to each other with fists, sticks and anything they could lay their hands on.

Suddenly the melee was shattered by the sound of two gunshots. The gangs separated quickly and the police, who had been keeping a cautious eye on the brawl from a safe distance, swooped. They found one of O'Brien's henchmen, John McKenna, lying wounded in the street. The sergeant, who knew McKenna, asked the dying man: 'John, who shot you?'

'Dick Croker,' he replied, and died.

Arrested and thrown into the notorious 'Tombs' prison Richard Croker was stripped of his plum job and facing the gallows.

Hewitt won the seat in Congress and promptly turned his back on Croker, while Honest John Kelly could do nothing for his favoured henchman and said he had to let events take their course. Jimmy O'Brien still carried considerable influence in the city and bitterly used it to have Croker tried and convicted of murder.

'I never carried a pistol in my life, and never will as long as I can use my hands,' Croker declared at his trial.

Some eyewitnesses testified that he had fired the shot, others that he had not. After 17 hours the jury gave their verdict – six for conviction on the murder charge and six against. A hung jury.

'Croker was thereupon released and he was never tried again. It was generally believed in later years that he did not fire the shot that killed McKenna, but that it was fired by his friend, George Hickey. General Wingate, who was Croker's counsel, said after Croker's death that the man who had fired the shot was standing next to Croker during the trial and was prepared to dramatically proclaim his guilt if the verdict had gone the wrong way,' wrote Croker's biographer Lothrop Stoddard in his book, *Master of Manhattan*.

Croker was back on the streets of New York but without a job. As coroner he had lived it up, lavishly entertaining cronies in the saloon bars and at the racetrack where he liked to bet on the horses. Now he was reduced to doing the rounds of City Hall in a threadbare suit trying to get some sort of a position to get back on his feet again.

One New York journalist described his predicament. 'I never see Richard Croker in these days of wealth and renown,' he wrote. 'He was shunned by men of his own class and was almost in abject poverty.'

Knowing there was a vacancy Croker even followed the mayor into City Hall but he just strode on by, refusing to talk to him. Eventually Croker appealed to Honest John Kelly to 'use his influence'. As he waited for word about a job Croker was a pathetic sight leaning against a lamppost without a coat or hat as the snow fell on the frozen streets.

Eventually Kelly came down to tell him he had got him a job as fire commissioner. It was a comedown from coroner, but it was a job. He was back in the gang.

Just two years later, in 1885, Honest John was a sick man and Richard Croker his right hand man in the Tammany organisation. To quote his biographer he had 'quit the brawling turmoil of ward politics and was moving in the shadow of his exalted patron Honest John Kelly.'

That is where Tammany wanted its 'Boss' to be and on the retirement of Kelly the emigrant son Richard Welstead Croker assumed the title of Boss Croker and became the most powerful man in New York.

A big barrel-chested man with a close-cropped black beard and penetrating grey-green eyes, he dressed well and looked every inch the commanding political figure who effectively ran the city through force of will and a network of political patronage, bribery and the absolute loyalty of the Irish working class, who he rewarded with positions in the police, the fire service and the parks department, and other patronage dispensed through City Hall.

He 'rarely touched liquor' but he was a hearty eater and constantly smoked thick Havana cigars.

Boss Croker's office was on the first floor on the right of the entrance to The Wigwam. It was a large room furnished with plain, straight-backed chairs. The only decoration was a life-sized statue of an Indian chief clutching a tomahawk and hanging on the wall, a large portrait of the one-time native American ruler of Manhattan, Tammany, the Chief of the Sachem tribe. In a corner of the room, almost symbolically, stood a big iron safe. At the back of the big room there was a pair of folding doors and behind them a pokey little office, the inner sanctum, where the Boss could discuss in absolute privacy confidential matters of state.

'At Tammany Hall he is perpetually surrounded by a throng of henchmen and in their midst is Croker, smooth, silent, bland. Yet there is not one about him whose measure he has not taken. In short it's a game, the game of politics. And Croker defeats these folks; and turns them, and twists them, and takes them in and moves them about and in all things does with them what one expert might do to children at a game of cards,' wrote one New York reporter.

His political philosophy has probably been mirrored and articulated ever since by devotees of the art of attaining and holding power.

'While most men sit around club windows, or at dinner, discussing political plans, I go among my people to find out what they are saying and doing. I don't waste any time on theories. I want reports that give me facts and figures. I don't make plans to be forgotten overnight. I never went to bed on a theory in my life. As a matter of fact I never went to bed at all if there was a plan to carry out until I learned whether it would suit or not. We don't have any theories in Tammany Hall,' declared the Boss in one of his rare interviews.

Enticed by a bribe or as they liked to call it, 'financial sweetener', Croker helped Grover Cleveland to his second successful bid for the presidency of the United States in 1892 and Croker nominees held the mayoralty of New York from 1888–94, 'during which time he took the graft and spoils systems to new limits'.

According to one observer corruption was endemic in New York: 'Property and planning scams, protection rackets, prostitution and saloons putatively fell under his control.' He allegedly amassed a fortune of $8 million, but he held such control of the political machine, the judiciary and the police that no illegality was ever proved against him.

But his enemies were circling, trying to find a weak point in his armour. Led by the Republican Tom Platt, himself the son of an Irish emigrant, they were finally able to establish the Fassett Commission in 1890 to investigate corruption in New York City.

In reality it was set up to investigate Boss Croker.

Croker knew that if he was ever brought before the commission he would be torn apart. Always one for the bold and decisive stroke he suddenly announced that due to ill health he was quitting all his official duties including his role as Chairman of the Treasury Committee of Tammany Hall and going to Germany, to seek a cure for his ailments.

Resigning as City Chamberlain, which carried a salary of $25,000 a year, and handing over the reins of Tammany Hall to Thomas F Gilroy, he sailed for Europe, putting himself conveniently beyond the reach of subpoenas and a summons to appear before the investigation – but still retaining control.

A newspaper reported at the time: 'Speaking of his condition Mr Croker recently said: "I am almost discouraged. I don't know what is the matter with me, but I am far from being a well man."'

The star witness before the Fassett Commission was Croker's brother-in-law and one-time friend and associate, Patrick H McCann. Croker had been instrumental in getting McCann the lease on a municipal-owned restaurant in Central Park. But proving that no good deed ever goes unpunished the ungrateful McCann later fell out with Croker, who then used the same influence to have the Park Commissioners terminate the lease.

McCann began by revealing that, six years before, Croker had shown him a brown bag containing $180,000 which had been contributed by some of the big 'Tammany Men' to have one of their friends appointed as Commissioner of Public Works.

However, proving the theory of 'honest graft', when Mayor Edson declined to appoint their candidate to the job Croker had returned the money to the various donors. But the 'whip around' proved that huge sums were available and that Croker was pocketing huge sums of cash for his considerable influence.

McCann then got personal by saying that when the same man, a Mr Grant, was made Sheriff through Croker's influence, he had presented Croker's six-year-old daughter Florence with several envelopes, each containing $5,000 and that on the day of the celebration the little girl was wandering around with $25,000 in her purse.

Croker promptly cabled a statement to the New York newspapers: 'McCann's charge is false. Would not believe him under oath and is a blackmailer.'

There is little doubt that McCann was telling the truth, but Croker didn't waste too much of his time on low-level corruption like that. He didn't believe in being bought on the cheap.

In the late 1880s and the beginning of the 'roaring' nineties almost every corporation wanted to do business with the bustling city of New York. Croker, they knew, controlled all the people they needed to deal with. Bribing him directly cut out all the other layers of corruption. Their first calling card was a sizeable block of stock to Richard Croker. As the city grew so did the values of those shares in utility and construction companies, and so too did the wealth of Richard Boss Croker.

Even though he was no longer running the day-to-day activities of Tammany

Hall his men were in all the most powerful positions in the city and he could pull the strings when required.

His next venture was to set himself up as an English gentleman. With his wealth he acquired a town house in London and a country estate in Wantage where he bred horses. Although reporters declared that he 'seemed perfectly at ease with the racing nobility' the blue bloods of the turf knew that they were dealing with the son of a penniless Irish emigrant and a New York 'ward boss'. The class system decreed that Richard Boss Croker, for all his money, was not just a man of low class, he was a man of no class.

But every so often he had to go back to New York – just to let the underlings know who was really in control. On 7 September 1897 Boss Croker dramatically landed back in Manhattan, an event which was greeted in the newspapers of the following day with the headline 'Croker Returns from Elba', comparing his return to the city with the return of Napoleon from his enforced exile.

'Dressed in a plain blue serge suit, a blue cravat was snugly tied at his low collar, a white Alpine hat was crushed down over his grizzled hair, and he leaned on a cane,' said the newspaper reporter who was on the ship coming into New York. 'His eyes were keen and lively. From under the shaggy brows he shot furtive glances at the jagged profile of the great city ahead, the outline of which was just beginning to be defined as the morning mist drifted away. Those who gazed at the Tammany chief knew that his brain was busy, and the hard, set expression of the face was some index of the thought.'

But none of the 'Braves' were on the quayside to greet him. The return of 'the Boss' had left the organisation in a quandary. Three years is a long time in politics and during his enforced absence others had become accustomed to dividing up some of the spoils for themselves. Now they were in no mood to hand over that power and wealth. So Croker retired to his farm in Richfield Springs to think things over. The election for the Mayor of New York was about to commence and Croker ordered that the Tammany ticket should be headed by a little known and obscure judge called Robert Van Wyck, a 'party man' who could be depended on to divvy up the spoils of office.

There was a lot of opposition to Van Wyck, but once he was added to the ticket Croker took over his campaign against 'Reformer' candidate Seth Low.

'I told you three years ago that when reformers got into office they tried to stand so straight that they fell over backwards,' said Croker and sure enough as he sat in the famous Murray Hill Hotel surrounded by admirers 'Boss' Croker had called it right – the Tammany machine proved victorious once again and made their man mayor of the greatest city in the world.

'Mr Croker returned from Europe to direct our politics and he made a good job of it,' said Tammany orator Thomas R Grady as the celebrations got into full swing. It was Croker's greatest triumph; as his biographer says, 'Richard Croker was indeed Master of Manhattan.'

Days after the election the Boss, with 'his' mayor, went to Lakewood, New Jersey, and established headquarters in the town's biggest hotel. 'Croker's Court' attracted trainloads of politicians, great and aspiring, and all classes of schemers and businessmen looking for jobs or favours from the city's new administration.

The Boss gave himself an air of royalty, instructing everyone to appear for dinner in evening dress, as he had seen during his time touring the country estates of England and Ireland.

'The results were startling, even ludicrous,' says his biographer. 'Tammany roughnecks struggled into "boiled shirts", grew apoplectic over high, starched collars, and tried to look at ease in "tux-edos" or swallowtails which, somehow, would not fit. Among this uneasy company sauntered the Boss immaculately tailored by London's best. Croker fairly flaunted his English wardrobe, his English manners, even his English valet.'

At noon on New Year's Day 1898, Tammany Hall took over, not merely Manhattan, but all of greater New York.

'The new regime burst in with much pomp and ceremony. City Hall blazed with light, effectually routing the gloom of a foggy winter's day. A band played, and the old building swarmed with Tammany men, surging exultantly through the flag-draped rooms and corridors.'

Boss cannily stood back and let Mayor Van Wyck take the bow. But when Croker sailed for Europe that year, as he did every summer, it was like royalty leaving New York, to the point that on this occasion a police boat preceded his ship and fired a 21 gun salute at the departing liner.

After Van Wyck's defeat by an anti-corruption campaign fronted by Seth Low in 1901, Croker's standing went into terminal decline and he finally ceded command of Tammany in 1902 before returning to his estate in Wantage, England to his horses and his prize bulldogs.

'I am out of politics and now I am going to win the Derby,' he declared.

Horse racing was among the expensive pastimes he had developed in America and now, in England and free of politics, it became his passion. The Boss determined that the only way to succeed in the game was to have his horses trained at Newmarket, the headquarters of racing. But his plan required the go-ahead of the 'Noble Lords' of the Turf Club who controlled horse racing in England. Despite his money and fame they refused his request.

Enraged, Boss Croker immediately sold his English estate and in 1905 moved himself and his racing interests to Ireland, buying the Glencairn estate in the foothills of the Dublin mountains near Sandyford from Judge Murphy and spending a considerable amount of money remodelling it as a baronial mansion.

With his imported thoroughbreds and his bottomless pockets, his dark 'Yale blue' colours flashed past the winning post with increasing regularity and he was the leading owner in Ireland in 1905 and 1906.

Meantime, Croker had officially separated from Elizabeth in early 1897, handing over his impressive Manhattan townhouse to his wife and making a generous settlement for her and their children, the eldest, Richard, being 19 at the time. While Boss Croker was indulging his passion for horse racing in Ireland, the 'fast' living in New York, fuelled by the money and power of their famous father, was taking its toll on his family. His son Frank was killed in a motor-racing accident in 1905 and Hubert, or 'Bertie' as he was known in the family, died of an opium overdose the following year.

Because he was spending so much time in Ireland, Croker gave his son Richard power of attorney over his affairs in 1907 and extended that two years later, giving his son complete control over all his property, bank accounts and trust funds. It was a move he would later regret.

But for now Croker had found the horse he believed would make his last great wish come true. Bred in England but brought to Glencairn as a foal, the colt was named Orby and Croker trained it with only one thing in mind: winning the Derby.

Always one for theatrics, Croker sent the three-year-old to the great race at Epsom with 17 'stout Irishmen' as bodyguards. Going at odds of 100 to 9 and ridden by the American jockey John Reiff, Orby stunned the British racing establishment by winning the thrilling race by two lengths to shouts of 'Orby wins – the American horse wins!'

Immaculately dressed in top hat and tails, Richard Boss Croker led Orby past the grandstand where King Edward VII and his son the Prince of Wales were holding court.

'Mr Croker raised his silk hat in silent acknowledgement, King Edward turned away,' said reports of the day.

Croker was not invited to that evening's Derby Dinner hosted by the British king. It may have been 'the Tammany Derby' but the British establishment was having none of Boss Croker. Instead it was left to the king's Irish subjects to celebrate, and they did so in style. Croker returned to Ireland to a hero's welcome, bonfires burning in the hills around Sandyford and it is said that Croker gave his £40,000 in winnings from wagers to local charities. The horse then went on to win the Irish Derby, the first horse to complete the double.

Richard Welstead Croker was truly 'back home' when he was made a Freeman of Dublin in 1908.

He won two Irish Oaks and was again leading owner in Ireland in 1911, but his interest in racing was tapering off and he settled into a sedentary life travelling between his homes in Dublin, New York and West Palm Beach.

His wife Elizabeth died in the late summer of 1914 while on holiday in Austria. Boss Croker joined his family at her burial in the Croker plot in Woodlawn cemetery in New York. After the funeral the family adjourned to their mansion off Fifth Avenue, but the once united Croker clan was thrown into complete disarray when their father announced that he intended to remarry. According to himself, his daughters cried and his sons swore at him.

Boss Croker had fallen in love – with a woman said to be 50 years younger than himself.

He had met her just six weeks earlier at a burlesque show in The Studio Club on Broadway. He was 73 and his new bride-to-be, a woman of Indian descent, was said to be just 23 years old.

Bula Benton Edmondson was born in Muskogee, Oklahoma and it was said her mother had come from the Indian Territory and had Cherokee blood. According to her own account she had immersed herself in Indian culture and given herself the name Keetaw Kelantuchy Sequon. Whether this was a genuine name or whether she adopted it for a number of vaudeville performances was never quite clear and would become a matter of some dispute in the New York courts at a later stage.

Private detectives hired by the Croker family maintained that, by the time she met Boss she was already married to a man called Guy R Marone and was 'a well-known street walker on Broadway', not the complete stranger in New York their father seemed to believe.

'She is a pretty girl and looks like an Indian when she is dressed like one, but she could pass in street clothes and no one would notice, or think she was Indian,' said one reporter when the scandal of her relationship with Boss Croker broke.

The Croker family, who were used to hearing their father described as a crook and a thief, were outraged by his liaison with the young woman. In response to their protests he initially postponed the wedding but then, less than two months after his wife's death, he married Bula on 26 November 1914 in New York. The couple were married at St Agnes Roman Catholic church on Lexington Avenue by a priest friend from Ireland.

'When a man does a good thing the newspapers never mention it; when a man does a bad thing the papers hound him for years . . . I never did anything wrong in my life,' said the Boss enigmatically as he left the church followed by a clutch of reporters.

After the ceremony the happy couple called on his good friend Mr Nathan

Strauss, owner of Macy's department store, before visiting Mrs Randolph Guggenheim in her Fifth Avenue mansion where she treated them to a wedding breakfast. Shortly afterwards they left for West Palm Beach for their honeymoon.

Despite his family's reservations and recriminations, relations between Boss Croker and his family didn't sour straight away. As he prepared to depart for Ireland on 2 April 1915, Boss Croker called his son Richard to his home and told him he was making a 'trip will' – a common enough practice for wealthy people in those days when journeys were lengthy and perilous. He told Richard that he was leaving everything to him.

'You are more acquainted with my affairs than any of the other children and for that reason I wish to provide that everything be left to you and that you will distribute everything I have among the children. You are the best one to do it.'

But relations between Boss Croker and three of his four remaining children deteriorated quickly after this gesture.

In 1917 Boss Croker accused the same son, Richard Jnr, who had looked after his financial affairs for years, of dishonesty, and tried to revoke a trust fund with $333,000 for his three younger children, Ethel, Florence and Howard, and get the money signed over to himself.

Richard Jnr, who already had property transferred to him, refused to break the trust pointing out that most of the money had come from the resources of their mother Elizabeth.

Boss Croker did not take kindly to being thwarted. He told Richard, in a letter dated 15 November 1917: 'I am tired and sick of this kind of thing. My main reason for revoking that trust fund was that I wanted to divide it between Howard, Ethel and Florence. To my certain knowledge you never sent Florence her share. Your conduct alone is sending me to an early grave. You never go to church – money is your God. You have been playing a great game with my money right along.'

He followed with another letter addressed to his children dated 1 December 1917: 'Richard in his whole life has never made a dollar of his own. Richard has been miserable all his life and has been playing a great game with my money, pretending that the money came from him. Since I have taken my business out of his hands he has become very impudent to me. You all have forgotten what a good father I have been to you. I have given you all the money I can afford. I wrote to Richard for $10,000 dollars some time ago and he refused me. I am glad I have lived long enough to find him out.'

But his other son Howard had a different version of events.

'In 1917 our father insisted that the trust be revoked and that the trust funds be sent to him in Ireland. We both [Howard and Ethel] visited our father for the purposes of discussing this matter and informed him that we were unwilling to have the trust revoked and wished to have our brother, Richard, continue as trustee and have the trust funds kept intact, so that the arrangement made by our deceased mother be carried out. A large part of the trust fund had been contributed by our mother out of her own resources. The purpose of both parents in the trust agreement was to provide for the three younger children upon the death of the parents. While our father was disappointed at our refusal to consent to the revocation of the trust agreement, he remained on most friendly terms with us and was quite friendly to us in the month of October, 1919.

'Prior to the attempted revocation of the trust, our father did withdraw from our brother, Richard, the control of his affairs in this country and had turned that over to his second wife. No one had any objection to this because we all felt our father was at liberty to place the management of his affairs where he pleased. It became evident shortly after, however, that efforts were being made by our father's second wife to turn him away from all his children and especially against our brother Richard, who was the most familiar with his affairs. We realise now that it was essential that the friendly and affectionate relations existing between our father and his children must be broken up if his entire fortune was to be diverted from them. We were familiar with the part our brother Richard had played in managing our father's affairs, as well as his management of the trust estate, and knowing the malicious influence being exerted on our father, we naturally supported Richard. Our sister Florence, who was not in this country for 15 years, was not familiar with the situation and did not know the facts as we know them. She was guided entirely by the suggestion made or the views held by our father and his wife and had no other source of information.'

Boss Croker and Richard Jnr met in the National Democratic Club in New York on 4 June 1919 to try to thrash out their differences. Boss said his wife Bula had gone through all the papers that had been handed over to them and discovered what he described as 'wrongdoing' on the part of his son.

According to Richard he told his father: 'This is a very disagreeable subject for me too and I don't intend to continue it any longer. I know everything is wrong and I don't wish to hear any more about it.'

As they were talking Bula interrupted, repeating: 'Daddy don't you have anything to do with it, they will swear your life away. Don't go and throw oil on the troubled water.'

He said that although they disagreed at that meeting the only one who used the word 'liar' that night was his father's wife, Bula.

'I was proud of him and had the greatest esteem and respect and affection for him as I have up to the present,' Richard would later say when six legal cases involving the family came up for hearing in New York and Palm Beach.

Boss Croker re-stated his belief that his son Richard had been cheating him and appeals by Richard that he was being deceived could not convince him.

'I told him there was but one thing left for me to do. That since he refused to give an opportunity to show that he was wrong I must take legal action in order to prove he had made a mistake.

'I said to him "I must serve you a summons" in three suits, he threw the summons on the floor and said "I won't accept service" and walked out the door.'

The following December Howard Croker said that he met his father and stepmother in the Savoy Hotel in New York in a final attempt to avoid litigation.

'My father took Ethel and myself into the bedroom and closed the door. He asked me what we wished to discuss with him. I told him that I had come to ask him to appoint another trustee to my brother's place for the trust fund. I told him that my brother wished to be relieved from his trusteeship. The reply was that my brother could not be relieved, that he had mishandled the funds in this trust and that until he accounted for the missing money he would not relieve him. We had only got started in the conversation when his wife entered the room and stood alongside him and when my father finished speaking and saying that he would not relieve my brother, his wife spoke up and said that we had just come to make trouble and that she would not stand for it and that she was going to call the police and have us put out. She went over to the telephone when my father stopped her and told her we would not be having anything like that.'

According to Howard, the old Boss 'looked at her in the most meek and appealing way, to ascertain whether or not what he had to say met with her approval.'

On 2 April 1920 Richard Croker Jnr, his brother Howard and his sister Mrs Ethel White filed an injunction in West Palm Beach, Florida against their stepmother Mrs Bula Croker, restraining her from disposing of any of her husband's possessions.

They claimed that by way of his 'enfeebled' mental condition she had fraudulently obtained control and management of all his property and while she was investing and re-investing his money it was 'with the intent and purpose of ultimately getting control and possession for her own use and benefit'.

They claimed that large amounts of property which the Boss had acquired in West Palm Beach had been reclassified in joint names, or in her name only. They would also allege that property which Boss Croker owned in West Palm Beach had been transferred into a company called Palm Beach Estates, controlled by a business associate, JB McDonald, to ensure that it was no longer part of his estate when he died.

'The defendant [Bula] has in her possession a large amount of cash and securities belonging to the said Richard Croker Snr, which she unjustly retains and which she has from time to time secreted and transferred out of the jurisdiction in order to prevent lawful process to reach the same within the State, that the defendant has large sums of money deposited in banks in her own name within the county of Palm Beach and elsewhere which sums of money rightfully belong to her husband, and from time to time she has withdrawn large portions thereof and forwarded the same out of the jurisdiction and beyond the

105

reach of the State.'

They claimed that when Bula realised their father was a man of 'large means' and 'wealth' she falsely claimed that she was a 23-year-old of 'royal Indian blood' and a direct descendant of Chief Sequoyah one of the great Cherokee chiefs and a woman of refinement and culture and reputation.

'And by reason of the charms and smooth manner, ingratiating ways, seductive methods and her subtle devices and deceit, she quickly worked herself into the confidence, love and affections of Richard Croker.'

As the legal wrangles continued the family had Boss Croker's and Bula's bank accounts frozen and got an injunction preventing them from leaving the United States for Ireland, as he usually did in the early autumn. His wife would later claim that they had only $5.67 in their pockets and for 26 days they were 'beggared' until the injunctions were lifted.

In late October 1921 Boss Croker sailed out of New York with his wife Bula for the last time, bound for Ireland and their castle near the Dublin mountains. He would never see New York or his children again.

They arrived in Glencairn on 21 November 1921 after an arduous and eventful journey. That evening, according to Bula, Richard came downstairs and asked her for the two 'trip wills' that had been drawn up before the journey. She gave them to him and he put both of them in the fire in their 'little Japanese room' in Glencairn.

Although seriously ill from 'a chill' that had developed during the voyage, Boss grimly fought back and saw the early spring arrive in Ireland. It is said that four days before he died he was wheeled out the front door of his Sandyford mansion to view his mausoleum, which had just been completed.

'Silently he viewed it, built among the rocks beside a shaded pool a stone's throw from the gravy of Orby. Then he whispered: "I am ready for it."'

Four days after his death on 29 April 1922 Boss Croker's funeral took place in Glencairn. The Requiem Mass in his private oratory was celebrated by an old friend, the Reverend Thomas Grennan of Aungier Street, Dublin, and the chief mourners were his wife, Bula, and his daughter, Florence, accompanied by her husband Major Norris who had travelled from England for the funeral.

'After the service a procession, led by a cross-bearer and acolytes, proceeded to the grave. The coffin was borne on the shoulders of eight estate employees. It was covered by a pall made of natural violets and evergreens' went the report in the newspapers of Friday, 5 May under the heading 'Late Mr Richard Croker: Private Funeral in Demesne'.

Croker, who had been a secret supporter and financial backer of the IRA during the War of Independence, was not forgotten by the new government: Arthur Griffith, President of Dáil Éireann was accompanied by his wife, while General Michael Collins was represented by Kevin O'Shiel. Among the mourners were his solicitor, James J McDonald, Sir Thomas Myles CB, Alderman Joseph McDonagh, Maxwell Arnott of the Dublin department store, Dr Cyril Murphy his physician, and the Right Hon. James MacMahon, Under-Secretary at Dublin Castle.

The divisions in the family were evident as the 'other side' – his sons Richard and Howard and his daughter Ethel – did not attend, but sent wreaths. Other wreaths covering the grave came from Lord Clonmel, 'The men of Carrickmines Stud' and 'The girls of the house'.

Boss Croker was hardly cold in the ground when the battle for his money began in earnest.

In his will it was thought that he left a fortune in Ireland, England and Florida, estimated at between $5 million and $10 million. But it would emerge that Boss Croker was virtually penniless when he died.

His wife Bula later described the day the will was drawn up. Mr McDonald arrived at Glencairn that Sunday morning 12 October 1919. Bula was asked to get 'a block of paper' while Croker and McDonald discussed the terms of the will. The will was then written out by the solicitor. The only part of the conversation she said she heard was at the end when her husband told Mr McDonald to be sure that it was made 'watertight'.

McDonald replied that he thought that it was watertight and he said that in a short will there would not be very much to 'attack'.

Mr Croker, who was lying on a couch, got up and came around to the table and read the will himself. He told McDonald that he had spelled Mrs Croker's name wrongly, that he had written 'Beulah' instead of 'Bula'. Mr McDonald made two changes and asked Croker to initial them.

When the will was signed and witnessed it was put in the strong box in their joint names. It was then brought to the Hibernian Bank and after Croker's death it was opened at Bula's request.

Dated 12 October 1919, the last will and testament of Richard W Croker was written on plain stationery, and headed:

> Glencairn,
> Telephone 10 Dundrum,
> Telegrams, Sandyford, Sandyford Station, Stillorgan, Co Dublin:
>
> I, Richard Croker of Glencairn, Sandyford, Co Dublin, declare this to be my last will. I hereby revoke all previous wills made by me. I hereby bequeath and devise to my dear wife, Beulah [crossed out and replaced by Bula and initialled RC] E Croker, all the property, real and personal, which I may die possessed of or over which I may have any power of appointment, absolutely. I hereby appoint my wife Beulah [crossed out and replaced by Bula and initialled RC] E Croker, to be the sole executrix of this my will, in witness whereof, I have hereunder signed my name this twelfth day of October, 1919.
> Richard Croker
> Witness.
> James J McDonald, 116 Grafton Street, Dublin.
> Thomas J Fleming, 13 Longford Terrace, Monkstown, Dublin.

Later reports said the will was 'considerably marked up with corrections' when in fact just two corrections were made. The will document was also accompanied by a second letter, written on the same stationery, but this time in the hand of Boss Croker's. It read:

> My dear Bula,
> I'm writing this note for you to keep in case you should survive me. I wish you would give my daughter, Florence, ten thousand pounds. She is the only one of my surviving children that has ever shown any gratitude to me.
> Richard Croker

While it was recognised as evidence in the subsequent court case it was not regarded as a codicil to the original will.

In the Four Courts in Dublin lies a small brown envelope containing about 10 yellowing documents, many with the original stamps of the period, which go some way towards telling the tale of Richard and Bula Croker and the sad disintegration of Boss Croker's relationship with his children.

Henry B O'Hanlon, a solicitor of 58 Dame Street, Dublin, who was now acting for Bula Croker, gives his own potted biography of Boss Croker in one of the documents which is dated 10 August 1923.

'His only hobby was racing and breeding of bloodstock,' he wrote, before revealing that in 1917 Richard Croker had conveyed his 'magnificent home and estate' known as The Wigwam and his property in West Palm Beach to his wife Bula. The following year he signed his house, Glencairn, and the surrounding estate into her sole name too.

'Richard Croker always claimed to be an American citizen,' continued O'Hanlon, who then quoted directly from the man himself: 'I never voted in Ireland; America is my country. I have lived there all my life and made my name and money there. I will never agree that I belong in any way to any other country.'

This is followed by a document signed by Bula Croker herself and entitled: 'In the Goods of Richard Croker'. In it she said that they came to Ireland for the 'summer racing' and repeated that between 1917 and 1918 he conveyed all his property in Ireland and Florida to her name.

'As of August [1918] he didn't own or possess any property in Ireland,' she said. 'All he had was a joint bank account in the Hibernian Bank in Dublin.'

On 17 April 1923 the American Consular Service wrote to the High Court in Dublin seeking a copy of the original will and soon after Richard Croker Jnr filed papers challenging its validity.

When the case opened before the Lord Chief Justice, Sir Thomas Molony, sitting in Dublin Castle on Thursday 31 May 1923, it caused a worldwide sensation. The case to overturn the will was taken by Richard Croker Jnr against his father's wife Bula E Croker. Mrs Ethel C White, Boss Croker's daughter was granted the right to be represented and was known as 'The Intervenent'.

Teams of the best lawyers in Dublin assembled to try the case, which was heard over two weeks with 11 full days of evidence and relayed by hordes of journalists and commentators to newspapers around the world.

Mr Richard Croker, the plaintiff, was represented by Mr Serjeant Sullivan, Mr JCR Lardner KC and Mr Kenneth Dockrell (instructed by Messrs Montgomery and Chaytor); and Mrs Ethel White (The Intervenent) by Mr Jellett KC and Mr Hubert Hamilton, instructed by Mr Valentine Miley.

Mrs Bula Croker was represented by Mr Serjeant Hanna, Mr Patrick Lynch SC, Mr Sullivan KC and Mr Costello (instructed by Mr HB O'Hanlon).

The case had everything – money, power and sex, bigamy and society.

Mrs Croker claimed that she had attended Chicago University in 1902 and been a schoolteacher in Cisco, Texas in 1911 and, after outlining the details of her life, she dramatically told the court: 'Aside from all the beautiful things friends of his said in this court, I can add that my husband Richard Croker was a saint.'

Mr David Ruttledge of the Turf Club recalled Richard Croker telling him as they strolled in the gardens at Glencairn before going to a race meeting in nearby Leopardstown: 'If I die tomorrow, all this belongs to Bula.'

However, according to lawyers acting for Richard Croker Jnr, from March 1912 until some time in 1913, Mrs Croker was living as the wife of Guy R Marone in Northampton, Massachusetts and later in New Brunswick, Canada. Marone's landlady and a number of other witnesses were brought to Dublin to testify as such.

When this dramatic fact was introduced Mrs Croker was brought back to the witness box to be cross-examined by Mr Jellett.

'Now, Mrs Croker, do you remember in October 1911 being in Northampton, Massachusetts?' he asked.

'No, sir.'

'Or at any other time?'

'No, sir. I was never in Northampton, Massachusetts in my whole life.'

'Do you know what Mr Guy R Marone's occupation in life was?'

'No, sir, I do not know anything about Mr Guy R Marone.'

She was then re-examined by her own counsel, Serjeant Hanna.

'At the time of Mr Croker's death were you his lawful wife?'

'Yes.'

'And you are now his lawful widow?'

'Yes.'

'And were you at any time during your whole life married to any person other than Mr Croker?

'No, sir.'

Witnesses Mr and Mrs Addis, who lived next door to the house where Guy R Marone lived with his wife, were adamant that the woman they knew as Mrs Marone was now Mrs Croker.

A Mrs McElroy said that in 1921 she was brought by private detectives working for the Croker children to the Adelphi Hotel in Saratoga Springs where they sat next to Mr and Mrs Croker in the dining room and she identified Mrs Croker as the person she had known as the wife of Guy Marone.

Serjeant Hanna then read the affidavit of Howard Croker regarding his father's bride Bula: 'She was not a person of culture, refinement, good character but on the contrary, she was lacking in refinement and culture and good reputation and had, prior to the said marriage, received the intimate attention and pecuniary support of other men.'

Turning dramatically to Howard Croker in the witness box he asked imperiously: 'What do you mean?'

Howard Croker declined to be more specific.

But it got worse as the week wore on.

'Was that part of the Palm Beach trial that your father's wife had been a well-known streetwalker in New York before she married your father? Was that part of your case? Answer the question, yes or no,' Mr Patrick Lynch, acting for Mrs Croker asked Richard Croker when he went into the witness box.

'The question you have just asked is a rather long question. Part is true and part is untrue,' answered Richard.

'What part is untrue?'

'That I said she was a Broadway streetwalker. I never said that.'

'You never suggested that?'

'I never suggested that in the terms you have put it.'

'In any terms?'

'I made a statement that my father's wife was well known on Broadway.'

'What is the meaning of that, sir? What did you mean to convey by that when you said Mrs Bula Croker was well known on Broadway before she was married?'

'Just what I said.'

'What is it?'

'That she was well known on Broadway. That she was living in a hotel near Broadway where people who are familiar with Broadway lived.'

'Did you mean by that to make an imputation on the chastity of Miss Edmondson? Did you believe that she was an immoral woman before she married your father, that she was an immoral woman in New York?'

'Whatever I have had to say was based on the information which I received.'

'Do you believe that Miss Bula Edmondson was an immoral woman in New York before she married your father?'

'I believe Miss Bula Edmondson absolutely deceived my father as regards her residence in New York and the representations she made to him before the marriage.'

The question of Boss Croker's place in 'society' was also raised in the case. He was portrayed by some of the witnesses as a fairly uncouth figure who, despite his money and power, shunned society. Not so, said his son Richard Jnr.

'He met people in all walks of life, in high society as it was called, swell society as he referred to it on many occasions; and he told me frequently that if he had wished for a social career he could easily have followed that as well as a political one, owing to his family connection and the old family in Ireland, and he told me that as he pointed out what was in the glass window installed in Glencairn, the crest of the Croker family.'

The matter of the various court cases in Palm Beach was brought up by lawyers for Mrs Croker.

'We are not going to try here what was the subject of eight other actions,' said Lord Chief Justice Sir Thomas Molony.

When it came to summing up the case the Lord Chief Justice spoke for seven hours, finishing his speech at 3.15pm on Friday, 16 June 1923 with the words: 'I have never felt more grateful to a jury for giving me and giving the various witnesses their undivided attention and taking an active interest in the presentation of the case, and doing everything to justify the retention, if not the expansion, of the jury system as being – as I have always believed it to be – one of the best handmaids of justice and one of the greatest institutions our forefathers have handed down to us.'

The jury was immediately sent out and returned at 4.30pm to read the Order Paper. They had to answer Yes or No to a series of questions that would determine the outcome of the trial.

Was the paper written and dated 12 October 1919 and alleged to be the last will of Richard Croker?
*Yes*

Was the deceased at the time of the execution of the alleged will of sound mind, memory and understanding?
*Yes*

Did the deceased at the time of the execution of the said alleged will know and approve of its contents?
*Yes*

Was the execution of the said alleged will obtained from the said deceased by the undue influence of the said defendant Bula E Croker?
*No*

Did the said defendant Bula E Croker make false and fraudulent representations to the said deceased as to the honesty, loyalty and affection of his children, Richard, Howard and Ethel?
*No*

Did the said defendant Bula E Croker by contrivance keep the said Richard Croker deceased from intercourse with his said children to the end that prejudice might never be removed?
*No*

At the time of marriage of the said Richard Croker deceased with the said defendant Bula E Croker was she the wife of Guy R Marone?
*No*

At the time of the said marriage did the said defendant Bula E Croker then know that she was the lawful wife of the said Guy R Marone?
*No*

Immediately after the chairman of the jury finished answering the Order Paper, which was a clear victory for Bula Croker, there was 'a loud outburst of cheering and hand-clapping in court'. The Lord Chief Justice, rising to his feet, said in solemn tones: 'I very much regret that the last scene of a great case should be disgraced by the conduct of people who ought to know better.'

Cheers of 'hear hear' were heard from more respectable members of the packed courtroom.

The Lord Chief Justice said he would grant probate of the will of Richard W Croker and costs against Richard Croker Jnr and Ethel C White. Each of the jurors was awarded 10 guineas on top of their nominal fee of one guinea for jury service.

Mrs Croker was 'warmly cheered' as she came down the courthouse steps and entered her motor car in the castle yard. She waved her hand in acknowledgement as she was driven away from Dublin Castle.

As well as hearing the case, the Lord Chief Justice received a document from EJ L'Engle of the Law Exchange, Jacksonville, Florida entitled: 'Opinion on the Validity of Will of Richard Croker Snr dated 12 October 1919 and if invalid the effects on the will of the same testator dated 1917.'

This document, on flimsy rice paper, reveals that in his original will of 1917 Richard Boss Croker had decreed: 'My wish is to be buried in dear old Ireland', but apart from a number of named bequests, he left his estates in Ireland and

Florida to Bula E Croker. These bequests were $1,000 dollars each to Florence, wife of Major JG Morris of Blewburton Hill, Berkshire, England; Ethel, wife of Thomas F White of Cedarhurst, Long Island, New York; Richard Jnr, Ridge Street, Port Chester, New York and Howard of Cedarhurst, Long Island, New York. He also left a sum of $5,000 to his solicitor in Dublin, Daniel O'Connell Miley.

*The New York Times*, which covered the story in detail, said that most of the oceanfront West Palm Beach property, which included his home, The Wigwam named after Tammany Hall's New York headquarters, was once worth $2 million but was now worth about $800,000 because parcels of land had been sold off to Palm Beach Estates.

On 11 July 1923 Ethel C White and Howard Croker joined their brother Richard Jnr in yet another attempt to challenge the will, this time in New York.

In the action against their stepmother, Bula Croker, and their sister, Florence Croker Morris, they sought to have a 'temporary administrator' appointed to their father's property in the United States, particularly in Florida. In a statement issued the same day they said:

> The copy of the will, as published in the newspapers, shows that no provision whatever was made for any of the children, even Florence. What the paper referred to as a codicil is merely a note written on the stationery that our father was accustomed to using in Ireland. In this note the suggestion is made that Florence be remembered. We are informed that the note is not part of the will and is wholly ineffective. The publication of the note apparently is made for the purpose of showing that our father had not turned against all his children.

Surprisingly, but perhaps very wisely as it turned out, Bula Croker did not fight the family on the issue of appointing an administrator. She agreed to the New York Trust Company to be 'temporary administrators' of her late husband's estate. Now, instead of suing their stepmother, Richard Jnr and Ethel had to enter into further litigation against the New York Trust Company. On 2 December 1924 a judgement was given in their favour for $235,456, which was to be divided equally among them.

But they were in for a shock that would drag the issue out for another few years. There was no money in the estate – at least for them.

According to a further legal judgement dated 22 July 1925 Boss Croker held title to one parcel of land in New York, but the mortgages exceeded the value of the property. 'There are no assets in New York of the estate of Richard Croker with which to pay said judgement [of £235,456],' said Judge Walker.

The net value of his estates in Ireland was given at £150 and his personal assets in West Palm Beach valued at £2,885.

What had happened to Boss Croker's millions?

Bula had not only taken all the cash and securities that the Boss had accumulated during his reign at Tammany Hall, but all his property had been transferred to his wife as well.

On 7 November 1917 half the property in West Palm Beach, which was approximately two miles of shoreline, was assigned to her. On 28 May 1918 the Dublin firm of Miley & Miley had been brought in by Richard Croker to legally transfer Glencairn into her name also.

When he died, Boss Croker the famous multimillionaire had little more in his estate than a small Dublin shopkeeper.

In Florida the property that wasn't in Bula Croker's sole name was held by Palm Beach Estates, a company established by their one-time friend, JB McDonald, who now claimed that he had an option to purchase it at a set price. The price of property in Palm Beach was going sky high, but McDonald claimed his option was legally binding.

This led to further litigation and according to *The New York Times* of 19 August 1929 Bula Croker lost her case against Palm Beach Estates.

She also lost an estimated $5 million, as a result.

The 'merry widow' Bula Croker died on 16 March 1957 at her estate in West Palm Beach, Florida at the age of 73.

After walking in triumph down the steps of Dublin Castle 35 years earlier, she had gone straight to Glencairn, packed her things and never set foot in Ireland again.

# Chapter 6

# *The Mystic's Muddle*

When Judge Paul Gilligan came to adjudicate on the last will and testament of the millionaire writer and philosopher John O'Donohue, he declared that the poet's last wishes 'unfortunately provided an illustration of exactly how a person should *not* make a will'.

O'Donohue, a former priest and the author of the bestselling spiritual books, *Anam Cara*, *Eternal Echoes* and *Benedictus: A Book of Blessings,* had left more than €2 million in his will when he died suddenly in 2008 just days after his fifty-second birthday while holidaying in France with his lover Kristine Fleck.

O'Donohue had originally executed a will in 1998 'with the benefit of legal advice'. But in February 2001 he decided to make another will, shortly before he was due to go on a speaking tour of Australia. This time he did so without the bother of consulting a solicitor, something which the legal profession made a fuss about, but which was largely irrelevant to the High Court case that would follow. It was the confused thought process behind the will that was responsible for the trouble it caused, although the lack of legal advice did lead him to make some very basic mistakes in setting out his last wishes.

In the new will he stipulated that he was leaving 'all my worldly possessions to my mother Josie to be divided equally and fairly among my family with special care and extra help to be given to my sister Mary.' He also stipulated specific gifts of money to be given to a number of other persons.

O'Donohue was survived by his mother Josephine (Josie), his sister Mary and brothers Patrick (PJ) and Peter but he also had a number of nieces and nephews who were named in the document, adding further to the confusion.

After writing out the details of the will he then committed what the judge called 'the classic error' of having it witnessed by his mother and his brother Peter, two of the beneficiaries. Legally, witnesses are not entitled to also benefit from the estate.

In the end, however, that turned out to be a minor flaw which the courts could overturn; the real trouble lay elsewhere.

When the will eventually came to probate in 2008 it was impossible to decipher exactly what were the intended last wishes of the priest, campaigner and philosopher who had made a fortune and counted many wealthy Americans, including Stephen Spielberg's wife Katie Kapshaw, as devotees of his unique blend of wisdom, mythology and philosophy all wrapped up in a binding of Celtic mysticism.

The result was that his mother Josie O'Donohue had to go to the High Court on 9 November 2011 to ask a judge to clarify exactly what her son intended in his last will and testament.

John O'Donohue was born to a farmer and stonemason Paddy O'Donohue and his wife Josie Dunleavy on 1 January 1956 at Caherbeanna, near Fenore, in the Burren of County Clare. For those who are not familiar with it, the Burren looks forbidding with flat sheets of limestone extending right down to the Atlantic Ocean. It is sparsely populated, but the local farmers are said to be well off because, although you cannot see it, there is a fertile sheltered plateau at the top of the rocky landscape and cattle can be 'wintered' without the farmers having to spend a lot of money on sheds and fodder.

John O'Donohue grew up speaking Irish fluently and was known as 'Johnny Dry' in the local national school. At the age of 12 he attended a Catholic seminary, St Mary's College, Galway as a boarder. At the age of 18 he decided to joint the priesthood and was enrolled in St Patrick's College, Maynooth. He graduated with degrees in English, theology and philosophy and was ordained to the priesthood in 1982.

He was assigned as a curate to the parish of Rossaveal in Connemara, a huddle of small houses and a harbour that accommodates the ferry boats to the Aran Island.

After three years of rural isolation Fr O'Donohue got leave of absence to go to Germany to learn the language and study. He ended up in Tübingen, the town where the philosopher Hegel had studied. There he learned German and was soon so fluent in the language that he completed a doctorate on the philosopher and his work, graduating from Eberhard Karls University with a PhD in philosophical theology in 1990.

He came back to Ireland in 1990 to be reassigned to his parish. But Fr O'Donohue was now more interested in writing his post-doctoral studies on the thirteenth-century Dominican mystic preacher, Meister Eckhard.

His bishop at the time, an austere prelate called Dr James McLoughlin, wanted him to give up his 'auld writin' and work full time in the busy parish of Knocknacarra in the Salthill area of Galway city. But Fr John O'Donohue, CC as he then was, had other things on his mind. According to himself he was trying to move his parishioners away from their rigid, traditional Catholic beliefs in favour of a more spiritual church.

'I was trying to refine their fingers . . . so that they could undo so much of the false netting crippling their own spirits,' he said, probably unaware that many of them depended on this so-called 'netting' to live the sane and normal life of an Irish Catholic watching their church collapse before their eyes as it became engulfed in sex scandals, paedophilia and official cover-ups.

His teachings and the fact that he wanted to be a part-time curate so that he could spend his time writing and studying, resulted in a head-on clash with his bishop. This led John O'Donohue to resign from the parish, but it would be another 10 years before he left the priesthood altogether.

'The best decision I ever made was to become a priest and I think the second best was to resign,' he would say later, although he didn't formally leave until 2000, several years after the publication of his most famous book.

He also said that he had 'a fundamental conflict with authority' which probably made him unsuitable for life in an authoritarian organisation like the Catholic Church.

O'Donohue moved to a stone cottage in the Burren and it was while filling in for an ailing priest in Carron in the early 1990s that he attended a public meeting called to oppose the building of an Interpretive Centre at Mullaghmore, described by some devotees of the area as 'the unique mountain that some regard as the very soul of the Burren'.

As the son of a stonemason who had lived most of his life in the rocky landscapes of the Burren where he was born and Connemara where he eventually settled, he knew a lot about stone and its influence on the landscape. 'Each stone has a different face,' he said once. 'Often the angle of the light falls gently enough to bring out the shy presence of each stone. Here it feels as if a wild, surrealistic God laid down the whole landscape.'

Like some old-style prophet, O'Donohue immersed himself in a campaign to prevent the Office of Public Works (OPW) going ahead with its plans for the Interpretive Centre and by 1996 he was chairman of the Burren Action Group. It was one of those typical long-running divisive Irish disputes where two sides try to do the right thing but, instead of working it out, both sides became locked in a vicious and seemingly never-ending struggle about the proper way of going about it. On the one hand was the zealot O'Donohue, convinced of the justness of not allowing the 'holy mountain' to be defiled by the Interpretive Centre, while on the other side, 'official Ireland' with its bureaucrats and blundering politicians was awkwardly trying to find a solution to what was threatening to become a real problem.

The OPW wanted to build the centre in a 1200-acre 'national park' so that there would be proper parking facilities and educational facilities to explain to the tourists flocking to this spectacular limestone landscape on the edge of the Atlantic exactly what they were seeing and why it was worth visiting in the first place. As it was, the narrow roads were blocked with tour buses, and tourists in their thousands were tramping through the fragile eco-system that includes delicate rock formations, wildlife and species of plants that grow nowhere else in Ireland.

'I'm fiercely proud of that group [the Burren Action Group] because I think they have behaved with impeccable dignity and courtesy and great honour,'

O'Donohue would later declare. 'We have attacked nobody and said nothing that we cannot stand over. We have no vested interest – money is not our goal at all. Our goal is a very innocent one – the love of that mountain, which makes us recoil at the thought that after millions of years it might be destroyed. The nice thing about it all is that a great community has been formed out of our closeness to the mountain and our awareness of the environment. Friends have been made here who'll stay friends for life.'

Despite the backing of 'official Ireland' for the project, O'Donohue and his allies, thrown together because of their love of the landscape, eventually got such national and international support that the project was abandoned. Even the concrete foundations for the centre, which had already been poured, were eventually dug up and the site put back the way it had been found. In the meantime much energy and millions of pounds had been wasted on construction costs and professional and legal fees.

The journalist Michael Finlan who profiled O'Donohue for *The Irish Times* in 1996 described him as: 'A tall, commanding figure with a luxuriant black beard . . . he has an Old Testament cast to his demeanour, or so you'd think until he explodes a bellyful of laughter at you, which he does frequently when he talks.'

He continued: 'At 37 John O'Donohue is one of a group of young Irish priests whose principled individualism cleaves to what older clerics might disapprovingly see as maverick behaviour but which really is concerned with the human side of their priesthood as opposed to the sacerdotal rigidity traditionally associated with the Irish clergy. As often as not, you'll see them going around in a gansey with no sign of a Roman collar tightening around their necks.'

Even then O'Donohue was making pronouncements that would later take shape in the Green movement, which he had probably encountered in Germany where the half-Irish firebrand Petra Kelly was a leading advocate. 'Landscape is the first-born of creation; it was here billions of years before humans came at all. One of our great duties is our duty to the land,' he told Finlan.

Yet those on the opposing side, who often found themselves vilified by O'Donohue and his followers, couldn't but like him. One politician said he would see the priest at meetings dressed in a designer coat from Brown Thomas in Dublin that cost over £600, surrounded by gnarled old farmers wearing their torn trench coats and Wellington boots. When he was challenged about it the priest just laughed it off, saying he didn't know it was a designer label and someone had given it to him as a present.

In the meantime his mixture of German thought and Celtic mysticism fused into his first book *Anam Cara*, subtitled *Spiritual wisdom from the Celtic world*. The Gaelic title translates into English as 'soul friend'. It was published to a largely indifferent audience by Harper Collins on 9 September 1997, around the time that Princess Diana died in a car crash in Paris.

He knew that Irish people had a distinctive suspicion of philosophical thought. 'It is not an intellectual society; we lump things together,' was one of his pronouncements. Yet the man who described himself as 'a poet and philosopher' would go on to astonish the publishing industry in Ireland and internationally.

'It is strange to be here. The mystery never leaves you alone,' the book begins. 'Behind your image, below your words, above your thoughts, the silence of another world waits. A world lives within you.'

It was a work littered with pseudo-spiritual quotations which, like his will, were either impossible to decipher or, alternatively, you could take whatever meaning you wanted from the words and phrases he had lovingly assembled.

'We do not need to go out to find love; rather we need to be still and let love discover us,' he urged. 'All the possibilities of your human destiny are asleep in your soul.'

Another passage went: 'When you cease to fear your solitude, a new creativity awakens in you. Your forgotten or neglected inner wealth begins to reveal itself. You come home to yourself and learn to rest within. Thoughts are our inner senses. Infused with silence and solitude, they bring out the mystery of the inner landscape.'

For some it was an astounding spiritual awakening and the discovery of what O'Donohue portrayed as a profound Celtic mysticism. To others it was a completely bogus pseudo-philosophy with a heavy dash of Celtic nonsense stirred in for a wealthy foreign audience brought up on atheism and unbelief and searching for the hidden meaning of existence; the type of people who found Buddhism too rigid and any form of organised religion outdated and unfashionable.

'His books, emerging every three or four years, were written in a kind of long-form prayer style which was impossible to read quickly and did not work for everyone. They were the distinct product of a life often spent in meditation and solitude. Not that he was not a gregarious, fun-loving companion, and mesmerising storyteller in the bar, but that his public presence grew from private silence,' wrote his friend Martin Wroe.

Whatever it was, it was a slow burner. For a few months *Anam Cara* languished on the bookshelves but gradually through word of mouth it began to sell, pushing its way to the top of the bestseller list as people began to ask, 'Who is John O'Donohue?'

To the astonishment of the publishing world it was reprinted 13 times in the following 12 months and went on to spawn an entire industry of books, CDs, readings and talks all over the world and in retreat centres in Ireland.

Devotees came in busloads to the Burren and soon John O'Donohue was lionised by wealthy patrons who wanted to be taken to these 'shrines' of Celtic knowledge by the author himself. Writers like Deepak Chopra and Larry Sossey favourably reviewed his work which helped sell his Celtic mysticism to a worldwide audience.

Yet O'Donohue was aware of, if never terribly comfortable with, the irony that as a contemplative writer critical of consumerism he himself was making a fortune exploring spirituality for people who wanted to find a path to some form of enlightenment.

Some of the more cynical observers regarded this form of Celtic mysticism as just another 'brand', but one packaged carefully for the wealthy and discerning consumer.

Yet O'Donohue could, without any trace of irony, say, in reference to the growing importance of the internet: 'I don't like to see knowledge treated as a product.'

Soon the mystical utterances of the priest became a staple of funeral services for all kinds of denominations, but particularly for those who had abandoned their Catholic faith and found in O'Donohue's words and philosophy a replacement.

He acknowledged himself that he was filling 'our modern spiritual hunger and questioning' and his themes of love and death, youth and ageing and the quest for solitude in the busy modern world were universal.

O'Donohue's timing was also perfect and soon he was in great demand, particularly in the United States where people connected with the 'Celtic mysticism' of the work, but he also travelled extensively in Ireland, Britain and other far-flung destinations, giving talks at Oxford and other centres of learning and expounding on philosophy and poetry. His thoughts included gems like: 'While experiences vanish, memory remains'; 'The narrative of an individual life is the secret construction of this invisible sanctuary of memory' and 'When at last the body falls and the visible life vanishes, the finished sanctuary of memory holds all the harvested possibility.'

Writing in *The Guardian* newspaper Martin Wroe, who knew him through the alternative Greenbelt Festival held annually near Cheltenham, added: 'O'Donohue found it amusing that pop stars and presidents had his book at their bedside, that Hollywood directors and household name actors sought his counsel. It confirmed his view that there is an intersection between philosophy, poetry and theology which can host an audience increasingly exiled from what he called "the frightened functionaries of institutional religion".'

Building on his reputation as a Celtic 'mystic', O'Donohue published *Eternal Echoes* (1998), a book of poems *Conamara Blues* (2000); *Divine Beauty: The Invisible Embrace* (2003) and *Benedictus: A Book of Blessings* in late 2007. But none of them repeated the success of *Anam Cara*.

Between bouts of solitude in his stone cottage in Gleann Treasna, Connemara, where he had moved because he could no longer find any time to himself with devotees calling at all times of the day and night, John O'Donohue was travelling the world, meeting important people and being feted as the great seer of modern secular society.

On one of his frequent visits to Oxford, O'Donohue met up with a homeopath, Kristine 'Kate' Fleck, around August 2007 and they became lovers. It was a new direction for the philosopher and poet and it was while enjoying a New Year holiday with her in Avignon, France that he died suddenly in his sleep on 4 January 2008, just three days after his fifty-second birthday.

His brother Pat described the moment when he heard the news: 'Christmas for me had always been a time of sweet tastes, of presents, presences and joy. Then on 4 January 2008 it was suddenly and cruelly transformed as it was overtaken by the bitter awareness of loss and grief. It was at that moment, 4.35 am, Friday morning, my head bent low into the phone searching for a mistake, that my eyes first caught a glimpse of the familiar ground vanishing at my feet. As a fog descended on my days, the only thing that settled in my heart was an absolute presence to John's oft-repeated statement: "There's a day waiting for you in your life when unwelcome news will breach your boundaries, whether through the measured sentences of an obligated physician or through the cold earpiece of technology, news of illness to you or a loved one will arrive."'

Writing in the London-based *Independent* newspaper another writer John Skinner described how he came to know O'Donohue 'obliquely' after O'Donohue contributed a prologue to Skinner's translation of *The Confession of St Patrick* (1998). In the prologue O'Donohue wrote: 'History is an amazing presence – it is a place where vanished time gathers. While we are in the flow of time, it is difficult to glean its significance, and it is only in looking back that we can recognise the hidden dimensions at work within a particular era or epoch.' Skinner then adds his own ending: 'Words that may well be applied to O'Donohue's own influence on a modern spirituality that more and more seeks to free itself from the shackles of organised religion.'

There may have been unintended irony in holding a memorial service for the poet and philosopher and former priest in Galway Cathedral, itself a monument to the monolithic nature of the Catholic Church which he had left.

Although to be fair to him he had always maintained that the Catholic Church, which he had abandoned, had many admirable qualities. Its treatment of women, however, was not one of them. 'It [the Catholic Church] would rather allow priests to marry than it would allow women to become priests,' he wrote. 'The awful mistrust of the feminine goes all the way back to Genesis where Eve is blamed for offering the apple to Adam.'

In keeping with his literary work and his Celtic heritage John O'Donohue was buried in the shadow of the ruined eleventh-century church at Creggagh, which stands overlooking the foaming waves of the Atlantic Ocean near Fanore, County Clare with the limestone sheets of the Burren looming in the background.

※ • ※

By the time his will, drawn up in 2001, came to be adjudicated on in the Probate Office in Dublin 10 years later, serious questions had arisen about the one-page document. Because of the amount of money involved, over €2 million, most of which came from advances and royalties from his published work and fees from his speaking tours, it was decided that it was a matter for a judge to decide exactly what the 'last wishes' of the former priest, poet and mystic really were.

A certain piquant urgency was added to events by the fact that the philosopher's mother, Mrs Josie O'Donohue, who lived near Ballyvaughan, County Clare, was herself terminally ill with cancer and it was vitally important for her son's estate to be put in order before she too died.

The court was asked to decide a number of issues. What exactly was the meaning and legal standing of the word 'family'; whether that meant only his mother, two brothers and sister, or extended to members of the wider O'Donohue family including nieces and nephews, as some of them were named in the document. There was also the matter of what was meant by the term 'special care and extra help' to be given to his sister, Mary.

When the matter first came before the High Court, Judge Paul Gilligan adjourned the proceedings because he wanted the 'eight or nine' people mentioned in the will to be informed of the legal proceedings and provided with all the relevant legal papers to see if they wanted to be legally represented at subsequent court hearings, where they might want to protect their own interests. People who were mentioned in the will, but not specifically assigned any legacy, could, after all, have a legal claim on part of the estate.

He also found that there was 'a myriad of background angles', including the tax implications for some of the beneficiaries which could include 'potential tax difficulties down the line'.

As well as leaving everything to Josie and 'special help' to his sister Mary, O'Donohue had also stipulated gifts to various named persons. Vinog Faughnan SC, the barrister acting for Mrs Josie O'Donohue, asked the court to specify what powers she had in her capacity as legal personal representative of her son John.

After the legal papers in the case had been circulated to all those mentioned in the will, Judge Paul Gilligan gave his verdict on Thursday, 1 December 2011.

In the first instance he decided that although two intended beneficiaries of the will, John O'Donohue's mother Josie and his brother Peter also witnessed his signature, the will itself was valid under the 1965 Succession Act.

He then came to the other issues that had arisen. He concluded that after studying the document he was 'unable to decipher the exact meaning' of the will, and that while John O'Donohue was undoubtedly 'a man of considerable learning' his will 'unfortunately provided an illustration of exactly how a person should not make a will.' As a piece of English he said the will was unclear and raised a number of questions, including how to interpret the 'mutually exclusive' intention that the estate was to be divided equally among the O'Donohue 'family' but his sister was to receive 'extra care and help.'

If the judge decided that it was to be divided equally among his mother, sister and two brothers, where were the gifts for four other named beneficiaries, two nieces and two nephews, to come from? And if they were to come from the estate, who would decide how much they would get and what would have to be taken off the other beneficiaries to ensure that the wishes were carried out. Such issues, said the judge, were 'a significant stumbling block' to ascertaining what exactly O'Donohue's intentions were.

The judge said there was only 'one clear fact' in the will, and that was that he intended a group of people to benefit from his estate, but what way the estate was to be divided was 'significantly less clear'.

The judge said that his task was to assess if various proposed modifications to the will were permissible in law, including the family's contention that Mr

O'Donohue's real intent was to create a 'hybrid trust'. The judge decided that there was no simple insertion or deletion of the terms of the will that would not involve 'remaking' the entire document. The terms of the will, he concluded, rendered it void 'for uncertainty'.

As a result the judge found that, technically, John O'Donohue died intestate (the same as if he had left no will) and because he was not married and had no children he was 'a bachelor without issue' and therefore the entire estate legally belonged to his next of kin, his mother, Josie.

There was also evidence from the Probate Office that in this case, letters of administration, where an administrator takes over the administration of an estate in the absence of a will or an executor, could be taken out.

The judgement was delivered by Judge Gilligan on Thursday, 2 December 2011.

On New Year's Eve, the eve of her son's birthday and just five days before the fourth anniversary of his death, Josie O'Donohue passed away.

According to John O'Donohue's website she 'crossed peacefully from this visible world into that invisible realm to which John preceded her by almost four years'.

The President of Ireland, Michael D Higgins attended her burial alongside her more famous son in County Clare. As fellow poets, O'Donohue and Michael D had been friends for a number of years and for his inauguration in Dublin Castle as President of Ireland he requested that 'Beannacht', a poem O'Donohue wrote for his mother, should be recited as part of the State celebrations. John O'Donohue was, said the president, 'a person of immense courage who gave witness to the truth'.

His only trouble was that he didn't know how to put his intentions about his €2 million fortune into clear English, a lapse that caused his mother a great deal of grief and unwanted publicity at a time when she was terminally ill.

# Chapter 7

# *Something for Sara*

As he lay dying, Cathal Ryan, the troubled aviation tycoon, set out to use part of his vast fortune to revisit a dark episode that had led to the lurid details of his private life becoming public property and to undo some of the hurt that had been inflicted on an innocent woman who just happened to be in the wrong place at the wrong time.

With the millions he made from his shareholding in Ryanair, Cathal Ryan certainly had the means to make amends to the woman at the centre of a celebrated drama that enthralled the Irish public.

Two days before his death at the age of 47, the heir to the Ryanair fortune signed his last will and testament, setting out how his vast €250 million estate was to be distributed.

While some wealthy people use their will as a weapon, Ryan set out to find an honourable way to settle his affairs and make amends for the dramatic events of the Rocca v Ryan legal battle that had peeled open the colourful lifestyle of the rich and famous country set.

Among the many bequests in the 18-page will, dated 18 December 2007, Cathal Ryan left €2 million to Sara Linton, the beautiful nanny whose brief encounter with Cathal Ryan unwittingly dragged all their lives into the public spotlight.

Since his death, which came just months after the death of his father Tony Ryan, the train driver's son who founded Guinness Peat Aviation (GPA) and later Ryanair, the wealthy Ryan family has maintained a low profile.

Tony Ryan himself had an ambivalent attitude towards publicity and journalists. On one level he hated the public profile but on another he couldn't resist the allure of newspapers – even investing in the ailing *Sunday Tribune* at one stage and losing £600,000, a considerable fortune at the time.

He once took a journalist on a week-long trek around Europe on his private jet, only to have a violent disagreement with him when he discovered that the intended article contained an inscription from the book he was reading at the time, *Cider with Rosie*, which was signed: 'To Tony – Love M'.

The M in question was his lover Miranda Guinness, the former wife of Benji Guiness, the Earl of Iveagh. Ryan immediately set about having the article 'pulled', going as far as ringing the proprietor of the newspaper. When that didn't work he enlisted a top-flight legal team and spent a small fortune finding spurious reasons why the article was a breach of confidentiality.

The article never appeared – but years later Tony Ryan entertained the same journalist to a mug of tea in the kitchen of his opulent home in Eaton Square in London and revealed that he was buying Lyons Demesne, the estate near Celbridge which he acquired from another tycoon, Michael Smurfit, and restored with an estimated €100 million of his own money.

Only his eldest granddaughter, the actress Danielle Ryan, who inherited Stacumny House, the beautiful manor near Celbridge where her father Cathal died, has became something of a reluctant public figure – mainly because it is difficult for an aspiring actress to stay out of the limelight. She has also used her name and her father's legacy to promote the budding Academy of Dramatic Arts in Dublin and the Lir Theatre near Grand Canal Square in Dublin, where she is a director.

But the family's jealously guarded privacy ended dramatically when former Miss Ireland, Michelle Rocca, went to the High Court to seek damages from her one-time lover Cathal Ryan arising out of an assault at a thirtieth birthday party in Blackhall Stud in County Kildare. The High Court resembled a photo shoot for a celebrity magazine with the Rocca sisters, Michelle's new lover Van Morrison, her friend Marian Gale, hairdresser David Marshall, and others parading through the halls of the Four Courts to relive a glamorous birthday party, which Judge Michael Moriarty memorably conceded would 'not fall within the realms of a vicarage tea-party'.

Even the 'bit players' in the drama, the celebrity lawyer Gerald Kean and his then wife Clodagh, Dr Stephen Murphy and Ryanair's controversial chief executive Michael O'Leary, added to the glitter and drama of that heady week when the most intimate details of Cathal Ryan's life with Michelle were forensically dissected by the lawyers Garret Cooney SC and Nicholas Kearns SC.

It all began five months after Michelle Rocca's biggest television moment, as co-host with Pat Kenny for the 1988 Eurovision Song Contest in Dublin, when she was invited to Tony Ryan's Tipperary mansion, Kilboy, for the annual 'barn dance'. This was a lavish all-night affair where beautiful models and celebrities mixed with his family, friends, business associates and staff of GPA, his airline-leasing company based in the Shannon tax-free zone.

Beautiful Michelle Rocca was the mother of two young daughters, Danielle and Natasha, by footballer John Devine, from whom she was now separated.

Cathal Ryan, a Ryanair pilot and the eldest of Tony Ryan's three sons, had been briefly married to Tess de Kertzer, whom he had met in Sri Lanka and they had two children, Cillian and Danielle. The couple separated in 1985.

At the barn dance Cathal asked Michelle if he could see her again and so began the tempestuous love affair that would enthral the Irish public for a week in 1997.

At the time, Cathal was based in England and Michelle was making a career for herself as a panellist on the musical quiz show *Play the Game*. Their romance was tempestuous, to say the least. She claimed that he attacked her in the bedroom of his home in England one night and in reply he claimed that because he was tired and wouldn't help her 'play out' her script she attacked him, scratching him so badly on the face that he had to wear a plaster for several days.

With her work commitments for RTÉ Michelle spent more and more time in Dublin and after various rows and recriminations Cathal said he got 'the impression' that the relationship was off.

But that all changed when she told him she was pregnant. They and their four children moved in together to a house in Brighton Hall in the leafy Dublin suburb of Foxrock.

Shortly before Christmas 1990 they had a huge fight and he took his two children and left, staying with his mother Mairead in Sandymount and terminating the lease on the house in Foxrock. Michelle, who was then working in public relations with the firm Wilson Hartnell, had to ring his father Tony Ryan to get the rent paid, and she later moved to a smaller house in Booterstown, County Dublin.

Their daughter Claudia was born in April, 1991 and Cathal Ryan attended the birth. They later went out socially on a number of occasions, including the lavish christening party thrown by the baby's proud grandfather Tony Ryan at his Tipperary mansion.

Then, on the night of 2 February 1992, Lucinda Batt threw a surprise party for her 'boyfriend' Tony Ryan in the Cashel Palace Hotel in Tipperary. An old friend of Cathal's, June Moloney, 'played cupid' and introduced him to her friend, Sara Linton, who was working as a nanny for a wealthy Tipperary family.

They went on a couple of dates and, according to Cathal Ryan, 'the romance flourished'. And so a few weeks later the happy couple were invited to attend June Moloney's thirtieth birthday party at Blackhall Stud near Clane in County Kildare. But when Michelle Rocca called to visit June with a birthday present days before the party the hostess found herself with a common party dilemma. Should she invite Michelle knowing that Cathal would be there with his new girlfriend? It was a difficult situation so, after consulting Cathal Ryan, June also asked Michelle to the bash. 'You are welcome to come – but only if you can handle seeing Cathal with his girlfriend and you promise to behave yourself,' June told Michelle.

'I always behave like a lady,' said the one-time beauty queen.

And that is how Cathal Ryan, Sara Linton and Michelle Rocca, in the company of about 20 other guests, ended up together at the birthday party that Saturday night in March 1992.

The food was late arriving but the guests enjoyed the lavish hospitality. At around 11.30pm, Cathal Ryan noticed his girlfriend, Sara Linton, was missing. It transpired that she was tired and had gone up to a bedroom to rest. When he found her he took off his jacket and shoes and lay down beside her and fell asleep.

Another guest, the well-known hairdresser David Marshall, who was playing golf the following morning with June Moloney's husband, Brian, came into the room and although he noticed that there was somebody in the other bed, got undressed and got into a second bed which he had been told earlier was his for the night.

Some time later the peace of the room was shattered when Michelle Rocca stormed in.

'Somebody was hurting me, hitting me in the face and screaming obscene language at me,' Sara Linton would later tell the High Court. 'She got me by the hair and hauled me around the bedroom. She was very frenzied and she got hold of my hair and I wasn't able to do anything. She wouldn't let go, she was hurting me. She flung me against the table and the lamp.'

Michelle Rocca conceded that when she went into the bedroom and saw the couple in bed, she called Cathal Ryan 'a bastard or a bollocks or something like that'. She then described how Cathal hit her, what she described as 'a haymaker', between the eyes, breaking her nose. He dragged her across the room by the hair, she said, punching her again and again in the face and chest and kicking her on the bottom, arms and legs.

'Every time I have to look at my daughter I have to realise that her father is a woman-beater,' she told the High Court.

During the legal action, Michelle Rocca claimed that Cathal Ryan was her fiancé, that he had asked her to marry him. She also revealed that when he gave the ring to her they were on O'Connell Bridge in Dublin and he asked her to throw her jewellery from other lovers into the waters of the Liffey below. Mr Ryan said he had given her a ring 'as a token of our love' during one of their happier moments, but it was only a gesture which Ms Rocca hadn't appreciated because it wasn't the real 'rock' that she was expecting.

Asked had she gone to the bedroom to track down Sara Linton, she replied: 'I was not entitled to track her [Sara Linton] down, but as his fiancé I was entitled to be angry if I found him in bed with another woman.'

'I want to make it clear that I had never struck a woman before that time in Clane,' said Cathal Ryan.

But he didn't apologise. That was left to his father, Tony Ryan, who arrived with a bunch of flowers to Michelle's house in Booterstown the day after the now notorious party. Later Michael O'Leary tried and failed to facilitate a deal to prevent the case coming to court.

The most intriguing aspect of the case was that it ever got to court. Neither side appeared to want to bring it that far, but it somehow gained a momentum all its own, leaving the door open for the media to have a field day as the lives of celebrities and the super-wealthy were laid bare by teams of battle-hardened lawyers.

A civil action for assault was heard before a jury which decided, after two hours of deliberation, that Michelle Rocca was assaulted by Cathal Ryan that night and he had used more force than was necessary. They awarded her damages of £7,500.

Oddly enough, the bitter courtroom confrontation seemed to drain all the participants. Cathal Ryan picked up the entire costs of the trial, estimated at £300,000 which he could have disputed because of the size of the damages awarded to Michelle Rocca. After his death Michelle Rocca said of Cathal Ryan: 'He was a wonderful father; he and I had a very good relationship over the past number of years. He will be greatly missed by all of us.'

In his last will, dated 18 December 2007, Cathal Ryan left Swordlestown Stud near Naas and a house in Chelsea to his son Cillian; Stacumny House to his daughter Danielle; €2 million to his daughter with Michelle Rocca, Claudia Rocca Ryan, when she reaches the age of 24; and the Villa La Rondine in Lake Como, Italy to Cillian, Danielle, Claudia and his fourth child, Cameron.

But he also left €2 million to Sara Linton, his date at June Moloney's birthday party, for the anguish caused to her by the attack and the subsequent publicity that she had to endure. The couple had stopped seeing each other shortly after the traumatic events of that night in Blackhall Stud and Sara Linton moved to live in Italy, returning to Ireland briefly to give evidence in defence of Cathal Ryan.

Another beneficiary of the will was his first wife, Tess de Kertzer, who was left €3 million, but with the condition that she did not contest the will.

Cathal Ryan left €10 million to be distributed by his trustees to children in need and the promotion of the dramatic arts in Ireland, and a further €25 million for children in need outside of Ireland.

He left his share of his father Tony Ryan's €95 million estate to be divided among his four children.

Cathal Ryan also set up a number of 'discretionary trusts' for his children, appointing his executors as trustees. He stipulated that on their twenty-fifth birthday each of his four children would get €25,000; €1 million on reaching the age of 30; €1 million on reaching the age of 35 and €5 million on reaching the age of 40.

Lyons Demesne, the stately home that Tony Ryan rescued from ruin, has been advertised for sale internationally at a fraction of what it cost to restore, and Stacumny House, which is owned by Danielle Ryan, is also on the market.

Perhaps the fear of reprising that courtroom drama in 1997 would deter most families from ever wanting to see the inside of a courtroom again. But that may be about to change.

Now, five years after his untimely death, the last wishes of the one-time pilot and major shareholder in Ryanair, Cathal Ryan could once again enthral the Irish public. The heirs of Cathal Ryan may not like this return to the limelight, but with an estate worth €250 million there is obviously a lot at stake for both sides in the impending battle of the trustees with the Revenue Commissioners.

At this point, all that is known is that solicitors acting for the executors and trustees of Cathal Ryan's will – his brothers Declan Ryan of Enniskerry, County Wicklow and Shane Ryan of London, and Ann Mulcahy, George Gill and Patrick Ryan, a partner in the solicitors firm Kilroys – lodged legal papers on 27 February 2012 indicating that they are taking High Court proceedings against the Revenue Commissioners.

In response the Revenue Commissioners indicated in documents lodged on

8 March that they intend to defend the proceedings.

The details are, as yet, unknown but they are unlikely to provide the prurient among us with the sort of salacious details that emerged almost daily during the Rocca v Ryan encounter.

# Chapter 8

## *The Wondrous World of Wills*

### Mr Coleman's Last Wishes are Frustrated

Patrick Coleman was a wealthy 'tea, wine and spirit merchant' whose family had a lucrative business since 1755 at No 2, Suffolk Street, Dublin, the present site of O'Neill's public house. Because of its location near College Green, the site of the old Parliament of Ireland, as well as the Stock Exchange and other financial institutions on Dame Street, Coleman's was patronised by a wealthy clientele.

Around 1875 the elderly bachelor sold the business because of ill-health. When he died in 1877 old Mr Coleman had amassed a large portfolio of property and investments worth around £10,000. His executors were William H O'Leary of York Street, Dublin and John O'Brien, a Roman Catholic clergyman of Loughrey, County Galway.

Possibly influenced by the priest, Mr Coleman desired to leave a large portion of his estate to a number of Catholic institutions but, instead, his will became the subject of a rather unique dispute when it was contested by members of the Douglas family, who stood to gain the Coleman fortune if the will were overturned.

The case was reported in the papers at the time:

## Cavan Weekly News 3 July 1878

A legal decision, involving the loss of more than £10,000 to various Roman Catholic institutions and charities in Dublin and elsewhere in Ireland, was given a few days ago by the Court of Appeal, consisting of the Lord Chancellor Ball, the Lord Justice Christian, and the Lord Justice Deasy. The question before them was as to the will of the late Mr Patrick Coleman, a grocer and publican, of Dublin.

About the end of '76 Mr Coleman, feeling ill, instructed a solicitor to set about preparing his will for execution. On the 2nd of January '77 the solicitor brought to him a document, endorsed 'draft will', embodying his wishes in regard to the disposition of his property. As Mr Coleman then appeared to be in a dangerous state of health the precaution was taken of having the draft will executed at once by him, in the presence of witnesses, as his last will and testament.

His health then seemed to get better, and it was not until the 24th of February that the will, copied out in the usual formal style, was duly executed by Mr Coleman. Now, it is to be kept in mind that the 'draft will' and the subsequent copy, or 'engrossed will', were precisely to the same effect – even in the same very words – and that both of them left the money in question to the several institutions and charities.

Well, on the 7th of April '77, Mr Coleman died. The Act of Parliament which governs the legality of bequests for religious purposes provides that, in order to be valid in regard to such bequests, a will by which they are left must have been duly executed three months at least before the testator's death. From the 2nd of January, on which date Mr Coleman executed the 'draft will' to the 7th of April, the date on which he died, the period elapsing was longer than three months, and therefore if the draft will was to be held to be his will, or even a part of his will, the law would decree that his money should go as desired.

But, on the other hand, from the 24th of February to the 7th of April was shorter than three months and consequently if the 'engrossed will' of the 24th of February – that document, and that alone – was regarded as Mr Coleman's last will and testament, all his bequests to religious charities would be cancelled.

The judge of the Probate Court decided that both wills, the draft one and the engrossed one, should be taken together as the last will and testament and, as this would give the charitable bequests the advantage of the earlier date, he decreed that they were valid according to law.

The three judges of Appeal have now decided the other way, to the effect that the document of the 2nd of January was superseded and, as it were, put out of legal existence, by that of the 24th of February; that the latter must stand alone; and, as the period of three months, required by law, did not intervene between the execution and the death of Mr Coleman, the charitable bequests all come to naught.

Among the institutions thus deprived of substantial sums, are St Vincent's Hospital, the Mater Hospital and Cork Street Hospital; the schools attached to the Roman Catholic Churches of Clarendon Street, High Street, Dundrum, and to the convents of Booterstown and Trim; the clerical bodies of Clarendon Street, Westland Row, Heytesbury Street and Church Street; and such institutions as St Mary's for the blind, St Joseph's, Glasnevin, the Orphanage of St Vincent de Paul, Glasnevin, the Night Asylum, and the committee for aiding the Sick and Indigent Roomkeepers' Association.

Had Mr Coleman lived seven weeks longer than he did, the will of the 24th of February would have defied attack, but the appellate judges hold that his death, on the 7th of April, deprived the last will he had signed of legal force; that that will, in its turn, cancelled the one preceding it, and that both wills utterly failed so far as regards the charities.

## From Trophy Home to Bleak House

On 11 August in the year 2000 Patrick Aloysius Duggan sat down at the desk in his study in 'Walford', No 24 Shrewsbury Road, Dublin and signed his last will and testament.

The seven-page document sets out in some detail a series of bequests to members of his family, his friends and his servants and even included £1,000 for Masses to be said for himself and his wife Carmel in Donnybrook Church 'at an honorarium of £100 for each Mass'.

A chartered accountant and well-known Dublin businessman, Patrick Duggan is all but forgotten now, but his home, 'Walford', has become an enduring symbol of both the Celtic Tiger and the economic catastrophe that has brought Ireland to its knees.

Patrick Duggan was the son and heir of Richard Duggan, a Dublin bookmaker who founded the Irish Sweepstakes, the man who recruited former IRA man Joe McGrath and another bookie, Spencer Freeman, into the enterprise that would make all three of them and their families vastly wealthy for much of the twentieth century.

Richard Duggan was the brains behind the operation, Joe McGrath sold the tickets illegally through a network of IRA contacts across the United States and Canada, and Freeman was the man who invested the wealth they accumulated in a variety of Irish enterprises.

Shrewsbury Road in Dublin 4 has always been the 'residence' of choice for Irish tycoons. Current residents include the Esat Digifone founder Denis O'Brien, members of the McCann family of Fyffes and a smattering of well-known legal eagles and professional people.

And it wasn't any different in the early part of the twentieth century. It was a road populated by men of money and prominent figures in the judiciary. When he died in 1935, Richard Duggan left Walford and what was then the vast sum of £77,604 in his will. His house and his seat on the board of the Irish Sweepstakes went to his son Patrick who also added to the fortune through his chairmanship of a related business, the Hibernian Insurance Company.

When Patrick Duggan died on 13 December 2004, he could never have been accused of squandering his father's legacy. His three children, Blathnait Crowley whose address was given in probate documents as Blackrock, County Dublin, Marion Van Den Bergh of Chateau de Cysoing, France and Neal Duggan who remained in Walford following his father's death, have every reason to be grateful to their father, not only for his legacy, but for the perfect timing of his departure from this world.

The Revenue Commissioners affidavit attached to his will gives the value of his estate as €58,113,711. He also had €4,573,898 in stocks and shares, €3,052,660 in cash in banks and financial institutions, and three life insurance policies.

But the jewel in the crown was Walford, his house on 1.78 acres of land in Ballsbridge, Dublin 4 valued for probate reasons at a staggering €50 million in December 2004. This was at a time when property in parts of Dublin 4 was outstripping in value property in Knightsbridge in London, Rodeo Drive in Los Angeles and other salubrious addresses around the globe.

When the auctioneering firm of Sherry FitzGerald put Walford on the market in May 2004 it carried what was seen as a more realistic estimate of €35 million. Although run-down and neglected, Walford, with its superb location and its vast gardens, was then regarded as the ultimate trophy home.

At the time, Ireland was said to have, according to Bank of Ireland research, 33,000 millionaires and speculation in the media was rife with big names who could afford to buy Dublin's most expensive private residence. Would the buyer be Denis O'Brien, or Michael O'Leary, or one of the many millionaires nobody had yet heard of? The answer was no, they were too smart.

At the auction in June 2005, Walford, described in brochures as 'the finest house to come on the market in Dublin', sold for €56 million, the highest price ever paid for a family home in the city.

Adding to the intrigue was the fact that it was officially purchased by a company called Matsack Nominees, which is owned by a firm of Dublin solicitors, Matheson Ormsby Prentice (MOP). But the real buyers, although they have never admitted it, are believed to have been the glamorous former social diarist Gayle Killilea and her husband, the property developer Sean Dunne.

Various plans were submitted to demolish the old house and replace it with grand Celtic Tiger homes fit for the billionaires queuing up to live on Shrewsbury Road. But in the end these schemes were rejected and planning permission was granted for a renovated Walford with two houses to be constructed in the grounds.

Meanwhile, the house decayed and, with the financial and property crash of 2007, Walford, along with the skeleton of Anglo Irish Bank's new headquarters on the Liffey, became perfect symbols of the madness of the Irish property boom and the reckless lending of the Irish banks.

When it was put back up for sale in late 2011, *The Irish Times* expert Frank

McDonald was dispatched to view the house, which was now on sale for €15 million, a price reduction of €41 million.

'Built in 1902, the Tudor-style Edwardian house was occupied by the same family, the Duggans, for 50 years prior to its spectacular sale in mid-2005,' he wrote. 'A brochure from that time shows that it was elegantly furnished and had two eighteenth-century marble fireplaces in the main reception rooms. But the fireplaces were taken by thieves while Walford stood vacant for the past six years and there isn't a stick of furniture in the house now. Black and white marble effect linoleum in the entrance hall has gone too, leaving just the concrete floor, and all of the rooms have bare wooden floors and stripped walls; this is Bleak House.'

It didn't sell and has since been taken off the market.

Meanwhile, in his will Patrick Duggan left the residue of his estate, everything that remained after the 31 individual bequests to grandchildren, friends and servants, to be divided among his three children, Blathnait Crowley, Marion Van Den Bergh and Neal Duggan.

Timing, it seems, is everything.

## The Greed of Kitty O'Shea

The real trouble started for Charles Stewart Parnell not with a petition for divorce by Captain Willie O'Shea, the cuckolded husband of his lover Katharine 'Kitty' O'Shea, as is generally assumed, it actually began with the death of Katharine O'Shea's wealthy old aunt, Mrs Anna Marian Wood, or Aunt Ben as she was better known.

When she died on 19 May 1889 at the age of 96, the family struggle over her last will and testament and ultimately what in today's money was a multimillion fortune, would not only tear the family apart, but would also bring down the man known as 'The Uncrowned King of Ireland'.

Imperious Aunt Ben had bankrolled Katharine's husband, the flamboyant and impecunious Captain Willie O'Shea, on his ill-fated business and political ventures, which eventually ended up with him acquiring a seat in the House of Commons for the constituency of Clare. Of the 13 nieces and nephews in the

Wood family it was Katharine she favoured, providing her with a safe house in the grounds of Eltham Lodge, her grand mansion in Kent, for herself and the five O'Shea children.

But this prim and elderly Victorian lady was never told that the youngest two, Clare and Katie had been fathered by Parnell, then leader of the Irish Party and one of the most influential politicians of his era. Nor was she told that Captain Willie and Katharine hadn't lived together as man and wife for years . . . indeed the aunt was led to believe that when Parnell stayed with Katharine in nearby Wonerish Lodge, it was as a house guest rather than lover.

Had she known of the deception, it is unlikely that her favourite niece Katharine would have inherited anything.

While the love affair of Parnell and Katharine O'Shea might not have been known to Aunt Ben, their living arrangements and the birth of three children to Parnell and Mrs O'Shea (one died shortly after birth) was common knowledge in political, social and media circles.

The real question was why the pair had never been 'outed', to use a more modern expression. Sometimes the best way to keep a secret, however, is to pretend it isn't one – and in this case it worked for everybody, except the unfortunate Captain Willie O'Shea.

The wily Katharine O'Shea made sure that her husband knew exactly who was in charge. But Captain O'Shea was more than happy to hold his tongue, in the expectation that his wife would inherit Aunt Ben's fortune, estimated at around £200,000 (at least £10 million in today's money) and after he had shared in this good fortune and a proper settlement had been arrived at, he would then consent to divorce her and they could both make their own arrangements to live happily ever after.

'O'Shea still had one strong reason for inactivity,' writes Paul Bew in his scholarly biography: *Enigma: A New Life of Charles Stewart Parnell*. 'He expected his wife's aged Aunt Ben to leave a large sum to her niece. If he remained Katharine's husband, O'Shea might reasonably expect a share in this windfall. In the late 1880s Aunt Ben's death was expected almost daily by the Captain.'

It wasn't to work out that smoothly, however.

Katharine O'Shea was one of 13 children of Sir John Page Wood, a distinguished and well-connected, but not very wealthy, rector. However, her Aunt Ben had inherited the impressive Eltham Lodge and a considerable fortune from her barrister husband. In her original will, which she made in 1883, she had distributed her fortune equally among her various nieces and nephews. Then in April 1887 when she was 94 years of age Aunt Ben made a new will, in which everything was left to her favourite niece Katharine O'Shea.

One of the first things Katharine did with the new will was to send a copy of it to her troublesome husband, Willie O'Shea, who was constantly threatening to divorce her because of her infidelity, a move that would bring disgrace on Parnell and ruin his political career in Catholic Ireland forever, and would also prompt Aunt Ben to disinherit her niece.

It was a calculated move by a very calculating woman. The contents of her letter, enclosing the will, left him in no doubt that if he made any fuss about her living arrangements he wasn't going to get a penny of Aunt Ben's inheritance.

'My aunt says she will not give one penny to me either for support of myself or the children, or of course for yours either,' she told Captain O'Shea in reply to a letter in which he threatened to take his children away from Katharine and Eltham.

But matters changed in March 1888 when Aunt Ben's other nieces and nephews, Katharine's brothers and sisters, learned, probably from the troublesome Willie O'Shea, that everything was going to Katharine and they had been 'cut out' of the new will.

Led by Katharine's brothers, the distinguished Field Marshall Sir Evelyn Wood and Charles Page Wood, they quickly brought a case to the Court of Lunacy to have their aunt declared 'non compos mentis'. Their case was that their sister, Katharine, had exerted undue influence over their elderly aunt to seize her entire fortune for herself and that the earlier will, made in 1883, should prevail.

Katharine O'Shea out-manoeuvred them in the first round of what was to become a family war of attrition. With the help of her lover and his considerable political influence, she engaged Sir Andrew Clark, who happened to be the personal physician of the then British Prime Minister William Gladstone, to examine Aunt Ben and declare her mentally fit. Eventually, and it is thought reluctantly, he produced a written opinion, delivered to Katharine O'Shea on 20 April 1888, which pronounced Aunt Ben sane and competent enough to make the new will.

Possibly Clark was 'leaned on' by his political masters to placate Parnell, because it seems the doctor was a most reluctant participant, and it would be alleged later that every effort was made to protect him at a later stage in the drama.

'To endure for nearly 10 years the triangular relations [Willie O'Shea–Katharine O'Shea–Charles Stewart Parnell] upon which he [Parnell] had embarked in 1880 was to invite humiliation and to risk a catastrophe which no responsible leader could be justified in incurring,' writes FSL Lyons in his book *Parnell*. 'To have prolonged the danger for so long as he did was especially condemnable when the reason behind it was Katharine's anxiety to lay hands on the whole of her aunt's legacy. To hazard his leadership and his cause for a pecuniary motive of such a kind exposes Parnell to the charge to which there is no convincing answer, that he had subordinated his judgement to that of his mistress and in so doing had recklessly jeopardised the important national interests committed to his charge.'

Plainly he accuses Parnell of bowing to the demands of his mistress 'Kitty' rather than the cause of Home Rule for Ireland.

When Aunt Ben died in April 1888, the legal case of her fitness to make a will turned into a dispute over the terms of the will. This caused Aunt Ben's fortune to be frozen until the matter was decided by the Probate Court, which the parties involved knew would take some considerable time – three years as it turned out.

Captain Willie O'Shea was left with a dilemma. He could wait in the hope that Katharine would be generous with him if she won the case, or he could file for divorce and get a settlement which would include some of the proceeds of the will. His strategy was to renew his threats to issue divorce proceedings against his wife.

Parnell's preferred solution was to 'buy off' his one-time supporter and MP for Clare. A bribe of £20,000 had already been talked about, in return for which Captain O'Shea would admit to infidelity on his part and his divorce from Katharine would go through uncontested. This might not be ideal for Parnell's political future, but it would provide some sort of an 'Irish solution to an Irish problem' and, because of his popularity, he might just carry it off.

But with Aunt Ben's fortune tied up for at least three years and Parnell's own estate, Avondale House near Rathdrum, County Wicklow, teetering on the edge of bankruptcy, neither he nor Katharine O'Shea had the cash to carry through on this solution.

So on Christmas Eve 1889 Captain Willie O'Shea petitioned for divorce on the grounds of adultery by his wife, naming Parnell as the 'co-respondent' or lover. The rest, as they say, is history. Parnell's reputation was ruined, the Irish party and the Irish nation was split, and on 6 October 1891 the Uncrowned King of Ireland died of exhaustion and pneumonia complicated by kidney failure, at the age of 45.

By 1892 the will dispute was still in the courts. Captain Willie O'Shea was an 'intervenent' claiming that he was involving himself in the case to protect the interests of his three children. Katharine O'Shea's two children with Parnell were discreetly left out of the proceedings.

As the O'Shea v O'Shea and Parnell divorce proceedings had not gone ahead, the media were now expecting all the revelations of infidelity, denied to them by the settlement of the divorce case, to come out in the Wood v O'Shea will case, which was due for a full hearing before the Probate Court on 24 March 1892.

But as the date for the hearing neared, frantic efforts were made by very powerful interests to prevent the case going to trial. More than mere publicity was at stake. Katharine O'Shea was warned by her barrister Sir Charles Russell that she could lose everything and it seems Prime Minister Gladstone was most reluctant that his personal doctor should be called as a witness to be questioned on the circumstances surrounding his decision to certify that Aunt Ben was sane and sensible at the time of making her will.

After hours of discussion in the days leading up to the case, the two sets of lawyers went into the chambers of the probate judge Sir Charles Parker Butt who was to hear the case which would be decided by a 'special jury'. An hour later the parties emerged to announce that the matter had been settled.

Of course, the first item on the agenda was the lawyers' fees, which were quite considerable, reducing Aunt Ben's legacy from £144,500 to £130,000 before a shilling was distributed.

The £130,000 was then divided equally – Katharine O'Shea and her five children getting £65,000, with her brothers and sisters getting the same amount to divide among themselves. Of Katharine's share, £15,000 was put aside to provide homes for herself and her former husband, Captain Willie O'Shea. Katharine O'Shea and Willie shared the remaining £50,000. This was still a considerable sum and was invested in Consolidated Stock, a very conservative investment in land or land mortgages which gave each of them an income of about £700 a year.

The judge also ruled on how the £50,000 capital would be shared out after their death, with their eldest son, Gerard, getting 40 per cent, their two daughters Carman and Norah getting 22.5 per cent each and Katharine O'Shea and Parnell's two daughters Clare and Katie getting 7.5 per cent each.

How much any of them got is now clouded in the mists of time but, in his book *The Laurel and the Ivy,* historian Robert Kee maintained that 'a dishonest solicitor and bad investments' had seriously reduced Katharine O'Shea's income by the time she died, inducing her to write what is considered an unreliable but sensational memoir to make some money.

After his untimely death, there was also Parnell's will to be considered. This too was a financial disaster for his loved ones. Although he had lived 'on the edge of bankruptcy' for much of his life, he still had Avondale, his house and estate in County Wicklow.

In a will, which he made before he married Katharine O'Shea, he willed it to his wife and two children, Clare and Katie. However, because he failed for some reason to re-make the will after their marriage on 25 June 1891 it was declared invalid on a technicality.

Instead, Avondale went to his brother John Parnell and Katharine never got to come to Ireland, the birthplace of the love of her life. But maybe she was lucky. Avondale came with huge debts, running to an estimated €2 million in today's money, so after cutting down as much timber on the estate as he could quickly sell, John Parnell disposed of the house and estate to a Dublin butcher and it later came into the hands of the Forestry Commission and the Office of Public Works.

Certainly Aunt Ben's legacy does not appear to have brought much luck to the extended Parnell family. But for her dramatic 'tell all' book published in 1914, Katharine O'Shea would have died in relative poverty in 1921.

Her children didn't fare much better. Her eldest son Gerard survived World War I before emigrating to Canada where he disappeared. The eldest daughter Norah contracted the painful disease, lupus, and died in 1923. Carmen married twice, developed a taste for fast horses and strong drink and, after indulging heartily in both, died tragically young the same year as her mother, 1921. Parnell and Katharine's daughter Clare died after childbirth in 1909. Their second daughter Katie married a soldier and went with him to West Africa. She ended up living in poverty in Camden town in London before coming to live in Dublin where she died unknown and unloved in an asylum in 1947.

Of Parnell's immediate family, one sister, Anna, joined Sinn Féin but then moved to England, calling herself Cerisa Palmer, and is presumed to have committed suicide when she drowned in the sea in 1911. Another sister, Emily, described by one of the family as 'somewhat deranged', died in a Dublin poorhouse in 1918.

Despite the tribulations, the meeting of Charles Stewart Parnell and Katharine O'Shea remains one of the great and enduring love stories of all time.

As for Aunt Ben and her money, who remembers?

## The €400 Million Developer Worth just €72,000

Liam Maye, along with his partner Joe O'Reilly, owned Castlethorn Construction, a firm which built a series of prestigious housing developments around Dublin.

They then went on to develop the iconic Dundrum Shopping Centre in south County Dublin, which, when it opened, was said to be the largest shopping centre in Europe.

When Mr Maye died suddenly of a heart attack at his Spanish villa on 5 May 2008 at the age of 64 it was believed that he was worth in the region of €400 million.

The will itself was made on 16 April 1998, 10 years before he died, when Mr Maye was living in Sydenham House in Dundrum, just up the hill from the shopping centre that would become so bound up with his business dealings. As well as appointing accountants Brian Wallace and David Simpson as trustees, he appointed his brother Christopher 'Christy' Maye as guardian of his infant children.

In his will he instructed his trustees to divide the residue of his estate among his children when they reached the age of 25.

The executrix of his will was his wife Mrs Anne Maye, and when she took out a grant of probate on her husband's estate a little over a month after his death, on 12 June 2008, the gross value of his estate was put at just €72,000.

The affidavit setting out Mr Maye's worldly possessions, which comprised of a number of cars and boats, was given to Allied Irish Bank by Mr Maye's neighbour in Foxrock, the much respected chartered accountant Mr Bernard Somers.

To use the legal terminology favoured by lawyers in such cases, this valuation caused 'disquiet' and 'grave concerns' at Allied Irish Bank, which had loaned one of Mr Maye's companies, Mayco Ltd, €58 million to buy a block of apartments at the Sweepstakes development in Ballsbridge, Dublin 4.

When the case came before the Commercial Court in July 2010, Mr Justice Peter Kelly said it was 'extraordinary' that alarm bells hadn't gone off in Allied Irish Bank a lot sooner when it learned of the difference in valuation between Mr Maye's estimated worth of at least €100 million (and possibly four times that) and the official valuation of his estate at just €72,000.

Originally from Cloncallow, a townland near Ballymahon, County Longford, Liam Maye was one of a family of seven. His brother Christy stayed in the locality and became the owner of a very successful property portfolio which included The Bridge House in Tullamore, County Offaly and the Greville Arms in Mullingar, County Westmeath.

Liam came to Dublin and worked in construction before teaming up with another Longford man, Joe O'Reilly, in a string of successful development projects. One of the best known and probably most lucrative was the Carysfort development in Blackrock, County Dublin built on lands sold off after secretive businessman 'Pino' Harris acquired the Carysfort Teacher Training College from Charles Haughey's government.

Even when they formed Castlethorn Construction in the early 1990s, Maye and O'Reilly were doing well. Back then Maye was living in Dundrum and O'Reilly a few miles away in Terenure. According to the first set of accounts for Castlethorn Construction, they had a gross profit of over £1 million in 1992, but came out with a loss of £43,000. At the time, they were developing the Carysfort lands and the three directors shared £302,000 that year, which was big money at the time.

Maye and O'Reilly owned 40 per cent each of the company while their partner John Fitzsimons from Maynooth, County Kildare had a 20 per cent stake.

Two major developments would make their name and make their development firm one of the first to have its assets transferred to the National Assets Management Agency (NAMA): the Dundrum Town Centre and Killeen Castle Golf Club in County Meath.

By then Maye and O'Reilly had moved to leafy Foxrock in south County Dublin. Maye bought 'Weaver's Hall', a large pile once owned by Seamus McGrath of Irish Sweepstakes fame, who named one of his horses after it and saw it win the Irish Derby in 1973.

The massive Dundrum Town Centre opened to much fanfare at the height of the boom, attracting as tenants a galaxy of top shopping names and brands from London and New York. Overnight it changed the shopping habits of Dublin's southside suburbs, but plans to extend it back through the old village faltered with the advent of the credit crunch.

Killeen Castle was supposed to be the ultimate playground for the new rich. Built around an ancient ruined castle that once belonged to the Earls of Fingall and which was burned by the IRA in the 1970s in the mistaken belief that it belonged to Lord Henry Mountcharles, it set new standards in golf club opulence.

The development comprises a championship golf course, top-class facilities and expensive houses discreetly built around the grounds. After spending €10 million to make the castle resemble something from a Disney set, it now remains an unused shell, while the business itself is controlled by NAMA.

It was when Liam Maye suddenly died that the whole saga began to unravel. His wife Anne was left in control of a crumbling empire at a time when Ireland was experiencing what is now recognised as the worst property collapse in the developed world.

Alexandra House, or Block C, in the Sweepstakes Centre in Ballsbridge was to prove a classic example. Liam Maye had borrowed €58 million to fund the family purchase of it through Mayco Ltd. His partners O'Reilly and Fitzsimons were not involved in the venture. According to AIB lending manager Brendan Hanratty the bank received 'periodic statements' from Mr Maye's financial advisors that he had personal assets valued at €100 million, so they were prepared to fund the deal. (Others believed that when his stake in Dundrum, Killeen Castle and a host of other developments and management companies were taken into account, he was worth about four times this sum.)

At the time, banks and other financial institutions were targeting 'high net worth individuals' with tax-efficient schemes to invest their wealth. Mostly these involved borrowing vast sums for property investments, in this case a block of apartments with a rent roll that could sustain the interest repayments. But to remain viable such investments needed to hold their valuations.

Then came the property crash.

This was quickly followed by the death of Liam Maye in Spain and the revelation that his estate was worth the staggeringly small sum of €72,000. It seemed that after a lifetime as one of Ireland's most prominent property developers there was nothing left.

AIB for its part said that it held 'many meetings' with Anne Maye in an attempt to resolve the situation. Mr Hanratty for AIB said in an affidavit that the bank had what he termed 'grave concerns' about the explanation given by Bernard Somers for the 'most unusual' process in which the grant of probate had been extracted.

After a year of fruitless negotiations and sitting on its hands the bank finally issued proceedings to recover its multimillion euro debt. On 26 July 2010 AIB appeared before Judge Peter Kelly to ask him to 'fast-track' a case before the Commercial Court. Why AIB waited over two years, from June 2008, when it was told the valuation of the estate, to July 2010, when it began legal proceedings against the estate, is a mystery that Judge Peter Kelly found 'extraordinary' when the matter first came before him.

He refused to fast-track the proceedings saying the bank had failed to show the necessary urgency to merit transfer of the case and it would have to proceed through the ordinary High Court list.

And that appears to be where it is stuck, like a lot of other legal cases that have surfaced in the Irish courts as a result of the property collapse.

According to documents lodged in Mayco's office on 13 April 2012 the Ballsbridge apartment block was 'written-down' in value by €13.9 million. This leaves the block of apartments valued at €35 million and Mayco Ltd with liabilities of over €23 million.

The accounts for Mayco Ltd also reveal that AIB has a first charge on the company property and rents and that it can demand repayment of €57,628,690 on foot of personal guarantees it has from Liam Maye and his estate. But if his estate is only worth €72,000 where are they going to get the money?

Unfortunately for Anne Maye and her daughters that isn't their only problem, or the end of the story.

Another lending institution, Friends First, has secured a judgement against her for €4.5 million after she gave a personal guarantee, dated 4 February 2009 regarding €1.5 million borrowed by each of her daughters, Emma Maye and Dawn Maye of Belarmine Park, Stepaside, County Dublin and Nicola Maye who lives at the family home, Weaver's Hall, Plunkett Avenue, Foxrock.

It appears that in April 2008, just a month before he died, Mr Maye had organised for his three daughters to borrow €1.5 million each from Friends First. Advised by Warren Private Clients, the money had been invested in a 'tax driven' fund which had been set up for Mr Maye, under which the three daughters would only pay tax when they exited the fund. However, when the daughters defaulted on payments to the lender the agreement was terminated in March 2010 and Friends First went after them for the money.

Again, Judge Peter Kelly was asked to try the case, in which there was no dispute, that the money was advanced to the three daughters and not repaid.

He gave a judgement against them for the sums involved.

Friends First then went after Anne Maye in November 2011 on foot of the guarantees which she had given, signed on 4 February 2009, to indemnify Friends First if her daughters defaulted on the loans. After she failed to honour the guarantee, Friends First went to the Commercial Court where Judge Kelly reserved his judgement, as the daughters' original case was being appealed to the Supreme Court.

According to *Phoenix Magazine* in July 2012, all the cases involving Anne Maye and her daughters Emma, Dawn and Nicola, have now been settled.

> Last year, Friends First Finance was granted judgements totalling more than €4.5 million against Emma Maye and her two sisters Dawn and Nicola Maye, arising out of loans given for equity investments. Earlier this year Friends First took High Court proceedings against their mother Anne Maye who, it was alleged, had guaranteed these loans in the event of a default. That case was settled out of court, however. The three Maye daughters each appealed the Friends First case to the Supreme Court, which was struck out last April. Phoenix understands that the High Court judgements were vacated after the three daughters paid around 80 per cent of the €4.5 million that they owed.

## A Case of Squatters' Rights

Property was obviously auctioneer Des Grogan's passion and he made it his business to know what was going on in his patch. He had an office in Drumcondra on the north side of Dublin city and his 'patch' was the surrounding suburbs of Phibsboro and Glasnevin.

When Mrs Alice Dolan died in 1981, Des Grogan, a canny 22-year-old auctioneer with an eye to the future, wasn't long in finding out what was going to happen to her solid redbrick house in Enniskerry Road, Phibsboro.

What he discovered interested him deeply.

Alice and her husband Patrick lived originally at No 36 Botanic Road, Glasnevin. When Mr Dolan died in 1969, Alice's sister Mary Williams moved into the house for company. She died some time later, leaving Mrs Dolan alone in the house once more. Then it happened that Dublin Corporation wished to acquire Alice Dolan's house as part of a road-widening scheme. The Corporation agreed that the people who then owned No 6 Enniskerry Road in Dublin 7, the Hoeys, would sell their house directly to Alice Dolan, with Dublin Corporation paying over the sale price to the vendors.

For some reason both the previous owner of the house on Enniskerry Road and Dublin Corporation signed the 'assignment' documents dated 15 December 1978, but Alice Dolan did not.

In some of the media reports that would surface 30 years after her death, Alice Dolan was described as a barrister, which doesn't seem to have been the case, as there is no record of her in the Rolls of the King's Inns, the official keeper of such records.

In any event, Mrs Dolan moved to her new home, No 6 Enniskerry Road, and lived there until her death in the James Connolly Memorial Hospital on 22 October 1981.

Her funeral was one of those seldom seen and sad events; hardly anybody came. Most of her friends were already dead, she had no close family and, as the young auctioneer Des Grogan observed, the only people there were a smattering of the old dear's neighbours. Alice Dolan didn't seem to have any living relatives.

Grogan kept a close eye on the house in the weeks and months that followed. Nobody came, or seemed interested. He made a few inquiries discreetly through people he knew in the area and there seemed to be no relatives, even distant cousins, interested in her affairs. Alice Dolan had simply died, she left no will and nobody was really interested anymore.

But Des Grogan knew a little bit about the law and, in particular, a term that is much used but little understood: squatters rights, or adverse possession as it is legally known.

The germ of an idea began to form in his mind. Other young men like him were going out and getting mortgages, shackling themselves to a monthly payment for the next 25 years. Young Mr Grogan and his wife Mary already had a house in nearby Russell Avenue where they lived, but now he could see a way of turning that into a nice little earner and allow him to live rent-free for the foreseeable future.

So one day in February the following year, 1982, Des Grogan went down the lane at the back of No. 6 Enniskerry Road, kicked open the back doorway and gained entry to Alice Dolan's home.

As stated in the Supreme Court case that would follow many years later: 'The defendant [Mr Grogan] learned of Mrs Dolan's death and the apparent absence of next of kin in the course of his auctioneering business, and broke into the premises through the back door in February, 1982.'

It must have been quite strange at first walking through the rooms, looking at the old woman's worldly possessions, her clothes, old photographs and mementos of 81 years of life, the knick-knacks and rubbish accumulated over a lifetime.

Des Grogan hadn't come to rob the place; he had come to take it over. He simply moved into the dead person's house and assumed it as his own. He changed the locks and secured it, which is one of the things that must be done to acquire adverse possession, and after that no one came to challenge his right to live there.

We don't know what happened to Alice Dolan's possessions, presumably he recycled the things that were useful and got rid of the things that weren't. Quietly he did up the place and then his young wife Mary joined him in Enniskerry Road where they quite literally 'made themselves at home'.

The weeks turned to months and then years and it wasn't long before people on the road assumed that Des Grogan was the rightful owner of No. 6 Enniskerry Road, Dublin 7.

The legal position when someone dies intestate and has no living relative with a claim on the estate, is that after a period it passes by law to the State.

But the State it seems moves slowly, in this case at a snail's pace.

It was 26 September 1997, over 16 years after the death of Alice Dolan, when the Attorney General, Mr David Byrne, executed a deed of consent allowing letters of administration to be granted to Michael A Buckley, the Chief State Solicitor of Dublin Castle to act as the 'nominee' of the government in winding up the estate of Alice Dolan. After this her house would be sold and the proceeds taken into government funds.

It took another three years before, on 21 July 2000, letters of administration were granted to Mr Buckley's successor as Chief State Solicitor, Laurence A Farrell, acting on behalf of the new Attorney General, Michael McDowell.

The authorities then discovered that the house was already occupied and so proceedings were issued in the Circuit Court in 2002 to have Des Grogan evicted in order that the State nominee could take possession of the house in Enniskerry Road.

But Mr Grogan wasn't giving it up that easily.

He disputed the State's right to take the house from him on two different grounds. Under the normal rules of adverse possession, a claim of squatters rights can be made if a person has been occupying a premises continually and without challenge for a period of 12 years or more. However, under the Statute of Limitations Act 1957 a State authority can pursue an interest in such property for a period of up to 30 years.

Mr Grogan argued that, as he had lived continuously in the house for 16 years and as he had secured it so that nobody else could claim ownership, it was his under the rules of adverse possession.

He also argued, up to the Supreme Court, that the Chief State Solicitor was not a 'State authority' for the purposes of the Statute of Limitations, 1957, which meant that the 30-year period available to the State authorities to pursue an interest in the home of Mrs Alice Dolan was not available to the current Chief

State Solicitor, Mr David O'Hagan (successor to Mr Buckley and Mr Farrell).

The three judges of the Supreme Court, Judge Niall Fennelly, Judge Fidelma Macken and Judge Joseph Finnegan were asked to decide complex and highly legalistic questions arising from the Intestates Estate Act 1884, the Statute of Limitations Act of 1957 and the Succession Act, 1965.

In their judgement both Judge Fennelly and Judge Finnegan held that the Chief State Solicitor was not a State authority under the Statute of Limitations Act, 1957 and therefore was not entitled to a 30-year period in which to claim the estate for the State. As it hadn't been claimed within the normal 12-year period the State could not claim the estate of Alice Dolan because Mr Grogan had been in possession of it for 16 years.

In a dissenting judgement Judge Fidelma Macken, while agreeing that the Chief State Solicitor was not a 'State authority', disagreed with the other judges and gave a minority judgement that the period during which the State could repossess the house was 30 years.

But Mr Dolan had won his case by a 2-1 majority.

Once the matter came to public attention the focus of the case switched from the highly legalistic Supreme Court ruling to 'who is Des Grogan?'

Now 52, the former auctioneer has turned out to be quite a colourful character. In the 30 years since moving into Alice Dolan's house he has done rather well for himself. Once the term of squatters rights had elapsed, he bought another house on Enniskerry Road and he amassed a considerable property portfolio including four houses in Phibsboro, two on Russell Avenue in Drumcondra and a property in Rathmines.

Along with his wife Mary he also owns the ABC Guesthouse on Drumcondra Road which consists of three houses joined together in a large bed and breakfast business. In addition, it emerged that he lives with his wife in a mansion on the Howth Road in Dublin overlooking Dublin Bay, complete with security gates.

He was also the promoter of a short-lived oil exploration company called Charter Energy Corporation founded in 2007 and dissolved in 2009. The directors included Grogan and Natasha Savelyeva, who, according to Thom's Dublin Street Directory, resides at his Howth Road address.

Judge Fennelly was asked to rule on the matter of awarding costs, to which Mr Dolan said he was entitled. Having won the case in the Supreme Court through what one of the judges called a 'clever' legalistic ploy, Judge Fennelly said that there was something 'egregious' or shocking about the application.

He was refused costs.

# Death of a Clare Farmer

Michael Davoren was one of the biggest farmers in County Clare. He and his wife, Grace, had a 269-acre farm at Ballycahill where they lived with their four children. Davoren also farmed the adjoining 623 acres at Ballyaben, Ballyvaughan, County Clare which belonged to his widowed mother Maura, but which he had worked most of his life.

As an only son he not only expected to inherit the family farm, it was already in his mother's will that he would get it.

When he fell ill with colitis, an inflammation of the lining of the colon, he was taken to University College Hospital, Galway where he was operated on by consultant gastroenterologist John Lee and consultant surgeon Oliver McAnena. He died shortly afterwards on 31 August 2003, at the age of 47.

Grace Davoren of The Barn, Ballyaben said that, following her husband's death, relations with her mother-in-law Maura Davoren deteriorated to such an extent that Maura changed her will to benefit her grandson, also called Michael. She subsequently changed it again so that her entire estate, including the Ballyaben farm passed to her daughter, Mary O'Regan.

This resulted in Grace Davoren suing the Health Service Executive, claiming negligence in her husband's treatment at the hospital and under Part 4 of the Civil Liability Act, 1961 that, as well as damages for loss of dependency, she had lost out on an expected inheritance of €1,312,275, the value of the family farm that her husband would have inherited had he not died before his mother.

The HSE's legal team argued that it was probably the falling out between Grace Davoren and her mother-in-law Maura that had caused her to lose the inheritance of the estate, rather than the death of her husband.

However, in his judgement, given in December 2011, Judge Iarfhlaith O'Neill said he was satisfied that Michael Davoren would have inherited the Ballyaben farm had he not suffered 'wrongful death' while in the care of the HSE and University College Hospital, Galway.

He also found that even if the falling out between Grace Davoren and her mother-in-law was the cause of Maura Davoren changing her will, this was directly due to the change in her state of mind caused by the wrongful death of her son.

He said he was satisfied that Michael Davoren's dependents would have inherited the estate of Maura Davoren if it were not for his wrongful death.

He ruled that Grace Davoren was entitled to €1,312,275 for the lost inheritance of the estate, as well as €184,271 to cover the loss of income from farming the Ballyaben farm following her mother-in-law's death.

He awarded a further €50,436 for the loss of rental income from the family home, on the basis that if her husband were still alive when his mother died they would have moved into the Ballyaben house and rented their own home, and he awarded another €44,975.79 in general damages, including the funeral costs and other expenses.

It all came to €1,591,957.79.

### The Wife Who Booked the Holidays and Bought the Wine

John O'Meara was a solid man, a cattle dealer and, according to reports, a 'renowned beef finisher' who lived on a 200-acre estate, Pitchfordstown Stud, outside Kilcock County Kildare.

Originally from Thurles, County Tipperary, the farmer and businessman was said to be worth about €80 million at the height of the boom. But he didn't have a high profile and kept mostly to himself, his family and his business affairs.

He started in the 'live' cattle exporting business with the well-known Purcell family before going out on his own.

His business was buying cattle in Ireland and 'finishing' them on his Kildare estate and other farms he owned in Meath. When they were ready for the market he shipped them to the lucrative markets of the Middle East where Irish cattle sold at premium rates. They were then slaughtered in the traditional 'halal' method as required under Islamic law.

Mr O'Meara went on extensive business trips but he wasn't very well known outside the niche business where he made his money. Apart from work he had a passion for horse racing and as well as breeding his own horses he had a couple of good prospects in training with Noel Meade. In one picture of him, taken with his horse Johnny Setaside and champion jockey Paul Carberry, he is a slightly stout man dressed in a sober grey suit and white shirt, the only splash of colour being a red-and-white-striped tie.

O'Meara was happily married. His wife Claire Swift, who kept her own name, was the sister of a well-known 1970s model and Miss Ireland contestant, Helen Swift. They had two young sons, aged seven and six.

Life changed dramatically for John O'Meara and his wife and family in the summer of 2008 when he was told that he had terminal cancer and had, at best, just 18 months to live.

Claire Swift, it was later maintained, was a 'stay at home wife' who looked after the house and her husband's domestic affairs. But she was also a director of one of his companies, Althorne Ltd, which had accumulated losses of €1.5 million that very same year. Obviously Claire Swift didn't have a head for business; she would later tell the High Court in Dublin that she had signed 'millions of documents' but she didn't know what she was doing at the time.

'I trusted my husband. There was nothing, nothing we ever wanted. I would have laid down and died on the spot for John. Signing something just wasn't an issue.

'I know nothing about the intricacies of what he did . . . we never discussed business.'

He had another company called Trenturo Ltd of which his aged mother, Mary O'Meara of Rathamanna, Thurles, County Tipperary, was a director.

Like many businessmen in the early years of the new century he dabbled in property, buying up a 'swathe' of development land around the town of Dunshaughlin, County Meath, as well as extensive farms around Dunsany in the same county.

He was obviously well connected and also travelled further afield and got involved in a Polish property venture with heavy hitters in the property market like Michael Holland and Paddy Shovlin, developer of the massive Beacon Centre in south County Dublin.

Because of his developments in Dunshaughlin he provided land for the local soccer club and was a great supporter of golf classics and other fundraising activities.

Claire Swift left the business end of things strictly to her husband. Her role, she admitted, was to 'book the holidays and buy the wine'. While she stayed at home with the children, John and Charlie, he took care of business, to such a degree that she never saw a utility bill of any kind.

After learning that he had just 18 months to live John O'Meara set about putting his affairs in order.

In his 18-page will drawn up on 20 May 2009 he appointed Gaye Hillary of Naas, County Kildare and Tom McParland, of Newbridge, County Kildare as trustees of the will.

Clause 3 states: 'In the event that my wife Claire should predecease me or die contemporaneously with me or not survive for a period of thirty days, I appoint my sister-in-law Helen Swift of Moy Stud, Summerhill, County Meath as guardians of my children under the age of 18 years at the date of my death.

In Clause 4 (b) he went on to leave his wife the sum of €1 million in cash from his assets; he left her Pitchfordstown Stud, Kilcock, County Kildare and all livestock, machinery, furnishings and payments from the EU Single Farm Payment and other EU payments he might be entitled to.

In three subsections to Clause 4, (c), (d), and (e), he left €200,000 to each of his trustees, Gaye Hillary and Tom McParland and €10,000 each to three of his employees at Pitchfordstown Stud, Seamus Maloney, Joe Flanagan and Rory Callanan, provided they were in his employment at the time of his death.

The remainder of the will laid out the various provisions of how the proceeds of this trust fund would be distributed when the time came.

He then set about providing for his wife and children. He told his wife that he was setting up a joint account 'for yourself and the boys, should anything happen to me'.

He did most of his business with Bank of Scotland and so he transferred €1.5 million in cash into an account at the bank. He is said to have told his wife that she was 'going to be very wealthy' when he died.

But John O'Meara must have got an inkling that the financial meltdown and particularly the collapse of the property market were taking its toll on his fortune.

In a codicil signed on 12 November 2009 and witnessed by an employee of the stud farm and Ann Corrigan, a lawyer with the large Dublin legal firm of Arthur Cox, he deleted clauses (c), (d) and (e) of the will – the bequests totalling €430,000 to his two trustees and his three employees.

When John O'Meara died just two weeks later on 27 November 2009 at the age of 48, his grieving widow was in for further shocks.

After a suitable period of mourning she called to Bank of Scotland armed with the details of her account to make her first withdrawal. But the 47-year-old mother of two was told by a senior official of the bank that they couldn't give her any money from the account as her late husband owed the bank €12.8 million and all his accounts with Bank of Scotland had been frozen.

Claire Swift issued proceedings against Bank of Scotland demanding that they release the money in the account he had opened in their joint names, which now became her inheritance.

The bank's case was that it had the right to take the money in the credit account as a 'set off' against money it was owed from other accounts operated by John O'Meara and his businesses.

But James Gilhooly SC for Claire Swift argued that if the bank ever had such a right, it had died with her husband in 2009 and, as his rightful heir, the €1.5 in cash now belonged to her.

Judge Mary Laffoy said that Claire Swift had perceived her husband to be a 'very wealthy man' prior to the economic downturn of 2008 and that perception 'may have been justified'.

She found that the cash in this particular account was 'jointly beneficially owned by Mr and Mrs O'Meara and that the funds passed to the plaintiff [Mrs O'Meara] by right of survivorship on the death of Mr O'Meara.'

The judge ruled that the bank was not entitled to 'set off' the businessman's debts against a family fund.

## The Secret Diaries of Sir Alfred Beit

By its very nature a will is usually a dry document filled with legal language summing up a life in terms of property and possessions rather than any outstanding achievement or even good deeds. In July 2006 when the will of Lady Clementine Mabell Kitty Beit of Russborough House, Blessington, County Wicklow was lodged in the Probate Office in Dublin, there was no expectation that her last will and testament would contain anything other than the details of her vast estates and trusts in Ireland, Britain and South Africa. Her husband, the late Sir Alfred Beit, had inherited a huge fortune made in the diamond mines of South Africa by his father Otto, one of the founders of the De Beers diamond cartel more than a century before.

Of course, the fate of the exotic contents of Russborough House and its fabulous art collection was bound to be of interest. But the Palladian mansion in Wicklow had already been put in the hands of the Beit Trust and much of the famous Beit art collection handed over to the National Gallery of Ireland.

Sir Alfred Beit died on 12 May 1994 at Mount Carmel Hospital in Dublin, leaving a will with a value of £3,299,708. His famous art collection had been plundered by both the IRA and the criminal Martin Cahill, known as The General, and, poignantly, his will included two paintings by the artist Guardi 'the said pictures having been stolen and not yet recovered at the date of this my will'.

Lady Beit died on 17 August 2005 in London, leaving an estate in Ireland valued at €7,143,892, and an additional €12 million in Britain.

Her will started along predictable enough lines with small but generous gifts to the Garda Siochána Benevolent Society, the Rector of St Mary's Church in Blessington and an equal sum to the parish priest across the road, along with gifts to the Kildare Society for the Prevention of Cruelty to Animals and the Wexford Festival Opera.

There were small bequests of personal possessions, such as a watercolour by Turner which was donated to the Apollo Foundation in London, a gold box made by Garrard's of London, a gift from her husband on the occasion of their golden wedding which she left to the Alfred Beit Foundation, and numerous other gifts of personal belongings and money to friends and relations in Ireland and Britain.

There were a pair of small pictures and a portrait of her father, Major the Honourable Clement Mitford DSO, MC, killed some months before she was born in May 1915 during the First World War, which were bequeathed to the Royal Hussars Museum, Peninsula Barracks in Winchester, England.

Clementine Beit, who was called after the father she never met, was a cousin of the famous Mitford sisters, the eccentric daughters of Lord Redesdale. One of them, Nancy, was a famous writer, another, 'Debo', married the Earl of Devonshire, owner of Lismore Castle in Waterford, while a third, Diana, was the mother of Desmond Guinness, whose second marriage was to the British fascist leader Sir Oswald Mosley. Clementine was closest to another sister, Unity, and in the 1930s the two of them met Adolf Hitler.

But it was the enigmatic Clause 8 of the will which has left a mystery that will remain unsolved during our lifetime, a mystery that historians of the future will unravel and which may throw new light on one of the great conundrums of the British Royal family:

> I bequeath my late husband's diaries to my executors and trustees to be held by them upon the following trusts:
>
> a)  To retain the same in their sole possession and custody under lock and key for a period (hereinafter called 'the trust period') which shall end 21 years from the date of death of the last survivor living at the date of my death of the issue of his late Britannic Majesty King George VI or for 70 years from my death, whichever shall be the shorter, and I direct that my trustees shall not allow anyone (including but not limited to a biographer of my late husband) to

have access to the said diaries during the trust period.

b) At the expiry of the trust period my trustees shall hold the same upon trust for the National Library of Ireland absolutely.

The burning question is, what is in the diaries of Sir Alfred Beit that they cannot be opened until 21 years after the death of Queen Elizabeth II of England?

Of course many wills contain what is known as a 'royal lives clause' meaning that something is to be triggered after a specified period after the death of a king or queen, or in some Irish cases after the death of Eamon de Valera. But these are usually to do with distributing the proceeds of a trust or fund. In this case there is a clear connection to the British royal family, as Sir Alfred and Lady Beit moved in such circles.

The answer to this mystery has been entrusted to Dublin solicitors Paul Dennis Guinness and Paula Fallon of 19 Lower Baggot Street, Dublin and whoever shall succeed them as trustees of Lady Alfred Beit's will.

What is almost certain is that the diaries contain intimate details of the court of His Highness Prince Albert Frederick Arthur George Windsor, Duke of York, Earl of Inverness and Baron Killarney, who unexpectedly became King George VI, the last king of Ireland, when his brother King Edward VIII abdicated on 11 December 1936 in order to marry his twice-divorced mistress Wallis Warfield Simpson.

Sir Alfred and Lady Clementine 'Kitty' Beit were described at the time as 'not merely the richest young couple in London, they were also known as the handsomest'. Sir Alfred was a Conservative MP for St Pancras and went on to become parliamentary private secretary to the Secretary of State for the Colonies.

In the 1930s the couple were intimate members of the future king's inner circle at a time when he was just the second son of King George V. 'Fred' was regarded as an unlikely candidate to ever succeed to the throne because he had married a 'commoner', suffered from a stammer and chronic stomach problems, had knock-knees and, although wrote with his right hand, he was naturally left handed and had been forced by his tutors to conform due to the generally held belief that left-handed people were an aberration which should not be tolerated.

Alfred and Clementine Beit had been friends and benefactors of the man who most recently achieved fame with the biographical film *The King's Speech*. But what revelations the diaries contain will not be known in our lifetime.

The Beits left London in 1945 after Sir Alfred lost his parliamentary seat. They went to live in South Africa but were appalled by the new policy of apartheid and wanted to return to London. Alfred Beit's mother died and left him an incredible collection of paintings, including Vermeer, Goya and many more, and they needed a house big enough to display their newly acquired art collections. As they sat in their estate near Cape Town leafing through a copy of *Country Life* magazine, they saw that the Daly family were selling Russborough House, built in the 1740s for the Earl of Milltown, near Blessington in County Wicklow and described by the architectural historian Mark Bence-Jones as 'arguably the most beautiful house in Ireland'.

They bought it by telegram in 1952, little knowing that in the years that followed it would go on to become known for some of the most notorious art heists in history.

## Was She Right to Be Paranoid?

Duleek House, a great grey pile, was built around 1750 and, according to the Knight of Glin, the architect was Richard Cassells, who was responsible for some of the great Georgian houses around the Irish countryside. Built by a wealthy MP, Thomas Trotter, it acquired a somewhat better pedigree with the marriage of his daughter Elizabeth to the 2nd Marquis of Thomond.

At any rate, although the estates were gone the once grand three-storey mansion was still standing proud near the town of Duleek, County Meath when the exotically named Maura de Souza and her family took possession in 1952.

Mrs de Souza had two daughters: Genia, a vivacious blonde and an accomplished horsewoman who hunted with the Tara Harriers and had a great interest in shows and the theatre, and her younger sister Shaheen who was born with Down's syndrome.

In time, Genia married a man called Wearen. They lived in Duleek House and had a number of children.

Maura de Souza eventually fell out with her son-in-law and on one occasion even accused him of trying to kill her. Although the house was big it wasn't big enough for both of them. The strain eventually led to Genia and her husband separating.

Around the mid-1980s, according to Genia de Souza, her mother became increasingly paranoid and delusional. She believed that the Provisional IRA was using Duleek House as a base and that the rooms were bugged. She even thought the television aerial was being used to pick up and transmit signals from the house to some unknown but very dark forces working against her.

She also believed that her car was being tampered with, the brakes removed, the wheels loosened and the keys interfered with. And she was convinced that certain members of the family who were living in Duleek House were 'conspiring' against her in ways that she could not quite define.

It was like something out of a horror movie except that, even if Maura de Souza was delusional, by a quirk of fate she would die in a tragic car crash.

On 30 January 1998 Maura de Souza arrived at the offices of Branigan and Company solicitors in Drogheda where she told Donal Branigan that she felt her life was in danger and she wanted to make an 'emergency' will.

They drew up the will that afternoon but, unusually, Maura de Souza decided to leave everything to her Down's syndrome daughter Shaheen, and nothing to her other daughter Genia, who had supported her and Duleek House with various money-making ventures throughout the years they had lived there together.

To add to Genia's later dissatisfaction she would learn that not only did her mother leave her nothing, but she also decreed in her will that on Shaheen's death the remainder of the estate would pass to her guardian, Tessa Gannon, a niece of Maura de Souza who lived in England and was also executrix of her aunt's will.

Curiously, the last will and testament was written out in Maura de Souza's own hand, and was not typed up in the solicitor's office.

'I appoint my sister-in-law, Ann Gannon, and Tessa Gannon, my niece, executors of this my will and trustees of my estate,' states the will. 'I appoint Tessa Gannon sole guardian of my daughter Shaheen de Souza.' She then bequeathed all her worldly possessions to 'the said Anna Gannon and the said Tessa Gannon' to hold in trust for her daughter Shaheen de Souza.

'On the death of the said Shaheen de Souza, I give and bequeath all my said property to Tessa Gannon', the will concludes.

The circumstances surrounding the tragic death of Maura de Souza in a traffic accident at 8.15pm on the evening of 22 April 1999 are now buried in the files of the investigating gardaí. It was just a few days short of 15 months since she had gone into the solicitor's office in an agitated manner saying her life was in danger, and some years after she had first said her car was being tampered with.

The details were reported briefly in *The Irish Times* under the heading: Meath Woman Killed in Collision with Truck.

> A 68-year-old woman, named as Maura de Souza of Duleek House, Duleek, County Meath, was killed last night when the car she was driving was in a collision with a lorry. The accident, which happened just after 8.30pm, occurred at a 'notorious' junction at the Commons in Duleek. Her body was taken to Navan General Hospital.

When the details of Maura de Souza's will became known, relatively quickly her daughter Genia mounted a legal challenge to have the will overturned on the grounds that her mother had not been fit to make a will and that she had been suffering from Alzheimer's at the time.

The case was heard in mid-February 2004. After outlining how Maura de Souza had come to him, solicitor Donal Branigan said that she was 'well presented and well reasoned' and if she hadn't been he would not have carried out her wishes to make the will.

He told the court that, in retrospect, the late Mrs de Souza was not enamoured of Genia's husband and Genia had been left out because of her husband. The couple had since separated.

Her doctor James Hayes, a GP from Navan, said that she had a mild form of

Parkinson's disease, but did not suffer from Alzheimer's as was alleged in legal documents submitted as part of the case. He said she suffered from 'chronic anxiety' and her 'compliance' with taking her medication was 'seriously in doubt'. He said he realised that relations between Maura de Souza and other members of the family were 'taut'.

Cross-examined by Mr Brian Spierin SC for Genia de Souza, Dr Hayes said that from his experience he believed the late Mrs de Souza had not been clinically of unsound mind.

Ms Tessa Gannon said the late Mrs de Souza had dedicated her life to Shaheen and was concerned that her child would outlive her. The will, she said, had 'split the family down the middle like the Red Sea'. The late Mrs de Souza had told her about making the will and of leaving her 'in charge'. Maura de Souza had said she had left Genia some land.

Ms Gannon said she regretted she did not have a more detailed conversation with the late Mrs de Souza about the will but she had felt uncomfortable and embarrassed at the time.

She was not even sure that the late Maura de Souza had been telling her the truth. She believed she was under a lot of pressure at the time. There was 'a bit of an atmosphere' in the house. Maura de Souza had visited her in England and it was like she had come from a 'war zone', Tessa Gannon said.

The terms of the will were harsh on Genia but it had been the late Mrs de Souza's way of making 'absolutely sure' Shaheen would be looked after.

After a two-day hearing, Judge Thomas Smyth said it was an 'unfortunate' case for all concerned, but he was satisfied from the evidence of the solicitor and the doctor that the will was executed in accordance with the Succession Act and was not open to question.

The validity of the will did not relate to its fairness, he said, or whether another parent would have done what Mrs Maura de Souza did. The case was about whether she had the capacity to make the will and knew the extent of her estate and who could expect to benefit from it. It was not at issue whether Maura de Souza discharged her moral obligations, he said.

He also said he regarded as 'very important' that Maura de Souza, believed that her niece Tessa Gannon would make a very good guardian.

Judge Smyth found that Maura de Souza had made a valid will and dismissed the challenge of Genia de Souza.

Written at the end of the will is: 'Maura de Souza v Gannon and others. This will was proved in solemn form of law before Mr Justice Smyth on 20 February 2004.'

Genia de Souza decided to appeal. Genia de Souza was reported as saying that the courts had overturned the earlier decision on Maura de Souza's will, and found in her favour instead.

Soon after came dramatic news reports of yet another misfortune to befall the family, the night Duleek House burned to the ground.

It was on the night of St Patrick's Day, 2008 and Genia was having dinner with friends Jim Flanagan and Sharon Keoghan in Oscar's restaurant in the village when word came that Duleek House was on fire.

The hero of the hour was her teenage son Kyle, who carried his aunt Shaheen from the burning house, helped his 14-year-old sister Megan escape the blaze and then released horses stabled nearby into the fields so that they wouldn't suffer from the plumes of smoke shrouding the Georgian pile as it was enveloped by the blaze. For his efforts he broke his toe.

Genia arrived at Duleek House at the same time as the fire brigade and managed to help dogs, cats and even a pet snake out of the conflagration.

In an interview given the following day to the local paper the *Drogheda Independent* she spoke about the will dispute and her appeal to the courts.

'It seems our luck has turned at last,' she said, referring to the fact that the family had survived the blaze. 'We had a good result in the court and then this happened. I do hope that there is nothing left to go wrong.'

## The Scottish Divorce

In a weak squiggly hand the will is signed 'D Romanes at Edinburgh, 9 May 2010'.

Eight days later on 17 May, Deirdre Mary Astrea Romanes died at the age of

60. She left behind a fortune in property and shares in the well-known Scottish newspaper company, Dunfermline Press, worth £4,176,782.

She was an unlikely media tycoon. Born Deirdre Donnelly on 11 July 1949, she was brought up in County Wicklow with her brother and two younger sisters before going to school in Navan, County Meath, where the family had connections in Philpotstown. After leaving school she emigrated to London where she trained as a nurse, and then moved to Edinburgh to do a midwifery course.

There she fell in love with Iain Blair Romanes, a newspaper executive and the fifth generation member of the family that owned the Dunfermline Press. When they got married, Deirdre Donnelly also married into the family newspaper business which he had largely inherited. The couple had no children and Deirdre became involved in the business, working her way up through the ranks to take on the role of chief executive in the mid-1980s.

When Iain and Deirdre Romanes divorced amicably, he got a multimillion settlement and went to live in Monaco while she became the largest shareholder and managing director of the Dunfermline Press.

Irish provincial newspapers became the unlikely target of Scottish interest in the 1990s, with media groups such as Johnston Press, Dunfermline Press and Scottish Radio Holdings attracted to the country by high readership figures and the boom in advertising.

Dunfermline Press, perhaps influenced by Deirdre Romanes's Irish background, were to the forefront of the invasion. During the 1990s she expanded into Ireland, paying a small fortune to buy up a string of newspapers including *The Meath Chronicle* based in Navan, *The Anglo-Celt* in Cavan and the *Westmeath Examiner* in Mullingar, all strong provincial newspapers which were branded under the heading of Celtic Media Group, a subsidiary of the Scottish-based business.

After her death, Deirdre Romanes's 2010 will decreed that £3 million of her fortune was to go to the Deirdre Romanes Liferent Trust which had been established in 1988, and the trustees were requested to 'use and apply this legacy to take such action as they think fit to secure the future prosperity of

Dunfermline Press Limited'.

Clause 4.4 of the will then added: 'This legacy and any tax on it shall be preferential to all other legacies and bequests under my will or otherwise and the following provision of my will shall take effect subject to it.'

In the next clause in the will she left £1 million to her sister Elizabeth Smyth, who lives in County Meath.

Mrs Smyth was not very happy about the terms of the will and when the trustees went to sell two properties in Edinburgh that were part of her sister's estate she mounted a legal challenge to prevent the sale going ahead.

She argued that under the terms of a previous will, dated 2 June 2008, her sister Deirdre had left instructions for her trustees to sell the two significant properties in Edinburgh, No 33 Heriot Row and an adjoining property in Jamaica Lane (known as the Heriot Row properties) and their contents, and they were 'to pay and make over the net sale proceeds to my sister, Mrs Elizabeth Smyth'.

This will also declared that Mrs Smith was to get 50 per cent of the proceeds of the sale of the two properties with the other 50 per cent going to her four sons.

According to the Schedule of Assets drawn up after the death of Deirdre Romanes, these properties were together worth £2,250,000.

In her statement to the Scottish courts, Mrs Smyth said that she was 'apprehensive' that if the estate was distributed under the terms of the 2010 will 'there will be no funds available to satisfy the legacy' to her after the payments of debts, inheritances tax and the 'preferential' legacy of £3 million which was to be used to prop up the Dunfermline Press, which by then was in serious financial difficulty.

She also alleged that her sister's former husband, Ian Blair Romanes, took advantage of his wife's weakness – she was suffering from cancer – and induced her to change her will just days before her death, in favour of the newspaper publishing company, of which he remained a director.

The will, she maintained, was made by Mrs Romanes at a time when 'she lacked the necessary capacity' and when she was 'weak and facile'.

In reply, the trustees of the will said that Deirdre Romanes 'did not intend the respondent [Mrs Smyth] to receive the two houses and their contents.

'The principle proof of that intention should be derived from the will itself. The words used by the testator were not to be altered or transposed if they were capable of sensible interpretation. Where, as here, the words of the will are unambiguous they cannot be departed from merely because they lead to a result that may be considered capricious, or even harsh and unreasonable.'

Mrs Smyth then argued that the intention of the 2008 will was that she would receive the proceeds of the two Edinburgh properties: 'At the date of the execution of the deed [will] the respondent [Mrs Smyth] was resident in Ireland and that would afford a reason for the deceased directing her executors and trustees to sell the Heriot Row properties and their contents. That was consistent with the direction being of an administrative one only.'

Pending a hearing of the full case Mrs Smith was granted an order in Edinburgh by Lords Reed, Hardie and Wheatley, preventing the executors from selling the two Edinburgh properties.

'The issue for our consideration is a narrow one,' said the judges, 'namely whether pending the resolution of the dispute the executors ought to preserve the Heriot Row properties and their contents in their present form or whether they are entitled in the meantime to realise these assets in the knowledge that they will be prohibited from distributing the proceeds of the sale until the present dispute has been resolved.'

In her will Mrs Romanes made various bequests, including another property worth £400,000, over £1 million in cash, and furniture and paintings worth £189,000 as well as a yacht based in the Channel Islands.

Unhappily, the death of Deirdre Romanes coincided with a rapid deterioration in the finances of the Dunfermline Press and the Celtic Media Group in Ireland. The company had paid more than £30 million for its stable of provincial newspapers in Ireland – but in her will they were valued at just £1.

The company was £28 million in debt by 2011 when it went into receivership. Although the company was trading, it couldn't sustain its borrowings and after Lloyds Bank agreed to write off £10 million in debt, the company was the subject of a management buy out by its directors, who called the new company the Romanes Media Group.

According to sources, the dispute over the last will and testament of Deirdre Romanes is still ongoing.

## A Case of Mistaken Identity

When a wealthy County Cork farmer died leaving a considerable fortune, the question that later arose was who did he intend to be the main beneficiary of his will.

Edward Godfrey, aged 79, of Newtown, Bantry, County Cork made the will in March, 1998. He left a number of small legacies to relations and friends and 'all the rest, residue of my estate' to 'my niece Mrs Anne O'Sullivan, 3 The Square, Kenmare'.

Mr Godfrey's estate came to at least €3.5 million.

The executors of the will, however, had to go to court to decide who should get most of the money. Should it be Farmer Godfrey's niece, who wasn't correctly named in the specific clause of the will, or should it be his sister, who was.

In the High Court in Dublin Judge Mella Carroll was asked to decide whether the will was intended to benefit Ann Godfrey of Elm Park, Wilton, Cork who was Mr Godfrey's niece, or Anne O'Sullivan of The Square, Kenmare, County Kerry who was Mr Godfrey's sister.

In an affidavit, the niece, Ann Godfrey, said it was her belief that her late uncle wished to benefit her brother John, who was in an institution, and herself. She said that her uncle intended that she should act as a trustee for John's share and look after him for life. She had also lived, originally, in The Square in Kenmare, before moving to Cork. The reference to 'Anne O'Sullivan', she maintained, was a mistake.

In her submission to the court, by way of affidavit, Anne O'Sullivan said she was the older sister of Edward Godfrey. She and the late Mr Godfrey were siblings in a family of seven and she and her deceased brother were always very close.

She said that the late Mr Godfrey regularly visited her and her family in

Kenmare and she and her late husband and her children had regularly visited him in the original family home in Bantry.

The executors brought the case to court to have the position clarified. They told the court they were adopting a 'neutral' position and said they would administer the estate according to the terms decided by Judge Carroll.

Although the case opened in the High Court, settlement discussions followed the first day of the hearing. Mr Brian Spierin, SC representing the executors of the late Mr Godfrey's will, said the parties had been able to come to an arrangement between themselves and had reached an accommodation on foot of that.

John Gordon SC for Ann Godfrey, the niece of the deceased farmer, said he was delighted to be able to tell the court that the family had resolved the issues in a harmonious and proper manner and everybody was leaving court on good terms.

It was agreed that the niece, Ann Godfrey, should get the entire residue of the estate, less a moiety of the proceeds of the real estate to be retained for John Godfrey, the nephew of the deceased, who was in an institution.

## A Voice from beyond the Grave

According to her brother Liam, elderly spinster Kay Ellison 'wouldn't spend Christmas'.

Miss Catherine Ellison, to give her full title, had never married and had no children. She lived alone on Dolphin Road in Drimnagh, Dublin city and was well known as a 'frugal' woman of routine and habit.

She had no central heating in her home and she kept warm in the winter with a two-bar electric heater. The house had fallen into disrepair and she often told relatives that if she had the money she would like to move to another area of the inner city.

Unknown to them, however, Kay Ellison had the money, and luck would bring her much more.

Described by relatives as 'a miser', it was discovered after she died that the frugal Kay Ellison had up to €600,000, most of it in cash, stashed away in various bank accounts.

If she worried about scrimping and saving during the week, on Saturdays she threw caution to the wind and made a weekly pilgrimage into Dublin. She liked to rummage around the 'euro shops' on Camden Street where she would buy a few items to keep her going for the following week. Then she would head on up the street to bargain with the stall holders selling fruit and vegetables to add a few meagre items to her purchases.

With the 'messages' complete she would call over to her brother Liam who ran a couple of companies called Rare Fashions Limited and Regency Marketing at No 11 Lower Camden Street.

He was used to these regular visits from his sister. They would chat for a while about money and investments, because Kay had by then amassed considerable savings and relied on him and his accountant for advice. He would then ring a pub he patronised across the road and two lunches would be brought across to his office where they would eat them together. It was Kay Ellison's big treat of the week.

In the family it was recognised that Liam and Kay were very close and that he was the one who would inherit whatever she had when she passed away.

Her brother said that Kay was a daily Mass-goer who didn't like spending money. Neither was she domesticated, he said; she didn't like cooking and relied on him for the big treat of the week.

Like a lot of old people, especially those without family, 'she had a horror of going into a nursing home' and so was very money conscious, saving every cent for her old age, little realising that it was already upon her.

After their weekly lunch, Liam would give her €4 and, before getting the bus back to Dolphin's Barn, she would go to the nearby Spar and buy two €4 'quickpick' Lotto tickets for the 'syndicate' they had going together.

She would then ring him on Sunday or later during the week and they would compare their numbers against the winning combination. This had been the routine for almost 18 years.

On Saturday 28 January 2006 Kay made her usual visit to Camden Street before going over to the Spar where she bought a Lotto ticket with the numbers

1, 9, 13, 27, 36, 38. Later that night, at about 8.10pm and within minutes of the Lotto draw finishing on the television, Kay phoned Liam at his home, 63 Templeville Drive, Terenure, Dublin to tell him excitedly: 'We've won the Lotto.'

They had, but they had to share it.

The jackpot for that night was €1,350,000. Possibly later that night or on Sunday morning Kay would have learned that they hadn't won the jackpot outright. They shared it with two other winners, each of the three picking up the tidy sum of €450,000 in cash.

According to Liam Ellison he immediately went around to his sister's house that Saturday night and told her not to do anything with the ticket until he got advice from his accountant, who had also advised Kay on her financial affairs. As it happens, neither of them signed the lotto ticket at this point, a curious omission for an otherwise careful businessman.

But things were not as they seemed.

Gary Ellison, a nephew of both Kay and Liam Ellison, says that when he called around to his aunt's house that same Saturday night, as he did every Saturday night, his aunt opened the door to him and announced: 'We've done it.'

Could it be that Kay Ellison was devious enough to conduct two different Lotto syndicates with her brother Liam and her nephew Gary, telling neither of them about the other? It was certainly possible, and it was something that a High Court judge would be asked to adjudicate on in the future.

For someone who was so careful about money it is curious that Kay Ellison left it for two weeks before making arrangements to go into the National Lottery office in Middle Abbey Street, Dublin, to collect her winnings. However, when she rang Liam to bring her in to collect the €450,000 cheque, he told her she had mixed up her dates and he couldn't drive her in that day because he had an important appointment.

It was to prove a costly move.

Kay Ellison was determined not to wait any longer, so she rang her nephew Gary, who lived not far from his uncle. Described as a former senior bank official, he had taken early retirement from the bank and now drove a taxi.

He collected his aunt from her home on Dolphin Road and they went together to the National Lottery office where they both signed the back of the winning ticket as well as a declaration form that he was part of a syndicate with her. However, the National Lottery cheque for €450,000 was made out in her name only.

He then drove her to the Bank of Ireland in Camden Street where she had an account and where the manager knew her. The money was lodged into an ICS Building Society account that was solely in her name.

Later, Gary Ellison would insist that he too was involved in a syndicate with his aunt, Kay Ellison, and that every week they did a €4 quickpick for the Wednesday and Saturday Lotto draws. He said he was happy to let her buy the tickets because she also had investments in Prize Bonds and had been very lucky over the years.

On 11 July that same year, 2006, Catherine Ellison of 29 Dolphin Road, drew up her last will and testament. She appointed her niece, Doctor Martha Ellison of Appian Way, Dublin and her brother Liam of Templeville Drive as executors.

She left her brother Charlie, of Templeville Road €10,000, his wife Christina and their children, Declan, Lorraine, and Sandra, €1,000 each.

She left her brother Bernard of College Crescent, Dublin 6 €10,000 and his wife Marie and their children Brendan, Yvonne, Gary, Ian and Fiona €1,000 each.

She left her brother Aidan of Knocklyon, Dublin €5,000.

She left her brother Liam €20,000, with €1,000 each to his wife Martha and their children, Deirdre, David, Paul and Martha.

She left her house on Dolphin Road and the residue of her estate to her brother Liam Ellison 'for his own use and benefit absolutely'.

The two-page will was signed and witnessed by a factory manager and a packer whose address was given as 11 Lower Camden Street, Dublin 8, the business address of her brother Liam.

Kay Ellison died of cancer at the age of 84 in April 2007.

When her will went to probate, Gary Ellison knew that the bulk of his aunt's fortune had gone to his uncle, Liam Ellison, who by then was in his mid-70s and had retired as a company director and his companies dissolved.

Gary Ellison, then 41, took a case to the High Court claiming that he was part of a syndicate with his aunt when she won the €450,000 and as such he was entitled to a half share in that portion of her estate. His uncle, Liam, contested the case saying that it was he who was part of the syndicate and he didn't believe that his sister was ever a member of a Lotto syndicate with their nephew Gary.

When the matter was heard before Judge Eamon de Valera in the High Court sitting, Gary Ellison said he was close to his aunt and she had been 'a great strength and support' during his separation and subsequent divorce from his wife.

He was asked why he had allowed the money to be put into an account in the sole name of his aunt. He said that he had 'no worries' about allowing her to have the money in her own name. It would 'give her comfort' he said, adding that although 'it might sound cold', he believed he wouldn't have to wait too long before he got his share of the Lotto win.

Liam Ellison who was disputing his nephew's claim said that if he had gone with his sister to the Lotto office to collect the winning cheque that day there would never have been a court case, and Gary Ellison would not be making any claim on the Lotto winnings. He said it was 'crystal clear' that he was the joint owner of the winning ticket and that he was entitled to hold on to his full inheritance from his sister.

Nor did he believe that Gary Ellison visited his aunt on the Saturday night in question, or was met with the words, 'We've done it.'

'The case my client will make,' said Patrick Hunt SC, counsel for Liam Ellison, 'is that you were asked to ferry your aunt to the National Lottery headquarters and that you opportunistically signed the back of the ticket and a declaration form.'

Mr Hunt SC said that Kay Ellison was 'speaking from the grave' in her will and her wishes were clear from her careful decision to bequeath just €1,000 to her nephew Gary, instead of the €225,000 which he was asking the court to award him as his alleged winnings from the Lotto syndicate.

Cormac Ó Dúlacháin SC, for Gary Ellison, said the existence of one Lotto syndicate did not exclude the existence of another. He said that Gary had not been 'singled out' by his aunt in her will, as she had left €1,000 to each of her other nieces and nephews.

The most important feature of this case, he said, was that Gary Ellison had signed the winning ticket and this was a 'definitive element' in any contract. The evidence of the case had not 'dislodged' Gary's claim over a half share in the Lotto win by virtue of him signing it. Kay had kept Liam's involvement in a syndicate secret from Gary, and it was equally possible that she had kept Gary's involvement in a second syndicate secret from Liam.

'It does not stack up that she is speaking from the grave by saying this,' he declared.

In his submission to the court Mr Hunt, acting for Liam Ellison, said that Kay Ellison was a woman of 'high moral principle' who went to Mass daily and it was inexplicable that she would 'double-cross' her nephew in this manner by doing him out of his legal entitlement to a half share of the Lotto winnings.

Newspaper reports of the case in Tralee said that it had also divided the Ellison family, which sat apart in the back of the court, some supporting Liam – who was always expected to inherit most of his sister's estate – others supporting Gary.

The case for Gary Ellison was summed up by Mr Ó Dúlacháin saying that it was possible that there were two syndicates and the only person who could confirm this was Kay Ellison, the woman at the centre of the drama, but she was now dead and it appeared that Judge de Valera would have to decide the issue.

He reserved judgment until the following law term.

However, according to sources close to the case, the judge and barristers involved did their best to 'nudge' the disputing parties to reach a settlement. Shortly after the conclusion of the court proceedings the judge was told that the Ellisons had settled their differences.

Details of the settlement were not disclosed.

# Chapter 9

## *The Black Widow*

Helena Agnes Blackall lived in what might be called 'genteel poverty' with her three elderly daughters in the family mansion, Marino Park, a large property secluded from the public gaze by a long driveway and woodlands, just off Mount Merrion Avenue in fashionable Blackrock, County Dublin.

Without telling her daughters, the elderly and bedridden Mrs Blackall, then 99 years of age, contacted her solicitor, James F O'Higgins, and asked him to call to see her at the once grand house which, like the old lady herself, was beginning to show its age. That day she instructed him on the details of a new will which she intended to make.

On 23 September 1976 while her daughters were elsewhere, the solicitor returned to Marino Park accompanied by an employee with the new will, to incorporate the wishes of his client. As she sat up in bed he read to her the draft document which he had drawn up. It went as follows:

> I, Helena A Blackall of Marino Park, Blackrock, County Dublin, widow, declare this to be my last will and testament. I hereby revoke all former wills and testamentary dispositions made by me.
>
> I appoint my four children, Eileen Blackall, Gerard Blackall, Irene Blackall and Rose Blackall as executors of this my will.
>
> I give, devise and bequeath all the property I die possessed of to my said children, Eileen, Gerard, Irene and Rose absolutely in equal share and I direct that my executors shall sell, convert and otherwise

> deal in my property real and personal and divide the proceeds in equal
> share among my said children after payment of all my just debts and
> testamentary expenses.

The will was witnessed by James F O'Higgins and Noreen Flanagan and bore what Judge Brian McCracken would later declare as 'an almost illegible signature, which is clearly that of a very elderly person'.

The events of that day in September 1976 would lead to a series of legal actions involving the validity of the will and the sale of Marino Park which then passed slowly and bitterly through the legal system for over a decade, almost beggaring her two remaining daughters, Eileen and Rose, then in their late 80s, and ending with a wave of public sympathy for them as they struggled to avoid eviction from the family mansion.

Perhaps old Mrs Blackall, originally an O'Brien from County Clare and who claimed to be a direct descendent of Brian Boru, knew what fate had in store for her daughters, because after the will was read to her the only thing she said to her solicitor by way of comment was: 'I think that's fair; one of them is a bit fiery.' She didn't say which of them it referred to, but it was probably Dr Rose the youngest of her three daughters.

Some months later, on 10 March 1977, Mrs Helena Agnes Blackall died. She was in her 100th year. After her death life went on as normal in Marino Park, the three elderly daughters pottering around the place as the house and gardens gradually fell into disrepair and which they just managed to stop a little short of outright dereliction.

Meanwhile, outside the gates the real world of which they knew so little was changing more rapidly than it had at any time since the Blackalls had first come to their secluded mansion in 1917 when it was just one of many landed estates in that part of 'the countryside' outside Dublin.

Marino Park, officially No 44 Mount Merrion Avenue, Blackrock was built on one of the few long, straight roadways in Dublin. Originally the carriageway of the Fifth Lord Fitzwilliam, Mount Merrion Avenue was designed to take him from the grand entrance of his estate on the Rock Road to his mansion on the elevated site where Mount Merrion Catholic church stands today. As it happened, the grand entrance and two wings of the proposed mansion were all that were built before the lord of the manor departed for his other estates in Pembroke, Wales.

Marino Park, a more modest eight-bedroom mansion, was originally built for the rector of the nearby Protestant Church on Cross Avenue. After he passed on it was rented to the Dowager Countess Mountmorres, now a forgotten figure in Irish history but who at the time was at the centre of a celebrated murder case that convulsed the British Empire.

On 25 September in the year 1880 her husband Lord Mountmorres, a minor landlord who lived at Ebor Hall near Clonbur, County Mayo, was shot and killed as he returned to his estate from performing his duties as the local magistrate. Mountmorres had refused to reduce rents for his impoverished tenants and was planning to evict those who were unable to pay. In the aftermath of the assassination his body was left lying on the narrow road and local peasant farmers refused to allow the corpse to be brought into their meagre homes.

'To these causes he undoubtedly owed his death,' said one of the many newspaper reports referring to the event and his plans for eviction. 'If any doubt of this could have existed the behaviour of the peasantry to Lord Mountmorres' unoffending widow and children would effactually have set it at rest. So strictly were they boycotted that it was not long before they had to leave Ebor Hall and take refuge in England.'

It was at the beginning of the land agitation led by Michael Davitt and Charles Stewart Parnell and such was the outcry from the British establishment that Queen Victoria had the widowed countess brought to Hampton Court Palace where she was given an apartment until a safe home was found for them in Ireland – which was Marino Park.

It was far from this kind of grandeur that Thomas Henry Blackall was reared, but he too was a man of ambition. The son of a large farmer from Kildeema, County Clare he was, according to the 1901 census, living in Kildeema with his parents and his first wife Jane aged 25. The couple may have had a child, George, however it seems his wife died shortly afterwards. Thomas remarried in

1905, his new bride the formidable Helena Agnes O'Brien from Kilfenora who was 25 at the time of the marriage.

As part of the marriage settlement it was agreed that any property they owned would be put into a trust fund for their children. This was one way in which a wife could protect her interest in the family home, something that wouldn't become part of the legal system until Mr Charles Haughey's Succession Act was passed by the Dáil in 1965.

Thomas H Blackall wasn't immune from land agitation himself. As well as being a farmer, Blackall, a Catholic, was also a Justice of the Peace and had obtained an appointment as the Estates Commissioner for County Clare. In April 1910 while he, his wife Helena and some friends were in residence at Kildeema the house was attacked by land agitators.

According to reports of the incident, the front door of the house was demolished and the inside 'riddled with shot' in an attack which seems to have been provoked by some decision he made about the division of land.

'The incident was very serious to the health of one member of the family,' said a report, which revealed that 22 panes of glass were broken in the dining room window and a bullet 'penetrated the piano'.

The attack is almost certain to have led to Thomas Blackall's decision to leave County Clare almost immediately with his family and move to Dublin. He obtained a position in the Estates Commission office in Dublin Castle and moved into a house in Woodstock Villas in Terenure. By the time of the 1911 census he had moved to No 9 Greenmount Road, Terenure with Helena, who was then 31, and George, who was now seven years of age.

Blackall, who kept two servants, a coachman and a domestic, is also described as a landowner / farmer, which presumably relates to his estate in County Clare. It seems that sometime around 1917 he had been promoted to the position of Assistant Land Commissioner and his prospects were looking up.

It may be entirely coincidental that the Rt Honourable James Owens Wylie who, as well as being a member of Her Majesty's Privy Council of Ireland, was Judicial Commissioner of the Irish Land Commission and Thomas Blackall's immediate boss, and lived in The Elms, a large estate on Mount Merrion Avenue, adjoining Marino Park, which at the time was up for sale.

Whether Wylie told him about it or he found out for himself, Thomas Blackall divested himself of his estates in County Clare and his house in Terenure and bought the mansion and adjoining lands, moving to this idyllic enclosed estate in south Dublin with his family and bringing some of his estate workers up from County Clare to tend the farm.

The eldest son George died, but the couple had four other children, Eileen, Gerard, Irene and Rose.

Life may have seemed idyllic but keeping up an estate with workers and servants cost a lot of money on a civil servant's salary and later reports said that Thomas Blackall suffered badly in the 'Crash' of 1929, which wiped out investments and left him seriously short of money and badly in debt.

It certainly wasn't the last time that the family would find themselves in such a position. To raise some cash, Blackall sold 10 acres of the estate and a small housing development called Hyde Park was built around the original gateway to Marino Park so that the new entrance to the estate was no longer on Merrion Avenue itself.

But even this wasn't enough to keep up the old place and Helena and her eldest stay-at-home daughter, Eileen, established Burton Hall Dairies in 1944 to supplement the family income by selling milk from the dairy farmers around Blackrock to the new suburban homes which had crept out from the city along the Stillorgan and Rock roads.

Things got even tougher for Agnes and her daughters when Thomas Blackall died on 6 May 1945 at the age of 76, leaving behind a widow and four grown-up children, Eileen being 34 at this stage.

Gerard, who had attended Trinity College to study medicine, dropped out after a year to join his uncle in the 'motor trade' and became a fairly well-known figure in the business in the years that followed. He married and left home and had a son called William, who was seven at this stage and would later become a chartered accountant. Rose qualified as a doctor while Irene became a teacher.

Gerard, who lived in Dale Drive in Kilmacud, lived an independent life and Marino Park became a house full of women with Helena as the matriarch.

They were still struggling with debts in the 1950s when the Bank of Ireland served an eviction order on Helena for non-payment of a debt. She and her daughters set about saving the house and it was said that, because Gerard didn't rally round, he became further detached from his mother and three sisters.

His behaviour, however, was quite understandable because by then he had his own family to take care of and in the 1950s the most sensible thing to do with Marino Park was to sell it off to a religious order or a property speculator, the two classes of people with money in those days.

With Helena getting on in years she made a will dated 5 August 1966 in which she left Marino Park and the surrounding land to her three daughters, Eileen, Irene and Rose. Gerard was excluded from the provisions of this will because his mother believed he hadn't really taken any interest in Marino Park, which was now beginning to fall into disrepair.

Only after she died did the three daughters discover that their mother had made a new will, which was held by her solicitor, Mr O'Higgins. This will was significantly different in just one aspect from the original 1966 will – it divided Marino Park among the four children, giving Gerard a quarter share of the 'ancestral' home, as opposed to the original, which left the place to the three daughters in residence.

Gerard Blackall doesn't seem to have concerned himself very much with this, continuing to lead his own life and run his motor business. His wife died and he and his son William moved to Stillorgan Grove also in Blackrock leaving his three sisters in occupation of the house.

However, that all changed in 1981when the elderly widower went on a trip to Scotland and met an attractive former lingerie model, Iris Bennett. He was 70 years old and she was 33, but they fell in love and within months they were married.

Gerard was soon to become a father once more. He and Iris had a son called Mark, and Gerard now found himself in need of money to fund his new married lifestyle and support his family. Quite naturally he went back to his surviving sisters to see if they would buy out his quarter share of Marino Park, as left to him in the 1976 will.

They told him that apart from the fact that they simply didn't have the money, they were relying on the 1966 will, which declared that the house and lands had been left to the three of them and he was not entitled to a share of the family property. Gerard disagreed and the arguments went back and forth for a number of years before Gerard finally went to a solicitor to begin proceedings to enforce the terms of the 1976 will.

Little did he know that it would lead to countless court cases over the next 10 years, he would be dead and most of the money would be spent on lawyers' fees and other expenses before the struggle over the last will and testament of Helena Agnes Blackall was finally settled.

Although not related to the dispute over Marino Park, the little enclave itself was becoming enclosed by housing developments, which had a bearing on the events that were to follow. Mount Merrion Avenue with its Victorian villas and estates like The Elms, Marino Park and Clonfadda was now a very desirable location for the new professional classes to live. One by one these big houses were being swallowed up for development. The Elms, once the home of the Rt Honourable Wylie, had been bought by a local developer called John McDonald who had demolished the house and turned its extensive parkland into a series of tastefully built apartment blocks. McDonald, who lived in nearby Waltham Terrace, had found the enterprise highly profitable and his development company Chessington Ltd was on the lookout for similar estates – preferably down-at-heel mansions which could be demolished and the attached lands developed.

Gerard Blackall was getting increasingly frustrated with the obstinate refusal of his sisters to honour the terms of their mother's will. They were all getting older and yet there seemed to be no resolution to the interminable wrangling over Marino Park. And it must have seemed even more urgent when one of the three sisters, Irene, died in March 1985.

Gerard Blackall finally instructed his solicitor Brendan Maloney of Bray, County Wicklow to issue proceedings against his two sisters, Eileen and Rose, to recover his quarter share of Marino Park.

There were several phases, taking in the Circuit Court, the High Court, the Supreme Court and back again several times, as 'the battle of the Blackalls' twisted and turned through the corridors of the Four Courts, going nowhere fast.

Gerard issued a Civil Bill against his two sisters seeking an order from the Circuit Court to have the house sold and the proceeds divided so that he could recover the quarter share that was rightfully his under his mother's will.

In a judgement dated 23 July 1991 Judge John Carroll found in his favour, ordering that the house should be sold and that Gerard Blackall's solicitor, Mr Maloney should be given 'carriage' of the sale, which was to be through the auctioneering firm of Lisney. The two sisters appealed this decision to the High Court in July 1992 where the case was heard by Mr Justice Lardner, who confirmed the earlier decision that the house should be sold.

But he put 'a stay' or delay on the order because he was told that the sisters were also disputing the terms of their mother's will, and the matter came back before the High Court in October that year. At this stage things were further complicated because, for reasons which were never divulged, Gerard Blackall decided to 'discharge' his solicitor Mr Maloney, who he said was no longer acting for him. However the judge decided that Mr Maloney should still have the legal responsibility of selling Marino Park.

After consulting with auctioneers and various bidders it was agreed to sell the house and grounds to Chessington Ltd, the company controlled by Mr John McDonald and his wife Patricia, for £400,000. Although it would later be called into question, it was a good and fair price. At the time there was a housing slump in Dublin and Marino Park was not attractive to many developers because it was effectively 'landlocked'. On one side was The Elms and on the other the housing development Hyde Park. Getting in to it to carry out building work was going to be very difficult for an outsider, but McDonald, who had developed The Elms had a ready-made access through this development to Marino Park.

To add further to the saga, Gerard Blackall died on 16 July 1994 at the hospice in Harold's Cross, Dublin, at the age of 82. His death notice mentions his second wife, Iris and describes him as 'father of Mark and William' but makes no mention of his sisters by name, simply saying 'sadly missed by his family'. Inevitably his death led to further delays and the matter was back in the

Circuit Court on 19 July 1995 when the contract for the sale of Marino Park to Chessington Ltd was approved by the High Court.

At this stage none of the Blackalls had signed the sale agreement. Gerard had refused to sign and was now dead, while Eileen and Rose had also declined to put their signatures to documents which they knew would inevitably lead to 'their' house being sold. So the judge decreed that the County Registrar could sign for both sides and he also ordered that the two elderly sisters should be given a further six months to find a new home before they left Marino Park forever.

Matters were further complicated when it emerged that Chessington Ltd had only paid 12.5 per cent of the deposit on the sale, about £4,500, instead of the £40,000 which would have been normal in the case of a property transaction of this kind. Inevitably this would form part of a new set of proceedings issued by the Blackall sisters to block the sale.

There was another catch. As they were also contesting the validity of their mother's 1976 will the two sisters argued that they should be left in Marino Park until that issue had finally been decided.

Because Gerard was now dead his share of Marino Park had passed to his widow Iris Bennett Blackall, dubbed by some sections of the tabloid press as 'the Black Widow'. She was now named in the various legal proceedings as his 'personal representative'.

In a judgement delivered on 28 June 1996 Judge Brian McCracken had to decide whether the will of 5 August 1966 was the legal will of Helena Agnes Blackall or whether the will of 23 September 1976 was the 'last true will' of the deceased.

'I am quite satisfied that Mr O'Higgins, Helena A Blackall's solicitor, initially took instructions from the deceased to draw up the will, and that several days later he returned to visit her with the will drafted and ready for execution. I am further satisfied that he read the will over to her, and that she indicated her approval, and then affixed her signature to the will, with some difficulty,' said Judge McCracken summing up 'the Battle of the Wills'.

In addition, he found that Mrs Blackall understood the contents of the will and that even though she was almost 100 years old at the time of making it, her doctor was satisfied that she was mentally capable of making a will at the time.

'I have also had evidence from a friend of the family who said that she might have been slightly hard of hearing but she was never confused; and from Miss Rose Blackall and Miss Eileen Blackall, I have to say that they both gave their evidence honestly, and the furthest that either of them went was the evidence of Miss Rose Blackall that in 1976 her mother had good days and bad days and sometimes was confused, but if things were explained to her she would understand. It is also clear from their evidence that for some considerable time they, and in particular Miss Eileen Blackall, had looked after her mother's affairs, as indeed one would expect in these circumstances.

'The picture which I have obtained is of a very elderly lady who was a little hard of hearing and had become almost bedridden, possibly partly as a result of a transient-type stroke, but principally simply due to old age. While she may not have been fully aware of all the legal background to her assets, which involved a family trust, she was clearly aware that she had disposing power of the house, which was her principal asset, and had clearly formed the view that the right thing to do was to divide all her assets equally between all her children. I think she was perfectly capable of making this decision, and of instructing a solicitor to draw up her will to that effect. While, like many people of her age, I would accept that she probably did have bad days, there is no evidence before me in relation to the particular day when this will was executed except that of Mr O'Higgins and therefore, based partly on his evidence and partly on the presumption of the validity of the will, I am satisfied that the deceased was of sound mind, memory and understanding when she executed the will.

'Accordingly, I declare the will of 23 September 1976 to be the last will and testament of the deceased. As it contains a specific revocation clause, it must follow that the earlier will of 5 August 1966 has been revoked.'

Defeated on the issue of their mother's will, the two elderly sisters then left the Circuit Court and went to the High Court to seek to have the order for the sale of Marino Park, overturned. Instead Judge Mary Laffoy in the High Court confirmed the sale in an order dated February 1997. She gave them a further six months to leave Marino Park and said the closing date for the sale should be 12 August 1997.

This was appealed by the sisters back to the Circuit Court. When it came before Judge Moran he ordered that Gerard Blackall's widow, Iris Bennett Blackall, should be given an order for possession of the house three months before the closing of the sale, provided she did not execute an order for possessions until 31 July 1997.

Rose Blackall then appealed Judge Moran's order and the matter made its way to the Supreme Court by way of a special summons to overturn the sale. Judge Francis D Murphy delivered his judgement on 18 June 1998.

In his summing up of the issues at the heart of the Blackall dispute there is a distinct tone of irritation at the never-ending litigation over Marino Park.

'For nearly 10 years members of the Blackall family have been in disagreement as to the ownership of the property known as Marino Park, 44 Mount Merrion Avenue, Blackrock, in the county of Dublin. More particularly they have been in disagreement as to how that property should be dealt with or disposed of for the benefit of those entitled to it. Unhappily this dispute has given rise to protracted litigation,' he began. 'Disappointed litigants may have a sense of grievance. They may wish to reopen a decision already made or to pursue by way of further appeal an adverse decision but every system of justice must, in the interest of the public and indeed in the interest of the parties themselves, provide some point of finality for all litigation.

'The die was cast once the final order for sale was made. It is not open to the [Supreme] Court to grant the reliefs sought by the applicants in this action. I refuse to grant the relief sought and I dismiss the special summons.

'What the lengthy history makes clear is that the proceedings in which this appeal is brought seek to reopen the issues as to ownership of Marino Park which was authoritatively and finally decided by Mr Justice Lardner in 1992. As Ms Justice Laffoy had anticipated in her judgement in February 1997, it is not open to the plaintiffs / appellants to invite this or any other court to review the question of ownership whether on the basis of different evidence or different arguments. That matter has now been finally concluded.

'I appreciate that the appellants, and in particular Ms Rose Blackall, still feel a sense of grievance. To the extent that she will have to give up the house in which she has lived for so many years, one could not but feel sympathy for her. On the other hand she in turn must recognise that her late brother Gerard derived no benefit whatever from the one fourth share in Marino Park prior to his death nor has his widow, the defendant / respondent, enjoyed any benefit therefrom notwithstanding the successive orders of numerous courts which determined the substantive issue, and most of the procedural ones, in her favour. Furthermore, very considerable loss has been incurred by the protracted and misguided litigation. Justice now requires that the orders made by the courts be implemented without further delay.'

But it wasn't over yet – not by a long shot.

Although they were due to be evicted, the determined sisters then went and found a new buyer for Marino Park themselves – one who was prepared to pay considerably more than Chessington Ltd. Property prices, especially in desirable areas of south Dublin, were now rising steeply and the sisters had found a developer prepared to pay far more than the £400,000 originally agreed as the sale price.

Back with a better offer dated 17 December 1998, the Blackall sisters appeared in the Circuit Court once again, this time before Judge Liam Devalley, who lived nearby in Frascati Park, Blackrock. He now decided in favour of the Blackall sisters, the first time since the lengthy litigation over Marino Park began.

His decision to overturn the original order for the sale was based on the fact that Chessington Ltd had only paid a portion of the deposit on the sale and so he believed the sale was invalid and the sisters could accept the higher offer, which was not specified in public.

The full deposit was received from Chessington Ltd on 18 May 1999 almost four years after the sale was first agreed. So the matter came back to the High Court and, in a decision dated 6 June 2000, Mr Justice Joe Finnegan in the High Court found, among other things, that the contract for the sale of Marino Park had not been terminated and the sale of the house and the distribution of the proceeds should proceed, with Gerard's widow, Iris Bennett Blackall, getting a quarter share of the proceeds.

'The delay in progressing this matter from July 1995 was due to the determination of the defendants [Eileen and Rose] that the sale should not be completed,' Judge Finnegan announced. He ordered that the sale should now go ahead.

On 15 June 2000 Rose Blackall, now in a wheelchair, was pushed into the High Court in Dublin for the last time to appeal to Judge Daniel Herbert to put a further delay on the High Court order enforcing the sale of Marino Park. Her sister Eileen was too ill to attend. Rose told the judge that she wanted the delay because the house, which had been sold for £400,000, was now worth €4 million, and that the decision meant it would be 'sold down the river'. The judge was sympathetic but without papers relating to the case said he could not take the matter further.

'I'm not descended from Brian Boru for nothing. He conquered Dublin a thousand years ago and now I'm fighting for Blackrock in the year 2000,' said Rose Blackall as she was wheeled from the court, where the matter was adjourned as the judge tried find a way to get the other parties in the dispute back into court.

But there was nowhere to go; the sisters had finally exhausted their legal claims on Marino Park and the patience of the judiciary.

On 19 October 2000, elderly, ill and frail, the two sisters finally left Marino Park for the last time, Eileen going into a home and Rose to stay with a relative in Blackrock.

The gates to Marino Park clanged shut for the last time and a lock and chain were bound around them. A digger was brought in to dig a trench which effectively meant that the avenue up to the decaying house was no longer in existence. Now semi-derelict the once grand home fell prey to vandals and thieves who stripped lead, chimney pots and other valuables from the crumbling mansion.

When the proceeds of the sale were finally disbursed on Friday, 27 July 2001 by Judge John Buckley in the Circuit Court, there was €475,000 to be divided among the various parties from the proceeds of Marino Park.

Gerard's widow Iris Bennett Blackall got his share worth €149,000.

Outstanding legal fees came to €139,000.

The Ulster Bank got €79,000 in repayment of a loan taken out by the sisters in 1998 to fund the ongoing litigation. A firm of architects was awarded €36,000 and two firms of auctioneers got €20,000. Eileen Blackall got €23,000 personally from the sale of Marino Park and she inherited another €20,000 due to her sister Rose who had died in the meantime.

It was a paltry inheritance from such a grand mansion, but in truth had they been more generous with their brother Gerard when he came looking for his legacy it would have been better for all of them. They would have saved a lot of money that went on legal fees and kept the family squabble from becoming a public spectacle and a legal saga.

Eileen Blackall died in August 2005, aged 94.

An attempt by the developers of Marino Park to demolish the old house was rejected by Dun Laoghaire / Rathdown County Council so, eventually, the builders went in and the house was renovated and converted into high-class apartments. The outbuildings were gentrified and became town houses and a row of other houses were built in the gardens which once had been the park where the Blackalls played as children.

On Thursday 16 October 2003, as the property boom began to take off, young professionals in Jaguars and BMWs created a traffic jam on the long driveway through The Elms and into Marino Park as they jostled to view one of the new symbols of Celtic Tiger Ireland. They were handed glossy brochures with fancy architects' drawings and impressive specifications which made no mention of the bitter struggle for the lost soul of the old house. Bidding was swift and behind the walls of the old manor the genteel poverty of the last owners of Marino Park was replaced by the designer opulence of the new professional classes who moved in to occupy the historic building.

It is believed that the entire development raised €15 million.

※◦◦※

Iris Blackall didn't look the part of the 'Black Widow', portrayed in the media as a woman prepared to go to any lengths to get her elderly sisters-in-law evicted from their Dublin mansion so that she could get her hands on the proceeds of the sale.

She was an anonymous figure who had never appeared in court or made any statements or even complained publicly about the denial of her husband's inheritance.

One day she called to the offices of the *Sunday Independent* to see me following an article I had written on the death of her sister-in-law, Eileen.

Perhaps I, too, had fallen for the sad story of the two old dears who were being thrown out of their ancestral home, as had most of the media. The facts were, of course, that Gerard Blackall was entitled to his share of Marino Park under his mother's will, but his sisters had frustrated every attempt made by him and later by his widow to get his inheritance.

Despite the difference in their ages, Gerard Blackall and Iris Bennett had fallen in love and married. They had a child, now grown up, and they were entitled to their share, even if that meant the sale of the ancestral home and the elderly sisters making alternative living arrangements.

As was proved in subsequent court cases, Eileen and Rose Blackall had borrowed heavily from the Ulster Bank to fund a series of legal cases, when they could have used the money to come to a settlement with their brother.

Iris Bennett Blackall was a small, slight woman, dressed in black and she spoke in a quiet accent with a Scottish tinge. Our meeting was brief and she didn't really know what she wanted to say. She was simply a little old lady, not the grasping widow she had sometimes been portrayed as.

We made arrangements to meet again so that I could get her side of one of the longest running sagas in Irish legal history, but I never saw Iris Blackall again. Her mobile phone went dead and she seemed to disappear back into the dark past from which she had so unwillingly emerged.

All that is left of the Blackall family now is a tragic tale of a family split, the bitter battle over their mother's will and the inevitable succumbing of a once grand family home to the onward march of progress.

# Chapter 10

## *Hail and Farewell*

---

'Just then the servant opened the door to ask me if I were at home to Mr Hugh Lane,' writes George Moore in his memoir *Hail and Farewell*. Moore, a noted author and gossip, a friend of the painters Renoir and Monet, was in the sitting room of his home in Ely Place, Dublin reading a book. 'And a moment after, there came into the room a tall, thin young man, talking so fast that I gathered with difficulty that there must be a great many pictures in Irish country houses which he would like to exhibit in Dublin.'

His visitor was Hugh Percy Lane, a Cork-born dandy and the nephew of Lady Gregory. According to Moore's description which scandalised Irish society, he was a transvestite who when he wasn't selling or swopping Old Masters for the work of the French Impressionists, liked to dress up in women's clothes.

As Moore breathlessly relates, the young Hugh Lane was at a house party in Lady Augusta Gregory's famous home, Coole Park in Galway, with Yeats and some others when he caught a glimpse of his aunt's dress, tailor-made in Paris.

'It is always a pleasure to a woman to hear her gown admired; but there was a seriousness in Hugh's appreciation of the hang of the skirt, and a studied regard in his eyes which caused her a moment's perplexity, and when they rose from table he stood watching her as she crossed the room. In the same afternoon she had occasion to go to her bedroom, and to her surprise found her wardrobe open and Hugh trying on her skirts before the glass. "Doesn't it seem to you, Aunt Augusta, that this skirt is a little too full?" he remarked.'

Lane's reason for calling on Moore that evening was more business than pleasure. Moore knew everybody worth knowing in Dublin, London or Paris. Lane was anxious to get an introduction to Moore's neighbour in Ely Place, just off St Stephen's Green, the eminent Dublin physician Sir Thornley Stoker, then far better known than his younger brother, the writer and theatrical manager, Bram Stoker.

Lane wanted to add Sir Thornley's name to the patrons of his latest project, an exhibition he was organising in 1904 'for the advancement of art in Ireland'. Stoker lived in Ely House, known to his friends as The Palace, and was an important figure in Dublin as well as a great collector of antiques and art which adorned his mansion.

Moore described the interior thus: 'The Chinese Chippendale mirror over the drawing room chimney-piece originated in an unsuccessful operation for cancer; the Aubusson carpet in the back drawing room represents a hernia; the Renaissance bronze on the landing a set of gallstones; the Ming cloisonné a floating kidney; the Buhl cabinet his opinion on an enlarged liver; and Lady Stoker's jewels a series of small operations performed over a term of years.'

But Stoker had a healthy dislike of the young art lover who would later become Sir Hugh Lane and wouldn't invite him around to his house. He believed his 'exhibitions' were merely a ruse to discover valuable old paintings that had been hidden away for generations so that he could buy them cheaply and sell them to astute collectors and museums on the international art market where he had already made his fortune.

'He could not, or would not, understand that though it is in Lane's instinct to make money it is also his instinct to spend the money that he makes upon art. Nobody that I have ever met loves art as purely as Lane,' explained Moore, who was normally much more cynical about people's motives. 'I have known many people who make money out of art, but it is generally spent on motorcars, women, cooks and valets. But Lane spends hardly anything upon himself. His whole life is absorbed in art and he would not be able to gratify his passion if he did not make money.'

Moore concludes by boasting: 'I am the only one in Dublin who knew Manet,

Monet, Sisley, Renoir, Pissaro – I knew them all.'

Sir Thornley Stoker wasn't the only one to distrust Lane. Lady Gregory later admitted that there were constant jibes about his motives and intentions, possibly because nobody could comprehend someone wanting to give £70,000 worth of paintings to the city of Dublin without attempting to line their own pockets in the process.

What they didn't realise was that Lane was different, and not simply because he was a wealthy and effeminate art lover with an unerring eye for beautiful Impressionist paintings at a time when they were scorned by the establishment. Like many men of the Victorian and Edwardian era – soldiers, explorers, writers and collectors – he had a burning desire to leave behind a great legacy: in his case a great collection of paintings housed in a gallery that would immortalise his name.

Many of the 'bit players' in this saga that would last until 1959 are now long forgotten. Sir Thornley's brother Bram Stoker is renowned as the author of *Dracula*, while gossiping George Moore is remembered as the writer of *Albert Nobbs* which was made into a film with Glenn Close, rather than as the author of *Hail and Farewell*.

But Hugh Lane lives on, remembered not only for his tragic death and his artistic legacy to his adopted city, but because of his last will and testament which led to a dispute between Ireland and England lasting 44 years.

At stake were 39 of the famous Impressionist paintings which he bought in those early years of the twentieth century and which he yearned to permanently exhibit in Dublin, if only the city would build him a gallery to show them.

❧ • ☙

Hugh Percy Lane was born in 1875 at Ballybrack, County Cork the third eldest of five sons and a daughter of the Reverend James William Lane from Cork and Frances Adelaide Persse who came from the landed gentry of Roxborough, County Galway.

Isabella Augusta Persse, Lady Gregory, was his mother's youngest sister and the second wife of Sir William Henry Gregory, Governor of Ceylon. The Gregorys accumulated a vast fortune from an ancestor who was chairman of the East India Company and built Coole Park near Gort in County Galway as the family seat. Sir William died in 1892 leaving his lady wife free to pursue her artistic ambitions for the next 40 years. These included the Gaelic Revival, writing plays, encouraging authors, establishing the Abbey Theatre and for the last 17 years of her life using her considerable influence in Ireland and Britain to have her nephew's paintings brought back to Ireland.

The Reverend Lane moved to England when the family was very young, first to York and then to Cornwall where Hugh Lane grew up. The marriage was not a happy one and the wayward clergyman seems to have been missing most of the time, leaving his wife to look after the growing brood.

According to his biographer Margarita Cappock, 'Hugh Lane's childhood was unsettled and he received little formal education, but at an early stage he showed a keen interest in fine arts.'

From childhood he latched on to his imperious 'Aunt Augusta' during his frequent visits to Coole Park, which was the centre of an artistic set that included WB Yeats, George Bernard Shaw, John Millington Synge and many others. For the son of an obscure clergyman the artistic energy inspired a love of beauty and art that would literally make his fame and fortune.

Lady Gregory wrote in her memoirs that 'he used to shrink from rough play, finding more content in the greenhouse plants that were in his care or the dressing up of dolls in such brilliant coloured silken scraps as came his way, or in decorating parish feasts or Christmas trees . . . he loved to look at pictures and ornaments, finger family miniatures and jewels and the like.'

Lane, who had little money and no qualifications, was 'searching' for something to do in life. He did not come from a wealthy family and could not depend on trust funds or the kindness of his aunt. So he began to put his interest in art to work. With London as the centre of the empire, he got a job there with the art dealer Martin Colnaghi in the Marlborough Gallery in London, a firm which specialised in Old Master paintings, which were then very fashionable and expensive, especially among the nouveau riche who were desperately trying to turn new money into old traditions.

Lane appears to have combined his knowledge of art with the natural flair of a salesman. He left after a couple of years and joined the Carlton Gallery in Pall Mall where he became one of the leading dealers in his field, travelling widely in Europe buying and selling paintings and amassing a huge fortune and a great collection of paintings – French impressionists, Old Masters and Irish artists such as Orphan, Lavery and John B Yeats, the poet's father.

By now a wealthy man he stayed with Lady Gregory in Coole Park for Christmas 1900 and the dawning of the new century. There he met Edward Martyn, Douglas Hyde, George Moore and other members of the Celtic Revival. Just as Moore had, after many years in England, returned to Ireland to revive the country's literature, Lane was imbued with a determination to play his part by promoting Irish artists and bringing 'great art' to the Irish people.

In 1902 he organised an exhibition of Old Masters at the Royal Hibernian Academy, which was then in Lower Abbey Street in Dublin. In early 1904 he became involved in organising an exhibition of Irish art, which was originally to have been shown at the World's Fair in St Louis in the US, but the event was cancelled and instead held at the Guildhall in London.

Later the same year he began organising another exhibition in Dublin of Impressionist paintings, some from his own collection and others borrowed from collectors and art dealers, including works he acquired on loan from the art dealer Paul Durand-Ruel, who was the first serious collector of Impressionist paintings, which he picked up for very little in the 1880s and 1890s.

It was for this venture that he attempted without success to recruit the influential Sir Thornley Stoker. But in the end the eminent surgeon went to this exhibition in Clonmell House in Dublin, if only to see the much talked about *Portrait of Eva Gonzales* by Manet. Lane had acquired this painting in the part swap / part sale of a couple of Old Masters he had bought at bargain prices from rundown stately homes during a tour of rural Ireland.

On 20 January 1908 Lane exhibited 300 paintings in Clonmell House in Harcourt Street, Dublin, the former city residence of the Earls of Clonmell. The house and gardens, now known as Iveagh Gardens, had been purchased by Dublin Corporation as an 'acting' Municipal Gallery and Hugh Lane was granted an apartment there while plans were made to build a proper gallery to house the unique art collection.

Lane was now such an honoured citizen that he was conferred with the title of Freeman of Dublin on 10 February 1908, although it is noted that 'he did not sign the roll' an omission that would lead to a lot of trouble for everybody in the not too distant future.

In 1909 he was knighted by King Edward VII for his services to art, becoming Sir Hugh Lane.

A competition was arranged to build Sir Hugh Lane's gallery. The design favoured by the art dealer was one by his friend Sir Edwin Lutyens, who had recently been in Dublin working on Lambay Castle on Lambay Island for Baron Rupert Ravelstoke. But in a city riven by jealousy and envy, however, the decision to build a gallery from the innovative design, which envisaged a Dublin version of the Bridge of Sighs (Venice) with the gallery housed in a beautiful building straddling the river Liffey, was postponed by the members of Dublin Corporation. Some were not impressed with the concept and favoured other designs but many of the aldermen, representing a city filled with slums, brothels and poverty, baulked at the enormous costs involved. One alderman even described the collection of French paintings it was supposed to house as 'not worth the price of their frames'.

Local architects were also jealous that such an important commission was going abroad and used their influence with the city fathers to have the plan delayed further. As the controversy continued Hugh Lane wrote to Lady Gregory saying: 'I hate this city, I hate the people and I hate the gallery.'

Not yet 40 and knighted for his services to art, he flitted between Dublin, London, Paris, New York and the other great capitals of the world. As befitting his wealth and position his main residence was Lindsey House in Cheyne Walk, Chelsea, a villa looking out over the Thames.

In 1911 he became briefly engaged to Lady Clare, daughter of the Fifth Earl of Annesley, whose father was a prominent Fermanagh landowner and mother came from County Cavan. Perhaps because of Lane's proclivities, the romance went no further and Lane became once more absorbed in his collection of paintings.

Tiring of the delays with getting a Dublin gallery he issued an ultimatum on 5 November 1912 that if a suitable site wasn't found by the following January he would withdraw his collection from Dublin.

The deadline passed and the controversy dragged on.

*The Irish Times* editorial of 24 June 1913 summed up the feelings of the more cultured Dublin classes:

> The project for a municipal gallery of modern art in Dublin is in grave danger. The Corporation at its meeting yesterday considered, and shelved, the recommendations of the Mansion House Committee and of Sir Hugh Lane's eminent architect, Mr Lutyens.
>
> The latter recommended, and the committee strongly endorsed, Sir Hugh's persistent scheme for a gallery across the Liffey. But he produced a new fact which greatly increases the cogency of the case against a bridge site. The Corporation has pledged itself to find £22,000 for the provision of a site and for the upkeep of the gallery; the citizens have subscribed £11,000 for the building of the gallery – £33,000 in all. Mr Lutyens now states that the total cost of the scheme will be £43,000 – an unexpected and most serious addition of £10,000. This means, as we have said, that the gallery project is in serious danger. The whole controversy will begin anew. Matters like the value and number of the pictures, about which no real doubt exists, will be reopened *ad nauseam*. The enemies of a municipal art gallery have been presented with an opportunity of which they will take full advantage.
>
> We believe that, on this question of a municipal art gallery, the citizens are divided into three classes – a large majority which is really grateful to Sir Hugh Lane for his generous offer and really anxious to accept it; a considerable minority which is ignorant and apathetic; and a very small minority which, for reasons that we regret and cannot appreciate, is bitterly hostile to the scheme. All these classes are represented in the Corporation. We said two months ago that Dublin strongly disliked the idea of a bridge site, but was extremely unwilling to offend Sir Hugh Lane. We appeal to Sir Hugh Lane to save the situation. In doing so, we wish to apologise to him, on behalf of the whole city, for certain cruel

and unfair things which have been suggested about his offer and the motives that have inspired it. Even if these pictures are lost to Dublin, the city will always be grateful for the munificence and patriotism which gave it the opportunity to lose them.

We are absolutely confident that Sir Hugh wants these pictures to remain in Dublin. We ask him, therefore, to add to his gift of art masterpieces a gift of self-sacrifice. We ask him to realise that the citizens, rightly or wrongly, do not desire a bridge site, and that the cost of such a site is now shown to be almost prohibitive. The pictures will be saved if Sir Hugh will allow the Corporation to revoke its acceptance of a bridge site. Beyond any doubt, the scheme of a bridge site is now dead.

It was. So was Sir Hugh Lane's interest in having his paintings exhibited in Dublin. He packed up the 39 most important Impressionist paintings in the collection and sent them back across the Irish Sea for storage in the National Gallery in London. He donated others, including Old Masters, to the National Gallery in Dublin and a gallery in Belfast.

While most commentators accept that Lane wanted his collection of paintings to go to Dublin it seems that Lane himself was not quite as certain. On the evidence of his will it would seem that the great art collector was playing off the two cities and the one which promised to promote his legacy the best would be the winner.

What he hadn't factored in was that the London establishment could be just as obstinate as their Dublin counterparts.

After withdrawing from Dublin Hugh Lane went back to dealing in paintings and making a great deal of money – yet still he brooded about having his collection recognised in either London or Dublin, and used his influence on both sides of the Irish Sea to see which of them would make the most effort.

The next episode in the saga of the Lane pictures began in 1913 when Sir Hugh Lane met with the powerful Lord Curzon, an influential trustee of the National Gallery in London, and offered his Impressionist paintings for an exhibition there. The gallery's response was that they were 'disposed to think that while some of these pictures are well worthy of temporary exhibition in the National Collection there are others which hardly attain the standard which would justify their inclusion.'

Angry at this rejection, which also deeply embarrassed Curzon, Lane told the National Gallery that they would exhibit all the paintings or none. After further discussion it seems that agreement was reached for the exhibition to go ahead and Sir Hugh Lane was asked to provide a list of guests for what promised to be a glittering opening night, 20 January 1914.

But the week before it opened to the public the full board of trustees of the National Gallery decided to view the exhibition and some of them, particularly the curmudgeonly Lord Redesdale, took a serious dislike to the entire project. Cleverly, however, he did not object formally on grounds of taste, rather he and some of the other trustees objected because Lane was a picture dealer rather than a philanthropist. Redesdale, father of the famous writer Nancy Mitford and her colourful sisters, compared some of Lane's collection, by artists like Monet, Renoir and Manet, to the work of a 'pavement artist'. According to Anne Kelly in her scholarly history *The Lane Bequest: A British-Irish Cultural Conflict Revisited* Lord Redesdale was so incensed by the collection that he protested at 'any portion of the National Gallery or the Tate being assigned to Sir Hugh Lane who is a picture dealer, for the purposes of holding an exhibition of his wares.'

Redesdale's remarks weren't too far from the feelings expressed by Sir Thornley Stoker to George Moore in Dublin more than a decade earlier.

As an extremely wealthy dealer and patron of the arts Lane had already made his will some time earlier in which he had bequeathed the 39 painting in storage in the National Gallery in London to that gallery. Now, the Irish artistic community, sensing an opportunity and anxious to lure the valuable collection of paintings to Dublin, appointed Sir Hugh Lane a director of the National Gallery of Ireland on 26 February 1914. Pleased by this latest honour Lane referred once again to the collection as 'the Dublin pictures' but wanted them exhibited in London, preferably at the Tate, to remove 'the slur' that had been cast on them by the National Gallery, before formally removing them to Dublin.

The First World War had been declared on 4 August 1914, but it seems to have been 'business as usual' for Sir Hugh Lane. He travelled to Dublin and then on to Lady Gregory's home at Coole Park for Christmas 1914. He later came back to Dublin and began making arrangements to travel to the United States where wealthy clients were clamouring for his 'wares'.

There the new oil, steel and railroad magnates didn't know what to do with the vast sums of money they were making and were anxious to acquire Old Masters and important paintings from Europe to furnish their great mansions and mock castles. Besides, America was not involved in the war and with the European market closed as the conflict raged across Belgium and France the great salesman Sir Hugh Lane decided to capitalise on the vast and lucrative new markets in America.

On 3 February 1915, obviously mindful of the trip he was about to undertake, he called his Dublin solicitors to an office he kept in the National Gallery in Merrion Square, and instructed them to add a codicil to his will, which would in effect make the older will redundant. It read:

> This is a codicil to my last will to the effect that the group of pictures now at the London National Gallery, which I had bequeathed to that institution, I now bequeath to the City of Dublin, providing that a suitable building is provided for them within five years of my death. The group of pictures I have lent to Belfast I give to the Municipal Gallery in Harcourt Street (Dublin). If a building is provided within five years, the whole collection will be housed together. The sole trustee in this question is to be my aunt, Lady Gregory. She is to appoint any additional trustees she may think fit. I also wish that the pictures now on loan at this gallery remain as my gift.

The codicil was signed Sir Hugh Lane. He also added and signed a further amendment.

> I would like my friend Tom Bodkin to be asked to help in the obtaining of this new Gallery of Modern Art for Dublin. If within five years a gallery is not forthcoming then the group of pictures are to be sold, and the proceeds go to fulfil the purpose of my will.

He travelled to Liverpool in mid-April and boarded the Cunard liner *Lusitania* and sailed for New York. There he sold Titian's *Man in a Red Cap* and Hans Holbein's *Portrait of Thomas Cromwell* to the American art collector Henry Clay Frick, whose beautiful mansion off Fifth Avenue is one of the city's great attractions to this day.

After buying and selling a number of other paintings Sir Hugh Lane made the fatal mistake of ignoring the advice of his wise old aunt, Lady Gregory. Aware from her many contacts in London that the war was escalating, she had advised her nephew to travel on a neutral American ship, as she thought this was safer. But Lane opted to travel once more on the *Lusitania*, the fastest and most luxurious liner plying the Atlantic at that time.

Travelling with the art connoisseurs Charles and Frances Fowles, Sir Hugh Lane was assigned the luxurious cabin D-26 for the journey. It is believed that his luggage, stowed in the hold of the liner, included a lead-lined container filled with paintings by Monet, Rembrandt, Rubens and other great artists which he hadn't sold and was bringing back to Europe.

Like most of the other passengers he was unaware that the climate of the war had changed. The Germans had mass-produced a new and deadly machine of war, the U-boat, and shoals of these efficient killing machines were patrolling the deep waters off the west of Ireland.

An altogether more sinister development was that passenger liners flying the Union Jack of Great Britain were now, in certain circumstances, 'legitimate targets'. Lane and his fellow travellers were unaware that the *Lusitania* would be marked as a target if the German U-boat commanders or their superiors in Berlin believed that she was carrying arms or munitions across the Atlantic for the British war effort. And what he and other passengers did not know was that the hold of the Lusitania was also carrying a cargo of arms, including over four million cartridges.

Lane was seen playing cards in the ship's salon with Marguerite, Lady Allan and Dr Fred Pearson on the morning of 7 May 1915 as journey's end neared. Then, as a thick mist lifted around noon and the ship sailed into bright sunshine, he and other passengers moved to the decks where, looking towards the southwest coast of Ireland, they admired the Old Head of Kinsale looming into view.

The sudden change in the weather was to prove fatal for the *Lusitania*. A German submarine, U-20, had already spotted the ship but then lost it again in the mist. When suddenly it cleared at around 2pm, the submarine once again got a fix on the great liner.

Sir Hugh Lane had just gone down to the dining salon with some other passengers when precisely at 2.10pm, 11 miles off the coast of County Cork and within hours of docking at Queenstown, Kapitan Leutnant Schweiger gave the order to fire and the torpedo was launched at the *Lusitania*.

What survivors later described as a massive explosion ripped through the ship, followed by a second equally devastating blast. Schweiger later insisted that he had only three torpedoes left and had fired just one, which means the second explosion was caused by the ships boilers, or as has been speculated, by the munitions in the hold detonating. Whatever the cause of the second blast, the direct hit was devastating.

The massive *Lusitania* sank in just 18 minutes, with only six of its 48 lifeboats successfully launched in the chaos and carnage that followed the explosions. Of the 1,959 passengers and crew, just 761 survived, saved by the lifeboats and local fishermen who went to the rescue in a trawler called *The Bluebell* and plucked survivors from the sea.

In all 1,198 passengers and crew were either killed in the two explosions or drowned in the Atlantic waters. One survivor later told of swimming for three hours, clutching a young boy, until the boy died in his arms and feeling that he was going to drown himself he let go of the body and watched it drift away. Only 289 bodies were recovered, 65 of which were never identified.

The body of Sir Hugh Lane was never found.

More people died in the sudden carnage of the *Lusitania* that May afternoon than in the entire Irish War of Independence, and such was the outrage in America at the sinking of the ship and the loss of many American lives that public opinion in the United States turned against Germany and the United States eventually entered the war on the side of the Allies.

Sir Hugh Lane's will was admitted to probate in London on 29 September 1915. The codicil, changing the terms of the will, which was found locked in the drawer of his desk in the National Gallery in Dublin, was not witnessed and therefore already deemed invalid. A High Court order of 25 May 1917 directed the executors of the original will to hand the 39 paintings over to the trustees of the National Gallery in London. The paintings included Manet's *Portrait of Eva Gonzales* and *La Musique aux Tuileries*; Monet's *Lavacourt Under Snow*; Renoir's *Les Parapluies*, Vuillard's *La Cheminee*, Pisarro's *View from Louvenciennes* and a treasure trove of other paintings, including a group of small masterpieces by Carot.

The collection that had been rejected by the National Gallery in London, despised by many of its trustees and described 'for the most part as the crazy extravagances of modern French decadents' by Lord Redesdale just two years earlier, was now viewed as a treasure that must, like the Elgin Marbles looted from Athens, be kept in London at all costs.

Over the next 44 years eminent figures like Michael Collins, Edward Carson, WB Yeats, George Bernard Shaw, Lord Lansdowne, Lord Curzon, Sean O'Casey and a host of political, business and social figures on both sides of the Irish Sea would become embroiled in what seemed like a never-ending argument over the Lane pictures.

The Irish side, led by Lane's implacable executor Lady Gregory and his friend Tom Bodkin, conceded early on that the codicil had no legal standing because it had not been signed by two witnesses, as was legally required. They argued instead that Dublin had a 'moral right' to the Lane bequest. This was conceded by many senior political figures in Britain, including, over the decades that followed, several prime ministers. But they were reluctant to pass legislation to legalise the codicil and even their wishes to return the paintings to Dublin were over-ridden by the trustees of the National Gallery in London who were adamant that they would keep the pictures for themselves.

The first course of action was an attempt to legalise Lane's wishes through an Act of Parliament, which would overturn the will.

In August 1919 James Macpherson, Chief Secretary in the British civil service in Dublin Castle began working on legislation that would transfer the paintings. 'There is considerable agitation through the whole of Ireland that this course should be adopted,' he told the War Cabinet, adding that 'all shades of political opinion' wanted what he described as 'a great national asset' to be returned to Ireland.

Viscount Long, First Lord of the Admiralty also added his support. 'I greatly fear that if it is definitely decided to have these pictures in England, irritation and annoyance quite out of proportion to the real merits of the case will be aroused in Ireland, and especially in Dublin, and I am sure my colleagues will agree that at this moment every effort ought to be made to avoid anything of the kind,' he said in a dispatch.

In 1922 during the Treaty negotiations Michael Collins raised the issue of the Lane paintings at the behest of Lady Gregory. But the trustees of the National Gallery in London pointed out that the National Gallery in Dublin and the Municipal Gallery in Harcourt Street (at the time) had already done rather well from Lane bequests, even without the 39 paintings at issue.

A friend of Lane's, Charles Aitken, also argued that Lane was totally disillusioned by Dublin's failure to build a gallery to house his collection and this was one of the reasons that he did not complete the codicil to his will by having it witnessed. Aitken argued that having drawn up the document it would have been very simple to have it witnessed had he really wanted to enforce his wishes.

The counter argument put forward by the Irish side was that Hugh Lane was in Dublin a few days before he departed for Liverpool and on to New York, and he had ample time to destroy the codicil if it was not his last wish.

In 1924 the Seanad of the Irish Free State passed a resolution demanding the return of the paintings and in the House of Lords in London Lord Edward Carson, the Unionist leader, supported the return of the pictures, asking if legislation was needed.

The British Government then appointed the Wilson Committee, composed of three politicians and headed by JW Wilson, to hear evidence from both sides, Lady Gregory and Tom Bodkin representing Dublin on one side and the trustees of the National Gallery in London on the other, and to adjudicate on the case. This committee eventually advised the British Government that it should not introduce legislation to legalise Sir Hugh Lane's codicil but pass a 'Loan Act' which would allow for the collection to be shared by the two cities. This was conveyed to the Irish Government on 14 May 1925 by the British Prime Minister Stanley Baldwin, but rejected out of hand by William T Cosgrave, President of the Irish Free State.

According to Anne Kelly's scholarly version of events, Cosgrave was also conscious that Dublin had still not provided a suitable gallery for the paintings and so even if they were available the city had not fulfilled Lane's principal condition.

The artist Sarah Purser had proposed that Charlemont House in Parnell Square, once the home of the earls of the same name, should become the new Municipal Gallery. This was taken up by the Corporation, but it would be another five years before it came to fruition and in the meantime a library designed by Dublin's most famous architect, James Gandon, was demolished to make way for an extension to the rear of the building, something which would surely be frowned on today.

In February 1929 the matter was raised in the House of Commons in a slightly opportunistic way by Colonel Howard-Bury MP, the Everest explorer and owner of Charleville Castle near Tullamore, County Offaly and Belvedere House near Mullingar, County Westmeath. When the Earl of Iveagh, a member of the Guinness family, died he left 23 paintings from his collection to the National Gallery in London. It was then discovered that his will had only been signed by one witness instead of the two required to make it legal. As a result, a Private Members Bill was introduced by the prime minister in the House of Commons to pass an act legalising the bequest.

'In view of exactly similar circumstances with regard to the bequest of the Lane pictures will he introduce legislation to enable the trustees of the National Gallery to hand these pictures over to Dublin and thereby carry out equally the testator's wishes?' Colonel Howard-Bury asked Prime Minister Stanley Baldwin.

The prime minister said he was not prepared to accept that the two cases were the same.

Colonel Howard-Bury replied: 'Is not the prime minister aware that it has always been said that if legislation were passed it would be establishing a bad precedent to alter a will; but, seeing that in the one case it is being done by a Private Bill, will he not withdraw his objection and have it done in the other case, and so establish the testator's intention?'

Mr Baldwin's reply was: 'The two cases are really not on all fours. In the case of the Guinness bequest, the legislation is not for the purpose of overcoming a dispute between two rival potential beneficiaries. That is the first and great difference between the two cases.'

Lady Gregory, who had spent virtually the second half of her life campaigning for the return of the pictures, died in 1932, leaving it to her wealthy American lover Tom Quinn, Tom Bodkin and others to carry on the campaign.

In January 1933 the charismatic Lord Mayor of Dublin Alfie Byrne wrote to Baldwin, who was once again British prime minister, suggesting that the long-awaited opening of the Municipal Gallery in Charlemont House on 19 January that year would be a 'suitable occasion' for the transfer of the pictures to Dublin for an unlimited period pending legislation making the Lane gift to Dublin permanent.

It was a good try, but it got nowhere.

When it opened in Parnell Square in 1933 the Municipal Gallery did not have the famous paintings but it did include a Lane Room with a bust of the art dealer, a reproduction of the codicil of his will and photographs of the 39 disputed paintings.

The onset of the Second World War led to the issue lying dormant for a number of years. Then Tom Bodkin wrote to Taoiseach Eamon de Valera in 1947 asking him to intervene, which he did, taking the matter up with Lord Rugby, the British representative in Ireland.

Lord Rugby reported back to the National Gallery in London: 'The Irish always confidently demand one hundred per cent as a proper settlement for any of their claims. They have much more respect for us when we make a stand. It is distinctly irritating when the issue of the Lane pictures is raised in an almost hostile spirit with the suggestion that we have no right to them at all and are withholding Ireland's rightful property from the owner.'

In the early 1950s the saga of the Lane pictures was constantly debated and referenced in the media. In November of 1953 when the National Gallery and Tate Gallery Bill came to be debated in the House of Lords, Lord Moyne (head of the Guinness family) and Lord Pakenham (second-eldest son of Lord Longford) tried to exclude the Lane pictures from the operation of the bill, which would ensure their return to Ireland.

It didn't work, but Moyne and Pakenham, two influential figures in the British establishment, had set in train the beginnings of what would eventually turn out to be a settlement of the long and acrimonious dispute.

But first it took another bizarre turn in April 1956 when one of the disputed paintings, *Jour d'Été* (Summer's Day) by Berthe Morisot was stolen from the Tate Gallery in London. Two art students Paul Hogan and Bill Fogarty from Galway, read about the Lane dispute in a newspaper article and, as Hogan told RTÉ many years later, 'decided to do something about it'.

They travelled to London and contacted the Irish Press Agency, which was an arm of the Department of External Affairs, telling them to have a photographer outside the Tate Gallery on the Thursday morning. They then got a taxi to the Tate, told the cabbie to keep the meter running and went in and stole the famous painting from the wall of Gallery 24.

Much to their surprise they escaped with the painting and, instead of the Irish Press Agency carrying a propaganda photograph of them being arrested on the gallery steps as they intended, an international manhunt for the fugitives began.

Five days later an unidentified woman walked into the Irish Embassy in London, handed over a package containing the painting and disappeared.

'I can only say I am delighted it has been recovered,' said Sir John Rothstein, chairman of the Tate, when the matter was raised in parliament. He explained that the orderly on duty had been assigned to other duties the morning in question and there was no security in that part of the gallery when the painting was stolen.

In November 1956 the Duke of Wellington, a trustee of the National Gallery, proposed a division of the collection between Dublin and London, with each half alternating annually between the two cities. He wanted any agreement signed on the Irish side by Lord Moyne and Lord Pakenham as well as the director of the Municipal Gallery in Dublin, because the two peers were 'as much English as Irish'.

The famous art collectors Chester Beatty in Ireland and Denis Mahon in Britain were also involved in trying to broker a compromise settlement.

Beatty told Tom Bodkin, who had taken charge of the campaign as chief guardian of the Lane legacy following Lady Gregory's death, that he should accept the deal which would divide the collection between the two cities. In London, Mahon told the trustees of the National Gallery that he was 'decidedly uncomfortable' about the circumstances in which they had acquired the Lane paintings.

Tom Bodkin was brought directly into the negotiations by Lord Moyne and Lord Pakenham during 1958 and it was he who advised the new taoiseach, Sean Lemass, that a loan arrangement between the two countries was the best solution. He was present at a meeting in April 1958 when a draft statement for agreement between the two governments was finalised. The pictures were to be divided and would alternate between London and Dublin every five years for a 20-year period, and both governments agreed that they would not support any campaign by any party to break the agreement.

Tom Bodkin said the controversy was 'ending honourably' after years of acrimonious exchanges between the two sides and the two countries.

A formal exchange of the paintings took place on 6 November 1959. Announcing the deal in the House of Lords, Lord Moyne said: 'I wish to express admiration for the tireless way in which Professor Bodkin has worked through the greater part of his life to give to Dublin the opportunity to enjoy the collection which his old friend Sir Hugh Lane originally formed for the city.'

On 12 November Taoiseach Sean Lemass thanked former taoiseach John A Costello, Tom Bodkin, Lord Pakenham and Lord Moyne for their 'unsparing time and effort' in finding a solution to a problem that had bedevilled Anglo-Irish relations. 'It is right that I should recall also the assistance given over the years by many other friends in Britain who have shown a constant anxiety to promote a friendly and equitable settlement of this question . . . We are sincerely grateful to them all.'

The agreement has been renewed and amended since. Apart from the eight most important paintings in the collection, which alternate between London and Dublin for periods of six years, the bulk of the paintings now reside in Dublin's Hugh Lane Gallery, named in honour of the man whose last will and testament led to a 44-year long international dispute and whose paintings have given endless pleasure to generations of art lovers.